!

@

#

$

%

^

&

*

( )

+

=

< >

;

" "

...

?

.

Advance Praise for **THE WILD TIMES**

For anyone who survived the 70s, or is curious about them, *The Wild Times* is the perfect guide book. Writing in the jingle-jangle urgency of the decade, Martin Perlich has unerringly captured the birds-in-a-storm whimsy of a journey navigated on too many drugs and too little sense of direction but precisely the ideal combination of curiosity and lust, abandon and longing. What a ride the 70's were and what a funny, sad and compelling chronicle this novel is. Right on, brother!

Ernest Thompson
On Golden Pond, 1969, White People's Christmas

At first, more fun than a barrel of monkeys—real or hallucinated—but ultimately, a story with real pathos. Martin Perlich is a true original—I loved the wild and woolly ride.

Sandra Tsing Loh
Depth Takes a Holiday, A Year in Van Nuys

Martin Perlich's *The Wild Times* revives priapic romps as peepholes, a la Henry Miller, in a gonzo spiritual quest to experience, manifest, and above all, know and get inside of a moment of time the likes of which we may not see again. The hypomanic, erudite, hedonistic, hilarious, compassionate and warped innocent sophisticate counter-hero Mitchell Hertz narrates his own Steppenwolfian descent into murky soul-seek through the portals of sound, sense and intellect in a uniquely Americana sensibility.

Perlich, with the adjectival acumen of the consummate wordsmith, blows syllables like Parker blew notes. Just when we have settled in to appreciate the trip, we are delivered a wallop that explodes and lays bare the easy assumptions of a lifestyle and an epoch that makes us wonder anew just what was it all about and what is its proper legacy?

Marvin Treiger, PhD Antioch College

Mitchell Hertz starts out as an amiable, irrepressible Holden Caulfield-style youth and transmogrifies into a lotus-eating, truth-seeking, long-haired hippie Trotskyist. He's a free spirit and a willing slave to good drugs, willing vaginas, and to the ever present heartbeat of music.

There would be no Sixties without such transcendently stoned mythological figures. Perlich plants his lovable Satyr in the ever shifting sands of the Culture Industry—straight jobs, where a man can get Income, or even better, Fired. Unafraid to follow his protagonist through the rat holes of failure or down any number of other, more sensual tunnels o' love, Perlich weaves his antic tale with great candor and comic twistedness.

Rita Valencia
White House Dogs, Style Vs. Content

Feverishly excavates the Boomer experience, exposing not only its tangled roots, but the complicated relationship between those roots and their perplexing, occasionally problematic, harvest.

Susan Key
American Mavericks

I laughed, I cried, I got a hard-on.

John Schneider
"Global Village" KPFK/Pacifica

The Seventies fell with a crash. (One name for that crash was "Ronald Reagan.") Perlich describes, with fine tonal accuracy, this collapse.

Sparrow
America: A Prophecy, Yes You ARE A Revolutionary!

For the Angelis
SoSo -

All my love
x y yx

6/6/06

Brentwood

THE WILD TIMES

THE WILD TIMES

MARTIN PERLICH

EMPTY PRESS
KINGSTON, NY

ISBN 1-933932-00-7
www.emptypress.com

Empty Press, P.O. Box 4371, Kingston, NY 12402

Book Design by David Perry

Printed in the United States of America
First Edition

For Tree.

PART ONE

Come, my friends,
'Tis not too late to seek a newer world…

Ulysses, *Tennyson*

Maybe it's the acid. Squinting my eyes one at a time. Blurs. Images. Faces floating in and out of the packed auditorium. *They don't see me. Their faces are floating. Beautiful white faces in rows.* I sit on an equipment box, staring off to the side of the big stage. *Can they? Will they? A whole new breed of people, becoming cows. Concert animals.*

Old for the first LSD experience. So old. Old. Doubt doubt doubt. Longhaired. Feel my hair. The Kids are so young! Feel the new beard. They're cows, like some dumb cows! Sweet, smiling garlanded cows! Sugar cows. They would be herd. Magic cows. Reindeer! Magic elk! Horns horns horns! Sacred cows. Big nautical eyes. Blowing their mooing horns. Youth's magic horns. They can't see me, but there they are, anyway, judging me. Slowly, softly, but in the end, where am I? Who?

The Kids. Contemptuous. *What do The Kids want?* The mocking mantra of corporate-hip young consultants.

Want? They want to buy. Sell to the cows.

Sure, sure, they have their fantasies and folkways. Calling each other Sunshine or Star or Rainbow. My friend Tommy Trout has a young assistant, a tall white kid from suburban Eriewood High. Butt-length hair, indoor skin, six-foot-six; they call him Tree. He seems to like it.

~

My first view upward at Timothy "Tree" Campbell was through the glass-door entrance of WEMP, the Top-40 radio station then dominating the ether surrounding Carnegie. He was ducking his head as he left the elevator, walking the rocking topple of a walk that growth-bursting young gawks often affect. Tree was answering phones for Trout, the first black pop-jock in a Top-10 market, passing on listener requests and assessing suburban hippie chicks.

Stooping to unlock the glass door, then unfolding to his full height, Tree's deadpan showed he was clearly expecting pubescent fuck-fans for Trout's maw. Instead he found a short, bearded older guy (over thirty, for sure, despite lengthening dark blonde locks) peering through the door. I attempted a *howdy, pard-I'm-okay-too* smile through the glass as he held it open for me, then glided in under his long denim arm, careful to tilt away from the curtain of hair.

"I'm Tree," he said.

"Great," I said as we eased onto the elevator.

The station was one of the hottest in the country, and Tommy Trout had just exploded. The city was crazy about him—especially, it was widely assumed, the white girls. His liberal, whitey admirers seemed to derive a perverse tingle, a bigot-absolving blip of long-trapped energy, in conjuring the vision of a trail of teenyboppers traipsing down to spend their innocence on this authentic paladin of color. Tree was serving his apprenticeship as Trout's producer, engineer, and *a priori* arbiter of Groupie-ripeness.

Tree was on fire for rock 'n' roll, radio, and a real life. I was the opposite, already a post-successful adult and a radio dilettante at best. But I was a glutton for great music in any and every form, and in 1970, it was rock. Rock anything.

Trout and I didn't talk much that night. He was too busy. I mostly hung on, *amazed* at his speedball pace. I was host of an "experimental" show on Carnegie's only classical station and defiantly innocent of most commercial radio operations, so I observed with gotta-learn concentration: how he swam the soundboard, manhandled the mic, flicked the faders, threaded the 45s, pumped the phones, eyes beaming wide-open. All in one smooth, dazzling, rhythmic power-surge. I watched Trout, and Tree watched both of us.

I saw Tree regularly at Trout's place after that, as I paddled out of straight life. Mutual friendship grew as we all got stoned together, and Tree was permitted to watch Trout and me "do" various women. One lawyer's wife in particular, kicking her heels and screaming on her family-room floor—her tiny children asleep upstairs in suburban seclusion.

"Now, Tommy! Now! Oh! Oh!" He mashed her knees to her ears.

"Okay, Judy."

"Oh, God! No! No! Stop! No more. Please!"

The TV gave us a silent Dick Cavett. Tree and I passed a roach, Albert King throbbing just above the level of audibility.

"Oh, God."

Tree took it all in, the high school senior. Then it was my turn.

Before the concert, we did the tiny pink tabs. Our little grouplet: Tommy Trout and his new girlfriend Sally, the Jewish doctor's wife, Bobby and Brenda Rich, and me, lying on Algerian pillows. Dropped the tab, then smoked a joint to ease the transition. We just leaned back into the deep Moroccan-blue leather couches and made an altitude adjustment, gently waggling our heads to Miles Davis' *Workin'* LP on the big AR speakers.

Going up.

First it feels just like Thai stick. Trout always has good weed. I'm smoking grass again for the first time since college, when I had to buy a bag of Bull Durham tobacco just to get the rolling papers. I'm gone from the house more, spending all my free time with Trout, getting high.

But this is really High. Really. Toeing the fine line between excitement and anxiety. Really. Really.

Riding to the concert, my head floats effortlessly yet ultra-active. Things look so *good.* People peep down at us from passing bus windows as we transfer joints from lip to furtive lip, the car sailing before the wind. The Riches in front, Trout's girlfriend on his lap, and me in back of the Mercedes. My wife Senta is absent.

I know where she is. Same place Sally's husband is: Off the Bus!

Senta. Lovely, red-haired, not-a-mean-bone Senta. Actors Studio Senta. Five-years-older, pregnant-again-after-all-the-dead-babies Senta. At home alone in her bower of bliss as I scramble for subterranean joys—my fuck-flight to Freedom.

Does she know? Can she imagine the perfidious heart her Mitch is hiding? Can I? Evasive maneuvers are now a way of life.

At City Arena we wait in a tight little foyer for Trout to be passed by security—two scowling, white, city cops. I'm in jeans and a black Emerson, Lake and Palmer T-shirt, a white bird soaring across my chest. Sally sits all-legs in cut-offs and suede vest, knees tucked under her. My eyes rivet on her puffy crotch.

The cops "proactively" gape at Sally. Watching gives me physical pain, as the drug begins its first big *whoosh.* The crowd buzzes gaily, swarming outside our little traffic chapel. The cops splay their noses in scrutiny on the glass, as the young, mostly white, crowd of late-blooming Midwestern freaks come trooping in.

Still no Trout. Marooned in the airless entry, captives of time.

"Another one with a nigger. Filthy cunt," grunts one cop.

"Fuckin' hippie."

"Looka those tits!"

"Animals!"

We're freaking from our side of the barricades. Cops freak from their side. The class-line, the culture, the other side of life—the wrong side.

Finally, just before opening act The James Gang finishes their set, Trout pops up, eyes whorling juicily, herding the apologetic promoter. He coolly waves us into the throbbing backstage hurly-burly.

The dripping band pushes past us, roadies parting the sea of suits on their way to the dressing room. Then my flaming brain hurls me headfirst into the action—the applause and screaming out front, the smell of adrenalated exhalation back behind the fire curtain. I feel it dragging me. *Who am I resisting? It must be the acid.* Though my mind is now in full rout, my feet creep slowly, retreating deliberately behind the stage curtain…

Where am I? Why am I sitting here? Will I lose myself? What is my self? Will it melt? Become powder or steam? Vanish into vapor and be lost? Can I die from this? Can part of me die? Part of me is dying. Which part? I'm glad. It's flying off me. Scampering into light and motion. Jaw tightening, sweat draws a line down my temple. *There's fire behind my forehead!* Ears drum tattoos. *Is it the acid? First trip. Old. Me. Old me—married with three kids. Goodbye to all that. Goodbye. Hello, everything else.*

Carnegie, 1970. A capital city in decline for the most part, population drooping down under one million for the first time since The Depression. Once-proud, home to Major League teams, Big Department stores and 24-hour industrial production lines, passed over by Big Capital, slowly sinking into rust.

Heat waves bend youthful audience faces. Rowdy. Midwestern. Bikers, greasers and 'ludes. Decompressing after a serious and extended pump-up, now sullenly at work against the second act—a lanky folksinger bowing shyly to an embarrassed speckling of applause. As the house lights come down, he saunters across the giant Depression-era stage to a solitary stool that awaits him in a pool of golden white.

I sit invisibly, staring out from my darkness into the hot-and-bothered faces as the new guy begins to speak:

"Hi, I'm James…" he mumbles unconcerned into the mic. He tunes his guitar (the way folksingers must always do, I surmise) and is slathered with the hall's hostility. Even though he signed with the Beatles record label, and his first album on Warner Bros. has been out for months, he isn't someone they gave a shit about yet. The nasty indifference in the hall is palpable.

The cows are moaning. Waves of heat jiggle the rows of young faces. *Just faces in the dark. Warping and shimmering.* Some dull, downer-dingied, regular blonde yeoman faces, others younger and fresher and open. First amped-up by the saloon-rock of The James Gang, then stupefied with boredom by this tall, thin sucker. Faces flit in the stage lights, then, from out of the darkened multitude:

"*BOO*-GIE!" A bikerish voice snarls. Then another contemptuous, born-to-be-bad heckle. And another. Above the scornful natter, James Taylor begins his country-campy blues.

I'm a steamroller for ya', Baby.
A churnin' burnin' chunka'…

"LOUDER!" from another voice.

How could I do these drugs? What is wrong with me? Looking out into the sneers, cringing for Sweet Baby James, for his friends, his record company. His mother. *What must the guy be thinking?*

Taylor stops and grins. "Ah cain't play no louder," he teases, "But ah c'n play softer…" leaning his guitar into the mic to pick some folksy accompaniment for his tormenters.

Bum-bum, diddle-diddle.

I swim in the sounds and sights of the crowd. Feelings and fear of feelings. Fear of…fear. *How did I get myself into this? Where am I going? What am I leaving behind? Will I ever return? Can I? Here, in this desperate clime, this place of great peril? This Great Hall! These lowing, threatening heifers!* My mind bursts with alien images undammed. Phosphorescent firefly effusions sail up and out of me, sunken visions unbounded set afloat. *Up, up, up! From my brain's own hermit nautilus. What on earth?* Slipping my anchor into a merciless sea of whoever these kids are. *Outlanders. Other people, new people's children. Different. I'm old to them. Old and in the way. Part of the problem. Standing in the doorway, blocking up the halls.* Anxiety soaks through me, palpitating terrors known and unknown. My shirt is drenched, my hair dripping Gorgon locks, ringlets of fire, greasy and forlorn, curling animal-like over my hairy ears. I shake my too-heavy head. My gut is tight—threatening spasm. I try to belch and a rank odor assails my nostrils—the stench of cave or jungle hut. Something bestial almost overruns me, and then turns on the crowd. *These days even the workers' kids have money to buy records and dope, and special muscle-cars. The color orange. Saffron. Mellow yellow. These cows!*

Outside all the rock 'n' roll concerts in America, the war in Vietnam rages on, undeterred by "street-fighting men." Blood on my baby sister's long blonde frizz, cracked open by Chicago cops at the Democratic Party Convention. I had set up a card table on the street in front of the main Bargain Records, Inc. store, where I worked at Public Square downtown. Doing my part. Raising money to get protesters out of jail. Showing solidarity.

Do these kids know? Do I get credit for it with them? Maybe they'll realize: I've always liked cows. Hated and deplored la Plaza de Toros. Always drank all my milk. And we all like ice cream, don't we? Right, kids? Eskimo pies? Drumsticks? And what about cheese? See? Think about pizza!

I look up and notice that now the crowd is *with* the down-homey Taylor, laughing *with* him. I let my grown-up body sway a little in the dark, head reeling gyroscopically, swaying to the gentle strum of a single guitar, at the corner of the huge, dark stage, sweat sliding down my living brow. I relax, free to rejoice in the certainty that my hair and I are safe here.

I somehow *am* this large kid audience, *am merged with* these lovely people I'd been checking out from my unaccountably attained perch atop an equipment case. At one with them, with the songs, not comparing this music to Pete Seeger, or Leadbelly, or Stockhausen, or Monk. *Wonderful new music. Music from now.*

I am part of the hall, the moment, the dancing night air. *The beautiful young humans. Now they're reindeer.* Swaying with Taylor and his soft, kind voice, his easy, generous way with word and phrase, his invitation to relax and sense a world embracing all truths at once, a universe shimmering in its place.

Wo-o I've seen fire
'n' I've seen rain…

I smile as he passes me on his way off stage. Smile and feel myself drawn into a vortex I'd always known was out there waiting—if only I could find that famous door marked "For Madmen Only."

I grope my way after him, and *bam!* A whiskey bottle skips across the floor like a flat stone, colliding with my anklebone. Hard. People dressed all fancy-rock, the way I've never seen up close, stagger-strut around backstage. The Who is warming up. *Crash! Yelling! Danger!* Working-class rowdies—rude, proud and drunk—hurl half-full bottles. *Out-of-control behavior! Powerful public anger!* A sheltering hubbub of retainers stumble about in the half-light. Men in suits. Fresh-breasted girls. Swirling concentric circles, crowding, desperate, furious with energy and abandon. *If this is the opening, what will the actual show be like?*

I am soaked and glowing wetly, temples throbbing down to the sinuses. My heart kicks against my ribcage, pounding everything. *Everything is pounding.* I pull back, off to the side of the high-ceilinged backstage. *Am I shaking?* I look up and staring back at me is Howie Meyers, the Decca rep from The Who's label, in a checked blazer, tight Sansabelts and a hairpiece. Why Howie is skulking the perimeter at what should have been his party soon becomes apparent. He calls something to me across an open dressing-room door.

"Howie! Hi. What?" I manage, conquering the dread.

He stares at me. *Tellin' himself I've changed. The last time he saw me I wore a silk rep tie.* "My generation!" he barks again.

What does he mean? Is he mentally writing me off? Am I a drop-out? A bum? I haven't worked in three months. *Cool it,* I tell myself tentatively, *you've worked hard—seven days a week. Take a break. Do some writing.* The record execs—my former suppliers—look at me over their shoulders. *There's Mitch. Cracked with the pressure…yatta-yatta. Blah-blah-blah. Woof-woof! Gone native.*

The kids bob like ripe harvest apples in a watery tub. Lines of young mammaries heave to the music, to the night, to the life caught within their tie-dyed clavicles. My mind gapes unbidden, recalling too-numerous affairs with the sassy young girls who were my employees. One tall dolly of a girl who turned out to have no clit. I looked and looked. "Really, it's okay," she assured me. "You go ahead…"

Runaround Stu on one hand, and devoted 'Jewish' father on the other. And the kids keep coming. *We are all marbled.*

~

It had only been six months since my life split down the middle—a cowboy between Indian ponies. *Which side are you on? The war. The Beatles break up. It's all the same. Falling apart.*

Back then—in January—my assistant manager at Bargain Records, Inc. reared up against me and I feigned mild concern. He may not have known it, but I was already washed up, a glass-jaw pug, looking for a graceful exit. Somewhere to throw the towel. A place to lie down. And here came my assistant baring the old dirk. Resentment, jealousy, and the sad facts of my disaffection blended into a moment's courage as we conferred with my owner in his office.

"Hertz doesn't care anymore." He looked over at me and quickly away. "Since he's back from England, he's not paying attention."

He was right. I was long gone, miles away on a planet called Bigger-Better, where I was creating, not pimping huge conglomerates' product. I was barely thirty-two. It was only two years since the Days of Rage in Chicago. Kent State and Jackson State and Attica had all happened. And when I'd gotten off the plane in London they told me about the Beatles. I'd bought Paul's solo album that day at Harrods. *Are the Beatles political?* I didn't know, exactly. I'd been writing a column in *Carnegie* magazine. *Maybe I'll write about that,* I mused. *Just go home and write.*

Meanwhile, my assistant pressed his apparent advantage. "Mitch *always* overbuys. Everybody knows it. And it's all the wrong stuff—this stuff that he plays on his silly hippie radio show. We spend half our time boxing up returns."

I took a long look at the two of them. My boss, in his brown-black herringbone sports jacket and gray flannels, looking weird and expecting a response from me that would set things aright, take him off the spot. My assistant, blanched in his perpetually starched white shirt and sensible tie. I felt no real threat from him.

Manager of a fucking record chain. Is that all I can lame-ass do? I got up and took the three steps that connected our offices, went to my cheap metal desk with the IBM-card dialer phone, and put a few things in my pockets.

"Like this new soundtrack—whatever it's called. Mitchell bought *a thousand* of it, and it's a three-record set."

"I got co-op advertising with the big buy-in," I offered with a Clifford Odets *Awake and Sing* kind of feeling, as if rousing myself at long last, about to burst into song. "It's called *Woodstock,* by the way," I said over my shoulder, "…that soundtrack."

On the way out the door, I remembered I'd left the Beatles album cover behind on my office wall—the recalled one, with the chopped-up dolls and meat. *Love to take that with me.* I shook it off and, lightheaded, strode up and straight out.

I had been a fairly big deal in Carnegie. Vice President and General Manager. Local radio phenom. Drove a Ferrari. A boy success with a big, romantic home in the flowering hip-trip development Winchester, where kosher fish markets had been replaced by *Nappy Water Beds* and *Whole Food Heaven.*

It was to this aging suburban redoubt that I retired. I bought a pound of decent Mexican weed for $300 and began to write for the first time in ten years. There was something about the solitary act of typing that recombined the halves of my bifurcated being, reacquainted me with wholeness. Unitary. Connected and alone.

Unless I was with my new friends—Carnegie upper-middle-class hipsters I'd met through Trout—smoking awkwardly hand-rolled joints down on the bridge in my front yard. On Yom Kippur, the day of atonement, we were wasted, listening to the new, relevant Rock: Jefferson Airplane, Santana, *Tommy.* The warm Midwestern night swirled with the smell of herb superb, and twinkled with women's laughter.

I'd gone up the stone steps to the giant living room walls lined with LPs from years in the business. Mostly classical. Nine different recordings of *Don Giovanni* (a *real* opera) alone. Ceiling-high cabinets presented thousands of alphabetically arranged spines. An Ivers & Pond parlor grand gleamed in the corner.

I went to my two heavy Thorens turntables alongside the mixer, changed the record, and turned up the gain on the Heathkit pre-amp, harnessing the huge, twin Macintosh 100's. I was heading back down with a fresh lid and some Ruffino, open to the flow of sensations, the freedom of the times…when a cop car pulled up onto the apron at the end of the long driveway.

The man getting out of the car didn't look like a cop. He had on a cheap suit. I walked calmly out to greet him. I saw another head slumped in the back.

"He gave us your name, Mr. Hertz," the detective was saying, looking over my shoulder at the assembled hip-lets, slyly sitting on their roaches on the Italian stone-masonry below. "That's all we could get from him. He's really out of it."

The "he" in question was Chandler Haig—scion of a fashionable WASP academic family, clerk in my main Bargain Records store and, alas, heroin addict. I helped load the lanky young poet-junky out of the back of the municipal Ford.

"This is the third time. His father told us to never call him again."

Bobby Rich and I drove the wasted Chan back to his fancy rehab tank in a lakefront manor out east of town, me in the back seat of Bobby's 230 SE, watching the proliferating fast-food franchises drift by, each in its neon penumbra. An epiphany about this new, emerging America, in the form of a poem, began to form itself in my mind:

Bob Dylan's Dream

While riding on a train going west,
I fell asleep for to take my rest.
I dreamed a dream that made me sad,
Concerning myself and the first few friends I had...

When I got home I began to type it out. I had ten or so neatly stacked pages when the phone rang. It was Trout.

"Doin' *what?* Writin' *what?*"

"A novel."

"A novel?! Man, you ever written a novel?"

"Come on, Thomas." I wanted Trout to like me. "I'm writing one *now.*"

"Now? Well, *now. Now* we need you back on the radio."

Trout was an escapee from the vicious Davis ghetto in Carnegie. His older brother was in prison for shooting a cop, and his younger brother had been killed by police gunfire. Trout was a Kent State grad. His satyresque smile and ready mammal surge made me love him blindly, but he was a master hypester, and I was always a potential mark.

"Who *we,* Trout?"

"The Carnegie fucking radio audience. They need your novel ass back on the airwaves, whether they know it or not. And they'll know it if they hear you."

"Meaning what, exactly?"

"Meaning how'd you like to be on WNBM?"

"Man, please. Those dog-brains don't want me. They want some schmuck talkin' bout *what's my sign?*"

"No, Mitch. You ain't paying attention. I *said:* how'd *you* like t'be back on the air again? Do y'own thing. Talk that weird shit you talk."

"They hire *you* already, or what?"

"No. But they call me a lot for advice. Think I'm a big deal. I told 'em: lose the plastic hippies; get Mitch Hertz over there!"

"Do I say 'this is Virgo Mitch Hertz,' or some lame deal like that?"

"Just get the fuck over there and apply. You *got* the job."

"That's it? I got the job? Then what?"

"Then you *immediately* help me get in as the fucking *Pro*-gram Director," he cackled. "Meanwhile, I'll see you at The Who!"

We'd seen *Woodstock* together earlier that year. Trout loved The Who.

"They didn't invite me. I'm out-of-the-industry."

"*I'm* inviting you."

"You?"

"I'm MC'ing."

Did I fuck myself forever? Quitting pre-med to study philosophy and musicology, Wittgenstein and Webern. Useless dogshit, just what dying Vietnamese peasants need: Arnold "I Hate Rhythm" Schoenberg and Bertrand Fucking Russell. My dad thinks I'm an asshole, I know he does. And I am. I certainly am. What's this all in aid of?

"Hey, Johnny! What'r you rebellin' against, exactly?"
"Well…waddaya got?"

Will they treat me like a hippie? A bum? A "white nigger"? Nice white people—Carnegie housewives, in fact—had spat in my face when I joined the Freedom Summer demonstration marching up Rockefeller Street. *My mother had danced with Paul Robeson. For that matter, whom am I serving? Whom! Whom! Whom! Would one of these younger radical kids laugh at the formality of the objective pronoun?* There's something so sweet about their "trip" that I want to just sneak silently onboard. *Am I giving up? Committing career suicide? Is this a mistake? An illusion?*

At least you're doing it voluntarily, says an oddly familiar voice.

I listen. *Am I? Or just copping another plea?*

You were never trained in business anyway, the voice says.

(What was I trained in?)

And Bargain Records, Inc. was growing to twenty outlets. And, you were, admit it...over your head.

No!

Yes you were! You never were a businessman. Just a good faker.

Running the swelling retail record chain with growing apprehension, fear of discovery—nostril-deep in my own brine. But my boss was equally unqualified, and looked to me for leadership. *Turn of inventory. Shrinkage control! Too much work. Between their bullshit and the radio station—too many hours.*

Our new units popped up randomly across America, metastasizing onto the new malls: Indianapolis, St. Louis, El Paso, Ventura, CA. *God! Just another franchise. Another place to grow money.*

I had my comforts—the scotch and the Black Beauties, and, of course, the welcoming arms of Placidyl. *O, Sleep, again enfold me.*

Back behind the curtain, Trout is smiling, gazing down into my newly-bearded face, whirling acid-eyes swimming gold and amber patches.

"Mitch Hertz, say hello to Roger Daltrey."

I behold a short blonde man in a vest, flowing gauze shirt and tight leather pants, who laughs, tilts a bottle at me and winks. He lets out a whoop, and jumps off to join the backstage boister. A more engaged, less altitudinous Me follows Trout as he trots off—his red, white and blue Sly Stone-rawhide fringes flapping gently. *My rescuer, my soul-pal.*

Trout heads back on-stage. The lights come down in the big house. Shouts of anticipation fill the dark hall. A spot picks up Trout:

"And now," Trout's big, husk-o-ramic radio voice booms out of the ceiling. "Let's give a big Carnegie welcome to...The Who!"

Immediately four bodies hurtle past me, and the scream that lofts to greet them is terrifying. I recoil, shrink, start to fade, ducking the high-sparking rockers and the ferocity of their audience. I am pushed backwards, head raging alienation, reeling to the side of the stage where I stumble over my former seat, the familiar equipment case, and am gently convinced by simple physics to sit down and stay put.

With the return to a safe haven, acid-fear recedes a hair. Then I realize that I can't quite see the band. Taking further stock—I am no longer hidden from the audience. The narrowly-parted curtains which had made me invisible during James Taylor's set are now spread wide, placing me squarely in the crowd's sight-lines. *Shit! What if they see me?* I decide to trust the darkness.

Sweating again into rapidly blinking eyes, I look out at the crowd and see only how different we are. *Different people. Wolves. Can I pass as one of them? A comrade? A fellow soldier? A fellow killer? Pull the wool...*

THWANG! My drug-reverie is shattered by a hammer stroke that must be a guitar strum, cracking forth from a huge stack of amplifiers I can no longer fail to notice behind me. Just as I turn to flee, I see a leaping, jump-suited devil dart out, wind-milling his pick-arm in a quixotic mid-air semicircle to smite the instrument, land on his nimble knees, and slide out across the apron. The energy is almost unbearable. Fascinated, I hold my ground, and despite constant blasts from too-close speakers, I find myself melting, not fighting— putting aside my own formal musical training and simply dissolving into the ocean of music: "I Can See for Miles," "Magic Bus," "Summertime Blues," and finally an hour-long version of *Tommy*. Climax. Climax. Climax.

Then the kids rush the stage. I come out of my mind-ballet with a gasp. *How long was I gone? Where have I been? What's that awful screaming?* The music ends. The roaring swells. Trout is on the P.A., thanking The Who and—*oh no!*—bringing them back for an encore before himself jumping down into the first row to enjoy.

Again the first thirty rows surge. I see Trout shoved forward by a mass of young bodies. Each time the crest is higher as Roger Daltrey wails...

We ain't gonna take it.
Never did and never will...

I am spellbound, brain swiveling…spiraling, splintering. A glimpse of Trout, *flick!,* like a struck match, borne forward, riding like a lure on a fly-caster's line, red, white and blue in the reflected light. Then swallowed by the roiling currents of sharks swimming upstream toward the stage, the sound, and some awful end.

Then I see the cops. A line of blue danger behind me, gripping billyclubs, grinding teeth. The song screams into a final climax and slams to a halt. An undifferentiated roar fills the vacuum. Bodies flare up over the lip of the stage.

I'm panting. Another roar from the crowd and *pop!*—a brilliant white flash. A huge bank of floodlights springs into life, blinds the crowd, and commands it into instant silent submission.

Sober and depleted, they file from the hall, leaving me standing stock-still, staring straight into the light.

There was a picture of me in an article in the *Carnegie Courier,* January, 1972, shot in a tiny on-air studio at WNBM-FM, me and Trout's first Carnegie station together. It showed a dreamy man in a turtleneck, lost under a dark, full beard. A strip of light from forehead to cheekbones created a contrast which made the long ash-blonde hair appear almost black. The accompanying story told of amazing ratings, listener loyalty, and pleasure with the prospects ahead. But all I saw, barely masked by the hirsute-suit, was the sadness in the eyes.

I'd broken my shoulder late that spring. In those pre-corporate days, radio accountancy was still loose enough to permit endless trade-out deals, barters and other fanciful schemes for self-enrichment. I somehow talked management into letting me slip in an improvised spot for a custom cycle shop on the West Side in exchange for a customized Triumph Bonneville. While they were building it for me, I'd do some kind of rap about them on my 8:00-midnight show.

I'd never been on a bike before. In high school, where I'd been a jock/hood, I'd subscribed to *Hot Rod,* longing for a chopped and channeled '32 or '34 coupe, or a Kustomized '49 Ford or Merc, totally de-chromed, with leaded headlights, Pontiac tail lights, and a 3/4-race mill. After I'd been thrown out of Baker High and was scrambling furiously to pass as "collegiate," I bought and restored a 1948 MG-TC, with right-hand drive and sixteen-inch bicycle wire wheels. My more affluent classmates' cars were chosen from the ranks of the Triumph TR-2, Austin-Healy 100, or ubiquitous MG-TD. Later, sports cars became the semi-official Fifties Ride among educated jazz and classical music people.

But now was rock 'n' roll, and motorcycles looked like rock 'n' roll to me. So I hung out at the shop with the greaser-hippies, asking dumb questions, picking up the lingo, watching them work.

The day of delivery I proudly mounted my candy-apple "Trumpet," kicked it to life, popped the clutch, and made such a fool of myself that the shop owner, Buzz, decided he'd better follow me home on his Norton, just to make sure the hot-dog deejay didn't off himself on their product.

We took it easy most of the way back to the East Side, and as we reached my bijou stream-side residence, I couldn't help but gun it heroically before turning into my driveway to make *la bella figura.* Buzz knew where I lived; he'd been there in his other capacity of drug dealer, so I didn't bother to signal. Stoned as usual, and pissed at being left in the dust by an upstart, Buzz came roaring after me in second gear, the Norton getting on the cam. As I braked hard to start the left turn, he rammed me right behind the thigh.

The bike popped sharply out from under me, hit the cement, and went clattering off down the street. I went straight down. Luckily we had helmet laws in the Midwest, and mine shattered as it absorbed most of the force of the road.

Supine in the middle of the street, I marveled and paused to express gratitude that I was not only still alive, but conscious. Then I quickly stood up, sufficiently aware of the approaching lane of cars, and surfed my still-pumping adrenaline wave out of the street and onto the lawn. Leaning heavily against a big maple tree, I breathed a self-congratulatory *whew* before I realized, from the pain radiating out from under my leather jacket, that my shoulder hadn't been so lucky.

A neighbor came charging up. "Are y'all right?"

"Sure am!" I said, and passed out.

⁓

With back-to-back air-shifts, Trout and I soon became sensations. And there with us was Tree. Tree had lived his life with his ear to a radio, loving all the voices who, he figured, advanced the medium. Growing up dad-less, he did this not so much out of social desperation as a need to stimulate neurology which might otherwise have lacked sufficient input from the environment. A typical Carnegie childhood, in other words.

So little Timmy listened when his mother drove him to school on those frosted lakeside mornings, when the car heater wasn't stoked yet, but the AM radio was: early Beatles, Dylan, Lovin' Spoonful—and he dug it all.

But for him the real magicians were the guys who lived the radio life—talked the talk, spun the platters, made harmless, idiotic jokes and dispatched news and weather as if they are barely tolerable nuisances. His fantasy about these AM guys was that they were warm, mildly clever middle-aged men who chain-smoked, drank coffee from mugs and were permanently pleasant, in a slightly arch but hearty insider sort of way. Yet they remained always just out of reach.

His father left when he and his sister were quite small. Morning-drive jocks have a way of sounding so chummy-cheery. He tells himself he can trust them.

Our behavior went well beyond Tree's childhood dream of comfortable breakfast table affability. Not that our AM predecessors hadn't partied. The mythical Top-40 speed kings always found some new end of the candle to burn. Still, rare indeed were those who went balls-out public with it all. After a while it was impossible for us to remember where the party ended and our air shifts began.

Tree followed Trout from WEMP to WNBM, creatively named after its corporate owner, National Business Machine, and perched in the penthouse of a major downtown hotel. The AM sister-station had already high-tailed it for the suburbs leaving us a playpen of Brobdingnagian proportions.

The young, blonde and relentlessly provocative daughter of WNBM's General Manager, Steve Gromek, came to visit one night just before I turned the mic over to our all-night guy, Harold Childs, a friend of Trout's from the ghetto. He played blues and 'Trane till dawn.

Jackie Gromek was pretty like her mother, clad in a Chicago T-shirt and tight bell-bottoms. "Gotta joint?" she greeted me, climbing the carpeted flight to our booth. "I'm old enough," she answered my doubting glance.

"But you're my boss's kid."

"What does *he* know?" she said as I turned to cue a record, and fished a roach from the Hot Tuna promotional ashtray.

"You've got a point."

"Match?" Jackie lit the tiny roach, inhaled gracefully but deeply, then slid it between my lips. I focused on her chest as I toked a solid hit, her hand on my face.

"I like your beard."

I exhaled with a sigh, leaned over to check the progress of Miles' "In a Silent Way," and squinted up through our common smoke.

"Nice hair." She pat-patted me like a puppy, smoothing down my substantial mane from the top of my head where the earphones had left a tangle to where it ended on my shoulders. To do this she leaned over me from the front, and the slight contact with her breasts caused a familiar reaction.

"What? My hair?"

"I like your voice."

I won't pretend that at this stage in my escape from *petit-bourgeois* domestic constraints I possessed a shred of principled restraint from dalliance with the young and willing. It was only that her father was a big Polish-American fella who hated everything I stood for and who could fire my ass cold.

"'Scuse me," she said, slipping her arm around my neck and sliding herself down onto my lap.

I thought about Senta at home—waiting out a sixth pregnancy, which might produce our third surviving baby. "In a Silent Way" ran out and I segued Pink Floyd. Jackie produced a roach clip and we mouthed the last hits, heads close.

"Don't you get off at midnight?"

Harold came in, grokked The Haps at a glance, and offered to take over early. I was still wavering but Jackie and my nether navigator were unanimous, so, since all other doors were locked, we found a small utility closet where we sprawled on top of a couple dozen unplugged hotel telephones and consummated with more passion than comfort. Then we said good night, and I went home to Senta.

Tree, our fledgling production chief, handled engineering, recording, editing, spots, news and PSAs. He was no less than brilliant, inspiring our whole staff with the rockish melodrama he brought to anything he touched. To have your voice underscored by Tree's silken envelope of sound, cut tight as the razor could cut, was to know perfection. Or a pinnacle of narcissism, at the very least.

After a few months, you could feel the city of a million souls begin to levitate, with the local audience getting its daily dose of the alternative culture. There wasn't much else happenin' in Carnegie, that, or any other summer, so radio, ya know, was it…

1972. Still the same us-and-them attitude of the 60's. The population divided between do-your-duty patriotic knee-jerky *support for,* and militant *rejection of* the colonial war in Southeast Asia. Youth radicalization crept in apace. The ruling class showed its willingness to kill even white kids to silence criticism of its policies. Trout heroically defied his WEMP bosses, putting his life on the line to play Crosby, Stills, Nash and Young's "(Four Dead in) Ohio" on Top-40 to uproarious civic affect.

Us and Them. Black against White, definitely. Always. Carnegie was outrageously segregated. Add to that antiwar youth versus the aging bullies who ran the land of the free, who benefited from its racism, its oppression of women, its Cold War and other imperial adventures.

The 60's and the early 70's were informed by the sense that mankind will finally flower again. Even so debased a concept as Flower Power was about that—so deeply obvious that a lot of seekers after subtlety may have missed the importance of this otherwise term of derision. Flowers in rifle barrels. The kids just want to be free, not die in Vietnam or Laos or Jackson State or Kent. Not in back alley abortions, either. Youth wants to smoke dope and fuck. Rebellion, yes. But also, pleasure. Free to feel again! The best revenge.

To be free, after all. To be integers. To become what Karl Marx, echoing the French Revolution, called "fully human." Enlightenment Now! To struggle with Nature, as common allies in the shared task of creating and developing human civilization to its highest fulfillment, to glorious achievements beyond our wildest dreams. Not locked, as we were, to a paradigm from hell (or was it Las Vegas?)—a social model of strip malls, fast food and profit, profit, profit.

Profit is not a dirty word in Carnegie.
The Founding Fathers didn't need food stamps!

—from local billboards, 1970

We were pretty radical at WNBM. Flippant, at least. Insolent, even. Subverting culture shibboleths. *Putney Swope* as an FM station, playing black music and white music of all genres, including gamelan and shakuhachi. Glenn Gould followed Led Zeppelin. Me, the designated militant, guided news policy, waxing anti-war, pro-woman, pro-student, anti-dress code, pro-gay, anti-Cop. *"Whaddaya got?"*

I went on the air to attack the Kent State Chancellor for trying to keep people away from a commemorative service for the student victims of National Guard bullets. The ratings were not slow to follow. Soon we were the first FM station to displace a major market AM Top-40 station. The Industry buzzed.

Yet even though the station was a smash, with our aggressive and obstreperous antics we presented something of a problem. Between Trout's sexual lighthouse charisma, and me challenging anything with authority anywhere near it, our on-air *pizzica-stuzzica* attack left few feathers unruffled. Endless calls from disciplinarian principals, churches, merchants, record companies, concert promoters, and finally, the Fraternal Order of Police (I'd played "Mr. Big Pig" by Country Joe) made management testy, despite the station's tripled billings. The home-office business machine boys over in Carnegie didn't want to hear about culture-clash in their only hippie FM station, and memoed as much. Trout rankled, told the General Manager to kiss his black ass. There followed angry verbal warfare, then an uneasy peace.

During this armed truce the Big Time came calling, in the person of Norman Woodehedd, the general manager of the other FM rocker, our ailing/failing competitor, WURB. The station was the runt of a fairly impressive FM litter spawned by corporate broadcast giant UrboMedia in the process of gestating the first and only "Progressive-Rock" network in American radio.

Woodehedd, called "The Head" by everyone who knew and therefore hated him, had previously blown it at hip, outrageous and failing-to-meet-corporate-profit-projections KURB in L.A. He was given an Official Reprieve: *Rescue the dead-loser WURB in Carnegie, and we'll think about sending you back to L.A.*

And he was fucking up. His on-air talent consisted of a couple of college-radio graduates and one pickled-and-fading old Top-40 speed-freak from Pittsburgh named Crazy Al.

Woodehedd called Trout and made an unrefusable offer. Though we both mistrusted silly The Head, Trout wanted to take his serious money. I held out for a contract or a signing bonus. They laundered me a Volvo with 18,000 miles as a perk. The deal was struck. Most of the WNBM staff—Trout, Tree,

I and a few others—departed, licking our lips, and moving our chips up the street to WURB. Bringing our audience with us, we became kings at The 'URB Superb.

In the glow of our first killer ratings book, Trout, ever the patient tactician, summarily told the despised Woodehedd to piss off.

"Beat it, Head. You're bad-vibing the whole operation. And your maroon fucking suits, man! Come back on payday to sign the damn checks. *We're* the reason we're number one in the ARB, not *you*," Trout sneered. "Now, g'wan home!"

Tree and I spent most of the summer of '72 together, segueing tunes from vinyl LP's with covers marked: "PROMO" or "FOR DEMONSTRATION ONLY." We played Emerson, Lake and Palmer, Allman Brothers, Hendrix, Neil Young, Miles' *Bitches Brew* or *Jack Johnson,* the Joni Mitchell *Blue* album, Dave van Ronk, the Fugs, Zappa—*Hot Rats* and *Willy the Pimp,* the first *Little Feat* LP, Ry Cooder's first LP, Randy Newman's "I Think It's Going To Rain Today," plus Leonard Cohen, Walter Carlos, Mahavishnu Orchestra, Pink Floyd, The Band, Woody Guthrie, The Byrds' *Sweetheart of the Rodeo,* a lot of Judy Collins but especially *Bread and Roses* and *Marat/Sade,* that wonderful whale-music, and Donovan, and Dylan, too.

Between tunes, often as not I inserted a spontaneous needle-dropped edit from a comedy album—Firesign Theater, early Cheech & Chong, *Beyond the Fringe,* Peter Sellers, and of course, Lenny Bruce, Lord Buckley and Richard Pryor. Beyond the later Miles Davis, the only jazz we played was Monk ("Well You Needn't" from *Monk's Music*—with Coltrane *and* Coleman Hawkins— was my favorite), Bill Evans, occasional Billie Holiday and Bessie Smith or King Cole Trio tunes with Nat on piano. We played Mississippi John Hurt and Buddy Guy and Muddy Waters and Libba Cotton and Freddy King as well as Leon Russell, Dr. John and Dan Hicks. And there was the inevitable Jefferson Airplane/Buffalo Springfield/Poco/Crosby Stills & Nash axis, orbited by Santana and Blood, Sweat & Tears.

I wasn't as crazy about the Stones as some, but I held *Sticky Fingers* next to my heart. I figured if the Kids dug it, fine—let's put it out there on the ether. And if the phones requested it and your gorge didn't rise when you listened to it, try to sneak it in: Black Sabbath, Jethro Tull (I turned off the monitors), early Fleetwood Mac (instant bad mood)—but as a point of honor we *never* played Chicago.

We provided the soundtrack to a humidity-engorged city belatedly beginning to actualize the social advances of the decade just ended.

Tree learned some things from me that summer. Texture, maybe—color and ideas and drama—but mostly timing. I also taught *myself,* forcing myself to formulate what otherwise might have continued to languish in my cannabis-drenched intuition. I learned something from my young colleague, too—acoustics, electronics, and other technical areas where I was thin. Before Tree, I couldn't cut tape, or record my own voice. Somehow, it worked perfectly. We improvised a dope-speak shorthand that allowed us to make unique sets gracefully, and for two years we inhabited a party-till-your-shift-starts-again, High-Middle Maoist, Rock 'n' Roll Heaven-on-Earth. Which you could only do if you got consecutive number ones in the ARB ratings. We got six straight. We were good. *Every*thing was good. People never stopped flattering me.

"Yeah. If I'm so good, what am I doing in Carnegie?" I asked myself, as I put down the studio phone. Someone had called to play flatter-the-jock. I took the roach that Tree passed me and toked up.

"Phones'r smokin' tonight," Tree said.

"Yeah. Let's shine 'em for a while. I'm bored with what they think."

"Yeah. Like, 'Too much of nothin' makes a man into a liar.'"

"You got *that* right," and took another toke.

"Thinkin' 'bout L.A.?"

"Yeah. And I don't even *like* L.A."

"What is it, then? Just challenge time? The old tick-tick-tick?" He took the microscopic joint back between his great, slender, editor's fingers.

"It's time. Yeah. I guess…well…if they offered us L.A.…."

Outside our small studio the steam of Midwestern night hung like chloroform over the city. Inside the booth it was cool and dark. Tree ran the board, 'slip-cuing' the tunes, sliding the pots to adjust the audio levels, taking records on or off the air as I instructed. I sat off to the side, holding announcer copy with my good arm.

Tree had, with no extra pay, been running the board for me—an act of solidarity unique in commercial radio history. All I had to do was occasionally open and close the mic switch. I was thus freed to do my mad little rap, read some live announcer tags and "rip 'n' read" newscast, night after night, until the plaster came off.

⁓

"Ma-an…" I began, and gazed over at the diminutive dark-haired girl seated silently on the carpet in front of the big record rack. "Hey Sherri, you okay?"

The teenager slowly sat up as I passed her a joint, stretching dreamily. The Beatles' "Across the Universe" filled our ears. As her arms came back, her extraordinary mammary development swelled underneath her Attica sweatshirt.

Sherri had first come to the studios as a guest of a record-nerdly regular. He was the kind of kid who occasionally turned me on to new music and obscure underground bands, sitting quietly, stonedly knowledgeable on the other side of the glass, nodding gently, punching, as it were, my hip card. Sherri was his date. It was first her splendid young breasts, then her oceaning eyes which commanded my glance, and relocated my attention to the detriment of that evening's show.

After the night of ill-concealed staring, she floated over.

"You're someone important," she offered in greeting. "I should know you."

It began: bubble, seethe, slosh and burn. "How old are you?" I queried.

"Twelve," she had snarled up at me, knitting the olive velvet of her forehead in splendid petty pique. I had barely controlled my awe at her insouciance and teenage mastery of time and place. Later, I finessed her age as covertly as I could from her erstwhile escort. He told me she was seventeen. When she showed up at the station a month or so later I sleuthed out when exactly she would achieve her majority, then pounced.

The day after her eighteenth birthday, I fired up a doob in Trout's Carnegie Heights kitchen, leaned on the avocado fridge, then dialed her folk's number in a striving-parvenu Jewish suburb abutting Baker Heights. Breathing quick and shallow, despite the THC just beginning to cut the adrenaline from my blood, I blurted, "Can I see you?"

"I'd like that." There was an easy conspiring quality to the smile in her voice. "When?" Her frankness was exemplary.

"How about tonight?" I gave up any pretense of subtlety.

A pause. Muffled voices.

"You'll have to pick me up here. Would that be okay?"

~

My marital situation precluded *too* much tramping about. Senta and I cultivated the appearance of happy Jewish house-mice, painting a picture of self-conscious munchkin bliss. It was easy. Senta was coy and impish—an actress, a singer, champion skier, and daughter of musicians, she was a perfect concert hall companion. Bed, however, was another country. For whatever reason, we never really sparked, relegating sex to blind, middle-of-the-night forays and sorties. And she'd been permanently pregnant. Careful not to lose yet another fetus! So, slowly initially, to slake my raging rapacity, I'd started stepping out.

Senta didn't catch on until we chanced to see Sherri at the Carnegie Symphony. Sherri was in a mid-thigh cotton A-line, darkly delicious, maybe 4'11" in boots, with buttocks-length bright black hair of Asian silkiness.

We engaged in intense mutual mooning, our eyes locked in interstellar cruise-control. I didn't really give a shit, fed up with my own insincerity and so desperate for authentic human response. "Fuck it," I thought.

So it was that this over-30 ex-businessman, preening behind full beard and newfound celebrity, married and spiritually encumbered—after what the Yogis might graciously call due deliberation—crept haltingly up the driveway, parked the repainted old Porsche convertible, and extended his hand to two people and a dog who knew that he had come to fuck their little girl.

Sherri and I smoked dope and watched a twenty-fifth anniversary Hiroshima memorial film on PBS, lying on overstuffed pillows on the den floor of Trout's pad. Fried corpses floated by on the screen while a test pressing of the first LP from a new singer named Elton John played over-and-over:

I hope you don't mind
I hope you don't mind

She wore shorts. I touched her smooth legs, thinking how firm her flesh was, tight, like a very young child almost. I asked her whether she'd ever made love.

"Once," she whispered, as I stroked the insides of her thighs.

My breath came quick and unreliable. I was unable to control my passion, as if she were the experienced one. It had been so long since I'd been with someone my body cared about. My hands shook as I slipped the panties away from her silken-haired sex, and the delicacy of her aroma.

From then on, late at night, after my air shift, aided by reefer, coke, mescaline, and the occasional pipe of opium, we hovered ecstatic. On the wet grass in Trout's backyard, tripping in starlight, the wet Midwestern air curling our hungry hair.

Once on the carpet in Trout's den, as I slid in and out of her nakedness, her wonderful pillowy mammae heaving, legs in high leather boots grasping my butt, a noise behind me pierced the veil of weed. Prisoner of the moment, I finally managed to glance over my shoulder to see Trout in the darkened hall, stroking himself as he imbibed the action, to which I immediately returned.

Sherri was in my studio, smiling a proprietary smile. I couldn't wait till my four-hour shift was over so I could at last ravish her youthful flesh.

"C'm over here," I wheedled…

She rose swanlike and lowered herself slowly onto my lap. My hand went under her shirt as her head came down on my shoulder. On the turntable Jefferson Starship crooned *"Can you see the stars tonight?"* to the darkened city. Her thigh pushed against my awakening tumescence. My left hand rose in an arc to smooth her sleek hair from her face. I kissed her forehead.

She was the symbol of my reawakening, of the snow beginning to melt from my sleeping body, and I dreamt often and deeply of running away with her. She would come back from Mt. Holyoke College to visit, a freshman on her tiny 175 cc Honda. We would rut furious and unabashed on Trout's desk at the station, later going out to our motorcycles into the night, my new Norton Commander riding off in tandem with her smaller bike. Endlessly fantasizing cross-country motel motorcycle madness—hacking my way, machete-minded, through the undergrowth of my strangled psyche. Slashing and plunging, an end to authority, to responsibility, to futures. Away from anger and thwarted sex. Emerging from deep within a body grown padded in the middle, and raggedly hirsute, the hair on my face obscuring the sneer of self-contempt my exposed cheeks might reveal, eyes glowing bright with trapped desire and lost chances.

My hand smoothed her cheek. Her dark eyes glowed under brows that were gentle and serene. I pushed her back, opening her white blouse. Warmth rose from her body in tropical waves. Breasts solid but soft, I lifted them from below, pressing them back into her, gently at first, then harder. Her mouth was small but very full, lips a true pink under a tiny nose. I slid a bra strap off her freckle-dusted shoulder. Flesh spilled its way to freedom. Then the other strap. I pulled her to me, dick pressing through my jeans into her belly. Her nipple rolled between my thumb and forefinger. One of her hands slowly unbuttoned my Levis, the other stroked the swollen denim. Lightning illuminated my groin. I squeezed her tit. Eyes closed again, she was opening her mouth.

BAM! The studio door flew open. A black man in cut-offs, a "Truth and Soul" T-shirt, and volcanoes in his eye sockets stood poised for a second, taking us in. Then, leaping into our cozy sphere, the veins on his neck popping out, he hallooed, "L.A., Motherfucker! Here We Come! We done *did* it now! Pack your bags, Mitchell! We's goin' to the Coast!" Tommy Trout *triumphans.*

On the radio, The Who sang:

Nobody knows what it's like
to be the sad man…

When I brought my confused young family to Los Angeles that late spring the city seemed tidy, sun-splashed and serene, a Shangri-la to us Rust Bowl refugees. Ocean, hills, palm trees in graceful civilized rows. The streets were clean, and everywhere, literally underfoot, bloomed exotic flora such as Carnegie only dreamed. Sure, it wasn't New York or London, with their cultural blandishments, or San Francisco with its hipper-than-anyplace patina and invigorating bay air, but what could care I, beholder of Paradise?

I was fascinated with the light, a special Renaissance Florence peachy-pink that licked the face of the city. Applied from without, but appearing to have come from within, as if Southern California had a deep glowing essence, a fiery core—a magic fire, which cooled on its way to the surface of things.

The city moved at a graceful, almost stately pace. The expression "laid-back" was the official modifier for the L.A. "lifestyle" among the rock writers and other Easterners, who still referred to my new home as "the coast." This designation seemed to apply mostly to the recent layer of chic new Hollywood hippies filtering onto the scene from privilege-points east: The East Village, Upstate New York (referred to sweepingly as "Woodstock"), Yale Drama School and everywhere else the new Beatles-born freedom-urge shook people from their inertia. They came trooping on in, and the Old Hollywood was waiting for them.

I came to Los Angeles following a dream, but a dream is in waking life not a conscious strategy so much as an unfocused *drive*, however fiercely repressed, to open something up. When UrboMedia offered me the coveted night-time slot on its struggling L.A. flagship, KURB-FM, I told Senta to sell everything we didn't want to take with us. I don't remember her voicing an opinion. But then again, I may not have been listening.

When our plane pulled up on the tarmac at LAX there was a big white limousine and a huge glittery "WELCOME" banner to greet us at the gate. We stared down, stunned at the white *Playboy* magazine stretch limo and the smiling face of the immoderately longhaired singer/songwriter Harmony ("just Harmony"), the girlfriend of Lance Guilford, president of *Playboy*'s new record label. She was an old pal from Carnegie who was living medium large in L.A., it appeared. We herded our kids into the limo and set off for our temporary new home.

The Head hadn't found us a realtor, much less any prospects as he'd promised. Then he became suddenly elusive, vanishing mysteriously like *ignis fatuus*.

Enter arboreal Laurel Canyon, a rural hillside paradise as different from the bland-but-nasty L.A. Basin as it is distant. Laurel was still home to the folk-scare end of Rock. We were staying with another friend from Carnegie, a tall, blonde 25-year-old Harvard-grad and Albert Grossman-road-manager-turned-film-producer named Jay Largent. On the floor of his poolside bachelor cottage, listening to a test pressing of *Goat's Head Soup,* and smoking what he told us was the Stones' dope, Largent ran it down:

"There're people out here who can see doing entertainment as art."

"Or vice-versa, I would imagine," I said.

"Those are the Old People. That's all they know."

"So who are the New People?"

"Me," he said.

"You." I repeated his confident flatness.

"And you."

"Me. Why me?"

"Because you're part of it; the thinking. New thinking. I knew it when I met you back in Ohio. You're a Producer."

"A producer." I wondered.

"Producer with vision."

It was great dope.

We lay there: Jay, filled with contented yearning, Senta, lost and anxious, and me, hovering between the Great Dream of Heaven and the Big Fear of Right Now, all of us ripped-to-the-tits (as our Hollywood Hills real estate broker would later describe as how she got after work) on world-class herb. The smell of jasmine appeared on the warm breeze crossing the pool into our new lives.

Senta fell asleep on a pillow. Jay and I went for a walk. Climbing to the top of Wonderland we looked out across the lake of lights of Los Angeles.

"You're doing the right thing," he said.

That night I had trouble sleeping. Drifting between threat and opportunity my mind began to take the measure of The Head's perfidy. He had done less-than-zip. No house, no agent, no car, no nothing. Just embarrassed looks when we arrived at the station to visit. Right out of the cab, we told the driver we were considering a place in Malibu. Noting our ragamuffinness, he said, "That's nice out there." (Meaning "Good luck, jerk-o.")

But in his dark office, The Head was diffident to a crime. We sat, squirming vacantly on his red leather couches, as he murmured into the phone, occasionally looking up in annoyance at our persisting presence.

"Gotta go, Mitch. Here's the keys to the station wagon. Drop 'em off to my girl Jodi when you're done. Have a good time in L.A." He shoved them at me with a now-go-away gesture.

A damp chill replaced the night flower scents as I fought to steady my diaphragm and deepen my breathing. The next morning, unburdened by our presentiments of disaster, our young host simply picked up the *L.A. Times,* found a listing for a place up in Beachwood Canyon, and drove us over in his Bavaria.

"Even hipper than Laurel. Quieter. Doesn't go through to the Valley, so less traffic," he filled us in, heading across Hollywood Boulevard to Franklin.

"What's the deal with the sign?"

"You know about the HOLLYWOOD sign."

I didn't, but nodded. He was driving faster now, aggressively, imperiously.

"Used to be HOLLYWOODLAND," he barked, as he jammed the silver sedan into a hole in traffic, sneering at a guy in a Maverick.

"That's the real estate company," I said, checking the listing. "Hollywoodland."

"Right."

He passed a line of cars going up Beachwood, under the stone gate, past the old Market, and way up into the cul-de-sac canyon under the HOLLYWOOD sign. The Mission Spanish-style house looked simple and undistinguished from the road, but ran four floors down the hillside. We met the owner, haggled briefly, and then bravely made an offer, which was accepted with alacrity.

So it was that this rugged Spanish stucco in Beachwood Canyon—the Nitty Gritty Dirt Band's ex-band-house—became ours. Summer of 1972. Time of the Big Rush—cocaine, multiple sex contacts, herpes, and Studio 54.

I had a week to settle in, so I mounted my big new Honda Four, put my oldest son Bruno, aged four and a half, up on the tank in front of me, and set off to explore the hills and streets of the city, cruising Sunset, immersing myself geopolitically. And I loved what I saw.

When UrboMedia offered me the L.A. gig, I had felt something calling out to me—a vaguely intuited counter-cultural sense of becoming something better, a renewal of self and a reaching out to others. A long-time reader of the *L.A. Free Press* (over and above the *Village Voice),* I'd been predisposed to the looseness, newness, even the shallow transience, the *plasticity* of L.A.—the cheese factor. In those Ron Cobb cartoons and Art Kunkin editorials I'd heard The Hymn of the Energy Ocean. Or something.

I tried to keep this feeling alive. Even as my life crumbled and fell progressively to bits, there was always a marvelous throb, a golden light, the rich Pacific offer of Life in all its fullness. I felt pulled into everything about my new hometown. There were 24-hour markets, gas stations, massage parlors, answering services, and dog-groomers who would come to your house.

The first night I reported for work at KURB, I opened the door of the broadcast booth and saw Garret "Professor Fermento" Manson, sitting at the mic, preparing to do what was to have been my 8:00 shift. I introduced myself, then Fermento explained in his Jolly Nerd persona:

"They're all in a meeting in The Head's office," he giggled. "Some kinda Programming deal, I guess. They asked me to sit in for you for tonight."

I made my way down the corridors and opened the door to a cloudbank, which wafted out at me like a nameless need. Seemed The Head had chosen this regular program department meeting to casually break the news to his talented staff—with his trademark clenched-jaw succinctity—of the firing of handsome and popular Martin Kooper.

"And, by the way, here's the new guy—Mitch."

Great.

They swiveled around to view me. I'd come in from Podunksville looking like a *muzhik*, a Narodnik peasant-out-of-water in this lotus land of tonsured beards and cowboy shirts, presumed to be the boss' butt-boy. With my last breath of bravery, I looked up. They regarded me with a salad of attitudes: amusement, disdain, frank indifference and contempt, all the while maintaining an invader-repelling banter.

I had no choice but to set up shop. On my first night I did one of my best shows ever—Allman Brothers to open, Johnny Winters, Freddie King, Leon Russell, middle-period Dylan, Pink Floyd, then Dave van Ronk singing "Cocaine."

In those richly innocent days, the station was helping to lead the country into a brief but memorable period of pan-erogenous sexual freedom: David Bowie's polymorphous *Ziggy Stardust* tour, Traffic's *Low Spark of High-heeled Boys*, Glam Rock. Sex, sex, sex, repackaged for the Hip Now. A big local band had a new album cover with a cute blonde in an apron proffering a pie. A big slice was already gone, and looking into the hole of its departure one found oneself staring into a vagina.

KURB offered its audience Barry Clear and Fermento, as well as the "Jive" Clive Levine, a manic digressive who speed-rapped a surreal mixture of Céline, Ginsberg and Sly Stone. But for all its artistic success, my new station was to make a programming transition. Despite millions of SoCal hippies stoned and listening, KURB was a corporate-poor relation to its big AM sister. KDRT— all Nashville, and a mile wide—had 20 to 30 *times* the annual billings of their upstart FM sibling. But UrboMedia understood that KURB had lured the kids, and, lo! The little freaks had money to spend.

In the first phase of its drive to push spot-rates to corporate profitability norms, the network wisely told their stations to play the cards they were dealt. The Head's mission, the reason they brought him back from Carnegie in the first place, was to plan and execute a multi-stage strategy, of which we were unknowingly facilitating the first link.

Initially he let us posture bawdy and bodacious, thereby expanding the audience we already had. "Stay outrageous," we were told, and did we ever, promoting a Mother's Day screening of the sensitive new independent film, *Deep Throat*—admission free if you brought your Mum. The Pussy Cat theater was jammed.

Next we staged an event for the whole family—the Sushi, Panties and Cocaine Parade (open exclusively to bearers of one of the above).

And finally, there was the famous Naked Wall, featuring candid photos of our dear listeners. We hectored them to send us nude shots for our in-studio display. Some were obviously just barely post-coital, with pink swelling lips and dripping skin-lassos. And so it went.

I was, of course, thrilled to take part in these *fêtes galantes*, flattered to be chosen to operate near the epicenter of the "counter-culture," to serve as a veritable strop for the cutting edge, and stoked to be on the receiving end of record company handouts. All of the blandishments, the traditional sweetmeats and comfits of Hollywood, as well as the special rewards for being part of the Hot New Stuff, helped me avoid the obvious fact that I was doomed from the start.

Every time I even *thought* of the station, my bowels jammed. Every time I saw, or thought I saw, a smirk—heard, or thought I heard, a snigger from a colleague—perceived a slight—felt myself excluded and marginalized—there began a cold panic deep in my GI tract, casting me back to potty-training. When I opened the mic switch to speak, I was visited with the presentiment of incontinence. The Diaper Terror. The Soiler. Gone the intrepid People's Radio Philosophe. Slain by fear. Aiming only to please. *Please, please, please let me keep my job.* Alone with my fears, my show wobbled twixt scared and too-stoned-to-care.

Then I found I couldn't reach Trout by phone. Originally we had been a 3-man team: Head, Trout and me, a management/talent package coming in from a runaway success at UrboMedia's Carnegie station to rescue our "losing" L.A. sister station. The blueprint was—with Trout at my back—I would reprise my Carnegie act: radical ideological mad-rapper of the FM airwaves gives the station shape, purpose, a reason to believe. But now it seemed that The Head, having strategically moved himself to L.A. first, was assiduously consolidating his power as GM. And I became the man alone, telling himself he'd be fine.

For the first six months up in Beachwood Canyon we had the constant interruption of three or four tradesmen—right-wing Riverside County hippie-racists, it turned out—alternately blowing us off and arbitrarily appearing for work when least expected.

Senta and I were clearly coming apart. She was only barely going along with what she considered my "concentration on the rock repertoire." She loved the general grooviness ethic, the democratically-open socializing that some hippie mothers were able to transform into a handy quasi-communal extended family, mixing sincere generosity with a keen *modus manipulandi*. Overwhelmed, she found a Guatemalan maid to sleep-in five nights a week with the three boys. That left her free to oversee the elusive workmen and the renovation that crept on eternally.

Alas, sexually, many factors combined to drive us apart. I loved Senta, but Romantic Love? Certainly *I* didn't know what it was, or what phylum in the taxon of affection it may have occupied. I did know I should not have married Senta. I married her for all the usual wrong reasons, was not *in love* with her. It was a reasonable decision to mate with a person I liked to be with, was stable, funny, talented, cute as a button. But just not *that*.

There had been other women, of course. Most of them products of the

Cold Pants, the Puritan analog of the Cold War. Most fucked you only to go psychotic with guilt.

One especially luscious blonde from Vermont, Lizzie Donaldson, a Barnard student-writer and friend of a friend. On her one visit to Carnegie she came to my basement bed, said she'd been a rape victim, and couldn't let me in. Such was her succulence that I just buried my face in her crotch and stayed for most of the weekend. She left me for New York with the distinct feeling of so-much-for-you, and I added her to the list of never-agains.

The week after I married Senta the phone rang late at night. I reached away from her to pick it up, leaning off the side of the bed to whisper into the mouthpiece. It was Lizzie.

"You got *married?*" she demanded.

"Well, yeah, I…"

"You got married without telling me?"

"I thought you…"

"Thought what? I slept with you and ran away? I was in Stowe with my Dad."

"How is he?"

"He died last Thursday!"

Senta woke up. I lowered my voice even more.

"I'm really sorry…"

"Who *is* it, Mitchell?" my new wife wanted to know.

"An old friend," I said, covering the receiver. I tried to get out of bed, but the cord was too short. The bedroom door was ajar, and Erie gusts chilled me back to the counterpane. *Lizzie, Jesus!*

"And I come back to school to find you got married? What's *wrong* with you?"

"Who is it, Mitch?"

Senta was pregnant. The wind rattled the panes above our bed. A frost swept across the linoleum in our ghetto basement bedroom.

"I gotta go, Liz, I…"

"How could you do this without even telling me?"

I hung up and closed the door.

~

My first innocently Edenic view of L.A. was the composite of all I could handle at the time, but there were a lot of things that didn't fit.

My new co-workers pretty much shut me out, both socially and professionally. Constant sarcasm, regional put-downs, rolled eyes, and general emotional pillage. Especially hurtful was the psychic stiff-arm by KURB's star, the brilliant "Jive" Clive. This sly rejection was new for me, and unexpected. To be preemptively gated out of existence by a jock whose Faster-than-Joycean, madder-than-mad rap left me devastated, disoriented, consumed with jealousy, and doubting my every thought and on-air utterance.

The Head repelled me with a passive-therefore-deniable campaign of almost complete silence, and I was otherwise pretty much pal-less, give or take a couple of record company guys I knew from Carnegie, who did what they could.

I partied with The Head's secretary, Jodi, and Don Hall, the station's one sub.

"He's even worse than you think," Jodi said. "I know."

"The Head's tryin' to ball you?" asked John, who also dealt coke small-time.

"*All* the time!"

"What do you do?" I wanted to know.

"I don't know. Push him off me. Sometimes he's loaded, so it gets tricky."

A baking L.A. mid-summer day in an apartment in decrepit Gower Gulch, where long-dead extras waited to be picked to ride horses past a camera. All Jodi's windows were open, and it was still hot.

"Didn't he beat up someone in Carnegie? That's what we heard when UrboMedia brought him back."

She did a line, pinching her nose. The silver Yamaha receiver gave us Steely Dan's new one, "Deacon Blues."

"I heard that, too, back in Carnegie. And that they found him fucked-up in his Continental. Beaten up bad."

"I got more shit on him than you could guess."

"Better be careful with that fuck-butt," I warned her.

"You, too," she said. "You, too." She hiked up her cotton sun-dress and sat facing me on my lap. She picked up the mirror and handed me the tooter. I did a line staring at yellow panties, the crotch faintly spotted with dry blood.

The phone rang. She picked it up and listened. "He wants you at the station."

The pressure was serious and mounting. Especially since freewheeling KURB was, in the fullness of corporate time, being set up for paper-training. Woodehedd, far from following and expanding our kaleidoscopic music and editorial policies from Carnegie, was quietly working to play-list the station, limiting the music to hits and what they insisted on calling "new product," and shunning all Black music except Hendrix.

After doing acceptably well 8:00-to-midnight, despite the trumpeted indifference of most of my colleagues, I was beginning to feel more relaxed on-the-air. I was puttering around one late afternoon, keeping an eye on our big pool where the three boys were for once not savaging one another, trying to figure out how to flush the pump filter, when the red push-button pool-side phone rang. I pulled the extra-long cord over to the diving board, sat down and picked it up.

"Just callin' to warn you, Mitchell." It was long-lost Trout.

"What's up?" I asked.

"He fuckin' fired me!"

"No!" That's all I said but the amount of real estate covered by my mind in the space between hearing and speaking was immense.

"I figgered the asshole for a lying sack of shit. Lying motherfucker been shining me righteously on all this time. Interim GM my ass!"

"You're s'posed to be here next month, for cryin' out loud."

"Yeah, an' when I called The Head to check the arrangements, I got Jodi, who gave me one of those 'Hasn't anyone told you?' deals."

Fuck! A reptilian vista appeared before me: desert and no life, myself a shriveled nub, rolling across the near horizon like a tumble-weed. *No job, no career, no family, no life, no…*

"Can't you call UrboMedia? They gotta know that you're the one who *made* that stupid fucking station."

"I talked to what's his name—Dinkle. He was full of 'we'll take care of it, Tommy,' and like that."

"So…?"

"So, shit, Mitchell! Wake the fuck up! It's all a corporate hustle. We've been ripped-off big time!"

"Yeah…"

"Well, at least I'm still in Carnegie."

"What's that supposed to mean?"

"You're a smart boy, Mitch. Figger it out!"

"Who you callin' *boy?*"

So now, on top of everything else, my one hope of salvation, the man primarily responsible for all three of us winning the right to come here in the first place would not be joining us in L.A. Trout, hip as only a black man among whiteboys could be, and tougher than nails, would be going to work as Elton John's publicist instead. Before I could regain my footing, I was summoned to The Head's executive cave.

"We'll be moving you to Morning Drive, Mitch. I think you'll be great," he said, grinding his jaw in the special way he had, and sweating, despite the a/c. No one knew whether he was aware that these little tics announced that he was lying, or whether he didn't care if we knew, or what. "Your special brand of political wit'll be perfect for the ride to work."

Sure.

Firstly, for the hippies, students, and rock'n'roll lay-abouts that were our core audience, "Mornings" began around noon. Secondly, The Head had recently broken the otherwise hermetic *omertá* between us to chastise me for the twist I gave my rip 'n' read newscasts: pronouncing the President's name "Noxin," awarding politicians the "Ferdinand Marcos Freedom Prize," sprinkling emerging tidbits about a certain high-rise D.C. break-in, etc., through the shift.

This reasoning was breathtaking in its insincerity—that the General Manager of a station commanding one of the nation's most massive baby-boom (and therefore anti-war) demographics, should be so obsessed with the mythical balance of the "Fairness" Doctrine used by the FCC to inhibit dissent.

"We'll call it 'Mornings with Mitch'…" The Head thought he was working me. I couldn't tell for sure whether he thought I was dumb enough to believe him, or whether he was just following standard big business prevarication etiquette: misdirection, executive ass-covering and corporate litigation-proofing. But I knew what it meant when they started moving you around in radio, until you became the dread 'jock who sits by the door': one day it would swing wide, and out you'd go. Down the floor, out the door.

I had one previous sit-down with The Head, in Carnegie when he was angling to steal Trout and me from WNBM to his failing enterprise at WURB. Then, an odd thing happened.

"How important is Trout, Mitch?"

"Meaning what?"

"Meaning we don't have big numbers in the ghetto."

"*We* do at NBM!"

There went his jaw, grinding away, a map of his mental mechanisms, scheming away. His doughy white face was otherwise inert, which would have covered his act perfectly, but his grinding told the tale.

"Come on, Donald. Say what you mean."

"We don't need that kind of input."

I found myself talking "street" to The Head. It gave me distance. "Is that the corporate line? UrboMedia tell ya ta say that?"

His double chin was bobbling. "No, it's…" gnashing and grinding. "It's…we don't need him."

"And I think we *do*," I told him and got up to leave.

"Wait, wait. I could get you 50K…"

"With Trout?"

He relented, and brought us both up the street to his barely floating wreck of a station. And since we got here the only real contact I had with this loathsome man was his weekly microscopic auditioning of the tape of my *Cunning Linguist* interview show. The endless barrage of memos "suggesting" more "mainstream" guests for my show: the Army, the LAPD.

I *did* have the L.A. District Attorney on the second week I was there, swearing up and down that *his* kid didn't smoke dope. "Aren't you worried about the lad? He must be tortured by peer rejection…"

One day on my new morning shift I realized, from an egregious entry on the program log: *9:00 AM "US Air Force: There's Victory in the Air,"* that it was the 4th of July. My god, I thought, our hippie-pinko station was offering its equally radicalized listeners, as a public service, nothing less than *a one-hour infomercial for aerial neocolonialism*. Fuck me! Naturally, I felt honor-bound to insert, into the quarter-hourly commercial breaks, the opening machine-gun blasts and first chorus of "Kill for Peace" by The Fugs.

~

We were on our second sitter. Anne-Marie was thirteen and mysteriously beautiful. I took the shyness of her youth as tranquility and projected it as wisdom in those horrible early KURB days when, for all I knew, she was my solitary listener, the only audience in the whole sun-baked basin. I coyly wheedled her for a daily critique of my on-air performance.

"It was de-sint," she would usually reply. She left us at the end of the summer to go back to school. Then I was alone.

~

After six fear-drenched months, The Head moved me for the second time...to the dread all-night shift. 2:00 to 6:00 a.m. I should have started exploring alternative employment, but then there was cocaine, don't forget cocaine. Yes, I had just been brought into the charmed circle coordinated by Codgers & Rowan, the hipper-than-hip rock/film PR firm who provided, to the privileged few, back-stage passes, bar and dinner tabs at the Troubador and Roxy, and connection to the drug of choice, the social wampum.

Yet, if I didn't pause to observe: "Damn! This is afflictive!" it wasn't just the anesthetic qualities of the coca leaf. I suffered daily anxiety attacks of such intensity that I was moved to take a black marker and write in big letters on my studio wall the *Bene Geserit* mantra from *Dune:*

I shall not fear, for fear is the mind-killer.

I needed to be reminded.

Gored, I nevertheless lowered my purely ornamental horns and plunged woundedly on, fashioning from those dire, dead middle-of-the-night hours a pastiche I called *The Tomorrow Night Show*—psychedelia, folk, interviews and live on-air performances and as much jazz as I could. Jesse Colin Young fell by and played for an hour after his Troubador set, "Animal" Eric Burdon came up and ranted about his label president, the proto-Reaganite Mike Curb. I did an all-night, different-drug-each-hour marathon with Frank Zappa's original Suzy Cream Cheese, Pamela Zarubica. Golden-voiced bluesman Donny Gildersleeve, who had his own show on KURB, would come by with admiring female fans.

My audience consisted of porno warehouse order-fillers, musicians oozing home from late-night gigs, surfers on dawn patrol, and other maniacs and social effluvia. I managed to establish a Hollywood underbelly of the air.

Up in the big, still un-renovated Mission Spanish house, dropping down the canyon face to a great pool ringed with avocado, grapefruit and the inevitable marijuana plants, things daily yawned further apart.

One night just before bedtime, Bruno, about five, started howling in his bed. Our third "nanny," a young Colombian named Aida, was finally losing it. Senta, having coaxed the kids into baths and pajamas, came puffing upstairs.

"Could you please speak with your son?" She looked old. She was five years older than I, and after the stress of multiple childbirths, motherhood and our new rock'n'roll "life-style," she looked worn and grim.

I looked away.

"Fine," I said, and followed the childish plaints down to the bedroom.

"Dad! Dad! Stay home, Dad!" Bruno was crying bitter tears.

"Shut up, Bruno," called one of his younger brothers, flat and disgusted.

"Shut up, Clifford, fucker-ass!"

"Come on, Bruno," I placated.

"Nooooooo!!" he screamed, sirening into full tantrum "Nooooooo!! Stay! Stay!"

"I have to go to work, baby." I crossed the Astro-turfed flooring to his bed and reached out to soothe him.

"No! No, don't! You don't have to go!" sobbing now, his face flushed and wet.

"Daddy has to work, Bruno. Give Daddy a good-night kiss."

"No! Go away! Go away!" He began pounding his pee-jayed little feet into the bed, running in place, stamping and screaming.

Working overnights for months, my psychic springs had unsprung.

"Bruno."

"Go away!"

"Bruno!"

"Go away! Go away!"

"Bruno! Bruno! Bruno!"

"Go…"

Snap!

I grabbed him wrathfully and began to shake. As I shook and shook, pleasure welled up behind my eyes like blood. God, it feels good! *He deserves it, the little prick! I'll smash the damned nuisance against the fucking wall!! YeeeaaaAAAHHHH!!!*

I heard my voice caroming off the bare plaster. Then silence, except for the hammering at my temples. A red lantern was lit in my head. Dizzy, I smelled the scent of smoke. Snorting, I suddenly saw the two younger boys, little Tony and Cliff, standing stock still in their cribs, staring wide-eyed at the sheer ferocity.

I scattered the coals of my self-indulgent fury and came to a full stop. I released the terrorized Bruno to the safety of his crib and took a step backward. Then a great deep breath came to me, which begat a sigh of relief, which broke over me in a mighty swell of revulsion, drenching me with the consciousness that *I'm doing nobody any good by staying in this house.*

Then I left.

There followed many dreary weeks of sleeping on friends' floors and couches. Sacrum-assassination. Sometimes I'd wait till they left for work, then slink into their still-cozy bed to filch a full night's sleep.

When I could stand it no longer—about the same time I had extracted the last drop of goodwill from the last of my friends—I moved into a splendid wraith of a place in downtown Hollywood, the infamous Lido Hotel on the folklorically resplendent corner of Yucca and Wilcox. One big room with a corner window overlooking the 24-hour-a-day traffic in human flesh and other illegal substances. Zappa's song "Willie the Pimp" looped endlessly in my head:

> *Standin' onna corner of the Lido Hotel.*
> *All the fancy ladies like the way I sell.*

I stopped by up in Beachwood once a week to have a "special time" with the boys. Once, we couldn't find Clifford. We searched and searched, mindful of the pool and its perils.

"Here he is!" shouted Bruno.

We ran to the kitchen. My beautiful, blonde middle boy, always smiling, was not on the floor. We looked up to the top of the refrigerator; a cardboard box faced open-end out. Inside the box was Cliff, offering a smile of apparent satisfaction.

"This is my Lido-hotel," he said. "My Lido-hotel."

They came to visit me once a week at the Lido. The primary population of elderly retired show-folk would make a big show of welcome to the boys when they came up to watch TV, have dinner and be taken to what they called the Clown Store, a huge and thrilling toy extravaganza on the south side of Hollywood Boulevard. A toy and a sleep on Daddy's couch.

⁓

The Lido was like my old hideout in my parents' basement, with its coal dust and dead medical machines. The solitude seemed a perfect circumstance to continue what I had begun, of necessity, up in Beachwood, my *War On Fear*. There at the tatty, raggedy-ass but plucky Lido I resolved to identify, locate and act-out every subconscious reluctance, every fear-induced impediment to prying myself open to Life in its Fullness. I would confront each and every hesitation, thus constructing a new, freed-up Mitchell, with unclogged circuitry expanded to allow the flow of pure vital energy in its totality. *Yes I could! Yes I would!*

This first big step on the road to self-re-realization was catalyzed dramatically by ingesting a cornucopia of exotic abusives. My favorite was lighting up a big bowl of Thai stick playfully smothered with a quarter-inch blanket of crystal flake, a pre-writing stirrup-cup I referred to as a Tin Roof Sundae. I chose to see myself as a person turning on the light in a dark room, staring the monster Xenophobia in the eye; one who had pulled all the electrodes from his brain, throwing off the domination of mere manners, taboos and other arbitrary social restraints.

Assuming the position, and spreading wide the cheeks of choice to a universe of adventure, I became, I told myself, *one who would DARE!*

At KURB, along with my now-attenuating all-night air-shift, I was busy attempting to people my interview show, *The Cunning Linguist.* I managed to snag Zappa and Lou Reed, and a slew of other radical well-knowns of rock-royalty. There were also those who would play roles in my life I did not, in my foggy perception of the business side of broadcasting, comprehend.

There was "The Fabulous Sascha" Strauss, a publicist for an outrageously pretentious Beverly Hills lady named Billy Kavilman. Sascha hungered after our audience at KURB. She realized hippies were the next big book-consumers, if enough of them could marshal sufficient brain cells for the task of actually reading, and pitched to me an array of potential guests.

Some were hotter than others, but most were usable: a famous radio shrinker, the guy who wrote *A Chorus Line* and, alas, 'Brat' Kavilman. Turns out Billy repped authors on book tours, including Bratilde Kavilman, her bright young daughter. Brat had just published her first book, a how-to self-helper, *The Guide for Returning Dropouts.* It was a well-written, witty essay on dropping back in, as the seventies marched inexorably onward, and sixties idealism was growing old to an entire generation of privileged Dropoutniks. Sascha pitched Brat to me. I read her book, and, needing a show that week, agreed to the interview.

At the taping session I'd praised Brat at length for her stylish prose and then came to the point. "Isn't your book addressed almost exclusively to an audience of your upper middle-class pals?"

Brat had not been happy. Her mother tried to block the show from airing, and I was left feeling self-righteous and ungenerous. Such was the fury of Ms. Kavilman, Sr. that I was sure I'd never see Sascha again.

Another notable contact was Sandy Durnit—an amazing ball of contradictions who introduced himself to me just after I arrived at the station.

He was taping nothing less than the History of Progressive Radio, and wanted to interview me. A roly-poly, messy kinda guy with a huge brain highlighted by giant angry red scars crisscrossing his shaved skull—the result of a car crash. Apparently he'd "forgotten" to turn the wheel at the one curve in an empty Arizona desert road and hit a huge yucca tree. Durnit drove the way he did everything else—not so much a loose cannon as a spinning 300-pound matzo-meal dreidel. He knew labor history, American culture, history of broadcasting and a frightening amount of other radical odds-and-ends—an alternative-culture maven extraordinaire. He was a moderately brilliant baboon with an unparalleled ability to come up with a decent idea, get it started, fuck it up, and end up sucking you in to doing the real work—then taking credit for the project. An idea man.

Both Sascha and Durnit labored under the misapprehension that, because I had this outrageous interview show on the super-cool revolutionary station, I somehow had power in the new, hip L.A.

I'd been following up a report in the *L.A. Times* of the bust, confiscation and banning by Orange County "authorities" of a tiny local underground weekly. The newspaper, called the *L.A. Star,* offered a unique blend of radical politics and split beaver. I quickly called the *Star* editors and set up a taping. On the appointed afternoon, we gathered in the KURB studio—first swapping obligatory expressions of solidarity, then my usual positive assessment of the value of their work, and then inevitably turning to address the more negative aspects.

"I gotta say that, while I defend your right to publish your views," I told them, "I have a hard time distinguishing *you* guys," (one of the three was a woman) "from the endless proliferation of sleazy porn rags currently choking Southland boulevards."

"You have something against pornography?" Leda, the woman editor, queried.

"Of course not, but if you're going to be puffin' yourselves up as so enlightened and unencumbered and everything, so…'liberated'…why do we see so few *men's* bodies in your ostensibly radical publication? The three issues I checked out had only naked *women*."

"We have a tough time finding men…"

"Please. In *this* town? Give me a break."

"Of course," she volleyed, regarding me as Epaminandas must have eyed the pies, "we'd be delighted for you to…*volunteer.*"

Grand pause, as I measured the windmill. I was not unattractive. I was relatively well-preserved at thirty-five. Graceful, even. I'd reflexively shaved my ratty proto-ZZ Topp beard to try to pass as a citizen the night Nixon was re-elected. I never worked out, but I did push a pretty big motorcycle around, so enough of the young jock tension remained in my *corpus*—especially when I inhaled and screeched my abs against my thorax. The bloodied beast I'd become since leaving Carnegie considered letting itself be petted.

"Well…sure…why not? What did you have in mind?" I smiled.

Early the next morning I was fetched at the Lido by a tall, blonde hipstress photographer in the first Honda *car* I'd ever seen, orange and shaped like an old-fashioned lace-up work-shoe. We headed off toward Malibu Canyon.

We sat scrunched in the tiny two-cylinder mini, cooled by the brisk Pacific morning. I stared dully at her blond hair, then out the tiny passenger window at the ocean. The station had okayed the shoot, even offered to make a calendar of the photo.

Silently, I oscillated between a great liberating rush of throwing off long-suffered constraint and hopeless suicidal depression. *At least I know what I'm feeling for a change. But, so what? I don't know what it means. Or when the feelings change. Perpetually. Moment-to-moment.*

Mitchell Hertz: a free-floating weirdo out of nowhere special, with not a whole lot to say. But that will change, I told myself.

The little Mother Hubbard Proto-Civic puttered north on the Coast Highway, the gulls skimming the heads of the wet-suited locals. We turned up Malibu Canyon into the hills.

Sometimes I lie awake at night and wonder
Where my life will lead…

Jackson Browne sang over the tinny, underdeveloped speakers. In 1973, a person living on the street was still called a "bum."

It's fear. I've been shaped almost exclusively by the single requirement: avoid anxiety. Pretty simple—"linear," they call it.

Drugs weren't helping, either. The obscurant effects of the cocaine, marijuana, mescaline, mushrooms and tequila that kept my immune system en pointe, my adrenals the size of brussel sprouts, were especially deleterious to the day's activities. The preemptive fear ate mind, heart—and nether parts, for sure. Scared limp.

The slow ascent of the practically powerless quasi-car gave me plenty of time, as we steadily *bap-bap-bapped* our way to the top of Malibu Canyon, to contemplate the presented impulsively jerked patella. *Dirty pictures. Cheap, cheap, cheap. Goodbye to all prep-school pretension of good taste. Farewell manly contempt for hot-dogging. Take your last mournful look at any vestige of nice-Jewish-boy self-concept particles you might have retained up to this point in your life.*

As we finally crested the top of the canyon, I beheld again the waiting Pacific, blue and abiding with expectation, gleaming with the first shafts of sun chasing night from the L.A. basin.

We motored till she found a suitably sylvan redoubt. I was still contemplating my genitals. The air was chilly and I wondered what condition my condition might assume for purposes of photographic impact. She, alas, was no help whatsoever. A diffident northern European artisan-class blonde, about five-foot-nine in stature, Shawna occupied a spot on a continuum between really classic horsey-WASP and neo-redneck hippie-chick. Her butt rolled deliciously beneath her *Chemin de Fer* bellbottoms. She pulled the Honda off the road into a meadow of tall grass.

She was polite, good with light and shadow, but there were none of the seduction games I somewhat expected. I was given to believe that it was always and only *me* "letting it all hang out"—at all levels of overtones and sympathetic vibrations. Just *me* just saying "Yes" as if it were my nature, not an attempt to save face by posturing.

"Come." She smiled shyly, not unpleasantly. "Stand over here?"

Her professionalism was casting my feigned reluctance into high and dubious relief. Too much contrast. But she made no attempt to put me at ease, no playfulness nor cajolery, no encouragement *at all*. Finally the reality of the situation registered—that she viewed me as a nuttso to be baring my Johnson so indiscriminately in what she considered a sleaze-rag. That she could barely bring herself to be civil. That I'd inevitably try to play hide the weenie with her if she gave me the slightest pretext.

As I dropped trou and bared all, I worried again whether my scrupulously unprovoked organ, given the chilly breezes from both sea and sylph, would manage to acquire for the camera what professionals called "wood." *Can't let down in front of my audience. What is the correct angle for these semiformal occasions?*

I sauntered over to where she set her equipment, trying to act as if I always walked around with my skin-metronome clicking off every step, swaying side to side. I shivered, only partially from the early morning dew. *Like Death eating a biscuit.*

When she removed her Santa Cruz Imports cowboy shirt, she revealed perky nipples bobbing aerodynamically beneath a faded dark Pink Floyd T-shirt, the logo moving languidly with her shifting mammal ballast.

"What do you think of, like, jumping?" Shawna asked. "Sort of joyous?" Every sentence was a question with her. Rising inflection *sobre todo*.

I had a side that would have made a good little German, ready to obey orders. I gave a tight little hop and my shriveled pee-pee thwacked against my belly like a salmon. I then repeated this lovely paddle-ball exercise a dozen times, vowing to insist on final cut to prevent any thought of using this dancing-dicky reel. *Too kinetic, man.*

She repositioned me. "Did you bring something? A prop…?"

The night before, she'd phoned to suggest bringing something with me: a hat, an umbrella, a microphone. I stopped at the Clown Store, where, on our last trip, Bruno had drooled over amazingly realistic scale-model guns in the front window. A Mauser machine-pistol looked more than authentic.

"Yes," I replied, and extracted the weapon from my Adidas bag. She smiled faintly and proceeded to move me around for an hour or so in the high grass, all business, squeezing off ten or twelve rolls.

The shot we chose as the centerfold for the May issue was classic. Above the caption, "KURB'S Main-Mic Mitchell Hertz," was me in a huge full-frontal pose, privates partially retracted against the brisk ocean breezes, arms folded in studied provocation, glaring insolently out from under long, allowed-to-blow-wild hair. Hips cocked and ready, eyes blazing with the preemptive bravado of raw terror, cold as the steel of the Mauser itself, dangling "carelessly" from my right hand. In short, a barely pre-psychotic, but not unflattering, portrait of me, my gun, and my outboard reproductive capacity. I told myself: *A magic time, full of promise—anything can happen!* And it did. Two weeks after the issue hit the stands I was fired.

I was out riding my big deep-blue motorcycle in the Santa Monica Mountains, late May, wind flapping my hair. I relaxed my weight over into the first of a series of slow esses and beginning to feel a little better. Margie, the shrinker Senta and I had been seeing to "ask permission" to split up our marriage, had told me to put back into my ultra-marginalized life only those things that *really pleased* me.

"But I can't *think* of anything that really pleases me," I told her.

"Nothing at all? Okay. Take a deep breath, close your eyes and see yourself smiling."

"Okay," I said, grimacing in attempted complicity.

"Fine. Now. Where are you right Now?"

"Well…maybe I'm riding my bike through Malibu Canyon…"

"So, go do *that*," she urged gently, "and then if, while you're riding, actually in the act of riding, you think of something else that seems pleasant, then do *that*. Add it to your life."

"Really?"

"Yes, Mitchell, but only if it gives you real pleasure. Don't do anything because you *have* to, or *think* you *should*, or feel guilty avoiding."

So I was climbing Old Malibu Road in search of gusto, joy, zest appeal. Pleasure, pleasure, pleasure. Alluring conceptually, I allowed, if I could only *find* some. Repeating to myself: *The sanguinary expectation of happiness that is happiness itself,* as Jane Austen put it, and she should know. Maybe I could, even in this depression, re-apply the same principle to pleasure.

I gently braked the big Honda. The pleasure principle, in and of itself. Here it was: my real life's only pleasure, a fucking mode of conveyance! Denial with dual disc brakes and matching helmet.

Riding, riding.

Riding my motorcycle was about all the fun I had. That, and lying on my bed in the Lido Hotel, endlessly plotting strategies to heat up my *Tomorrow Night Show* enough to win back a daytime slot on KURB; trying not to think of my wife and children, who'd waited a few months for my return then moved to a modest cottage in Venice. But when I got on my bike, giddy with the effort to handle my shame, the pure exhilaration of motion-for-its-own-sake popped me up and out of my old depleted self, into the new life of freedoms that beckoned. I told myself to mount up, ride out and meet it.

⁓

The next week I sat in the waiting room Margie shared with a few shrinker colleagues in a modestly modern office building on Westwood Boulevard between Wilshire and Santa Monica. Looking up from the issue of *Vanguard Workers* I'd been reading sincerely, but a little self-consciously, I beheld a glossy dark-haired beauty in brown suede, jeans and leather sandals talking to a wide, wild-haired Mosaic matron outside in the entrance hall. *Probably another shrinker if degree of earthiness is any indicator.*

"Put pleasure in your life!" I heard Margie's voice in my head.

I stood up, ran my hand through my hair, walked over and asked to borrow her pen. Intending to ask for her name and phone number as step two, I was daunted by the pre-echo of my own crudity. I struggled to think long range, turned away, doodled a little whiffet on my wrist as they continued their conversation unaware of my rejection fantasies, and returned the pen with what I hoped was a charming smile.

Later, in my session, I told Margie of my near break-through. "I know it's ethically equivocal, but aren't we trying to make me better? Give her my phone number at least. That way if she *doesn't* want to call she's safe from my unilateral affections."

"I just don't feel comfortable…"

"You *did* tell me to put pleasure back in my life," I reminded her.

"But that was…"

"You can ask for her number…" I prompted, swatting moral flies. "She can refuse."

"We'll see."

I waited a week with rare and barely constrained hope for the longed-for data. At the next session I discovered my shrinker had actually *forgotten* her errand of mercy.

"Margie, *please! Go* with me on this one. Please *do* this for me! I need to win one for once. *Fav*or me."

The next week my thoughtful therapist waited until the session was over, and for me to ask again. Only then did she open her purse and hand me the goods:

ADRIENNE DRESSER
(213) 650-5555

Dialing her number on the wall phone next to my tiny dry bar at the Lido I doubted my memory. *Could she be as luscious as I remember? Was I so cranked that day I'd have fucked a cocker spaniel?*

"Hi! This is Mitch."

"Uh-huh."

"From…the waiting room. Uh…I borrowed your pen…" Silence. "Remember?"

"The guy at Rachel's."

"In the waiting room. Remember me?"

"I think so. You're the thirty-six-year-old married disc jockey with three children."

"Thirty-five…" (Muffled)

"What?"

I tried to shoot the shit briefly and then blurted, "How'd you like to come over here; no, I think I'd like to be someplace natural with you, Adrienne. Outside, maybe. Could you pick me up at my hotel? It's a little nippy for my motorcycle and…"

"Beg your pardon?"

"…and my Cadillac's in the shop." *Oh fuck, what a cheese-ball!*

My old black '68 Fleetwood had "TONGUE" license plates, in honor of *The Cunning Linguist.*

"I don't *think* so, Mitchell," she made herself clear.

This sounded not at all cold, I decided, steadying myself for the approaching kiss-off—not pissed, but somehow admirably *firm* and remarkably *even.*

"But you're welcome to come *here.*"

So, I went calling to her upstairs quadruplex on Orlando in West Hollywood. It was spring, toward the end of the rainy season, still cool and green, with jacarandas beginning to blossom. I backed the bike into the curb and kicked the side stand down. Adrienne answered the door, a close approximation of the goddess I'd envisioned. Dark, serene and model-stunning, she held herself like a forest creature, I decided, aloof but solid. Built like a swimmer, with broad shoulders, hourglass waist and the legs of a golden goddess. Adrienne smiled pleasantly but not effusively as she welcomed me into the upstairs rooms she shared with her younger sister Lana.

She spoke very little. As the afternoon unspooled, a parade of visitors kept me verbal while she floated on the perimeter. There were more sisters, a brother, an ex-boyfriend who knew me from the radio, a member of the Beach Boys who dated her baby sister Honey. Fine Hollywood herb and music-talk went round the room for hours. Adrienne, however, the one I'd come to see, confined her activities to circulating, emptying ashtrays, and staunchly maintaining an open window policy in the freshness of new April. I shivered and caught her eye, yet time after time she looked away.

After a few hours, I said to myself, "If she doesn't make some kinda move soon, I'm conclusively outta here." I got up and put on my jacket, and looked down at her on the couch by the front door.

"Well, 'bye."

"Bye."

"Nice to meet all you guys," I waved to the others.

A chorus of farewells and then I glanced back down at her just before I turned to go, and saw her eyes. There, suspended in the depths of her dark brown orbs, I was sure I could just make out the word "please," bubbling up from far down under. I felt commanded by the cry of something chained, calling out.

It has always moved me to replay in my mind the vision of my own hand gliding out, without conscious effort, and touching her cheek, holding the smooth fresh skin for a moment before she reacted. Then Adrienne calmly reached up and covered my hand, and to my delight, pressed it to her face. Smiling, she hopped up, linked arms and walked me down the stairs and out to my bike.

Jacaranda blossoms had fallen on the tank and saddle.

PART TWO

In the Beginning there was the Worm.

—Wilhelm Reich (adapt. M. Hertz)

I always worshipped my father. Hard to admit though, because I feared him as well. Maybe they went together—a functional unity. I would figure that out later. Mostly, as a kid, I thought he was the best. An underdog-rooting kinda guy, and, in his role of dedicated physician, a great moral example. He had been an authentic healer in a time of canasta, country clubs, and Cadillacs, a housecall-maker who retained no accountant, business manager, *nothin'*. He'd send you a bill for ten bucks and if you paid it, fine. If not, well, he'd work something out, if he could remember to do it. Not just a country doctor in the GP tradition, but a dedicated chest specialist as well—and as they all were, I suspect, in those days before tuberculosis was considered conquered for all time.

My dad was also a medical professor, acclaimed diagnostician, and a lonely but heroic proponent of the singularly unpopular concept (in the HUAC-friendly fifties) of socialized medicine. He would have been a tough act to follow even if he hadn't been so very handsome. Virile, Slavic and compact, with an ex-gymnast's short muscle-articulated body. Intense barely began to describe him.

He was a Russian Jew, brilliant in a practical-scientific-radical, as opposed to speculative-artistico-theoretical way. But very needy, too—a master brooder and pouter! My mother said he'd been victim to his mother's preference for his older, jockier-soshier brother, and that he'd come to romance in search of maternal energy. So jealous was he of my lovely mother that the most consistent guidance for successful adulthood he was able to give me was: get outta here and get one of your own. Sent me on a hunt.

My mother was really curvy and cute as a firefly, in a tiny Mediterranean kind of way. A micro-Sophia Loren, I came to believe. The youngest of nine children in an Eastern European immigrant family, she somehow seriously *dressed*. She was so elegantly turned out I was forever at pains to show her off to my friends. But it wasn't just her post-Boopoid sexy good looks, extra *élan vital*, so to speak. She was dedicated to my father. Had forgone college and sold hats to put him through medical school. He wisely let her dress him: the cashmere suits, brown herringbone and French blue. Later the Ivy-League stuff. Sharp for a Carnegie doctor.

To this very-much-in-love couple, the Medical Resident at Daisy Hills Tuberculosis Sanitorium and his beautiful young wife, did I come, the firstborn, in the pre-War fall of 1937.

After a traumatic premature potty-training—which left me, at nine months, believing that my anus and sacrum were one and the same—there followed a classic Jewish superchildhood. Which meant: Enlightenment philosophy through the prism of science and the French Revolution, respect for reason and therefore history, casual but earnest etymology, adherence to scientific standards of proof and definition through all family discourse. It also meant "Cheder," a well-intended but lame attempt to transmit Jewish values through Hebrew School run by the Temples.

Carnegie Playhouse Children's Theater, Carnegie Art Museum Saturday classes & Film Society—*Beauty and the Beast, Alexander Nevsky*, Chaplin, Harold Lloyd. All "E"s in school, the child athlete, etc. through sixth grade, when my testicles descended from on high to claim me. I was caught in the cloakroom with a redheaded classmate's twelve-year-old breast in my hand.

Then, at a crucial point in the first semester of seventh grade, we bought a nice old Tudorish house on the border of then-posh Baker Heights, and I took a major dive. Though the hormones carbonated throughout my being, my humbler origins immediately spun me off the social matrix to the far lonely perimeter of my new school's social whorl. My *arrivisme* at mid-year relegated me to the company of nerdly guys with thick glasses and belt-slung slide rules, proud members of the Stage Crew. I was reduced to building model planes in their basements and bedrooms.

Up to that time I'd been something of a musician: piano lessons at four, French horn with a Carnegie Symphony member. At fourteen I was able to hold down the second-horn chair in the All-City Orchestra. So, another locus of my new life among the unpopular at Baker Jr. High was in Band, with all the other misfits.

Unaccountably, the next year I was invited to join the WASP-dominated jock service club called "Leaders." Members of the Leaders club were popular, went to parties, and got good mentions in the "slam books" that were a circulating measure of one's social prospects. But Leaders, like Band, was extracurricular, and they both met sixth period.

Once to every man and nation
Comes the moment to decide.
—Old Welsh Hymn

I agonized for days, but the siren song of status proved hypnotic to my neediness. I turned my back on Orpheus. A great divide had been crossed, the road not taken. I thought the athlete world would get me a girlfriend, and by the time ninth grade ended and high school came around, I was starting Junior Varsity quarterback.

I did make one actual friend—Maggie, the tomboy younger sister of Marjorie "Crunchy" Kravitz, whose daddy owned an advertised-on-TV carpet store. Maggie was a year behind me and popular. Despite her butchy, athletic, flat-chested permanently preadolescent body, Maggie had inherited her older sister's prominence in the Jewish crowd, and a regular slot at Flo Berman's Dancing School. I, as an outcaste transfer student, was perforce excluded.

It was in Maggie's dancing class group photo that I first espied the dark felinity of the exquisite Emily Evans in a scooping V-neck gown. At fourteen, Emily was already a more dangerous Liz Taylor, reaching out, her hot C'mere Eyes whispering, "Wander no more." Maggie offered to query my Enchantress, and a few mornings later, walking to school, she told me, "Emily *likes* you."

That afternoon, I presented myself at Emily's tall brick house. She made it easy for me. The first thing I saw as her loveliness appeared behind the screen door was that she was already smiling her sly secret-knowing smile.

"Hi."

She wore a loose sleeveless rayon blouse and the shortest cotton shorts I'd ever viewed close-up, baggy and revealing. She'd even rolled the legs up in impromptu cuffs. And her breasts, for a ninth grader, were wonderfully full and weighty-looking. I glanced heavenward and accepted fortune's smile with my own disbelieving grin of gratitude.

We strolled from her home to a nearby lot where a two-story house was under construction. We entered the structure's deserted framing and gingerly inspected the first floor, eyes darting to each other, then back to the tools, stacks of lumber and other underfoot hazards.

In a spurt Emily was mounting the workmen's ladder as I scurried, giddy to keep up. Glancing up to gauge my progress, I found myself staring straight up into what could only appear to my innocence as meat surrounded by bristly shrubs—her tender teenaged labia, lost in thickets of luscious black ringlets. Stunned, I worried: *does she know I'm looking?* Promptly I lowered my gaze and kept climbing. But when I dared to look up again it was to see her smiling and reaching her cool hand down to help me up. My heart raced. *Does she know?*

Still not certain of having escaped detection, I let her direct our strolling feet through the skeletal form, out through the mounds of unlandscaped dirt and ball-bundled bushes in the back yard, and all the way down to Baker Lakes

Park, where we rested on a small grassy slope beside still, green water. Emily crossed her slender legs into a tailor perch slightly above me on the incline, where I had to incline my head in order to see her. We chatted absently about our respective schools. I would be a junior at Baker High in the fall, she a sophomore.

We rambled on, she in her breathy confidential contralto, me in total transfix. Absently, I looked down to pull a clover from the fresh-cut hillside, and, as I raised my eyes up to her again I couldn't help but observe—incredibly— that while we'd been making polite conversation about English teachers and cafeteria Sloppy Joes, she'd been gradually allowing her pink cord shorts to gape to one side. Now, as I watched incredulous, the beautiful Emily Evans was proceeding, slowly but certainly, to stretch her leg, and with it the elastic leg-band of her cotton panties and, as demurely as this can be done, exposing herself to me, her pretty mouth turning up in a furtive smile as she revealed her sovereign pubic luxuriance.

It was late spring, her lovely dark legs parting gracefully, the late afternoon sun gilding over the lake. She smiled slyly, still talking in a low throat voice, and slowly let her pink nether lips ease apart for my ravished first-time eyes.

It lasted a brief, delicate moment, this elemental vision. Then, like Brigadoon, it was gone. Emily re-crossed her legs, and we resumed our casual, teenage chat.

Before we met, Emily had been dating one of the token old Jewish family boys at elite Collegiate School—tall, blonde, a tennis player, and rumored to have already been intimate with the girl of my dreams. But once I started coming around I never saw him again. I was hooked. Sotted. Blasted by love at last.

Just as our passion began to flare I had to leave on an eight-week official Baker High football camp trip to Canada, imaginatively named Camp "Oiratno." My math teacher, a partner in the camp, had come over to our house and flogged it to my parents as a way of advancing my football career and, incidentally, my grades in trigonometry.

That miserable summer in the forests of Clinton Bay, Ontario, I taught myself to play piano by ear. One dead, endless afternoon I found myself pining for Emily and, since they didn't turn on the generator till night-fall, there was no passive entertainment to divert my maudlin attention. I'd heard "our song," "Once in a While" by Ray Anthony, on a truck-stop radio during the bus trip up to camp from Carnegie. Now, in the mess hall common room, I morosely mulled the verse:

ONCE IN A WHILE
Will you try to give one little thought to me?
Though someone else may be
Nearer your heart?

Stirred I went to the battered rec hall upright piano and began to pick out the melody with two right fingers.

ONCE IN A WHILE…

Not that tough! Add the left hand. A chord? Wrong chord. Wish I knew some theory. Still the tune began to emerge. *Try the chorus:*

In love's smoldering embers
One spark may remain…

The song's contours began to take shape:

Oh, I know that I'd
Be contented with yesterday's memories
Knowing you'd think of me,
ONCE IN A WHILE…

Actually, I feared, *she's not thinking of me at all! Dating seniors now, my little entering sophmore!* Dating older guys at Baker High who drank highballs, had drivers' licenses, and daddy's '52 Roadmaster or '50 Olds 98 or even Caddy convertible to squire her about. *Meanwhile, I'm trolling for northern pike and black bass, memorizing the Varsity playbook, and eating out my heart.* But I stuck it out, and at endless summer's end came home a still-distant contender for starting quarterback and desperate for the object of my Canadian imaginings.

It took a semester to achieve full genital embrace with Emily, despite her attempts to catalyze the process, and my own burgeoning, albeit stumblebum, ardor. My prior experience with girls was rookie at best. Previously Mr. Marginal, I'd spent my time with a small number of male friends, occasionally double-dating with a social straggler, going to movies to cop an episodic feel.

Emily and I went to a make-out party at someone's parents' basement rec room. No one drank alcohol. No one I knew. Dope was still for musicians and other Negroes. Only the dancing and the sensory overload of her presence fogged my young mind. Before I knew what was happening, my sojourning hand was ascending the flesh of her splendid young thigh.

The week before, she'd matter-of-factly taken this very hand (we'd been sitting in the front row balcony watching Les Paul and Mary Ford live on the stage of the Castle Theater in Downtown Carnegie) and casually placed it, without apparent calculation, palm down on her wool skirt, right over where, I calculated and recalculated through the night—through *How High the Moon, The World is Waiting for the Sunrise* and even *Mockingbird Hill*—her vagina surely must reside. Her vagina. *Vagina.* It meant "scabbard" or "sheath" in Latin, *"wa-ghee-na"* in the preferred academic pronunciation—"resting place of Roman swords."

Slowly I had repositioned my hand, stealthy and inexorable as an inchworm, cell by cell, muscle by burning muscle, undulating so slowly, imperceptibly, making the tiniest, but most earnest, rubbing gestures on the ridge of her pubis. *Touching it! IT!! The fabled honey-pot. Too good to be true, especially with the prettiest sophomore girl by miles!* Yet, there was one leg, there was the other. *This must be the place.*

That night as we moved together closely on the crowded Rec Room floor, slow dancing to polite white dance music, I found this self-same hand magically gliding across the surface of warm skin and presently, without impediment, disappearing lubriciously into a remarkably hot, very wet place—like a baked apple, I decided. Emily closed her eyes, but when I beheld her darling dark face, haloed by deluxe Mediterranean curls, her lids parted, and a shaft of arc light blinded me for an instant. Then she smiled and the evening became the warmth of her juiciness and the voice of Nat Cole.

They tried to tell us we're TOO YOUNG...

When I came home from Canada there had been an immediate transitional period of biology class groping and exploring. But always there was a powerful unspoken accord, composed of both devotion and obsession, that we were meant for each other. She seemed as rabid as I, making explicit the secrets of her heart with the maniacally passionate Frankie Laine commitment ballad, "When You're in Love," played as loud as possible on her parents three-speed Victrola.

It was a first for me, being drawn to another; locked, inseparable. As a duly constituted couple, I found we were popular in a way I certainly never would have achieved as the terminal loner I had been. We went to the usual parties, conspiring to end up alone, kissing and groping her orlon sweaters into balled-up messes. Our lovemaking evolved through a succession of partial near-insertion strategies—me cumming so fast there was no question of effecting full penetration. Every time it was closer. *Was I in? Will I know?*

Noon and night, between brutal two-a-day football practices, with endless wind sprints beneath the August sun, we staged almost-shtupathons, as our compulsion took control. Finally, after marathon rec-room extra-heavy petting, I admitted to myself, walking home down the Rapid Transit tracks, *we must be doing it. This must be it! IT!* And I first knew adult anxiety.

I'd tried to use a "safe," as we had called condoms, a number of times at first. But I lacked experience with the surreptitiously-obtained contraceptives. My father was the world's shyest living post-Victorian male, so I was left to my own devices. Plus, the damn things kept slipping off, you know, during or after our frequent exertions. It was Emily who finally gave up, telling me to forget about using them. Honest.

I always managed to ejaculate somewhere I rationalized as "outside," which would turn out to be my key tactical blunder. I was so lame at sixteen that I was terrified of peeping to discover my unprotected cock's actual location *vis-à-vis* the fertile receptors of my dusky partner. Though we only actually shared a regulation bed twice in those perfervid years—once getting caught in best friend Dick Deutschmann's attic—we must have screwed hundreds of times.

Before meeting Emily, I had not only been a virgin, but was so retrograde as to have not yet discovered even the solitary joys of self-abuse. When I confided this fact to people later, they smiled knowingly. *Right! You got laid first, then jerked off only to relive the magic! Uh-Huh.*

But it was true. I would discover masturbation only later, by accident—reading an article in *Sport* magazine warning young men of the evil strength-sapping habit of "fondling." I read feverishly hoping to see the act described in detail, for the knowledge without which I felt like such a pitiful gleef.

Far from the sassy sexiness of *Happy Days* or *Grease,* the fifties were a dull and benighted decade of gross and hypocritical sexual repression. So I experienced a major shock of the new when, sitting there on the toilet, idly exploring my privates, I got a rod-on. *Damn!* I thought, months after my first blissful couplings with Emily, *this is like screwing! Let me try that again.*

Late winter of 1955—Emily's first year in high school. I was a junior and hanging out with weirder and more dangerous kids, "racky" elements. I always felt a distance from the smooth and weak Jewish and other white boys who were my classmates. My father, with his belief in socialized medicine—outrageously daring for a practicing physician in the mid-Fifties—had given the finger to the country club life, where I might have hung out with those "crowds."

So I'd begun running around with borderline sociopaths and hoodlums from the lower rungs of the Baker acceptability-ladder. Some were poor kids, like Don Rustig, from the immigrant fringes of the ethnic Kinsman area, who'd gone on to some success as a catcher and a fullback. Nice guy, short but powerful with huge calves and thighs. Good smile. No visible dating pattern, not at school anyway. We heard he went to whores.

And rich kids, too, like the barking Ralph Redding, from a hopelessly wealthy old family of WASP alcoholics, with parents who were vicious, race-baiting and mean. Ralph was crazy. Talked to himself, laughing his way down the hallways at Baker, breaking himself up, snorting and wagging his head wildly as he found his way to class.

Handsome Ronnie Blue, younger brother of Dan, Varsity wrestler and halfback. Ronnie would go on to eclipse his three-year older brother, making all-state at one-hundred-forty-nine pounds and going on to play in the backfield at Michigan. When he ran with us he was just a quiet kid.

We'd issue forth on date-nights, three or four of us bush-league bullies in Ronnie's '41 Olds club coupe, maybe meet another carload at Ronnie's father's drive-in, and look for trouble. Drag races, fights, minor vandalism, some party crashing. At a huge popular people get-together at Nadine Pepper's, Ronnie, who'd been trying to date her for months, drank some Booth's and decided to pull out his pecker. While the taffeta-girls squeaked their disapproval in the grass-cloth breakfast nook, he flipped open the Pepper's new electric oven and pissed on the big ham.

One night we motored to distant rustic manorial Pepper Pike, where the more worldly and ever-vigilant Rustig had discovered (and presumably auditioned) a rich blonde "nympho." She came out to the car smoking a Lucky, acting drunk. Plump, her black velvet gown fell away from her chest.

"Hi, boys." She gave us a dead, ash-laden breath.

Maybe she was crying. I didn't get a good look, but Rustig and Blue pushed her into the garage. I waited outside in the driveway. Yelling and laughter, and then just the huge Ohio sky over the looming mansion.

I never really had the nervous system for these sub-lunar forays and border-raids. With Emily pumping to pump, there was no compelling reason to complete my apprenticeship in idiocy, but it appealed to a side of me I had to respect, if not honor.

Accordingly, between continued evening love-banquets with Emily and constantly stupider scrapes with my fellow mini-churls, my schoolwork fell to uneven, at best. I did tie for first in the State Latin exam, and my English, history, and even math were often fairly decent. So when Mr. Boris, the Guidance Counselor, called me in for evaluation, I was startled to be informed that I was not smart enough for college. That's exactly what they said. My mother was livid.

My best male friend at Baker was the sweet Dan Rosario—son of a Spanish Jew, a short dog-like dealer in precious stones, and his statuary wife—who had the use of his father's '51 Olds Holiday 98, a huge but slinky two-door in two-tone gray. Emily and I doubled with Dan and Nancy Fryman, a squat, dark, pointy-breasted girl with an open, smiling face, much like her boyfriend's. She lived with her mother in an apartment near the Carnegie Light Rail. Mostly we avoided school functions, going to movies together: *From Here to Eternity, The Big Heat.* Necking in the car.

After one such elaborate soiree, we drove back into Baker around midnight. I was dozing on Emily's lap on the leather backseat when the car swerved, throwing us into the well behind the front seats. I heard Dan open the door.

"We've had enough shit from you punks tonight!" yelled an adult-sounding voice. Or was it "Jew punks"?

Emily was gasping. I tried to sit up.

"What's wrong?" I heard Dan asking. Pushing up onto a knee I saw two college-aged guys.

"Dan!" I pulled at the latch.

Night and the presence of violence. Horses were biting each other this night. Lightning should have appeared.

We had been forced to stop sideways in the center of a major intersection, deserted at this hour, blocked by their convertible: a black '54 Lincoln with an eggshell top. Above us, a traffic light blinked late-night orange.

One of the college guys walked up and without stopping just hauled back and slugged Dan in the face. As if he'd been planning to do it all along.

Dan grunted and fell.

For a moment the night was still, with just the bizz-ing of the warning light over our heads.

I stepped a foot onto the pavement.

"Hey!"

One of the guys had what looked like a club. I shoved the door open. He swung.

The sound of whatever it was hitting Dan's skull was unimaginable, a loud, dull *pop!* Then the guys were gone, peeling off in their Lincoln. There were girls in the car, too. Two blondes with big eyes.

I got Dan back in the car, and drove the single block to the Baker Heights police station.

I was being fucked-with, not by some low-life from my recent highwayman past, but while playing the game, going straight, passing for Jewish, for middle-class, for civilized, for "worth something." Only to be afflicted with these sons of Episcopal landowners, keeping us in our place, as it were.

At the pin-neat little constabulary the night desk officers were polite, even solicitous. By the time the brief interrogation was done, Dan was returned from a nearby emergency room with a diagnosis of a simple concussion. A bright white bandage covered multiple stitches in his scalp.

When his parents arrived, the cops showed real concern. "These boys need to pay for this."

"Couple of rich bastards. Need to be taught a lesson!" I put in.

The detectives looked at each other; on their salaries *we* were the rich kids, too. Then my father pulled up in his Jaguar, looking helpful but pissed.

Emily was contained, as usual, but cute little Nancy was in shock. "My mom won't believe me. She'll say it's my fault."

Nancy was poor for Baker, lived in a cheap apartment, and was known to be generous with her adolescent charms. Fast. Dan's wealthy parents were not pleased by her liaison with their only heir. In their presence, Dan found himself unable to muster much in the way of emotional support for the person he described to us as his girlfriend.

As the midnight crowd grew, a detective lieutenant finally appeared.

"We've got the kids who did this," he told us. *Kids?* I thought.

"And they're really sorry. Their parents want to have a meeting with all of us to work this out."

I found this somehow inadequate. But the grown-ups seemed to be saying okay.

The story played big for a couple of weeks. Dan and I were minor heroes at school as the community girded for the big trial. The story appeared a couple of times on local TV. Then a reporter came from the Baker *Sun Dial*. The picture his photographer took of Dan with his head bandaged somehow never made the paper. The promised trial of the two *shgohtzim* never came off. I guess they figured they'd buy the Yids off. And they did. Must have been the Rosarios, I guess. The lesson in power, if not completely assimilated, was Q.E.D.

⸏

One rainy day in March, Emily came home with her mother and father in their red and black Olds Holiday 88. I'd been waiting in the kitchen with Louise the maid. The three of them shook off their raincoats, avoiding my eyes as they passed the kitchen doorway. At length, a flat-looking Emily took me aside and covered my hand with hers.

"They say you have to leave. My parents want you to leave."

"How come?"

"We just came from the doctor," she shrugged. "He told them I'm pregnant."

In my youthful depths my colon reversed direction, seized up and stayed stiff.

"What does that mean?"

"It means I can't see you any more," she said.

"What are you going to do?"

"They told me they're gonna be the ones to take care of it. You better go now."

I walked home through the rain under sycamore, maple and elm—leafless still in the early spring—and the barely budding forsythias, wondering about what was real.

There followed the oddest period I'd yet experienced in my fifteen-and-a-half-year history—a hazy, silent-secret month of mumness in which the ineluctable abortion was arranged, but never mentioned, by my own shy daddy. My mother was let in on the secret only years later.

Isolated from the process as I was by both fathers, I had little feeling about what we'd done. No real pain, no humiliation, really, because of the secrecy implicit in the illicit procedure. Just the dull awareness that I'd fucked up again. Just numb.

After what must have been a hospital abortion, Emily was forbidden to see me. Weekends I'd park and wait with muffled oars for her to be driven home from whatever sizzling school sock-hop or soda shop she'd been soldiered off to. Her ostensible consort on these dates, and generally assumed new boyfriend, was Cary Dawson, the Class President, state champion diver, and all-city fullback. "Collar-ad handsome," people could be heard to say, a classic Norman yeoman, many times removed. Perhaps not that many.

She'd say goodnight to Dawson at the front door, then come skipping out the back into my father's Olds, which I learned to hot-wire with a hairpin.

We'd cruise to somewhere safe and dissolve into each other's bodies, pitching guiltless woo on back seat leather. It still seemed, despite what anyone thought, that she still cared only for me, sloughing off anything truly serious with this Dawson fella.

A few weeks later, while voiding bladder in the second-floor john at Baker High, I looked over my shoulder in midstream and found Dawson entering with the Mangiacavallo twins. They whispered, grunted, and finally snickered. I heard my name repeated in taunting tones, "Mitch-chull, Mitch-chull, Mitch-chulllll..." and I shot them a quick scope.

There my dashing rival stood, 6'1", 180, smirking obscenely, flanked by the *vitelloni* Mangiacavallo twins: Marco, 235, starting Varsity tackle, state heavyweight wrestling champion and lacking discernible neck; and Mario, 210, starting Varsity guard, heavyweight wrestling runner-up, and equally neckless. Hulking, slouching shoulders and open-collared white dress shirts showed acres of chest carpeted in dense wire brambles. I was turning back to my just-slackening stream when Dawson stepped forward and shoved me into the dripping urinal.

A single shocking Click, next stop Amygdala City. An infrared glow in my R-complex.

It just so happened that only the day before, a Sunday, I'd had a long confab with Jimmy Fisher, a bland but solid classmate I knew mostly from sports. We'd been watching his father strip the finish from a Chickering spinet, and Jimmy allowed that he hated fights where two guys just kept pushing each other, shoving back and forth without purpose.

"One guy says: 'Yeah?' and the other guy goes 'Yeaah!' You know, 'Yeah?' 'Yeah!' forever. What a crock'a shit!"

"Yeah. Gotta go for the cold-cock," I testified, summing up my slender childhood fight-wisdom.

We agreed that the *only* thing to do, should someone presume to mess with you, was unleash your deadliest "bolo" punch from as close to the floor as you could get your knuckles. As a kid I'd learned from regular confrontations with neighborhood Catholic hoods the truth of the adage:

He who fights and runs away,
lives to fight another day.

I did, perforce, a lot of running. But sometimes you had to stand there and get your ass kicked. It happened to me maybe once a month all through grade school, and I'd pretty much lost my fear of juvenile beating in the process.

Without waiting even to shake off my dong, much less button my 501's, I reached back and launched my best preemptive right, aimed at my tormentor's square, dimply, Anglo jaw.

Dawson's head snapped back, caromed off the marble wall, and followed the rest of his astonished Student Council President's body to the tiled lavatory floor as at least one tooth popped bloodily out into the warm spring air.

In the ensuing vacuum, I met the eyes of Dawson's pals as they looked up stuporously from their fallen mate. Sensing the Mangiacavallos' disinclination to detain a mad dog further, I stalked past the matching pugs to the lavatory door, and kept walking. By the time I reached the baseball practice field I realized they'd never let me come back.

I expected some form of *lex talionis,* jaw-for-a-jaw, but it appeared sufficient that I was expelled the following week. My mother convinced my father, a true believer in public education as a guarantee of a democratic society, to allow me to apply at Crockett Academy in a tiny town about an hour from Carnegie. It was a snotty little Episcopal prep school with only three Jewish boys out of a student body of two hundred and twenty-five.

Meanwhile, released from school obligations in early April, I went to work in my Uncle Saul's shop, making indescribably miscellaneous metal parts with fascinating machines for contracts from nameless government agencies.

I'd worked since I was twelve or so at paper routes or caddying at the exclusive Hathaway Country Club, and for Uncle Saul, when he was still a coin-op distributor, before the Mob took over. I serviced the Make-Your-Own-Photo booths, pinball machines and jukeboxes.

My mentor was a Hungarian named Lukas. We drove our route in his dull red '41 Chevy Fleetline: empty afternoon midways, amusement parks and, especially in the ghettos and working-class areas, creaky old roller-skating and bowling establishments, most built in and of the excesses of the mid-twenties. The great gilt rococo *Trianon* on 105th and Geometer, the big Negro *Playland* on Fairmount and Lebanon. We had fun. I helped refill the developer on the photo machines, and collect nickels from the baseball card, skee-ball and pinball machines. Lukas was the first workingman I'd spent a lot of time with. He told me things.

"These *Feketes,* Mitch. People say they're bad, call them Nigger. One shot at me. Shot my car, shot my hat. People say they're not smart persons."

"They shot you? When? What happened?"

"Long time ago. Maybe six months. They try to rob. Try take money box. I say no. This not yours. He shoot driver window. Glass everywhere. My good hat."

"Where was this, Lukas? What did you do?"

"Right here. I drive very fast away."

We were parked in the alley behind *Playland.* A dark Ohio winter evening. Black people, mostly older women and men with steel lunchboxes, getting off the No. 10 bus, pushing into the wind off Lake Erie. Christmas music from a record store. Billy Eckstein bringing White Christmas to the Chester ghetto.

"Did you call the cops? What did they do? What happened?"

"I tell your uncle. He say forget about it. I'm okay. Money safe. Gave me cash for fix car. Nice man."

"Think so?"

"Very nice man. Nice bonus for Christmas. He say things about *Feketes,* the colored people. He hate colored people. Sometimes at work…"

"What? What about work?"

"He hate colored people."

"He's from the South. A Jew from Florida."

"Sometimes he's mean to colored people at work."

"Like how?"

"Nothing."

"Like what, Lukas?"

"Sometimes he make colored ladies do things."

"What things, Lukas?"

"Things."

"What things? I won't repeat it. I'm not close with him. I won't tell a soul."

"One time I go to office late with collection box. Hear voice of Dinah."

"What was she saying?"

"She yelling 'No, please!' Then, when I open office door, see him holding her down on his big desk. She is crying."

"Shit!"

"You stay in school, Mr. Mitchell. You smart young man. You finish school."

Coming back to Sherman now, ostensibly a high school dropout, I thought, *is this how adults live who are not doctors?* Seeing real people, the kind who were my father's patients, working-people. Black and white. Eastern Europeans, mostly, some Appalachians. They only fronted a friendly attitude; I was the white-boy relative who'd fade after a couple of days of real work. Give 'im something hard to lift and harder to fuck-up. I knew.

I lifted heavy railroad tie-like lengths of metal, fastening them and watching while Raynor, the young Negro I was helping, measured and cut the basic hunks or "blocks" that would begin the journey to further precision cutting, countersinking, beveling and polishing, all to faceless federal specs.

Raynor was sincerely sweet. "Y'know Louis Jordan, Mikey?" he asked when it was his turn to rest and my turn to move the railroad another couple of inches.

"Who?" I was lifting, trying desperately to overcome the friction of metal-to-metal to slide the rail along.

"That 'Open the Door, Richard' song, Mikey? Know that guy?"

"Yeah, I know it," I said, trying not to drop my end too hard.

"I love that song, Mikey. Love to sing it like Louis Jordan." Raynor smiled. Even his teeth looked happy. "Maybe you could learn it on the piano, Mikey."

I ended the day tweezing steel slivers out of my cracked, bleeding hands, washing in solvent and taking the bus home, feeling glad to be numb. No girlfriend. No friends at all, really, now that high school was behind me. Lukas learned English in night school and left for a union job on the line at Ford. *Could I take his place? Did I want his life?*

"What will I do?" I heard the words bounce off the metal in the cramped, oil-coated men's locker room.

As I dragged up my parents' driveway, I carried the nagging, dislocating fear. I didn't know the word "anxiety," but as I slouched from world to world, both feet scraping the ground, I never stopped questioning. For the first time in my life, I doubted, and knew that I was doubting. I had played the role of boy in a family, but now what? Sometimes it seemed as if I'd be lucky to make mountain goat. I knew I needed direction, but I didn't know where I should be directed to. I didn't even know how to *imagine* a way to find out.

That night at the dinner table, dog-tired from the day on the shop floor, I heard my mother say they were looking for volunteers at Camp Sage.

"You might go down and apply for Junior Counselor. They have two and three-week openings. So you could leave if you didn't like it. In short order." She seemed so fresh and young, slicing her signature brisket. "You know, it's where I first met your father." I'd seen the pictures of them in their bloom— wool bathing suits and firm bodies of their youth. "It could be a new slate."

Then I had one of those moments, the ones where you feel invincible and as if you might vomit at exactly the same time. Suddenly, the future is where it's always been, rushing straight at you and nowhere at all. For a brief moment, you get things straight. Clear and right. A shaft of light slanted through my teenage fog-bank.

The next day I took the bus to the Red Feather office, far from Baker Heights, in a ghetto-bordering East Carnegie brick walkup, took a deep breath and smiled at the solid social-welfare lieutenant across the desk. I supposed they didn't have many young men applicants, much less presentable student-athletes, and I was engaged *gratis* on the spot. My mother was happy that night at dinner; my father heaved a sigh of relief: I was out of danger for the moment—and more importantly, perhaps, from where he stood—out of the house.

Camp Sage was the turnaround I'd hoped for. I threw myself into learning about child development, the new orthodoxy of "Group Theory," and being as agreeable an aid to the paid staff as I could in the two week stint I'd signed on for. So successfully did I seem to transform myself that I was offered a position for the rest of the summer at the munificent sum of $200 for the remaining seven weeks.

I started out as a "tumbling" counselor. I knew absolutely nothing about gymnastics, but from my varsity sports experience managed to fashion a passable exercise routine at least, adding various vaults and rolls, culminating in showy galas with campers somersaulting over piles of expanding numbers of other campers. There were floodlights. Music from a scratchy LP upon which I had recently fixated: the Rachmaninoff Second Concerto. We also ran a lot and did what I could remember of football calisthenics. I tried to avoid fixating on their little bodies. I was two years older, sexually initiated and when they did leg lifts, it gave me trouble. I wanted to see their little pussies. I knew they were up there. *Open AND Close AND Open.* Pink panties and wisps of hair. *Hold it! Keep 'em open!* I wondered if they knew what I was up to. Did it turn them on? They were obviously too young to be conscious of the magnetism of their potent nubility, especially in that benighted pre-Playboy era. Still, some of them beamed fiendishly at me as they spread their sacred girlhood for my delight and delectation. A storehouse of images.

Some nights after evening activities I found reason to visit the darkened Rec Hall from whence to peep the older girls through their cabin windows. Nothing serious. Brand new swelling nipple nubbins, the occasional teenage butt-crack succulence, and little else. They were too modest to display themselves to one another, so the shot selection was rather limited.

There was, blessedly, sex at night. Well, not sex exactly. Necking and dry-humping, on a blanket out on the cliffs above the huge lake. Sixteen-year old JC's from the poorer Jewish families. The big sky, the surf and semen spots on my khakis. It kept me going. There were a few I would later invite to my prep school dances, but only until I learned better. Turns out there were Jews, and then there were Jews.

I mostly worked on attitude, trying to shake that loser feeling, and that comfortable pain-avoiding arrogance which I could come to confuse with my best self. I got great responses from my supervisors, counselors, and the kids, and was invited back the next year as a full-time paid counselor. In the end, I rose to Music & Drama Counselor, producing and directing my own truncations of *Macbeth, Julius Caesar, Romeo and Juliet, H.M.S. Pinafore,* and even *The Wizard of Oz*. It fell to me to play piano and lead singing at all assemblies. All the Yiddish *shtetel* songs, the WWII Soviet solidarity anthems, like "Meadowland," and great American Labor songs: Woody Guthrie, Paul Robeson, the Weavers, talkin' 'bout:

> *Listen while I tell you that the very folks you hate*
> *Are the very same people made America great.*

I learned to accompany Israeli folksongs, Zionist songs, and folk dancing as well. But the most electric moments were accompanying our head-chef Willie Franklin in spirituals. Not knowing the tunes, I watched her nodding encouragement to me across the stage as I struggled to fake arrangements to "Deep River," "Balm in Gilead," or "Sometimes I Feel like a Motherless Child."

"Son, you're good!" she told me after one such painful exhibition.

"Please, Willie. I'm embarrassed enough! I skipped half the notes." I was more ashamed that she felt compelled to lie.

"You'll get it," she said. "Just give yo'self time, chile. An' don't give up!"

I came home to pack for Crockett Academy with a notable absence of steel filings under my cuticles. Before leaving for the new school I went to Blount Brothers at Baker Square, and with my $200 I bought enough Ivy-looking stuff to ease my passage amidst the gentlemen's sons. Oxford button-down collar shirts in white, blue and blue-and-white stripes; ties in regimental stripes, wool paisley and silk foulard; a Shetland crew-neck in "wheat;" a pair of charcoal brown flannels; a pair of the new khakis, each with the *de rigueur* (but function-free) belt in the back; a pair of Bass Weejun five-eyelet ties in black.

Two days before I was scheduled to leave for Crockett I got a call from Arnold Cashman, my co-anti-McCarthyite friend. A nice, very smart boy, but a bit stiff. Arnold was the first person I knew with horn-rimmed glasses. When he called and suggested a movie the next night, I was surprised.

"*The Defiant Ones* is at the Colony. Wanna go? I'll pick you up." He pulled up in his father's '49 Dodge. Good to see old Arnold. "I left my history book at Julia Stockman's. Mind if we stop? It's on the way." Their school year, like the expensive hooker of legend, had started without me. "Come on in with me," he said as he muscled the coupe into the fir-lined driveway.

The Stockman's was a cozy English cottage in the Lynnfield area of what I considered Upper Baker, while we Hertzes were barely on the fringes of Lower. I had pursued the perky Julia, their only child, the year before in the lakeside resort of Lucerne-on-the-Lake. Julia had given the signs that she was interested. She was in my class, unlike the younger Emily, and the idea of spending my senior year dating a classmate, with all the social acceptability that would confer, was not unappealing. I was equally ready to grapple with Julia's apparently endless cleavage. Her girlfriends had counseled, in the parlance of the time, *she likes you*, but by the end of the visit, Julia had shown total disregard for my presence, and I wasted no time in taking off back down Route 20 to my Emily.

I was not anxious to re-encounter Julia that night. I lamely straggled along after Arnold, hoping to escape with a cursory wave from the front walk. I gazed off down the cozy tree-lined street as he rang the doorbell. The very first cool wind of autumn chased a few early-dropped leaves across the trim lawns. I heard the door open.

"Hi, guys! Come on in!" Julia yoo-hooed to me from the stoop.

Head slightly hung, I drug my feet into the dark house and was startled by a scream and bright lights, as the living room exploded:

"SURPRISE!!!"

You could've bought me for a nickel. Here, shouting my name, were assembled every major potentate, satrap and Pasha of the new Baker Senior Class, foregathered as to a court wedding, conjoined to bid me ritual farewell. I steadied myself and looked around:

Rolly Denske, my desk mate in homeroom, my favorite receiver as a sophomore, and car-racing magnate to be. Ron Beauchamp, a vaguely Kerouac-resembling French-Canadian, and a favored running back. Rick Pesaro, later a famous painter and art historian in Indiana.

Pesaro, Beauchamps and I had neighboring lockers in JV Basketball, and compared cocks. Pesaro proposed us as the official penis-matching squad, challenging visiting teams to dick-offs. He even developed a costume based on the heraldic flag below the pages' court trumpets that unfurl and drop down to flutter heroically in the twelfth-century breeze.

My heart was seized with shock at the goodwill in the room. Months ago I'd written them off as having written *me* off, yet here they were, blind-siding my all-but-departed ass. Class beauties, jocks, Leaders. It was the perfect zephyr to fill my sails for a calm sea and prosperous voyage deep into the world of the American ruling class—as a tourist, make no mistake, but First Cabin.

When I arrived at Crockett Academy in the fall of 1954, the preparatory school's student body consisted of 225 young men divided in four forms nestled into the tiny village that bore its name. The Academy had been founded in 1820, a boarding school for sons of Carnegie supremos who, for one reason or the other, had decided against Choate or St. Somebody's.

Among a welter of other activities that year—including Orchestra, Pep Band, and the school paper—I also did sports. Varsity football, wrestling and baseball. I was okay for a 5' 8," 145-pound person who only took it seriously in the moment, or until the right girls noticed. I sensed that you got less points for athletic prowess at my new school, but at least you got some, and I knew no other way.

If you introduced yourself to somebody smartly on a football field with a good *pop!* to the helmet, you stood a good chance of gaining some instant respect. *Plus,* I surmised, in this backwater of the Interstate League, referred to as a "silk stocking league" by the national sports media, *I might even be able to walk on and start.*

We played what Head Coach Merriwell "Mel" Tibbett called a "multiple offense": a fairly brainy perpetually recombining synthesis of single wing, unbalanced "Straight T" and the new Bobby Dowd-pioneered "Split T." It was my job as quarterback to:

1) Call the plays
2) Call audible shifts to other formations; and
3) Execute the play called, as either:
a) blocking back (in the single wing), or
b) under center (as T-formation quarterback); in either case:
i. hand off the football,
ii. run the football, or
iii. pass the football.
4) Play Safety on Defense.

On the gracious New Englandy greenswards where our practices unfolded twice a day, it was fun again—no coaches cursing and bouncing pigskin off your skull. The uniforms were old-fashioned, but somehow not embarrassing—dark green jerseys, gold pants and helmets. A photographer from the school paper wanted a shot of our team captain, Don Brown, for the Opening Day issue. Don wanted to be shot in a cross-body block pose, and chose me as the demonstration dummy. The resulting photo showed me standing relaxed and happy, looking into the camera, while Don, face obscured, leaned formally into my thigh pads. The caption in the first issue of the new school year read: "Captain Brown demonstrates blocking," with the result that I was taken for the football captain by all new students and didn't have to wait tables or perform the other odious kitchen duties assigned to all newbies.

Where at Baker I would have played defense at best—my calves weren't beefy enough, and I refused to lift weights on principle—here I began to think I had a chance. I found myself in the running for starting quarterback. Incumbent senior Tim Blanchard was about my size, tough, a decent runner and a fourth-year classmate for most of the other starters, but he couldn't throw the football. My passes had helped to give our Baker JV eleven its first winning season in a long enough time to make the achievement notable. I could throw long, short and had somehow never thrown an interception. So, as a transfer, I was considered almost a secret weapon coming into the season opener against Fillmore Academy, a traditional landowner-Catholic boys school in exurban Bates Mills, Ohio.

The week before the opening game I got a letter from my mother reminding me of the looming Jewish high holidays. I jumped to my calendar: Yom Kippur was the Thursday before the Fillmore game. I called home to plead for dispensation and came up feeling guilty, so I asked Coach if I could miss a day of practice.

Coach Tibbett seemed a fair enough guy to me, a tiny dynamo of a man in his sixties who could still do anything but block and tackle better than any of us. I already sort of loved him. To let me go for a day, come back, and *still* take Blanchard's job would have been morale suicide.

"Not and start against Fillmore!" he said.

"But, I've got the playbook *cold,* and it's only one day."

Was there an element of anti-Semitism? I don't know. I was one of two Jews on the team. Who could tell for sure? Probably no more than the school at large, where my co-Mosaicists numbered a total of three. By demonstrating filial piety, I would be giving up a certain social *quantum athleticum* I'd worked hard to earn. But I went home, to honor the most solemn of Jewish holy days. My parents were thrilled. I took my little sister Lily's hand and marched into Kol Nidre service, the height of the Day of Atonement ritual, in which Rabbinate and Congregation check off their sins of the past year.

"And for the sin which I have sinned before Thee by covetousness;
And for the sin which I have sinned before Thee by stiff-neckedness…"

Every year I sat there thinking, *You talkin' about me? I did that?* as they ticked them off. *Or that? No, no, okay, yeah, no, no…maybe. Definitely.* I used to weigh each consecutive sin on the list, as the rabbi intoned, to try to calculate mea culpabilitá as every year I become more morally attuned. That hot, sticky mid-September evening I tried to concentrate on the heart of the Hebraic Code of Ethics to drive the Fillmore game from my mind. *It is right to honor thy parents.*

I was sweating in my new tweed jacket next to Lily, who was sweet and silent on those occasions, reading the incoming sin-stream. The music that followed was heartfelt, even sublime. But then young Rabbi Pincus Goodblatt got up to deliver the sermon, and I made the mistake of paying close attention to what he said. Most of my co-congregants seemed, from the vacant signs in their eyes, bored to stupefaction. After bungling a low-level scholarly exegesis of some minor sacramental term, the young rabbi launched into his text proper, and twin themes emerged:

First: "The Germans are a race of Huns. As a nation they have produced nothing of lasting value…"

Now, I was student-conducting the Beethoven *Fifth* at the Academy, using Bach *Choral Preludes* on the chapel organ to teach myself to phrase without the sustaining pedal in my piano studies, and running down to the Crockett Historical Society Library daily to check out the Toscanini complete Brahms *Symphonies*, or the Casals Festival *Brandenburgs,* or Wilhelm Backhaus' Beethoven *Sonatas.* So this notion, drifting down from the pulpit like a bad odor, struck me as ignorant, small, mean and contemptuous of the truth—and the congregation which employed him to know better.

"This is dumb," I whispered to Lily. She was only thirteen, but not stupid. Then the Rabbi slammed the door and locked it.

Second: "For all right-thinking Jews, the United States is just a stopping-over place, on the way to *Eretz Yisroh-el,* the Land of Israel."

BAM! I snapped my prayer book closed, grabbed Lily's little hand, jerked her up abruptly, and tugged her behind me as we bumped past the thirty or so outraged kneecaps that lay between us and the end of the row.

I spent the shank of the afternoon adrift in confusion. I'd gone off to the Academy concerned about sticking out as a Yid. Now I was walking away from it; was I running? Didn't I believe in God?

I simply found nothing personally useful in this social structure and its take on the Old Guy With a Beard. I worried that what I had done would somehow hurt my parents—yet they simply had to understand. *This Jewish business isn't me.*

To allay my anxiety I took out my copy of *For Whom the Bell Tolls,* my English homework, and was blissfully absent, off manning a machine-gun nest on a Spanish hillside till I heard them come up the driveway.

My parents listened to my challenge that if they couldn't defend the ignorant statements which had driven me out of the temple, they could consider me an atheist for good. Lily, I conciliated, could think for herself.

"Tell me I'm wrong!" I demanded. "Tell me you agree with what the Rabbi said." They stood there, resplendent in High Holy Days finest.

"No, son," was the unmediated reply, G-d love 'em. "You do what you believe is right. You can always change your mind."

I didn't start at quarterback against Fillmore, but Coach appointed me kicker. On the opening kickoff I teed the ball up sideways, toed way under it and lifted the ultimate dipsy-doodle all-over-the-place knuckleball floater which spazzed around at no greater an altitude than maybe thirty feet and came down at the 35.

There, by tenacity and dumb luck, I managed to find myself directly underneath it as it came vectoring down, caught it on the fly and kept running. I didn't go all the way, but I managed to advance the ball to about their 20 before getting buried. Blanchard came in and called three running plays, then I came back in and kicked a thirty-yard field goal.I took over the offense in the third quarter and threw for two touchdowns. We went on to win 24-to-14. I fight. I lose. I win.

The Academy was tough. Classes were Monday through Saturday. We read *all* of Shakespeare, both Bible Testaments, and wrote five pages every night. Honors English brought the totally whacked English Masters (as they were called in privilege-land), under the direction of "Black" Bart LaSorde, a maniacal syntax-enforcement official, and Patrick Michael Bearden, a defrocked goliard we called "Jiggs," who, with wit and whimsy, licensed us young tweedies to exuberate.

I did well in my new setting, where feeling superior was the main priority, save one. In that male-only dominion, pussy proximity led the list. After discovering sex with Emily, then having the door slammed abruptly on my dick, I rebounded by seducing one of her friends, sixteen-year old Mildred Merman—round, virginal and so luscious—and was hot on the trail of tall, blonde Francine Paley, the doctor's daughter. We were playing duets on Francine's living room Knabe, sitting snug on the piano bench, braiding our arms for the cross-hand passages—with the attendant rubbing and bumping of breasts—when her mother coolly delivered the resolution emerging from an unofficial *ad hoc* council of concerned parents: Beat It. I'd been barred from their daughters' environs. All of them. *No to Mitchell. Out now!*

For the periodic Academy tea dances I was left with no alternative but to revisit Baker High girls I'd never dated—rich girls who looked good, but wouldn't fuck me under any circumstance. Then just before graduation, I met a prep-school girl from suburban Rockford.

I got my first peep at her at the Academy Junior Prom, just before Christmas break, in my senior year. That year my friend Robin Feld (the other Jew in my class, and one funny mother) and I had put together a crudely generic singing group, based on some of the mildly satiric parodies and skits I'd been trying to fashion as drama and music counselor at Camp. We sang at school dances, did bush-league Stan Freberg routines, and garnered sufficient plaudits to persevere.

For Junior Prom, Feld and I penned a pre-modernist mini-musical pastiche. We got some laughs, pulled a few japes, worked up a sweat and when it was all over, repaired backstage in the senior coffee room to change. There I beheld the elegant cameo loveliness of Vanessa Heller, a Junior at the fashionable Rockford girl's school, Elder Pike. As I stripped the officer's blouse from my just-getting-fuzzy chest, I looked out into the still-buzzing crowd and saw her eyes on me. From across the room they seemed very wet.

Throughout my athletic career at the Academy, whenever I crossed the formal lobby of the Field House—with its trophies, pennants and balls painted school colors—I would study the award plaques, scanning the names of all the captains. Staring up at the succession of guys, I wondered how my interloping Jewish ass could possibly fluke into a place up there.

By my last semester at the Academy I'd earned five Varsity letters for football, wrestling and baseball. I'd been a decent quarterback and defensive back. I quit the wrestling team and spent the winter learning four-wall handball with my friend Duke Burberry, who dumped varsity swimming to join me. We earned the extreme displeasure of the Varsity "R" Club, which tried to throw us both out.

It hadn't helped that in an extraordinary Chapel Debate I'd been the one to argue the case against what I considered a fascist proposal to require compulsory attendance at official league games, and won the contest over two varsity stalwarts.

I was a little surprised when the expelling faction failed to carry a majority, saved perhaps by a winning football season in which my name had appeared in modest headlines in the sports section of the Carnegie papers. On the last play of the season I'd run back an interception for the winning touchdown against arch-rival Collegiate School.

But the debate cost me whatever points I'd scored with the coaching staff, and by spring term I was nobody's hero, just an average utility baseball player whose balls were under suspicion. Anyway, the baseball season opened my senior year with me batting second and playing third base. As the game with our most contemptuously considered opponent, Collegiate, approached, the team had no captain. Last year's stars had graduated and none of us returning lettermen had enough authority for the job. Leaderless we played well enough to beat a few college freshmen squads and to tie for first in the league.

I was doing okay, batting about .280 or so, getting on base a lot—singles and doubles, mostly, the occasional long-ball, but plenty of walks and hit-by-pitchers—scoring runs and not committing egregious blunders in the field. I had "hustle," a quality which was beginning to win back the confidence of my mates. We were coming together in time for the season finale with our arch-rival, who had creamed us in all three winter sports.

The night before the Collegiate game, the skies over Crockett unzipped, dropping torrential spring rains, felling trees, and leaving a quagmire where our infield had been. The game was called and, as decreed by tradition, entered the league standings as a dreaded tie.

We were pissed—enough so that Coach called Collegiate and re-scheduled the game for two days later at their field in fashionable goyish-suburban Carnegie. Strictly un-official, as far as the league standings were concerned—a pure grudge match. We hated the sneering soon-to-be-Yalie arrivistes.

We arrived that afternoon in late May, 1956, in the mansion-lined *haute bourgeois* preserves of upper Baker Heights, not prepared for the huge flash-crowd that greeted us. Blonde, long-legged girls from Arrow Greene or Pine Manor School, in pastel shirtwaists. Sandy-brownhaired guys in chinos, button-down shirts, Haspel cord jackets. But lots of them. More than we'd ever seen at a school contest. And noisier. I tensed up and threw a few in the dirt during infield practice. Third base was no more than fifteen feet from the home stands, and I could hear them mocking me, sing-songing my name in feeble falsetti. I threw the next one over Bill Roberts' head into the street. *That* got 'em going.

"MITCH-*ULL*! MITCH-*ULL*!!"

After warm-ups we assembled dispiritedly in the visitor's locker to plan whatever strategy one can in high school baseball. We sat fidgeting, awaiting Coach's last terse hound-blessing of our schoolboy athletic careers. I felt myself beginning to lift off into a weightless mind beyond nervousness, beyond care, beyond survival. Just a strange, pure Being There, digging the moment, with all these guys, sharing their mental and physical fields, appreciating it all.

"As you fellas know, we've played this season without a captain." Coach's voice visited my dreamland head. "This is the last game for many of you seniors. Maybe the last time you'll ever play organized sports."

I looked around the room foggily, watching the others lean forward on their benches to form a large sit-down huddle of respect and concentration. We all loved this sweet little man.

"But this is the Collegiate game. And today you need a leader on the field. Today you need a captain. *Think hard about the guy you elect.*"

I don't know how I got nominated, exactly. My Hebraic designation alone might have disqualified me—but in my mild state of alteration, I took the news placidly enough, with a deep sense of acceptance and gratitude, as one welcomes the Sabbath Queen, or the sodium pentothal, counting backwards, "a hundred, ninety-nine, ninety-eighhhhhh, neynnnddddeeee…"

Coach passed out neat squares of ruled paper, and pencils. There were only two nominees, he announced, Jim Scotland, our altogether decent second baseman and, *mirabile dictu*, me. Somehow my mild trance told me I would win; not because I was a better player (we were about even, but he couldn't really hit for distance), but because he was a sycophant of the Academy Old Boy-clique, and no one wanted an ass-kisser for a captain. I remember seeing Scotland's face when my name was announced. His lower jaw sort of mashed against his neck, like Andy Gump.

Now it was the top of the seventh, the final inning of high school baseball games. We were trailing, 2-1. I came up with two out and two men on base. I don't recall what I'd done in previous at-bats, what the count was, who the base runners were, nothing, except that their pitcher threw me a stupid pitch: straight and not as fast as he hoped, chest-high, what we used to call "at the letters."

When I swung my Lou Boudreau-model Louisville Slugger there was a certain effortlessness, a remnant of the golden reverie in the locker room. My bat connected with the ball as it bisected the plane of the pitcher's face. Oddly, there was almost no sound—none that I heard, anyway. Just the sense that the ball was launched, as from a catapult, and that it was climbing almost straight up, still climbing as it overflew second base, and finally, well beyond the center fielder's head.

I stood there at home plate, fascinated by the grand arc of the pill. Then I started running. As I departed the batter's box, one runner was already crossing the plate and the second rounding third, yelling his appreciation.

"Home run!"

I picked up the other runner as a blur in my peripheral vision. I made a luxuriantly wide swing around first base, and floated toward second when I began to notice fielders scrambling, our bench screaming my name, and the Collegiate shortstop on a collision course for second base! Out of instinct, I hit the dirt in a headfirst slide just before the ball arrived with a resounding *thwack!* in his mitt.

Safe! But what's the deal? How did they get the ball back so fast? Where is my game-winning home run?

It's relatively easy to reconstruct what *did* happen. The big storm had sluiced lakes of water all over the field two days before. Our own home field was a veritable rice paddy, a cranberry bog. The ball traveled 400 feet in the air and came straight down with a plop in a still-wet spot and, instead of bouncing and rolling all the way to Toledo, as it would have under normal conditions, the ball just stopped, stuck in the mud. The centerfielder, after only a moderate run, reached the ball, exhumed it from its creek bank and made the throw to the relay man, who completed the short shot to second that almost nabbed me.

I picked myself up, pissed at being held to a double. The first baseman came hopping down the base path, hollering for the ball. Then, taking the shortstop's obedient flip, he trotted insolently over to first, stepped on the bag and yelled, "OUT!"

I saw the umpire lift his right thumb and give the time-honored pumping gesture, and I fucking went *nuts!* First robbed of my monster homer (which, by custom at least, would have made touching all the bases unnecessary), and then unceremoniously thrown out on what should have been rendered a technicality. I leaped up, bellowing, and charged the umpire, who immediately turned his back. I picked up a glove and threw it.

"I was robbed!"

The stands erupted. For the first time in my life, I actually saw the color red. Out of control. Raging veal.

Then Coach appeared at my side, firmly but gently pinching the nerve in the elbow known only to coaches and cops, and steered my butt towards the sideline.

"Come back to the bench," he soothed under his breath.

"Bullshit! I was fuckin' robbed!"

"*Come* with me. You knocked in two runs." He moved me away from the ump, who now appeared ready to take punitive measures. "We're ahead. Come on."

We held on in the bottom of the seventh and won 3-to-2, so I'd knocked in the winning runs, and qualified as a semi-hero. But this Rube Goldberg victory quickly dissipated in the welter of the pre-commencement activities, finals, and proms which filled the last few weeks of my senior year.

With high school done, New York was waiting. I had been to New York before. My mother's favorite sister, and my favorite aunt, Ruth, lived with her husband (my favorite uncle) and her kids (my favorite cousins) on Long Island in a town named, ominously, Lake Success. I'd been taken for a New York "Season" for two weeks every year since I was born, even attending the last pre-war World's Fair in diapers.

I loved the big city. Every day, we'd join the grey-flannel commuters on the Long Island Railroad and zoop off to a Manhattan adventure such as my tiny midwestern eyes had never seen: the Sky-View taxis, the Rockettes, skating in Rockefeller Center, Macy's, Gimbel's, and especially Saks Fifth Avenue, with its fairyland Christmas windows. In later years I was treated to Carnegie Hall, the museums, and the fabulous Met.

My father couldn't abandon his patients, hospitals, x-rays, autoclaves and fluoroscopes, so it was just my gorgeous sweet mother and me. We went clothes shopping and I snuck peeps at all the ladies changing—their bras, slips and especially the mechanistic world of the girdle. And the smell!

Once I could read, I would scour *The New Yorker* for "Goings on About Town," exhibits and operas, shows and parades for weeks before we arrived. Not that we were sophisticates, or anything like that. My mother "couldn't understand" abstract art, and preferred Richard Rogers to Mozart, but she was of that first generation of Jews who figured they owed it to their kids to "expose them to art." I had my grounding in all those art/music/drama classes in Carnegie, but here I was in Gothamite heaven, where the real thing could be found in every gallery, swank restaurant, and art theatre. They even had foreign movies! So when it came time to pick a college I chose Columbia over Penn or Cornell, and never looked back.

I waited with my anxious parents in Carnegie's WPA-muralled terminal for the *Empire Express*, then sat up all night in my coach seat trying to shut out the squeals of the hundred homeward-bound *yeshiva bocherim,* returning from summer camp in Michigan. Prinked in skullcaps, spit-curls and prayer shawls, they punctuated my fitful interurban slumbers with goosing and gossiping all the way to New York.

Early Sunday morning we finally arrived at Grand Central and I took the IRT to Morningside Heights where I found my room on the sixth floor of Hartley Hall. I peeled off my sweaty clothes and sat naked at the end of the bunk bed, awaiting my steamer trunk, staring down meditatively onto the red bricks of Van Am Quad, until I passed out.

I awoke with four New Jerseyish faces goggling down the pillar of my prominent erection. Gaping open-mouthed was my new roommate—a physics major from Newark—his mother and sister with big shiny braces—and the father, curling his mustachioed lip with unpracticed furiosity.

Columbia required every entering freshman to suffer two full years of Contemporary Civilization ("C.C"), an exacting five-day-a-week survey course which assigned comprehensive readings in original sources from Plato to Marx to Vance Packard. They loved to pile it on: seven books of the *Republic* on the first night of school. It was at Columbia that fall that I got my first hungry look at the writings of the Great Thinkers, thinking *"Wow! This is the real deal, the basic rules!,"* and thereby separated my destiny from the Jewish pre-Doctors choking on the big lecture classes. I started as a pre-med, as family mythology directed, but it took less than a semester to figure out, what with competition from supercharged young Jewish science aces on the Eastern Seaboard, and my own lack of dedication, that my path lay elsewhere. By the end of freshman year I'd switched majors to Philosophy with a minor in Music.

I went out for Freshman Football, but it was too grueling—taking a subway to Baker's Field after chemistry lab seemed a lot more suffering than an undersized walk-on should reasonably undertake. I figured there *had* to be better ways to meet girls. I frantically blind-dated, otherwise hanging out at the West End Bar, where Beat luminaries were rumored to hold occasional court. And I went to mixers.

Mixers inspired the usual dreadful social anxiety for me—everyone on the make, me hoping aloof would pass for confident. At a Barnard get-together on the grass of their one little quad, I spied a girl sitting at the top of the library steps, legs open, undies on parade. I stared, convinced I was beholding the forbidden, making off with something of immense value—the purloined panties. She saw me. Flash Girl smiled shyly, but kept her legs spread. I smiled back, and she cocked her head quickly to one side, in the time-honored "come hither" gesture. So I dog-paddled through the tweed and flannel and was within hailing distance, when she stood up and sauntered off with a tall guy with red hair.

Later that day, isolated and in darkest despair, I laid down a sacrifice bunt; I pledged the hippest Jewish fraternity.

Lonely, I wrote a number of times to the probably unattainable Vanessa Heller, my Rockford debutante. I managed to book some dates with her for my first Winter Break back in Ohio. Nothing intimate: certainly not New Year's Eve, the biggie, but she did agree to go to the Settler's Ball, the shnoofy Academy alumni dance, and the Princeton Triangle Show. We doubled with my old pal from Baker, Dick Deutschman. He'd been one of the centers whose butt-cheeks I, as a Baker quarterback, had no choice but to spread.

Dick's mother, a sweet Southern Ohio blonde, had scrubbed for Dr. Daniel Deutschmann, Dick's father, in a WWII emergency trauma surgery somewhere in Germany. After the war the brawny surgeon, completely bald from his two years in hell, bought a big house on South Woodland Boulevard near Baker Lakes, and began to decompress. First Big Dan married his little nurse, fathered three handsome sons, then walked off into a life of terminal unwinding; drinking, whoring and drinking some more, all from within the bubble of his surgical practice.

His poor darling wife, Dorothy, a classic American dolly from a farm near Dayton, began to fade before our eyes. While Dick's two brothers, their friends and I did the dating quadrille through their house, "Dotty" Deutschmann lost her silken rural skin, her youth, her kidneys, and her mind.

One day Dick came home to find his mother in her blood-drenched bed, a carving knife in her whitened grasp. Dick called his father, then went outside and launched himself from the saddle of his speeding motorcycle headfirst into a backyard tree.

He and his younger brother were shipped off to expensive East Coast prep schools, but Dick and I remained pals. Now, as a sophomore at Princeton, he would be my guide to window shopping in the new big world of Old Family American Money, my first Ivy League Christmas.

It was one hundred percent white people. The dominant coterie was Episcopalian, for whom overt and casual racism was not an issue. I pretended I didn't hear "nigger, nigger, nigger" and "wop, wop, wop" and a deaf ear would have to be temporarily turned to "kike/yid/sheenie" as well. I stood there, sipping brandy and feigning indifference. Dick's date was a Bucks County shicksa and he himself was only one-quarter Jewish, by the usual Nazi reckonings, but he belonged to a Jewish country club. I was Jew through and through, which left me in my Brooks Brothers charcoal gray shantung tux, searching for clues.

What I saw was alcohol! Hard liquor! Boozers, these animal WASPs! Dedicated! Total stay-drunk-for-the-holidays guys. No concern for consequences.

Fuck it! Write a check! We're all gonna be lawyers or judges or something. Driving juiced, they never got arrested. Dining juiced, they abused the waiters. And loud?! What could I feel but awe for these scions of Good Family Mid-Eastern power and position at their natural, oblivious, festive best?

Yet I really didn't want to deal with their society shit. I didn't need them to get where I was going, because I wasn't trying to go anywhere in particular. They'd go to Yale Law School or wherever their families decided was most advantageous to go. Not me; I had no long-term goals. No plan. No agenda. I had no idea what my life might become. I just wanted the wet-eyed girl from the dance hall floor, Vanessa.

Our correspondence was polite. Her letters, tiny cursive characters on powder blue stationery, always gave me some small hope of something, but it was hard to tell exactly what. No mention of friends, school interests, areas of activity, love of sports, the arts, even fashion. Our phone calls were exasperatingly brief, non-committal and completely without focus.

"How's school?"

"Fine."

"Your parents are well?"

"They're fine."

"Have you decided where you're going next year?"

"They want me to go to Vassar."

"And what do you want?"

"I'm not sure."

Vanessa was a beauty, with sculpted features beneath a short dark cap of glossy black waves, a tiny, birdlike nose, and a delicate but not ungenerous mouth, which seemed to act as a strainer for large words or complex ideas.

Not that I was any deep thinker or anything, only desperate for some indication, some hint, some encouraging word. At the same time, there was something about her distant, self-contained, proto-Jackie Kennedy demeanor, something *misteriosa* which I couldn't help but find alluring.

"My parents say Columbia's not really in the Ivy League." That was as chatty as her sculpted lips allowed.

Finally I connived her to New York for Spring Weekend, and we ended up in the back of somebody's mother's Country Squire, soaked with endless martinis, bouncing up the West Side Highway to Scarsdale. I found myself with both hands somehow under her taffeta, palms sliding up her pressing thighs, then claiming her precious glutes from behind as she began humping me like a goat. My hand slid under her creamy globe, then under her panties and, *oh!* Into the fertile crevice.

Then, through the Beefeater haze, my slumbering Idmonster awoke, *sprong!* and a sudden ferocity forced a rhythm from my loins. Hump, hump, hump. My fingers driving to pierce her inner lips, claim them, gasping. *Oh! Oh! Oh! Right there...Oh!* Cataracts of semen filling my flannels. After that night there was something in the way she looked at me. A different eye-beam frequency, speaking "acceptance."

That summer, back in Ohio, in the crowded ballroom of the Seiberling Country Club, we swayed with simulated detachment at her Commencement Formal. My former Academy classmates, and other sylphs and swells glided by as the band played ballads. "Jalousie," "String of Pearls," and Ray Anthony's "At Last:"

> *At Last*
> *My love has come along.*
> *My lonely days are over*
> *And life is just a song.*
> *I've found a dream that I can cling to,*
> *A dream that I can call my own.*
> *I found a thrill that I can cling to,*
> *A thrill I've never known.*

Vanessa looked up at me and offered with larcenous indifference:

"I'm horny!" Smiling.

"Whuhhh?" Coughing and confused.

"Let's go someplace." That simple.

The paneled country club was jammed. White dinner jackets, pastel gowns. Blonde sons and daughters of commerce. Bouquets, balloons and bowties. We fought our way across the sea of celebrants out to my father's D-500 Dodge convertible with its crossed checker-flags nameplate on the trunk. Top down, duals crooning, the moon swollen and low in the abundance of sky.

"Over there," she pointed, and we rolled off the tree-lined lane we'd been gliding along over to a stand of maple.

Quiet in suburban wherever we were. Cooler than summer nights often are in those parts, and less humid, so that I did not stick to my new, baggy, Ivy suit.

"I missed you," she said.

Yes.

She was seriously swanked up for the occasion, and defoliating her many layers of summer fabrics, garter belts and nylons, finally to the sweet land of lips, took some furious prestidigitation. I was never quite sure that she wouldn't stop me at some sweet and precipitous moment, adding to the one-step-ahead-of-the-posse quality of our love-making.

I still didn't know what I was doing sexually, and the thought of coming in or around Vanessa spun me toward delirium. Kissing her was like breathing the night air in Mill Valley, a hillside in Fiesole, the base of Mt. Fuji or somewhere. Her liquid flesh lips, her mouth opening to a starry sky of dreams—*anything* seemed possible.

We had the front seat—an old-fashioned American bench—and there stretched ourselves out in our finery. I lifted the yellow chiffon to her waist. She gracefully helped my buzzing hands as together we slid her white silk panties to her knees, the heat rising from her belly, thighs, and the silky tendrils covering her vee as it disclosed itself. *Ah! Ah! No time!* I just pressed myself down on her, groping at my fly, grappling for my means of connection, surging man-root, fighting the resisting tab. Cutting my knuckles on the zipper. *Unh.*

I wasted no time. No rubbing or squeezing or skin on skin, not a cuddle to spare. Just drive—*Go!*—*Lunge!*—the tidal surge, unbearable, unstoppable.

Except for the zipper on my spiffy new suit pants.

I should have known better; I should have taken my time. The young beauty on her back, the young-me too crazed to savor her heat, her intoxicating bouquet, the sense-consuming gift-of-herself. I would have liked to just lie there cradling her for a few hours, stroking her outlying areas of fleshy richness, and kissing her time without end. Bury my face in her center; make it my world, my gift of love to her, to all women, to myself. Then when it came to entering her with my own body's messenger, my meat-Mercury, let it slide on her silent commission, her wet processes, breathing me in so slowly, so dearly, so full of feeling that all I could do would be to look at her, drawing the world in from her endless depths.

But on that night in this humid Ohio glade, nothing but insertion mattered. Dominance? Pleasure? Release? None of that on my mind—simple frenzy, driving me toward the elemental act of mounting. Her hips were quaking, thighs starting to tremble. *She wants it. She wants me. Dream of dreams! Here we go!* With one thrust I will change everything! *Make her mine! Fence in the South Forty! Now!*

But try as I might, my fly wouldn't budge. Oh, I dribbled away my sticky nucleus somewhere inside my suit pants, poor caged Johnson-head grating against the zipper-back, champing and chafing. *Shit. Flub.*

Twin impulses arose: to suppress my self-loathing and barely contained humiliation on the one hand, dive into Fifties forgetfulness, i.e. avoidance, or plot to get her alone as soon as I could change pants on the other. I knew she was waiting for me to seize the moment. *Carpe puellam!*

When I turned the ignition key and goosed it, the big Hemi *brrrwaaahhh-waahheded* to life, covering the darkened lane of love with pure potentiality.

The very next night I blistered old Route 18 at speeds of 90-110 mph all the way down to get her, bring her back to Baker in two desperate hours, and lower her to the floor under the writing desk in my father's study, while the rest of my family watched *Maverick* in Grandpa's room directly upstairs. We just *did* it. Just slid my grateful gland into her, fast and furious, as she puffed out little puppy-barks, and I even restrained my climax for a brief, but meaningful, period.

Many sex-drenched nights followed, and days, too. One series of afternoon encounters at Deutschmann's father's new apartment on Baker Boulevard stood out for the donkey-like way I'd walk out of a room, go into the TV room and wait for her to excuse herself, and join me. I would proceed to blitz-fondle her, *inhale* her face and within minutes be bumping around with her panties down, blushing lips and dewy bush to the open air. I'd just ease it in, just a little, just the head and maybe an inch or two of the shaft. Then I'd grab her firmly by the back of her lovely head and kiss her so hard she shook, feel her teeth, the pulse pounding in my lips, relaxing and then kiss her savagely again so that I tasted my own blood. I know *I* had visions of planets and secret gardens.

We'd put back on the few articles we'd removed and drift back singly to join our friends for a rubber of bridge, gin and tonic, and the early Stokowski recording of "Swan Lake," which Dick revered and we all came to associate with him and our visits to his father's current old money *pied-a-terre.*

I lived to share her body. She'd been accepted to both Vassar and Sarah Lawrence, and, though we'd just started seeing each other, at my urging she had chosen Sarah Lawrence, which was closer to New York and arguably hipper. After a summer of gin drinks, inter-urban speeding, and primary missionary sex, we went back East and slept together at least once a week.

~

One warm night in our crowded little Hartley Hall room, all three of us roomies were there, studying for finals and listening to WQXR on my mother's dark red Motorola, hearing the famous "Abscheulicher" aria from Beethoven's *Fidelio* between "Every day is Bargain Day on everything at Barney's" and the Delson Merry Mints jingle, when an authoritative knock was heard.

"Hertz? Mitchell Hertz here?" It was one of the *machers* in the one "secret society" that Columbia allowed to flourish.

"Yeah," I said, turning down Kirsten Flagstad. "Who wants him?"

"We want you to audition for The Speech. We need someone really snotty."

I knew The Speech, a satirical *droits du Seigniorial* jape, the traditional welcoming to the entering freshman class on the first night of their orientation week. The elegant Guy Manaster—an unstable fusion of Jackie Mason and Oscar Wilde—had delivered The Speech to our entering class.

At first I was shocked: how had I come to deserve such a reputation? *Snotty? Me?* Then I quickly came to see the value of the circumstance, and emboldened, grabbed a Haspel cord jacket to match my khaki bermudas, slid on a pair of mangy topsiders and went off to wow the small panel of ring-wearing tradition-maintenance men. I got the gig.

I arrived back in New York right after Labor Day to check into my new fraternity house digs. The TBZ house was a decrepit but serviceable four-floor brownstone on 113th Street, half a block west of Amsterdam and opposite a very busy fire house. I had joined for a number of reasons, none of them good.

One, it was the best Jewish fraternity, which is to say, the richest. TBZ brotherhood was drawn from upper-middleclass families, most of them from outside New York. New Yorkers at Columbia were viewed as expendable, cannon-fodder in the army of advancement through contacts. Especially Brooklyn, Bronx, Long Island or New Jersey Jews—a permanent underclass of brilliant, but socially unwashed locals whose parents couldn't afford Harvard or Yale. Obsessed with upward mobility, they sought a degree to transform themselves from tenement toilers into suburban professionals. These boys were not sought after by TBZ.

Two, both of my roommates (from fancy Jersey suburban prep schools) were thrilled to death to be invited to join.

Three, I wanted a place to sleep with Vanessa.

So, against my better judgment and democratic roots, I joined. Some of the brothers weren't too bad. A few were into be-bop and Kerouac—prefacing sentences with "like," used words like "scene," "man," "cat," "fall-by," and "crib." Most, though, were simply sons of privilege and willful parental neglect who would have their fling with bohemia and depart for Johns Hopkins or the Ford Foundation.

Rushing had been easy: they wanted me, recruited me and treated me better than my station in life would have otherwise entitled. In their eyes, I was a midwestern preppie, and that's all that seemed to matter.

As Pledge drew to a close, the surviving Pledges were informed of a tragic scandal that had emerged in the local TBZ leadership: Myron Faulkner, the treasurer—and a guy I sort of liked from playing in a recorder ensemble and singing in the Columbia Chorus with—had been caught embezzling large sums. These funds had gone to pay for a still-illegal abortion for his girlfriend Dinah, a negress whom many of us freshmen knew and liked.

The Brotherhood was divided to the point of violence on the issue of whether and how to bust Myron—expel him, call National in, have him arrested, or what. A meeting was scheduled. All of us were sworn to secrecy. The neophytes scrambled to discuss the matter, meeting in dorm rooms, the Lion's Den and John Jay Hall cafeteria. Sides were taken, positions formulated, heels dug in, with the predictable result that the Pledge class was divided: most for throwing Myron out, with shades of severity based on everything from readings in pre-law to family history to the Word of God as conveyed by someone's rabbi in Beaver Falls, PA. I was for leniency—the poor guy had a pregnant girlfriend for godsakes! A few other guys agreed, including the poorer of my two Jersey dorm-mates. But we were heavily out-manned.

At the next night's emergency meeting, chairs were set up from the dining room all the way to the sitting room windows. Brothers we'd never seen, or very seldom came to meetings, joined the regulars in nervous rows. Discussions became arguments, voices were raised, shouting turned to pushing. I was baited by the snobbiest members. I was on my feet.

"If it was you, you'd expect us to help you, not kick you when you're down!"

"I say call the cops. The guy's a common criminal." This from Stanford Ochs, son of a Wall Street banker.

"Let him pay the money back," I said.

"Let him sell his nigger baby," sneered Stanford.

I swung on him. I admit it. I broke his glasses. Blood poured down Stanford's cheek onto his flannel Chipp suit pants. A general mêlée ensued. Chairs were overturned. Lamps came crashing.

Suddenly, from the top of the stairs:

"Cool it! Hold everything! Here's Myron."

Silence was instantaneous. I found myself holding the shirtfront of a guy I didn't know, the son of someone famous from King's Point. There was poor Myron.

Then, "Fuck him!" and "Where's our money?" etc.

Then, "Let him talk! Let him talk!"

We all looked expectantly to Myron, who by now had descended the stairs halfway and stood surrounded by Chapter officers and a few national types. For a moment it was silent. Myron looked ready to cry.

Then, "RAT FUCK! RAT FUCK!!"

Then gales of laughter and extravagent back-slapping as Brothers threw themselves upon Pledges in expressions of congratulation as the whole sorry episode was revealed as a sham, a final last gasp of the hazing experience designed to bring the new and old members together in fraternal bonhomie. The Rat Fuck. Go figure.

So now it was time to occupy my TBZ quarters, a huge single room glossy with fire-engine red walls, around the corner from the famous V & T Pizzeria on Amsterdam. I now burned with the need for privacy, since the fraternity, short on expensive Manhattan living space, had ruled that no fewer than *four* brothers were to share the room. Luckily my roommates were all from the metropolitan area and mostly split for their easily commutable homes on weekends.

It was hot and close in New York, early September. I arrived a week ahead of my three roommates, absent my luggage, which had been mistakenly diverted to last year's dormitory. I had no climate-appropriate clothes, just the heavy olive tweed Brooks suit—vest and all—I'd brought to wear for The Speech.

Nothing was air-conditioned in 1957. Deepening my discomfort was my first-ever *Mal di Venere*—body lice, or *crabs*, in the parlance. Vanessa theorized they'd sprung unbidden from a toilet seat at the Sunset Drive-In on the old Rockford Highway. Now I itched full-time and was summoning the courage to ask the corner pharmacist at 110th and Broadway for a delousing remedy or a swift hemlock substitute. I ended up shaving my crotch hair and smothering my pubis in some kind of lethal Agent Green.

When the night arrived for The Speech I listened to my flowery introduction, then got right up there in front of six or seven hundred entering Frosh in their powder blue-and-white beanies and gave them what-for:

"Good evening, gentlemen. Although it's probable that, in the case of most of you refugees from the IRT, the salutation is spurious, at best, not to say presumptuous, in point of fact." Straight-from-the-shoulder material.

Here I paused to light a cigarette, casually assessing the mood of the crowd, feeling pluperfectly cool. It wasn't an act, really. I did feel superior. Organized athletics, especially football, had left me predilected toward the Adrenaline Moment. I simply sprang onto the stage with no more than the skimpiest preparation. "Well, what do you collection of Flatbush flotsam have to say for yourselves?" I sniffed.

The formal, dark-wood Livingston Hall dining room murmured, some tittering nervously under dimmed lights. It was a more than adequately humid night. People cleared their throats. My nuts were on fire with insect-death, razor burn and the masticatory effect of the hardiest of occupying mites. Deliberately, I stationed one of my Clarks cordovan oxfords up onto the chair, tamped a du Maurier on my Ronson, lit up and inhaled. My eyes swept the big high-ceilinged room, freed from its daytime cafeterial chores. I smiled and exhaled.

"So, this is your first step on the road to Doctor World? I'll bet your mommies are so proud they're telling everyone at Hadassah. Or is it a lawyer that little Schmuel is coming to Morningside Heights to become? Money, money, money! Fight your way out of the tenements and tract homes! Yes! Crack those books! Yes! Cram! Yes! Yes! Beat the curve! Pray your classmates to fail! Yes! Scratch your way into Med School! Law School! Okay!! Yale! Harvard! Okay!! Here it is!! Come and get it!!!"

They sat there aghast, expectations of gentlemanly Ivy League camaraderie dashed. Watching their affronted faces, I thought to ask myself, *why am I doing this?* Maybe there was a deep vein of contempt I secretly *did* harbor for these unwashed New York strivers, these grinds and geeks with their BOAC bags. Fewer than half of them were actual commuters, of course, but as a sizable self-doubting minority clot they presented an irresistible target. For a Midwestern *geschmatnik,* with my prep school tweeds and newfound Ivy pretensions, I could rely on all the personal disdain I could muster for these huddled masses of driven Gotham achievers and their dreams of salvation in the professional class. I looked out at them, amused by their passivity, evidence that my act was being taken for good coin. *I'll get broader, let them figure it out as the gag becomes obvious. In good time.*

"So, I've been asked to take time out from my busy schedule to welcome you to Columbia College in the city of New York, your first peek at A Bigger World. The University motto is—pay attention:

IN LUMINE TUO, VIDEBIMUS LUMEN

"Those among you with a serviceable secondary school education will have already translated—if not necessarily understood—the Latin, which says:

In Your Light Will We See The Light

"Get it? *Not* that 'by your light we'll see Cornell Medical School,' or 'Wharton,' or 'a ranch house in Great Neck or Montclair,' or 'some country club' or 'an Austin-Healey,' okay? See the Light!"

"Yes! I know! Your parents escaped from the Cossacks. Gentlemen, I'm here to ask you 'So what?' Does it follow that it's your job to restore some karmic balance? That if you work your little butts off that your families' lives will have been redeemed? That the Nazis and the Czar and the swarms of anti-Semites in Eastern Europe will somehow fade into oblivion? Does it mean that you can take the role of victim to the bank? If you grind, grind, grind for your entire college career, through law or medical school, and the rest of your life, for that matter, that God will look down at you and say '*Dayenu*,' basta, 'Es ist genug?' No, fellas, it doesn't. You're not here for that. You're here to open that big Nice Jewish Boy brain of yours and let that desperate, driven quality out. Let some of that Columbia *lumen* in. If you're really men, and not just some hysterical, poverty-aversive mothers' sons. Well, *are* you?"

They're not all Jewish, for God's sake, I reminded myself. *Not at all. Why am I stressing the Jewish part? What is my problem?* I stopped, and ground the du Maurier under my heavy English heel, then looked away from them with boredom and disdain which was only half put-on. I had to get this straight for my own sake.

There was something else, too, a feeling that I was actually lecturing myself, that I dared to hope, behind my ludicrous man-of-the-world posturing, that *I* had the guts to pick up the gauntlet, to live in The Light, inhabit that Greater World I visited every time I was with Vanessa in the bright white of orgasm, or when I listened to *Don Giovanni*, or Glenn Gould or Thelonious Monk, or when I read *The Brothers Karamazov* or the first lines of *Howl,* and my nervous system churned and bubbled, my innards lit up. I would go There, to that illuminated spot: a bigger, better, brighter place, more inclusive, broader, generous, wet, warm and well lit.

A light for us all. Here I was, free-associating in public, asking myself rather risky questions without knowing the answers. *How am I different from these hopeful new freshmen, other than this "'feigned" arrogance? Am I any more enlightened, in either Rousseau's sense or the Buddah's, than any of them?*

It became, there on the podium, obvious as life itself that of *course* every member of my audience must be capable of having that larger experience. Throwing wide my net, I took a few cursory swats at the non-Jews in the assembled freshman class, with no particular visible caricatureability. I decided to wrap it on an up-note:

"Fellow seekers of truth," and here I unleashed my flashiest smirk to "reveal" the irony of my former condescension. "Look here. Wherever you came from, we all come from *some*place. The point is not your place of origin but your destination. Whoever tries to pin you to your background really wants to keep you from where you're going—which is to become Universal Man, if you can identify that goal, even in your deepest slumbers. As for Columbia—the moment finds you in a perfect place to discover your dreams, if you will but search for them. This college—this city—this time to give what the Yogis call 'due reflection' to fundamental matters—*this Moment* is a great place to start your search. If for no other reason than that you're already here. Gentlemen of the class of 1961: I welcome you to Morningside Heights!"

For some reason, the applause caught me off guard. I waved gallantly in recognition, and stumbled out into the relative cool of the evening on Van Am Quad. I knew they'd remember me as a symbol of the challenge—or something like it—and suddenly my scrotum was on fire! I ran back to my W. 113th Street digs, ripped off my smoking under-drawers and buried my balls in the sink.

Vanessa soon arrived with a severely tonsured pubis—but within a month we were once again regularly swapping genitalia with re-assumed impunity. Out from under the pre-med onus, I was studying music: symphony and opera with Maestro Moore and theory with Hubert Boris. There were gorgeous long hours in the Music Library with the still-new "long-playing" records, and some leftover 78s: the Symphonies of Mahler, Bruckner, Vaughn Williams, Sibelius, Shostakovitch, Mozart, Haydn, Beethoven, Brahms, Schubert, Schumann,

Dvorak and all the rest. Wearing the old-fashioned Bakelite headphones, I followed along as well as I could in the full orchestral scores. My afternoons were spent strolling the shady paths through classic symphonic architecture, exploring the parallel depths of music and my own unmapped psyche. As fall turned to winter on the West Side of Manhattan, I looked up between *Andante* and *Scherzo* to see the November sun sinking into the Hudson a little earlier each day.

As I assessed the great religions and philosophical traditions, I also reassessed my own Jewishness. I was a beginning philosopher, a person uniquely placed to know how little he knows. In fact, I was just barely beginning to get a sense of what the questions might be. I doubted Judaism's claim to the Master Theory. Fretting daily over my ignorance, I spent the winter term reading and re-reading: logical positivism, aesthetics, and, especially, the philosophy of history.

My old handball mate Burberry had transferred down from Cornell, and was now a Columbia sophomore majoring in theology. Duke talked me into taking a class called something like Theology Survey for Philosophy Majors, and taught by no less then William Bass, Dean of the Cathedral of St. John the Divine, whom I found frank and often inspired.

I figured that all religions had to claim to have the "answer," insisting that they and only they could and did operate the best-performing franchise. In fact, they all put forward unblushingly the notion that "God told us to do this to y'all, understand? Don't fight it, you'll feel *better*."

The other factor was the very Jewishness of Columbia. All the cutthroat pre-med sharkos, with their big noses and New Yawkese, and their call-on-me hands perpetually waving in the professor's face. Partially, my quitting pre-med was a response to the unconstrained garrulity and open acquisitiveness with which these sons of Eastern Europe's *shtetls* approached the knowledge-gathering process. And, there was the fear of having to compete with them in the sciences. *Feature me versus a graduate of Bronx Science? Please. Do I look as if*

I need a new asshole? That Jewishness.

Oddly enough this played itself out not in a classroom, where I might have hoped to cross verbal swords with some brilliant Erasmus intellectual, but in gym class. I couldn't find enough hours in the day to continue freshman football, so one day, after a practice that ended in the dark, and an hour ride on the subway from Baker's Field to my dorm, I simply quit. Within days I found myself unceremoniously deposited in Phys Ed 101 with a bunch of Grand Concourse geeks.

Although most had no native athletic talent, and even less physical coordination, they were terrifically aggressive on the basketball court. The gym teacher was a JV fencing coach who couldn't have given less of a shit about us stumble-bums, with the result that endless fouls went uncalled and thus undeterred. One particularly obnoxious tall guy with really sharp elbows charged me one time too many, and I simply went berserk, grabbing the ball and putting on something of a master class in illegal moves, fouls and general bad attitude. I sneered, traveled, charged, elbowed and sneered some more. Yes, it was anti-Semitism, the kind that only other Jews could understand, the kind of condescension that spanned generations of wealth. That Wittgenstein had for Karl Popper. That privileged Viennese and German Jews in Europe—and later in America—had for their less fortunate Eastern European brethren. I had ball-player chops, and they didn't. So, for a few weeks I ran amok, smashing into my classmates, and snarling contemptuously at their damning spasticity. Finally the gym teacher noticed and whistled me to the bench.

"What's going on, Hertz?" The teacher was a working-class guy about thirty, plainly not amused. He had thick black stubble and a bald spot.

"I don't know, coach. It's been a long time since I've been in a *gym* class!"

"Well, this is very disappointing behavior from a boy with your background. You should be ashamed."

And indeed I was, upon reflection. But not till later.

About then, Duke was talking all this religious shit while I was just starting to gather, through arduous catch-up study, an inkling of what the real philosophical questions were. The rules of motion. Causality. Logic. Critical thinking. The development of thought.

"Let me take you to High Mass this Sunday." Burberry sounded hopeful.

He was a classical music fanatic too, so we'd spent a lot of time turning each other on to great things: the Bruno Walter's Brahms *Symphonies* on Columbia, Vaughn Williams conducting his own *Antarctica Symphony*, with John Gielgud and a wind machine. And a maniacal conductor named Hermann Scherchen, on a new label called Westminster.

I thought about lumpen-prole Mahler. Not like silver-spooned Mendelssohn, who had it easy. The family became Germans before he had a chance to know—much less decide for himself—all the advantages that his family would get by renouncing the Faith of their Fathers. I thought his music was nice but nothing like the intensity of risen-from-poverty Mahler.

Back in Crockett, Burberry had sat me down in front of his Webcor three-speed-turntable for a revelation: Raphael Kubelik conducting Gustav Mahler's First Symphony. I stole the LP and listened to it a hundred times. He also introduced me to the *Fifth*, the *Seventh* and finally the *Fourth*, a vision of the Divine. Mahler was wound too tight for longevity. A mover-upper through the minor league opera houses in the Germanish provinces, then Vienna and New York. Always conducting his perfectionist productions, composing during summer vacation in a wooden shed. It was Mahler who once remarked: "I put the whole world into a symphony."

And we seemed to get a whole world *out* of them. It didn't feel arty, or weird-for-guys or anything, just a couple of Academy fellas listening raptly, not one-upping each other on which was the "definitive" recording, not quoting *Saturday Review* or *High Fidelity*, just letting ourselves dissolve into the deeper unity of the music. I figured, this must be how it is among bigger people. This is why people spend thousands of dollars for fancy schools for their kids. This makes sense. Everybody in my class must be doing similar shit. Except my Academy classmates, these titled heads of Northeastern Ohio, were listening to "Annie Had a Baby," "Rocket 88," or, later, this cracker named Elvis.

Where am I in all of this? What is Jewish? What is it to me, anyway? What is loyalty? The same as trust? Or is it cowardice of a more or less acceptable kind?

At the start of sophomore year, Burberry once again became my classmate. Despite the appearance of innocence his boyish softness lent him—he would pull his horn-rimmed glasses off his patrician nose and nibble them—the Duke could throw them back. He could easily surround eight or ten martinis at a sitting, and then perform the amiable ruling-class Pass Out (wherever one was when one finally succumbed). And nevertheless chose theology as his Path: contemplation, investigation, and ultimate involvement.

"The Cathedral has the best music. Wait till you hear the postillion trumpets."

He had a sincere winning shyness about him, as if he didn't realize how attractive he was. I could feel his heart open up for me in his invitation to sit with him in the huge Episcopal Cathedral of St. John the Divine. I accepted, of course, and privately approached it as a kind of spiritual date. That Sunday we had breakfast at the counter in the St. Regis Pharmacy and walked the few blocks down Amsterdam.

The excellent chorus gave us a Bach Motet *a cappella*, the organist contributed Arne and Charpentier, then both joined forces in what sounded like a *Canzon* by one of the Gabrieli: responsorial, in a rising antiphonal surge that climbed from intense to off-the-scale, before plunging into a full-stop grand pause, silent except for the reverberation that seemed to hang in the scented air for eternity. Then *BLAAAAAAAAAAAA!* The downward-pointing state trumpets brandished some wild Spanish fanfare pointblank at the back of our heads. *BLAAAAAAAAAAAA!* I dived as if trepanned, dropping straight to my knees, as if dumped by Divinity, rather than merely floored by physics.

Dean Bass's Sermon was learned but accessible and actually *about* something—civil rights. The feeling in the great church was not as I had feared—off-putting and austere. Not alien, suspicious, claustrophobic or mean-minded, like my most recent Jewish "worship" experience. It seemed to be taking place in a new spaciousness, and in this space was available a choice, a voluntary gesture, respectful and challenging, offering clarity, warmth, and relaxation such as only complete concentration can bring. "Follow your heart," it whispered, and it felt good. "But not good enough," I reminded myself, "to live a lie." I looked into the glow in Duke's irises and thanked him for a great getting-up morning.

I did not believe in a god in any way I could acknowledge, and I was not looking for another delusional snare to replace it.

⁓

Four of us were sharing the large square room with the brilliant scarlet-lady walls on the third floor of the old brownstone BZT house. Our single piece of furniture was a couch decaying before our very eyes. Alex Lugash, whose parents owned the department store chain Chevette's, got his mother, who had a Renoir sketch in her bedroom closet, to donate last year's sofa and a pile rug and buy the paint if we'd lose the candy-apple.

We all wanted to be adults. Only Maury Douglas, with his sperm-encrusted 100-sock piles, was "youth culture." He hammered out fourth-rate Jerry Lee Lewis licks on the fraternity dining room upright, to the annoyance of the brothers, who preferred George Shearing, the Weavers and Alfred Deller. Physicist-to-be roommate Jerry Linden called him a "primitive."

We finished the last coat of adult-tan paint about two on a bitter-cold morning in late February, and then turned to the task of laying the luxuriously piled all-wool rug, only to be confronted with the presence of a mangy old green couch so close to the terminal stages of miliary tuberculosis that, when we tried to move it, readily began to mitose, regrouping itself into two or three stinky clumps while spraying generations of college-boy debris, not to say pestilential filth, to the corners of the room, thus endangering our wonder-rug.

At about this time came the *Il gran Balletto della Sofa*. I'd been up for three days to read *Crime and Punishment* cover to cover; unable to put it down until I found out what happened to Raskolnikov. I was rapidly tiring of this late-night gentrification initiative, figuring: *who gives a shit, really, we're just a bunch of dumb kids. What do we know, anyway?* I was far more interested in finding a place to take Vanessa for delights of the flesh. We'd been consummating more and more often, and, at least on my end, with mounting delirium. I resented this whole makeover deal; a harbinger of maturity, emblematic of the drawing nigh of adult functioning norms.

So I had an idea.

"Let's just lower this baby out the window, into the trash." I told my mates.

"Man, are you nuts?" said Linden. "It's three floors down at least."

"The trash is right below the window. We just drop the sofa straight down, right on top of the cans—no big deal. Do you have any scientific reservations? I mean, it's not gonna float away or *fall up* or anything, is it?"

"Why don't we wait till morning?" asked Lugash, the natural conciliator.

"Because we're at critical mass," I said, especially to Linden, Boy Physicist, "and, besides, it's so late, there's no one on the street to get hurt or even give a shit."

"Yeah," said Douglas, our crude hard-minded rocker. "Let's be done with it."

Sometimes I loved him for precisely that attitude. This was one of those times. I turned like a herd-dog to the two hangers-back and barked, "What do *you* wanna do? Carry it outta here in little paper bags for the rest of the night? Come on! Open the damn window."

The other two shrugged emptily and capitulated. Carefully, and with a certain surly stealth, we lowered the steadily disintegrating couch out of our third floor 113th Street window.

Lacking a rope, we simply used our hands, slipping first the back and arms, using two wooden legs as handles. All of this went fine until we let it go. Then its weight shifted, lurched, twisted, tumbled, and swung back clumsily into the front wall of the brownstone. Inside the second floor den directly beneath us a small group of brothers were watching "The Late, Late Show" *Whack!* A sofa leg launched a respectable *jete'* through the bay window.

A *crash!* and they scattered.

The leadership called a special meeting to dispense justice. The assessment:

the cost of a new window plus a fine for "irrational behavior." At first all four of us agreed to pay the repair bill, but resisted the additional $100 levy. Our actions were not irrational, we bristled. We paid the window part, and refused the fine. Then, under pressure, Linden agreed to pay, then Lugash, but I didn't buy it. It was my idea and, by all that's holy, it wasn't irrational. *Let 'em go bay at the moon.*

Then Douglas paid, and advised me to do the same. "Just go along with it, Mitchell, you idiot."

"Fuck no, man. They know it's ludicrous..."

"So was dropping the damn couch, *n'est-ce pas?*"

"Come on. Don't cover your retreat with banalities." That told him.

But they folded their tents on me. I was threatened unofficially with stiffer and stiffer fines, as the weeks of my resistance passed, then national censure, and (hint, hint, nudge, nudge—GASP!) expulsion from the fraternity.

"Do it," I told the national Treasurer, some big Windsor-knotted Wall Street shit-biscuit in his early forties, Irv, who delivered the ultimatum. "Expel me."

"You'll regret it for life, Mitchell. You'll be blackballed nationally. No one will do business with you." He postured paternal.

"What business do you think I'm in, for the love of God?" I asked him. "I'm just a poor fuckin' student!"

"When you *grad*-uate, you'll have no *con*-tacts. Don't be a *schmuck.*"

That did it. "I appreciate the advice," I said. "Thanks for taking time to come all the way up here to see me."

I beat a path straight to the Columbia Dean of Men and, in a tone of injured innocence, bled my conscience of the whole incident. He was very understanding.

"Of *course* you can quit! Just keep us informed. You made up your mind?"

"Sure. Why not?" I said and I really meant it.

Within a week I found a place across the street, in the building next to the fire station, a single room in the apartment of a paranoid Croatian crone. The widow Novotny made free with my un-lockable premises—rifling my desk, defiling the sanctity of my mail, leaving me notes critical of my housekeeping and, most dire, absolutely forbidding female visitors.

As much as I loved defying the harpy by sneaking Vanessa into my rented cell, it was too strenuous for my nervous system, like jerking off in silent running mode with roommates feigning sleep. Afraid to breathe, much less scream encouragement. *Uunnhh! Pinch it off! Ooooh! Meter it out! SSSsssshhhhhhh! Don't feel it; fight it! Beats nervous interruptus, or not doing it at all.* I was tired of waking up early enough to precede the old lady up and out, over to Broadway for breakfast at Chock Full o' Nuts. Just before spring vacation, in a fit of pique, I moved out.

My Long Island cousin Elizabeth Ann Barker, a wonderfully intense, melodramatic actress living in Cambridge, was dating a young Irish-American poet/songwriter named Brian Lafferty, who'd just gotten himself thrown out of Harvard College for something romantic. Lizzy, who was my sister's age, couldn't wait to show him off. We got together, drank grasshoppers, and taking an immediate shine to each other, agreed to become roommates in a fourth-floor walkup I'd found on 89th Street between West End and Riverside. In the evenings someone sang songs in Spanish. Brian was mostly gone. He had a pretty racy circle of rich men's sons he ran with, and I found myself being invited to drink away more and more of my afternoons with them.

The centrifuge began to turn. School drifted out of focus. Pre-med studies far behind me, I was every day more desperately in love with music, spending every sober minute I had obsessively mastering the standard literature, the great works of "classical" music, while at the same time striving mightily to give myself a grounding in the foundations of philosophy. But mostly I was contriving meetings with Vanessa. West 89th Street was twenty blocks from campus. Every day I felt more alienated from college life and all that that entailed.

We more-or-less found out she was pregnant back in Ohio over Easter vacation. Dan Deutschman did a urine test in his University Circle office, but had already let me know that, from his manual observation, she was almost certainly in the earliest stages of that most perfect process of regeneration. My mother, who was fond of valentine Vanessa, sweetly informed me that she could tell from her eyes—a certain "swimming" look. I figured they knew what they were talking about.

It was warm when we got back to New York, an early spring suffusion drenching Manhattan in blossoms, dressing dull urbania in the fresh colors of life re-emerging from the months of glacial carpet. Sap beginning to thaw, blissfully flowing the flow. After Vanessa's exam, we walked down Madison from her gynecologist on 72nd Street. I had hand-carried the specimen to the lab and awaited the results of the just-to-be-sure test. Positive! For some reason, I could hardly wait to call my folks.

We walked slowly into the fading afternoon light, adrift in the swirls of people in their premature summer wear; shorts, Madras ties, women in button-down cotton shirtwaists called Villagers. New Yorkers are always ready to jump the season. Outer wraps come flying off and bodies emerge into the newfound sunlight like the Prisoners in "Fidelio": *O, welche Lust*, and all that.

We had subscription tickets to a series, Six Modern American Operas. That night was *Trouble in Tahiti* by Leonard Bernstein. We'd decided beforehand that if she was Positive we'd simply accept the honorable imperative of a wedding, quick and simple. After all, we loved each other, didn't we? I was floating down the pavement, squeezing my bride-to-be's hand, grinning at the passing throngs.

At 65th Street I pulled over to a small wood-faced apothecary, and went in to call my parents in Carnegie. My mother seemed unabashed if not upbeat, gave both their blessings, and with preternatural calm expressed simple best wishes for our forthcoming nuptials. I bounced out to join Vanessa with a too-big smile. Back on the avenue we again held hands (in what I had been taught to think of, but now dismissed from mind, as borderline deviant—tourist—behavior) and drifted southward toward City Center. Occasionally I tried to break the mood by urging her to call *her* parents.

"Unh-unh," she shook her head.

"Why not?" I persisted, "We *have* to tell them."

"Not yet," she insisted.

"Why not?"

"I'm not ready, *that's* why," she told me, and sank back into a reverie oblivious to the rolling rhythm of the rush-hour press.

Finally, somewhere down around the mid-Fifties, she succumbed to my nagging, and we entered a small dark old notions shop and found a phone booth. She closed the wooden door and dialed Rockford. Peering through the glass and trying to concentrate, I watched her lips speaking silent movie-like to her mother. Then a long wait, as she listened but did not speak, glancing up at me only once and then putting her elbow down on the booth ledge and drooping her head down to be supported by her palm. And she listened.

I drifted back outside to gaze at the passing parade and calm myself enough out of emergency mode to contemplate my—our—new future. I was good as out of school now. I hadn't been keeping up with Harmony with Hubert Doris, or Logic with Morgenbesser. Only Opera with Douglas Moore and the required core curriculum. *Might as well give up.* That feels shitty, giving up, taking a dive. I did it once in wrestling. *Forget it. Just do it! Marry her. Then what? Quit Columbia and beg a $60/week job as assistant buyer from Lugash in his family department store chain? Ugghh. Back to Ohio? Can't see us in that world. But what about the baby? In Carnegie we'd have some help at least.*

Vanessa had just turned eighteen. My calm had blown over, my mind spinning around inside its own circuitry as I waited. *Schmuck! Are you fucking asleep, or what? You knock up two Jewish girls in a row? What are you? Some kinda idiot?* I couldn't consider, much less succumb to self-doubt (or any form of reflection at all). For some reason I knew what I was doing. *Have to do this. In control. Nobility of purpose.* Even heroic, I was beginning to feel. *What is this wheel that is turning me?*

Evening rush hour faded with the sun. People leaving work were more relaxed now, or just tuckered out. I was calm again, too, fortified with the confidence born of moral certitude. Or inexperience. Or both.

When Vanessa finally did come out, she was having trouble catching her breath between sobs. She looked as if someone had slapped her, hard. When I asked her what had happened, she just shook her head. We walked on about a block, her mouth a thin straight line, an occasional wobble around the jaw. Another block, I asked again. Her head shook. This time she closed her eyes. When she opened them, she found me staring at her. She looked away.

"They're coming. They'll be here tomorrow," sniffling back the dripping from her tiny, down-curved nose.

"What did they say?"

"They said I'm not."

"You're not what?"

"They're not letting...I'm...I'm...they're having an abor..."

"What?"

"A procedure..."

"What do you mean *they?*"

"Donny's coming down from Boston to do it..."

"Your brother-in-law from Mass General??"

"Yes." She started walking again.

"Look," taking her arm, steering her away from a moving taxi, "this is bullshit. We're old enough to get married if we want to. Do we *want* to get married?"

It was a full block of wide-eyed crying before she could focus on me, nod her head "yes," and start sobbing again.

City Center loomed. Her reaction was something totally new. Shocked awake at last, I was unable to prevent a flash-visit from Emily Evans, whispering urgently and low, "My parents want you out of the house."

I hadn't seen Emily cry, if indeed she had at all.

"Look," I whispered again, when we were seated in the orchestra section, "we'll be fine. My parents are really happy for us."

Why were they? I asked myself, and under that, *were they really?* My mother, who had fielded my call solo despite the presence of my father, seemed pleased enough. Vanessa was smiling distantly.

"It'll be fine," I told her. "We'll be together. They can say whatever they want."

The tears came again, quietly, and I looked away at the fresh crabgrass. By the end of the first scene, a satire of suburban decadence, she was sobbing so loudly we had to leave the theater. We took a cab up to my place on 89th Street. Lafferty was there, lying on the couch, but took one look and flew off into the night.

I helped Vanessa into bed and lay there beside her till her sobbing sank into the darkness and we both slept. I was dreaming something far away and fabulous, feelings in some perfect harmonious movement toward the great whatever…until I awoke and saw her above me. A terrifying sight, head thrashing from side to side, a look of dementia ringing her slack jaw, flames licking her irises. Riding. Galloping, galloping, galloping. Riding me. Up and down on my swelling dick, now rising high above my thorax as she posted, sliding down *hard* with her pussy blazing, spraying fragrant frothing juices across the sheets, bouncing her lovely firm breasts with the tenderest pink Queen Anne nipples, as she rode on and on, lighting up the night, the room splashed with her shadows. Riding. I watched as she spurred herself on, then lost consciousness as she began to *screeEEEEEEAAAAMMMMMM.*

In the morning we hove to, and prepared to face the music. Her parents would be arriving at La Guardia at 9:00. We took the train to Yonkers/Bronxville to try and head them off at Sarah Lawrence. But when we called Vanessa's room from the station, her in-on-it roommate notified us that "Dr. & Mrs. Heller, of the Rockford Hellers," had taken a suite at the Plaza, where they awaited us even as we spoke. We walked back under the tracks to await the New York-New Haven train, and the sun assumed command, briefly, of the early spring morning.

Mrs. Heller greeted us woodenly at the door. "Your father is in the next room," was all she permitted, then turned to finish hanging clothes in the closet.

I opened the bedroom door to a fair-sized room on the eighth floor of the Plaza, facing the park. High ceilings, white walls, and Currier & Ives prints. But whatever self-possession, whatever clarity I may have mustered in my twenty year-old mind was quickly scattered by the first icy utterance from the society doctor's mouth.

"What have you done to my daughter!?" he asked, in the manner of a movie rancher confronting a pesky, smalltime cattle rustler.

I had an insane impulse to give him the obligatory "It takes two, etc." but I stifled that, and instead addressed his daughter.

"Come on, Vanessa, let's get out of here. All we have to do is walk."

"And *keep* walking," her father said in a voice as cold as death.

"No problem, *Sir*," I assured him, "My life's been fine without you thus far…"

"Mitch!" she cut me off, "My daddy's upset."

"Like *we're* not upset. What's the deal? Tell him what we decided!"

"I…" her eyes began to close.

"Tell him we've decided to get married."

"I…"

"But how will you live?" Dr. Heller slid to his gentlest, most caring voice.

"We'll be fine," I began. "I'm going to…"

"We've made all the arrangements. Vanessa's brother-in-law is flying in." He shifted back and addressed the room as if we were in another borough, a different time zone, a puff of smoke. "We'll do the procedure tomorrow at Mt. Sinai."

"Bullshit," shooting Vanessa a look of deepest supplication.

"I…" Now the bedroom door opened and Mrs. Heller's gracious face appeared, with the hint of a thoughtful smile.

"You kids look hungry. May I take you to lunch?"

The soft-cop's turn. She took us to one of those small white-tiled cafeteria-style places still popular in the mid-Fifties, on 58th Street, across the street from the hotel and next door to the Music Hall (where I'd just seen Brigitte Bardot in

And God Created Woman with Burberry one rainy night that seemed a life ago).

We lacked discernible appetite. I ordered a fresh fruit salad, which in New York at that season was pretty basic: citrus, cantaloupe, a few soft yellow bananas, canned pears, and maybe a maraschino cherry. We ate in silence. I shoveled in my salad without looking up. Finally her mother rose to pay the check. I knew we simply could not go back to the hotel.

"Come with me now."

"I don't know…" Her eyes were once again swimming, head shaking slowly.

"I'm walking out of here. Come with me and we'll be together."

"What can I tell my father?"

"It doesn't matter. He'll come around if he sees we're serious."

"No, he *won't.*"

"*Come* with me, Vanessa. You can do it. You *want* to do it."

"I can't." She started to cry again.

My peripheral vision detected motion. Her mother was approaching. I got up. "Come on, I'm leaving." She looked down at her plate. "Come with me."

I didn't really expect her to come. I stood up, took my J. Press raincoat, and started walking before her mother reached the table. The place was almost empty. The cashier looked at me expectantly as I passed on my way to the door. I stepped into the street and turned west, reaching 6th Avenue before looking back.

I could have saved myself the effort. 58th Street was uncrowded, and it would have been a small matter to pick her out, even from a block away, had she been there. I turned my heavy Clarks cordovans northward, up Broadway to 72nd Street, where I crossed to West End, and headed north again. Suddenly, at 74th, I was seized by a stomachic earthquake which drove me sharply to my knees just in time to watch my fruit salad reemerge into the atmosphere, spray the wall of a church that happened to be there, and form a fragrant pool on the sidewalk.

Some oranges had stuck to the wall.

In the two weeks after the Plaza Hotel events I oscillated between desire and despair, bypassing hope completely, a kicked dog. I missed Vanessa so physically. Everyone but me knew what hospital she was in. I staggered around New York trying to hold onto my sense of purpose. Even the path of survival was obscured by clouds. All I knew was that I did not want to hurt.

I began running around with friends of Rafferty—sons of rich Jewish businessmen-gangsters—cutting Harmony 101 to sit around in Upper Eastside apartments listening to the first Mort Sahl and Lenny Bruce LPs and downing pills with gin. My decline quickened. Before I'd noticed, I'd missed a month of classes. Columbia insisted I see a psychiatrist if I were to stay in school. When I applied for one at Columbia's clinic at St. Luke's, they said there was a five-month wait. Finally, my parents found a shrink on Park Avenue that would take me.

In a particularly demoralized moment, roommate Brian and I tried to join the Marines on the buddy system, but the examining officer picked me out of a crowd of hopefuls and sent me to the Park Avenue shrinker to get a letter before they would take me. Lacking money or a token I walked uptown from the Battery, hiking up lower Broadway in my college-boy tweeds, wilting in the spring heat and offering to sell a copy of Camus' *Nausea* to passersby for a pay-phone dime. My doctor took one look at the willing conscript I was so earnestly trying to be and sent me packing back to my parents, trailing a Leave of Absence from Columbia.

Tail only just emerging from between my legs, I slowly resurfaced back in Carnegie, seeing yet another therapist, and working as an orderly at the venerable Physicians' Hospital, where I took pulses, scrubbed butts and lubed a lot of bed-weary bodies. I rose at 4:30 a.m. and took two buses to work. My body felt pummelled from the inside. I worked wearily alongside a twenty-five-year-old Appalachian who referred to himself as a "hillbilly" and called all Italo-American male patients "Pas-Kuh-Wall."

My first morning alone I stood tentatively bedside a 290-pound Polish-American giant, a rectal thermometer planted knuckles-to-the-sphincter. He was an ex-steel worker with big troubles, lying in a forest of IV vines, pressure masks and an oxygen tent. He lay there semiconscious, his breathing so radical— eyes popping open wide—NOW!—then sliding back under—then suddenly snapping upright in his big bed, the IV's ripping out with little red *poot*s.

Suddenly my hand and the thermometer it held were blown backwards with the powerful discharge of his bowels. The glass rod flipped back over my excreta-covered shoulder to *ping!* in half on the wall behind me, then begin its return to dust on the linoleum floor.

My hands full of his bulk, I learned the meaning of dead weight, washing what were now his remains from head to toe before wrapping him in sheets for my first ride behind a gurney to the "freezer" where he would wait for the "meat wagon." He was heavy.

I helped a medical resident pump fluid from the distended belly of a bright yellow FBI agent. The guy had an advanced liver cancer and was carrying an inland sea of toxicity. The doctor, a Filipino with very little English, soon ran afoul of the mechanical device intended for pumping out the bilious liquid. First, he found the puncture tube tip too dull to break the layers of flesh required.

"We give him Demerol," he said to no one in particular.

I stood there holding Special Agent Patrick's hand, as the resident stabbed away at his thorax, until, after a series of jabs, the tube sank home and he could begin to lower the level of distension. But it wouldn't work. He got the pet-cock set wrong, and every in-stroke sucked back the same vile liquid the previous outstroke had removed. The resident jiggled the valve, then tried again with the same results. Each new failure brought a pitiful moan from the poor yellow guy, as the liquid squirted back into his terrible tight belly. Finally I fled out into the hall, skipping down to bring help from someone who knew what to do—the head nurse. I was stunned by the wisdom of the giant tortoise-like nurses. The hospital was profitably run by a group of surgeons, including the rumored-to-be-inebriated-in-the-operating-room father of Dick Deutschmann.

Early morning starts meant getting home to enjoy the unique pleasure of spending an hour with my own convalescing father, confined to his bed with a case of his own nemesis, tuberculosis—the scourge that my father and his fellow Chest Men worked so hard to conquer. In an era when an MD was a passport to Country Club Heaven, getting involved with the patients, as my father did—making house calls, letting them come to his house, cooling their sputum in the kitchen refrigerator, being close enough to contact their common guest, the tubercle bacillus—was a badge of honor.

That summer I would walk home from the bus stop in time to join him in his otherwise cloistered bedroom for a full hour of Barnabus on Channel 6. Barnabus was an original—a Carnegie "coast-defender," in Fred Allen's graceful phrase—a local favorite from the earliest days of live TV who dressed up in a vaguely elfin outfit, including a straw boater and the cutest pointy ears, and hosted a daily *Popeye* festival for "kids and shut-ins." We sat there, my infected father and I; he flat on his back with prism glasses to watch the cartoons from supinity, me kneeling next to the double bed.

After about a month we had achieved the rank of minor historians, noting changes in Bluto's beard, Miss Oyl's *sopranino* croon, the proto-psychedelic flights of Max Fleisher, the random episodicity of Wimpy's appearances. All this we communicated in brief, hurried exchanges—a sentence followed ultimately by a grunt, mostly. Maybe twelve extremely well-chosen words per hour. Cleared throats with occasional laughter. Closeness adjacent.

About the time my father was declared cured (the tubercle bacilli had been surrounded by calcium), I was peremptorily fired by Physicians' Hospital after straining my back lifting a cardiac patient's bed up onto an elevator that chronically missed the floor by seventeen inches, below or above. When I returned to work after a one-day leave I was informed I was a bad insurance risk. "Good-bye. Here is one day's pay," or something like that.

So, figuring I might as well get back on track to finish my degree, I obtained Freudian Number Two's permission to sign up for some summer classes at Ohio College. That summer I bought my first car—a 1948 MG-TC, rusty black with ratty red leather, red painted bicycle spoke sixteen-inch wheels, and only one running board. A thousand dollars, as was. I drove it through most of the year with the top down, except on Carnegie's cruelest deep mid-winter days. No heater was provided.

I was still on a medical leave from Columbia for my psychic disintegration of the previous year. When the summer session ended, I enrolled for the fall semester full-time at Ohio College. It was not a very good school, so my Ivy League background conferred otherwise unattainable instant status, especially in the excellent three-man Philosophy Department. They liked my writing and gave me more credit than my woefully inadequate philosophical grounding merited, but I was from Columbia, and had studied with Nagel and the amazing Sidney Morgenbesser.

After class and weekends I went to Bargain Records in downtown Carnegie. This was their new location, opposite my father's office in the Lily Building. My father had discovered Bargain Records for us when I was still in high school, when he was buying the LPs he saw reviewed by Irving Kolodin in *The Saturday Review*. Beethoven chamber music, the Beecham *Prague* and *Jupiter* Symphonies, Ralph Kirkpatrick's Scarlatti harpsichord sonatas in many volumes on Westminster, The Casals Prades Festival Brandenburgs, Joseph Fuchs playing both Bach *Violin Concertos*, the Koussevitzky Tchaikovsky *Fourth* after he took my mother to hear the old man play it with the new Israel Philharmonic on tour. Lots of fluffy stuff, too: Rossini/Respighi: *Fantastic Toyshop*; *Dance of the Hours* and some ten-inch Decca records of Sousa marches, when I was in the Baker band. Plus lots of Benny Goodman's smaller groups with Teddy Wilson, Hampton and Krupa, and all the Louis Armstrong he could find, even going so far as to track down some early pirate ten-inchers, on the Jolly Roger (get it?) label. He loved Satch.

But it was the Rodszinski recording with the Carnegie Symphony of the Shostakovich *Fifth* that dug the deepest groove in my teenage nervous system. This had been the first piece of modern music I'd ever heard. I would sprawl out on the light green living room carpet completely absorbed in the third movement, lost in a vast winter tundra of the soul, in the snowy Ohio darkness.

My mother would come in from working in my father's office, cock an ear and tell me, "No wonder you're so depressed, listening to that music."

"It's the other way around," I would say, annoyed. "I *start out* depressed, put this on, and by the time it's over, I'm a sparkling sunbeam."

In the early summer of 1960, I stopped to pick up a present for Deutschmann, who was graduating from Princeton. I went there in search of the complete *Marriage of Figaro* with Erich Kleiber and the Vienna Philharmonic, which was in the special series on London Records that came with a complete vocal score as well as a libretto. Not many record stores (Sam Goody's and The Record Hunter in New York, probably) would carry this in regular stock, but Bargain Records was famous for completeness; they simply carried everything.

I asked a clean-cut, older guy behind the corner for the Mozart set.

"Oh, yes, the Kleiber *Figaro*: London A-4406, with Siepi, Corena, and, who *is* the Countess? Hilde Gueden, as I recall. No, Lisa della Casa." This white-shirted Slavic-American, with striped tie, slicked-back reddish hair, shark-skin suit pants and oxfords was Dan Manyak, the store manager.

"Anything else, sir?" he beamed.

"I'm interested in Handel opera," I said, extemporizing. "Isn't there a new *Semele*?"

"No, still just the old L'Oiseau-Lyre set," he said and looked genuinely chagrined.

"With the same cast as their *Sosarme*," I stated wisely.

Manyak was now eyeing me with interest. I walked to the front counter, opened a Schwann catalogue from the pile on the desk, and began to browse. I was wearing a short-sleeve Madras plaid button-down, khakis with a belt on the back and Sperry "Topsiders" with no socks. Feeling his eyes on my back, I turned and caught him grinning.

"Where did you learn your opera?"

"At Columbia, I…"

"But you're from Carnegie?"

"Yeah, my parents live near Baker Square."

"So do we; you home for the summer?"

"Starting summer school here next week—Beginning Italian."

"We could use part-time help…"

Dan Manyak was the manager of the local outlet of the burgeoning national Bargain Records, Inc. chain out of New York, with stores in Chicago, L.A. and San Francisco, as well as the very successful Carnegie location. I looked at his open smile, then cast a glance around at the large open room with thousands of LPs stacked spine-out on floor-to-ceiling metal library racks, as well as records face-out in aisles of bins marked Chamber Music, Opera Highlights, Vocal

Recitals, Avant-Garde, and Poetry & Spoken Word. The Shostakovich *Ninth* was playing on the house system. Followed by Sonny Rollins. Nice.

"I'll take it," I told Manyak.

"Can you start immediately?"

"Like tomorrow?"

"Like, right now. Here's a dollar; go buy a tie."

Bargain Records, Inc. was not what I considered to be On My Path. My intent was purely academic; I set my cap on a PhD in Philosophy and applied to the University of Chicago. The letter informing me of my acceptance, pending a formal interview, arrived the same day I met Ron Cook, an operatic tenor and friend of Rick Pesaro, my old Baker dick-matching buddy now a painter in Michigan. Cook was back in the states from Italy to sell some cattle on his farm in nearby Defiance, Ohio and Pesaro had brought him to my parents' house for a casual-seeming visit one wintry day. I'd been fascinated by the tall dark-bearded Cook, given to tweed capes, and interlarding his speech with Italianisms: *"come mai"* he would exclaim, or *"perché no"* or other devastatingly sophisticated-sounding interjections that gave him just the aura of weltschmerziness I knew I lacked.

When I mentioned the letter, Cook scoffed; said he'd just left the U of C Comparative Lit department in disgust over their stodginess in general and conservative taste in American literature in specific. No Beat stuff. No Kerouac. No Burroughs, Ginsberg, Corso. Maybe it's different in Philosophy, I suggested hopefully.

"Yeah," he snorted. "If you're arrested at Aristotle."

He was a big man, maybe six-four, and I didn't really know enough about the Chicago faculty to contend the point.

"We're driving west this weekend" he said into the silence. "Why not come along? We're picking up women in Chicago on the way to Iowa."

He was right about Chicago. The Philosophy Department looked gray and tired. The assistant who interviewed me displayed less energy than a pseudopod. I was beginning to think of academia as a cop-out, someplace to hide from life. Was this, too, fear of failure? I drove on with Cook, Pesaro and the two women from Chicago to Iowa City in Rick's '57 Ford Fairlane. The snow had stopped. The road west was dry through vast white-blanketed fields, the sun bright and warm. We heard the Met broadcast of *Don Giovanni* and Cook regaled us with tales of Tuscan indulgences. It was the time of the Cuban Revolution and our women companions' support for Fidel was met with barbed impatience turning abruptly to personal attacks. I stayed quiet.

In Iowa City we all stayed with a writer friend of theirs, Ian "Bulldog" Dangleson, an assistant professor and prodigious drinker. My memories of the one night of partying we shared with The Dog and friends are unreliable: gin, sex, and fighting, mostly. Tipsy, tired and still in deep contemplation of my future in or out of Academe, I slunk into my sofa-bed and fell into sleep. Sometime around 3:00 a.m. I felt a hand on my leg. I moved away. It followed. Felt a beard on my neck. I tried to roll over. The hand was fondling my balls through my nightshirt. I grunted. The beard was between my bare thighs. I feigned sleep, and received my first blow-job. The girls I'd known didn't *do That* and I was surprised how good it felt, despite the bristles scraping my scrotum. I didn't come—alcohol? embarrassment?—but Cook was very loving, and I was soon back asleep.

Back in Carnegie the decision loomed: College Professor or record clerk. My future looked as bleak as the slush-and-rock-salt filled Ohio winter. Nights alone at my parents filled with new audio components—and the new stereo LPs that were flying out of Record Company vaults to animate them— nevertheless seemed a dreary, desolate reminder of having lost my way. Friends faded into collegiate memories. My sense of failure grew with every medical school acceptance or law school admission by an erstwhile college chum. I hung out with my fellow clerks, once caught myself staring at their crotches. Was I a fairy?

One night at Orchestra Hall, home of the Carnegie Symphony, I beheld a young woman usher: slight and very tight, Sarah Browne, with a Hester Prinne sort of New England submerged maniac look around the eyes. Somehow she exuded a challenging quality of repression; the pent-up energy, lying coiled, waiting for the hot snap. I pursued her, finally loutishly extracting her innocence on my parents' bed, upon whose white spread she left a small group of dainty red spots. She had a girlish bottom with luscious upper body, and she was so tight her legs literally snapped apart.

Then the letter came from Settignano. Cook was writing to invite me to stay with them—him and two young women, whose photos he included—in the hills above Florence. As luck would have it, my mother was signed up for an Academy of Medicine Doctors and Wives tour of Western Europe, and I wangled a ticket for me and my enormous steamer trunk for $100 one-way. In two weeks I was in Rome, then by train to Florence, where Cook picked me up at the *stazione*. That first night we argued till dawn about whether D. H Lawrence was bi-sexual. Having read only one of his novels, I was at something of a disadvantage, but I didn't let that bother me. It gave me the opportunity to see a man who preferred the *ad hominem* to all other debating strategies. Attack minded, but fair enough when challenged to admit his error, if not change his ways.

There were, as he had said, two young American girls sharing the house, which turned out to be a neat two-floor cottage with three bedrooms. I had one, the sun porch actually, while Cook and his apparent mate, Saundra, shared the big front bedroom, overlooking the thin line of a garden, and the miracle pink of the Tuscan hills on their way to Umbria. The other bedroom was the resting place of a classic WASP enchantress Veronica Surrey with her flirty dark eyes flashing mischief and *prima facie* dismissal by turn. On-off. On-off. Dine-Dance. I was struck silent by this horsy apparition, her camellia-bud breasts coasting along in front of her, calves for days and dignified-but-playful medium brown hair to her shoulders, but worn up to the advantage of her broad and soul-stirring forehead. I liked Ronny, and she liked me. She loved me to play for her Scarlatti and Mozart Sonatas, Handel Suites that I would read through in a late afternoon when Cook and Saundra were down in Florence and we had a few hours alone together. A few popish jazz tunes, "Lullaby of Birdland," "Misty," and standards like "A Foggy Day," and "It Never Entered My Mind." Ronny would sit on the one couch at the back of our small living room, her skirt hiked up to mid-thigh, reading Paris *Match* or *die Stern*, or letters from her large family of prominent bankers in Connecticut.

We'd wait in the waning sun in late Italian spring, not exactly in each other's sphere, but not separate, either. In these few musical afternoons, I managed to find a kind of limited romantic involvement: safe and terminal. Ronny had a fella. A large blazer-wearing Florentine named Ricardo Fierro—tall, full and ten years her senior, with very white skin and true black hair on scalp and lip.

It was 1961. The Italian economy had just started to reemerge onto the world stage. Gucci, Alfa, and the divine Federico. *La Strada, La Dolce Vita, Otto e Mezzo*. Ronny's *inamorato* Ricardo drove a *Cinquecento*, the smallest Fiat, 500 cc. Half a litre, with terrible brakes. He would skuh-weeeeeeeeeeeeeee to a stop at appealing roadside shrines. Cook called him *Commendatore* in light tauntric mode, or *Admirale*. After we bought our five-year-old Lancia *Aurelia GT* he would refer to us as *I Lancisti*, "the Lancers," or more precisely, colloquially and not without irony, "the Cocksmen."

I was on the little sun porch overlooking the creek listening, in the stillness of the Settignano night, to my friends croon the timeless *canzon' d'amore* while the headboard thumped the ancient stone wall. At least I got some reading done. I discovered Olympia Press and its flat green paperbacks. *Naked Lunch* first, then *Thief's Journal* and anything by Genet I could find. Cook loved Kerouac and other Beat writers, especially Corso, who came to spend a week with us. There was a lot to read. Cook and I took the train to Milano to bring the rascal/poet's work to the attention of publisher Mondatori.

I was encouraged by the Corso visit, which I had initially dreaded somewhere deep down in my ego-structure. What new forms of withering ridicule would the Attack Poet concoct to dispatch poor little tenderfoot me?

But it was a shocker: Corso was generous and encouraging with me, but tough with people in general. Maybe, I thought, it goes with the territory: a poet could actually live what he wrote and write what he lived IF and ONLY IF he grew tough enough to stave off the opinions of others while protecting his own thoughts, ideas and especially feelings.

The week proved transformational. When Corso left, I sat down at my tiny Olivetti portable with a stove-top espresso at the ready, and without sketch, outline, or draft began to type:

La Storia della Borghesia in Italia
Teachers petting in lurid slick covered luminosity growing
awkward mustaches and erections of the Lower Soul.
Swans diving for aldermen in a cold lake of undrunk fraternity beer,
Pinning their crotches with great solemnity and fester.

Later I attempted writing short stories, while teaching English to bank clerks in Montecatini, and accompanying opera for Robert.

His singing teacher, the great Allessandro di Roberti had been Toscanini's favorite lyric tenor, thirty years before at La Scala. At lessons in his house near the Piazza del Duomo in Florence I accompanied Cook with equal insensitivity to what I did at home in Settignano. I never really bothered to study the piano score; I just sort of cruised through each (mostly Verdi) aria, playing as much as I could of the fills and under the voice, just a few approximated chord changes plunked out in the appropriate rhythm. Cook had a cannon of a voice. Metal was everything to him. The bones of the head, _la voce di testa._ When he sang _Di Quella Pira_! even the plumbing got to rocking.

We'd go by train to Milano for _der Rosenkavalier_ at La Scala, Venice for Luigi Nono and a fascist gang shouting out in La Fenice "Viva la Polizía," and the Rome opera for almost a whole season, as well as a _Falstaff_ in Sienna, and the Menotti festival in Spoleto. My education was beginning. I was being proposed to by opera-queens: "Come live with me in Oberlin, Mitch; I'll draw your milk baths." Cook knew a lot of "art-faggots" as he called them, insisting upon his own *bi*-sexuality. Horny as I was, I let him sleep with me on our opera travels, picturing the body of Ronny while he expertly brought me and himself to orgasm. It seemed okay while it was happening, but I worried. Once I told him it was "tawdry."

One hot afternoon in the square in Sienna, waiting for the *Palio* to commence, I was thinking, my mind in my coffee cup. *How can I possibly become a writer? I've had no real life thus far. All I know is words: history and theories about the world. I will have to get a life.* Then I ran out of money. I drove the Lancia to Southampton, and sailed for New York.

Back in Carnegie one more time—broke, with no work and no prospects. Flat-ass bummed. I fell back briefly into clerking at Bargain Records, and slipped into the shallow bohemian existence of a provincial Midwestern town. The place didn't even have a decent restaurant, but the Art Museum was impressive, and the Symphony was world class and cool. The job paid okay. I had a little apartment on the fringes of the black "ghetto," as they were just beginning to call them. Work was tiring but endlessly stimulating. Meeting the public was a challenge for my inner-Ivy League snob, but the records themselves were a huge turn-on: Bartók string quartets, Thelonious Monk, Mozart piano concertos, Stravinsky, Charlie Parker, Schönberg solo piano music, Lennie Tristano, Handel operas. The Miles Davis/Gil Evans *Porgy and Bess* had just been released. So had the original cast recording of Leonard Bernstein's amazing *Candide*. A new technology called "stereophonic sound" was just hitting the market. Exciting. *Ping-Pong Percussion* was a hit, but so were *Jazz Samba* and *Peter, Paul and Mary*.

But by night it was still the Midwest and there was not much action for late-blooming beatniks in the early '60's. A couple of coffee shops. One solitary folk club of dubious distinction, and jazz only in the black slums.

Sexual liberation was still a gleam in Hugh Hefner's, or somebody's, eye. Young women wept after sex, or, more likely, near-sex. Diaphragms and hysteria. My black friends sometimes would get me weed. We sat around drinking wine, listening to Lenny Bruce, Lord Buckley and a new-to-me tenor player called John Coltrane.

One late fall night I had no plans, as usual, and let myself be drawn along into a loose agreement to join the store manager and two fellow clerks for a night of drinking beer in assorted East Side bars.

The new manager was Frank Brogan, a strapping thirty-five-year-old Irish-American, suffering from over-ingestion of Mickey Spillane. A middle-class good ol' boy gone bad and loving every slumming minute of it. Frank was maybe 6'2", 240 with a red crew-cut that stood up straight in front. All attitude and a mile wide. I have no idea how he'd gotten the manager's job from the group of Jewish would-be intellectuals who ran the famous national chain of retail record shops out of New York City. *What must they have been thinking to hire this pug?* Frank's m.o. was to start a fight and run. Provoke two other people and back away. "Would have been a great cop," someone said.

The two other guys were Rod Vincent, a large, gangly twenty-year old from a small town someplace in Ohio with slicked-back ducktails and a loping, swaggery walk, and my old college friend and current roommate, Bill Boswell. Bill was about twenty-three, and still trying to identify his sexual proclivities after a long, slavish affair with his (male) Greek professor. He was a brilliant but exceptionally low-key kinda guy, with passive hostility written all over him. A sweet hairless boyish white face and a head of thick dark locks.

So we cruised up the main drag of our largish city, through the Negro areas and just before the University Circle, where there were a few dumpy, over-lit bars catering to nobody in particular. We parked Brogan's odd choice of vehicle for a Great Lakes winter—the first Alfa Romeo sedan I'd ever seen outside of Italy—and chose an anonymous saloon at what seemed to be random. Ray Charles' "Georgia" was playing as we entered the dead smoke-soaked storefront.

Other arms reach out to me.

One or two patrons looked up. I was feeling too 'existential' to notice much else. *Why am I doing this?*

Other eyes smile tender-leee…

A thumping and ringing from a couple playing on a full-size skeeball set-up. *Why am I here?*

Still in peaceful dreams I see—

The four of us found a booth and slid in noisily. I did not like the looks in my two larger friend's eyes. Glinting. Smiling at each other. Mean looks. Then, laughing, they jumped up and pushed each other boyishly toward the bar.

I've lived in Florence and New York, studied Wittgenstein, played Bach, read Camus, and sung in a madrigal group. Sounds from the bar. I heard Brogan's loud voice, yelling at the bartender. *Why am I here? Maybe I'll just get a bus home.* I looked over at Boswell, who seemed lost in the song.

…the road leads back to YOUUU…

They brought drinks back to the booth. Seagram's with beer backs. They threw back their double shots. I lifted my draft beer—Leisy's Light, Carling's, P.O.C., maybe Stroh's—and took a quick sip. The big guys grabbed their beers, slid to their feet again and bounded over to the skeeball game. I looked over at Boswell. His face was serene. Distant and, in a strange way, demure. A handsome boy, with a thin layer of baby-fat and downcast eyes. Measuring his beer, apparently inert.

"What d'ya wanna do?" I asked him.

"Wait," he said, and turned to check out the sudden noises from the back of the tavern. Shouts and scuffling from the skeeball area. I looked over. It was darker back there, but I see people pushing other people.

"Wanna get outta here?" I asked him.

"I dunno," he said, a crinkle of anxiety flitting across his handsome flat face. I stood up, looking for my coat. The noises were louder as I located my scarf and put it on. I left Boswell to deal with the night's trajectory.

There was a certain rowdiness; an angry uncoiling of hateful energy that was building as my cohorts grew increasingly ugly, pushing other patrons around. Seeing how far they could go. I told them I was tired and walked out onto Chester Avenue and caught the uptown bus.

I transferred at University Circle, where the midnight bus finally came and I was soon home again, lonely and depressed as usual in my tiny basement digs. Mercifully, I was asleep in ten minutes. At about 2:30 a.m. the phone faded in through the fog I'd managed to crash my weary retail body into, and yanked me mostly awake. It was Brogan.

"Got any money?" His voice was not drunken, not sober.

"Whuhhhh?"

"Hundred bucks?"

"I guess…" I'd just been paid.

"Bring it. Mt. Sinai Emergency. They been cut pretty bad. They need a hundred to admit 'em. Hurry." Then he added: "Both of them."

I got a cab to take me down there and handled the business, then I sat in the waiting room while they were given surgical attention. Brogan sat there next to me. They had gone rumbling through a couple more bars, it seemed.

"Yeah. On the way home, we were right out here driving past the hospital. Around the front, and—coming onto the circle—some big Cadillac wouldn't let us in, so we cut him off. Big, black '58 Coupe de Ville."

Brogan was a sports car aficionado. Tweed caps and driving gloves. Car coats.

"Yeah. We got out and it was a *schwartze,* bigger than me."

The guy turned out to be a bouncer for one of the fancier Mob nightclubs. About 6' 3", bald and very dark-skinned. Black as the night that covers us.

"Had a big knife. Caught Roddy's ear. I saw the blood. Took the ear right off."

Very quickly, despite the heavy cashmere topcoat he was wearing, the 300-pound bouncer had sliced Rodney across his charging face. *Snick!* through the center of his right ear. *Snick!* across the forehead.

"What happened to Boswell?" I didn't want to hear.

"Caught 'im right in the corner of the mouth. Opened him all the way down the jaw."

"You talk to the doctors?"

"They'll be okay. A lotta blood. They think they can put Roddy's ear back on."

"They found it?"

"I saw where it bounced to. So I went and brought it back here."

He ended laconically, wistfully almost, the unscathed provocateur subtly distancing himself from the unfortunates who lay waiting to be stitched into lifelong facial scars. He asked me to drive his Alfa to my house and keep it for him. Seems the bouncer had immediately gone to the precinct and filed a complaint for Assault. The cops wanted to talk with Brogan.

I walked out into the hospital parking lot. It was not quite dawn. A cold midwestern morning, dark and heavy with the scent of snows yet to come. Brogan's blue Alfa *Giulia* was parked in the middle of the "Doctors Only" section. The door handle was frozen. I beat on it with the meat of my gloved fist. The door creaked open on reluctant Mediterranean hinges. I got into the cracked leather bucket seat, jiggled the ignition key until the starter caught, second-guessed the choke knob and finally the engine fired, coughed and fizzled. By the time I got the revs up and idling, the sun was creeping tentatively over the Cancer Building. I managed to get it in Reverse and twisted myself around to back out of the space.

One of the best things about working at Bargain Records, Inc. was the endless stream of free LPs from promo men and record company sales reps. Boswell had taken home that night a copy of the new *Salome,* Richard Strauss's operatic shocker with Birgit Nilsson. The bulky two-record boxed set—with the sizable grimacing soprano, Ms. Nilsson, reclining in costume on its cover— was lying on its back on the Alfa's floor. In the dim light, I saw the cover begin to move, twisting and waving. I braked to a quick stop and heard a sickening, sloshing sound.

At that moment, the sun cleared the Emergency marquee and illuminated the head of John the Baptist, looking up, disbelieving, into the eyes of Salome, daughter of Herod, partially submerged and gently rocking in a small pond of blood from the bodies of my wounded friends.

In the spring I'd had enough and went "Off to Philadelphia in the morning," as John McCormick sang. I accepted an offer to join my friend Brad Barth and an integrated group of activists in Philadelphia in setting up The Philadelphia Children's School for Music & Drama, in the South Side ghetto. Our oldest actor was twelve.

I lived in Brad's girlfriend's modest but decorous apartment on the West Side near Penn, with her too-friendly cat, a small cardboard box of LPs (*Alexander Nevsky* and the *Brandenburgs*) and fabulous paperback editions of five centuries of world drama. I read a lot, sweated, ate the occasional peanut butter and white bread sandwich. We all lived on amphetamines dispensed by the girlfriend's doctor-father. I fought off the welcoming claws, and read. One night the phone rang.

"Hi, Mitch, it's Sarah. I'm at the bus station."

"Sarah?"

"Sarah! From Carnegie!"

"Oh, hi, Sarah…um, what station?"

"Trailways!"

"No, I mean *where*?"

"Right down*town* from you. Don't you live near Penn?"

"You're in *Philly*? What're you doing in Philadelphia?"

"I came to see *you*, Mitch."

I drove my not quite-BRG Morgan Plus 4 down to the depot to get her. Sarah still had this quietly hysterical slipped-her-anchor quality about her, totally in conflict with the reasonable, nay, formal aspect she showed the world. What I felt was this mother-puma ferocity sort of floating behind the scrim of her, not New England, but Nob Hill, it turned out, propriety. Prim-on-the-way-to-prissy.

And small, tiny, like fucking a child, I'd decided. That was one of the parts I liked, of course, that and her white-girl skin and vaginal grasp, as it were.

"Are you glad to see me?"

She was very quiet, but beneath that reserve, you sensed her power. She knew I wasn't glad to see her, but it didn't seem to matter much. She simply wanted me. It was an intense turn-on to slip it into her, her childly tightness, generous pink-nippled breasts, and her sheath dripping a clear mountain stream of pleasure. I smoothed the back of my hand up her thighs, soft and helpless under white skin, warmed by tiny blonde hairs. Clear but distant blue eyes gazed out below gently tossing bangs, and flashes of got-to-have-it desire flared up in plumes. It was almost too good to be true. I *knew* she had to go.

Sarah rubbed against me. I smelled bath soap and bus grime and the self-defining smell of rich-girl's hair. I got hard. She sat down on the side of the bed looking demure. Like a Breck ad, for Chrissake. She hoisted her faded Madras skirt to show the vee of her crotch.

I helped her take off her sleeveless shell and oddly threadbare bra, laced with sweat stains, and lowered my cheek to her chest, rising and falling in shallow huffs. She had a neat little rose of a mouth, not severe or mean, but not generous, and as I glanced up at her from her own bosom, I saw the too-tight smile of satisfaction tinged with dominance, beaming down at me.

I could smell her as she hurried out of her panties: the smell of bones and marrow, of the centuries of a certain kind of woman-rearing. I pushed my shorts down and bridged myself up onto her open body, pussy now expanding to become the flowering All, or, at least, the Immediate Future. I looked at her glowing face, then to her immature limbs akimbo, then back to her face—her eyes were closed, permitting the sensorium to feed on the moment—and then to the low table behind her straight blonde hair. There on the dark wood surface were a collection of plays by Jean Annouilh, an old alarm clock, Sarah's panties in a ball and a brass candelabrum holding a thick red candle.

There was nothing base, nothing hateful, nothing monstrous, nothing even remotely pleasureful in the act of carefully and respectfully servicing my young visitor with a surrogate. If she ever noticed the candle, she never let on, and the act came to a successful conclusion.

Afterward, her sweating nakedness close to me in the barely diminished heat, she was still smiling. Relieved of obligation, I was able to relax as her breathing stabilized, and I listened to her elaborate plans for a cross-country bus trip. The next morning it was raining as I kissed her good-bye under the umbrella at the 30th Street Station.

In that summer of '61, in the City of Brotherly Love, my car was set on fire. The money we were promised by various foundations ended up in the hands of the Junior League Drama Circle, who presented Mainline housewives impersonating chickens and foxes in fables for (as opposed to with) children. No money equaled no food. I lost five pounds, ten—I was always hungry. I couldn't eat promises, I told Brad, who was comfortably ensconced in his girlfriend's parents' Schuylkill side grandeur. No, he said, they had no money either, but she could forge her father's signature on script. So I began an amphetamine habit which accelerated with the passing of every meal. My prior drug use had been confined to the occasional speed-and-downer tweak from my father for cramming purposes, and the occasional joint with my Negro friends in Carnegie. Serious pill popping was new to me; I knew not whereof I ingested and what the consequences might be. I knew only that when I wolfed down the tiny pink tabs, the pangs receded to insignificance in a flaming world of right here and right now!

As part of our tiny integrated crew I was now able to work round the clock preparing the cast of fifth and sixth grade South Philly ghetto kids for opening night of Jean Cocteau's *Orfée*. The Ford Foundation had promised to attend.

But the stage had yet to be built. We'd been given an abandoned office building below South Street, the former home of the African Methodist-Episcopal Bishop of Pennsylvania who had vanished, coincidental to the disappearance of the Church treasury, some years before. The six-story building, perpetually vandalized all these years, was now ours to do with as we saw fit.

We scraped and painted, painted and scraped, but as opening night approached we had not finished converting the top-floor cafeteria into a performance area. Brad and I were building risers out of office doors, and stage machinery out of rusty business machine parts. I took the task of installing window curtains made from donated church robes. Since no rods or hanging hardware were available, I simply cut the robes to size and nailed them to the top of the floor-to-ceiling windows that encircled the large cafeteria area. I would climb to the top of an old ladder, holding the heavy robes and placing the nail with one hand, and swinging the hammer with the other. I would then get down, move the ladder a few feet, re-scale the heights, and try to miss my thumb for a change.

On the second night of this torture, blasted on speed and hallucinating, I backed down the ladder that was holding me, and instead of stepping off onto the riser, walked straight out the sixth floor window. Pure instinct caused me to hoist my trailing arm as my body crossed the sill and grab the open window—smashing all the panes and cutting ribbons down my arm.

I watched the sold-out *Orfée* premiere in miles of white ER bandages. The next day I got on a plane and went back to Carnegie, still in shock from the sudden withdrawal, but at least I had some Percodan.

In the psychosexual climate in which I was steeped—tenderized like a cheap cut of beef—you couldn't *just do it.* The early Sixties were as repressed as the Fifties, and sex always entailed melodrama. Girls were forever weeping after sex. There was even a theory of post-coital depression to disinform us that it was natural to feel bad after daring to produce an orgasm. So when I met Senta Laendler—small, cute, funny and five years older, a Wellesley grad and Actors Playhouse alum—I was so charmed that I managed to get her, too, pregnant.

I'd known Senta in passing, although our first-generation parents shared the same general Eastern-European-Jewish economic co-prosperity sphere. The first time I met her I watched her laugh at a party for a dancer I was dating, Theresa Thesanofolos, a lithe Graham-style soloist who had to be cajoled into bed, then sobbed us both to sleep in her Orthodox guilt. She had invited Senta to a small gathering of mixed-hipsters. Hearing a tinkly, musical laugh, I located Senta's cute red-haired face through the crowd. Eric Dolphy was playing soprano. We were introduced, both saying the usual: our parents know each other.

A week later I was ringing up a sale for *Ping-Pong Percussion Goes Hawaiian*, tearing off the proper amount of Ohio sales tax stamps, when the phone rang.

"Maybe Mitch knows," I heard Mike say.

"Knows what?"

"You subscribe to *High Fidelity*, right?"

"Yeah?"

"Do you have…she's looking for…here, I'll put her on."

Senta was looking for an article that Glenn Gould had written on Richard Strauss's piano music a few months back. I told her I had the piece; come over and get it. It was an obvious ploy. Of course, I was always horny.

So Senta came over. Ancient winter was making its move on Carnegie, snow gauzing down the narrow streets of my peripherally-dangerous neighborhood. My apartment had been the janitor's residence in what had been, in my grandparents' day, middle-class Jewish multiple-dwelling units. A typical basement, dark and overheated by the hot water pipes which hung down into all the rooms except the long railroad-flat hallway, lowering the headroom to a posture-defying cramp.

Senta seemed to have had a nose job. Purple semicircles capped her cheekbones, lending her eyes a beautiful, tormented Russian cast. She was so sweet; I had so much to share with her. We listened to Bach together. Gould, mostly, but also the *B Minor Mass* on Westminster with the divine Hermann Scherchen. And Mozart with Rudolf Serkin, Dennis Brain, and our own Carnegie Symphony, where her father played cello. I could get free LPs, and I bought a lot more.

She was teaching then, and acting, but putting away extra coin by home-tutoring. We had fun together. So I capitulated to what seemed the inexorable pull of destiny. All my friends—Deutschmann, Feld, even Burberry—had gotten hitched. I went along with the program, over my long-held resistance to "bringing children into this putrid and chimerical world," to marry her in January, 1963. I firmly expected to enter the Babbitt Brotherhood of family and business I had thus far managed to avoid.

I'd never really wanted children. While we were weighing the options, she miscarried. That decided it. *She would have children!* It would be good, Senta told people, good for Mitch to be a parent. Maybe even engender a modicum of human wisdom in this classic adolescent prince, increasingly absorbed by multiple and contiguous jobs, to have something to enhance his home life. I felt bad. I'd become promiscuous in an only fairly discreet sort of way. Businessmen did that then—maybe they still do. Bargain Records stores had been full of some of the farthest-out white-chick sales clerks in town. Young Beat babes flirting with jazz and the dark side.

Despite the hormones the doctors were giving her, Senta lost the next two babies too. She had to carry the little corpses around inside her for months till her uterus re-hardened, and they could at last be scraped out of there.

My father recommended a fertility specialist—the head of Ob/Gyn at St. Duke's Hospital, a giant teaching facility where, with the aid of massive hormone intervention, Bruno was born—the only survivor of his mother's first four fetuses—in April of 1968, three days after the assassination of Martin L. King, Jr. Senta was so blown away by her stunning procreative comeback that she was reluctant to bring our firstborn home.

The ghettos had erupted. And St. Duke's was Black Community-adjacent.

"Is it the protests?" I tried to reassure her.

"No, it's just that he feels so fragile. I'm scared to bring this tadpole home." She was beautiful as a mother. "I just know I'll break him."

She looked up at me with an odd light in her eye. A beam that passed me something. A message? A miracle? Magnetic wave? A moment of magnitude, just for me. Something.

"I'll take the little tyke home then," I offered, and it wasn't just a cheap rhetorical flourish. I got with it, spending time with Bruno, getting up to feed him or walk him or just hold him, entranced by his tiny humanness. I was stunned by how satisfying it was, with Bruno sprawled on my belly, just to sit there, Be There Then, and enjoy my beautiful boy.

I'd get up to feed and change little Ronald Bruno Hertz, roll a joint of Mexican weed from a shoebox lid and stand the grinning infant on his rubber jammie toes. We'd dance, the two of us giggling the nights away, as the Carnegie winter covered the tree-filled ravines of my front yard. I was in love with Bruno, simple as that.

Flushed with success and, at thirty-seven, a not-quite-but-almost-motherly five years older than her spouse, Senta had proceeded to get re-knocked up in a hurry. The next two boys, Clifford and Tony, were born at intervals of fewer than eighteen months each, their mother fighting the sifting sand and winning.

Yeah, I loved 'em all. Shot a ton of Super-8 film of the three of them toddling naked about the Carnegie Heights back yard. And, before I knew what smote me, I'd joined the hoary ranks of the patriarchs.

～

The role of authoritarian father held no attraction to me. So why did I allow myself to enter into the very serious world of child-rearing two more times? For one thing, I was trying to pass as a businessman.

Bargain Records had just gotten a new owner. Don Goodman had been the Great Lakes wholesaler for Columbia Records since the Fifties. I'd just been elevated to assistant manager of the smaller, older store in a declining neighborhood, near my father's old office. The rumor was that Dan Manyak, my store manager, was slated to host the show on WCAR. "I can do that," I said to the cash register. I contacted the station for an audition.

I had never spent one minute in broadcasting. Nevertheless, I found myself pretty much at ease behind the microphone in the tiny production studio, sight-reading a foreign name and title-clogged page full of "Theresa Stich-Randall, Paul Badura-Skoda and Dietrich Fischer-Dieskau" or *Le Marteau sans Maître, Die Entführung aus dem Serail, Il Ritorno d'Ulisse in Patria* and so on.

The audition went swimmingly, and I, as if in a dream, was rewarded with my first job in radio. It may have helped that Dan, my only competition, was gay and a trifle too fluorescent for the room. I got a weekly two-hour show airing Sunday evenings at seven called *The Listening Post*. For the first full year I was unpaid and earned every penny.

I became something of a personage, reviewing new records which—I would self-mockingly but effectively point out—were available for sale "at a Bargain Records, Inc. shop of your choice," followed by a list of store locations. Then intro Benjamin Britten conducting his *War Requiem* (US premiere broadcast) or Terry Riley's minimalist manifesto, *In C* (1965), music rising over the ubiquitous "This is Mitchell Hertz."

Then Fred Glick died. Freddie was my owner, Don's brother-in-law and partner in Great Lakes Distributing, which, after losing Columbia, flourished briefly as an independent, handling Atlantic, Dot, Vox, Mainstream, Roulette, Riverside and assorted others. This, in a valiant effort to piss successfully into the winds of change. Freddie had been kind to me as a student working at Bargain Records in the late Fifties when he was a Columbia salesman laying samples of new LP releases on me and my fellow clerks. Freddie was always laughing. Even as he grew thicker and sicker, smoking Chesterfields without end, stamping around his Erie office, threatening, cajoling, ranting and railing on the phone, turning red, I'd walk in and he'd say, "Mitch, how do ya keep a Jewish girl from screwing? Ha! Ha! Marry 'er. Ha-ha! Ha! (Coughing fit)!"

Then, "Are Chinese girls different?"

"What?"

"Are Chinese girls different?!"

"Why?"

"Are they different?"

"I don't know."

"Ask me."

"Okay. Are Chinese girls different, Freddie?"

"No!" Hacking and gales of laughter.

Then, "'Rastus Ginsberg,' asked the pretty white teacher. 'Are you

Jewish?'"

"Me?"

"Yes, Rastus. Do you happen to be Jewish?"

"'Naw. Ain't ah gotta 'nuff trubble bein' a Shwahtzeh?'"

More laughter and coughs.

After Columbia pulled out, Great Lakes Distributing went staggering its independent way with Don and Freddie trying to be distributors and retailers at the same time. They looked for the store managers, Dan Manyak and me, by then age 24, to give them their retail chops. We contended for leadership. I was young, Ivy League almost-educated and interpretably Jewish, and Manyak was ten years older, Slovenian and queer. I don't feel guilty—merit may have played a part as well as privilege. I've never been particularly homophobic, even letting Manyak's "wife," a black executive chef named Quincy, get drunk and put his face in my crotch when I occasionally took my dates over there for a visit.

I rose in what loosely passed for an organization. First store manager, then General Manager of two stores, then a third very successful spot in Gentry Center, Jewish Carnegie Height's first big department store-anchored enclosed mall, then the fourth in Eriewood on the segregated West Side. Success after success bred expansion, which I accepted as the American Way. We kept growing. Now I was having trouble with controlling inventory *and* employees.

I had always been a working manager, trying to lead by example, a habit picked up, I guess, in team sports. I spent most of my time downstairs in my cheaply re-decorated basement office, with cheesy royal blue industrial carpeting and walls barely covered with a single coat of sky blue paint, leaving the underlying rough plastering bumps and cracks to fend for themselves. Neon lighting completed the skimp-till-you-bleed decorating amidst which I did all the buying, advertising and hiring/firing for the whole chain, which, before I stormed out, had grown to eighteen stores in seven states. It was there that distributor's reps called to show me the "slicks" (cover art without cardboard) for the new releases, as well as take re-orders and plan marketing. Endlessly.

But when they were busy on the upstairs sales floor I flew into action, like the quarterback I have always been, in my heart's mind at least. Selling, wrapping customer purchases, recommending "best" versions of classics, checking in new merchandise from the packing slips, even taking deliveries with the two-wheeler. I did this six days a week, Christmastime being the worst.

The best thing about the job, of course, was music. Classical and New Music, folk, blues, even "International" (as we called what is now world music), and especially jazz. All of it was ultimately enriching, expanding, even ennobling. I learned a lot. Not "learned" in the academic, techno-analytical way, but just what various musics sounded like, and what they "meant." I got deeper into jazz, where when a player was really wailing he was "saying something." That kind of meaning, plus what it might mean socially, politically, historically, even emotionally.

Everything in music was fermenting, ready to explode. Modern classical music seemed to be frozen under the ice flow of Serialism, the radical sounding, but by the mid-Sixties, quite old-fashioned "scientific" or mathematical atonal twelve-tone composers—the so-called "Second Vienna School" of Arnold Schönberg, Alban Berg and Anton Webern and their spawn. Impossibly complex, intellectual music that had already driven international audiences screaming into the streets, and threatened to kill classical music forever. Jazz, too, was in turmoil. With the advent of the Civil Rights Movement, be-bop had split into twin tendencies, both with their claims upon the soul of the movement: the brainy "Hard Bop" of Miles Davis, Bill Evans, Coltrane et al., and the gospel-based "Soul Jazz" of Cannonball Adderly, Jimmy Smith, and Art Blakey. Now in the Black Rage of the Sixties it was entering its no-return phase of "out" new jazz playing, overleaping the bounds of traditional blues or standard pop chord changes, and sailing out where no audience would dare to follow, absent the psychic shoehorn of drugs.

It was into this environment of harmonic opacity and rhythmic stasis that first folk music and then the new "rock" (as opposed to the old pop or rock 'n' roll) came strolling in—with the British Invasion, with its return to Black American blues—and the hippy rock scene of San Francisco, Los Angeles and New York: Jefferson Airplane, Buffalo Springfield and Velvet Underground. That did it for me: Art music that swang (rocked) and "said something" about racism, war, love and to a certain extent, spirituality.

In classical music, the minimalists were restoring the primacy of rhythm after years under the domination of harmony. Steve Reich came out on stage alone and simply started clapping his hands in simple patterns, which expanded as other clappers, then drummers emerged to elaborate. A return to first principles was alive in the land. And it was this new "rock" that was doing it.

~

Don Goodman and I were on a turnpike trip to Chicago to visit our trans-shippers—major suppliers alternative to our local outlets—when we heard of Freddie's heart attack. We knew Fred had been playing Type-A run-around cocksman on his shallow, pretty-but-whiney wife Sally, an icy *parvenu* who wouldn't fuck him for money (or maybe *only* for money), so we weren't surprised. But we didn't turn Don's navy blue Wildcat convertible around and drive back to Carnegie to visit him in St. Charlotte's. We went on to Chicago and called when we got there.

When we finally got back to Carnegie I drove over to see him, but before I could plan another visit, he simply died. Thus, having out-regularized Manyak to become General Manager, I now more-or-less inherited a vice-presidency from the departed Fred Glick, and learned the lesson of his life: try to get over excessive planning. "Too much projection from too little data."

I just expected things to keep getting better, not just for me but for everyone. The imperial trance of Permanent Progress. America walks a little taller, sees further down the road of history. We earned it in The War. Get used to it. We are a true meritocracy. Think modern.

"Yeah," I thought. "This is how life is."

And in the spring (traditionally in Carnegie a period of perhaps eleven days duration), something actually sprang. A new-releases show for a new classical FM station, setting up shop and looking for sponsors. Why, they reasoned, shouldn't the leading local record shop have an interest in sponsoring such a show, say, weekly?

When WCAR called and asked me to interview Leonard Bernstein, I figured it was what happened next in life. Get used to it. No big deal. Again, the sanguinary expectation of success that is success itself.

~

"Everyone on my staff is afraid." It was William Bennett, WCAR Program Director.

"Afraid of what?" I was ringing the register on the large sales floor at Bargain Records at Public Square.

"We all think you're the best person."

In the year that I'd been doing *The Listening Post* we'd had little more than the usual sponsor/broadcaster relationship. They told me I was good, but I was paying their rent. So this request gave me a new sense of professional competence.

"I've never done an interview before, Bill," I said, wrapping a stereo ($1.00 extra) copy of Jazz *Samba* for a waiting customer.

"I'll be your engineer. You just talk to the Maestro."

"About what? Music? Records?"

"It's the first Philharmonic local appearance since 1920 or something. Buffone's bringing him to Music Hall in two weeks."

"So I hype the concert?"

"Mitchell, he's Leonard Bernstein. Anything he *says* will hype the concert."

From the second he asked me I knew I would do it. Ready to get out of the role of Mr. Jewish Businessman, as I was fast appearing to become in a semi-conscious drive to bond with the Goodmans, consolidate my leadership of "the stores" and generally expand the horizon of my *Weltanschauung*. We spent long hours being merchants—at least fifty hours a week—not including listening, writing, driving, and taping *The Listening Post*. Being swept up and out of my basement office into the wider world of classical music was just fine with me.

Senta drove me to Carnegie International Airport in her new R-8 Renault, a cute little black four-door with welcoming Frenchy seats. She dropped me at the gate, where Bennett was waiting with his Ampex and his Pan Am bag.

"What are you going to talk about?"

"His tempi in the Schumann *Fourth*."

"Okay…are they fast?"

"Slow…especially for him."

The visiting maestro was in his heyday with the New York Philharmonic, a career surge—as conductor/media figure/hetero, as opposed to a composer/activist/homo as the current micro-biographics would have it. He was on a binge to record everything he could get his hands on. This included the basic repertory as well as the areas of special concern to himself; fellow young American composers and the *Symphonies* of Gustav Mahler, among many. His new releases on Columbia of the Complete Schumann *Symphonies* had occupied hours of record-nerdly activity. I followed the new Bernstein interpretations with scores of each symphony, comparing them to other conductors' versions: Carnegie's own Béla Czar, Walter, Klemperer, maybe Karajan.

It was the first VIP Lounge I'd ever seen or heard tell of. I don't know how many of these the City of Carnegie maintained, given their distance from the big time, but this one had the biggest table I'd sat at to date. Bennett set up the mic and plugged in the recorder. I was thinking Schumann would be a good starting point, because the ads for the concert announced "Schumann, *Symphony No. 3, Rhenish*" and I was sure he could talk long enough for me to pick up something from his answer to lead to my next question.

I said "TEST, 1-2-3" for Bill and noticed in a mirror on the paneled wall that the part in my still-wet hair was crooked as Hansel and Gretel's path in the woods.

A wave of energy came off him as his party entered our lounge, four or five overdressed Fifth Avenue types. He was smaller than I'd expected; shorter than I! He beamed a big grin, and I grinned back.

I said something like: "I should have known I'd love your Schumann."

"Yes? Good. The slow movement of the *Fourth* wasn't too fast?" He was smiling radiantly, maybe forty-five, and sooooo good looking.

"It was fast, but not too fast." *Was it too fast? Did I know the difference?*

The next thing I knew it was an hour later and I hadn't noticed the passage of time, the importuning faces of his retainers, even Bennett signaling he had to change tapes. Only this beautiful, warm, sweet man who looked a little like my father and communicated a similar pureness of heart. I felt the whole time to have lived in a dreamland, a weightless world of higher purpose, a secret island in the ocean of his superior presence. I remembered a line from the one song my father had been able to play on the tonette, "Old Black Joe."

Gone from this life to a better life I know…

A better life. Life of the international world-view, and the inviolable universality of the language of great music. His life called out to me: "Keep rising." I didn't, in my Midwestern straightness, dare think that I might be falling in love with him.

"Well, it does seem a very conservative program."

"Conservative?" he showed mild surprise. "Who else would play the Schuman *Third?*"

"The *Rhenish Symphony?* Even Czar plays that and he's nobody's pioneer."

But, of course, by mid-sentence I knew. It came in one of those thank-God-I-figured-it-out revelations: Impresario Buffone had gotten the wrong composer and was out there advertising the *Third ("Rhenish") Symphony* of the German master, Robert Schuma*nn* (2 'n's), an arch-Romantic work of 1850, instead of what Maestro Bernstein and the Philharmonic were prepared to perform: the *Third Symphony* of his colleague, the distinguished American composer William Schuma*n*, (one "n") an occasionally dissonant, almost neo-Stravinskyan work of substantial weight and duration.

Not a pleasant surprise for a large, barely-middlebrow Midwestern audience expecting a jovial orchestral field trip to the Rhineland. I let the truth of the matter sink in and the interview sputtered and died. Struck by the stupidity and moderately aghast, he rose in distraction and began to allow himself to succumb to his handlers. But then the Maestro shook off the various camel's hair sleeves that had swallowed him up as he'd left the table, and came back to grasp my hand in both of his.

"Please come back to the hotel."

"I'm riding with my wife…"

"Bring her." And off he went to Carnegie's waiting limo.

The Schuman/Schumann confusion was the cause of significant audience-buzzing, as well as a certain amount of huffy walkouts during the Symphony. Worse, there was a thirty minute discrepancy between start times as printed on the tickets and those listed in M. Buffone's advance publicity, so advance subscribers tended to walk in during the quiet sections of the Berlioz Overture *Roman Carnival* that opened the star-crossed event. And I said so in my first-ever radio concert review, broadcast and rebroadcast on WCAR in the course of the weekend that followed:

"For Leonard Bernstein and the New York Philharmonic, a triumph of music-making. For *M. Buffone Presents*, a veritable festival of ineptitude, a blundering travesty of concert-giving that can redound only to the everlasting shame of this most musical of American backwaters: that its leading impresario can't find his zipper…" Or words to that effect.

This provoked a shit-storm. Buffone's daughter, Azucena, had called Bennett threatening to cut the station off cold. He'd been concerned, but realized WCAR was, like Buffone, the only game in town. Then Buffone himself called me at Bargain Records, and demanded to talk with the owner. He frothed away with the air of a man giving himself to swatting wildly at a pesky winged critter; pissed and too proud to stop.

"Who are *you?* Who are *you?*" he demanded rhetorically, stressing an almost German o-umlaut "u" sound. I was clearly not expected to respond. "I am Buf-*fone!*" he insisted

"'F*o-ne;*' I understand," I echoed.

"For years I bring de gr-reat stars to CAR-negie," he trumpeted. "Who are you to make de critic?"

"I understand, caro signor Buffone."

"Va-at?"

"For year I paint de paint-ing," I was remembering the joke: *"do they call me ze artiste? But suck one cock…"* Trying desperately to envision life without my job.

"Give me OWNER!" he screamed.

"I'll have him call you, Mr. Buffone," I temporized, never having felt this threatened-therefore-powerful before.

"Who are *you*?! I'll have your job!"

It turned out Don Goodman didn't give a shit what Sgr. Buffone—who, under his artfully constructed Italianate persona, was a Romanian Jew—blustered about, so I rallied to do more of whatever it was they thought worth defending.

Don was a wonderful guy to work for, but as the Vietnam War dragged on, and I became more an outspoken opponent of our involvement in Southeast Asia on the radio, a fissure began to yawn between us. There was, for example, my support for a local Beat poet, g.a. levin, whose radical paper the *De-classed Dharma Diaries* I helped to encourage by conning record companies to do co-op ads in it. We distributed the *DDD* on the front counters of our main record stores, where they were snapped up like catfish at a Baptist wedding.

They later found g.a. levin dead in his one-room ghetto apartment, on top of a hunting rifle.

One night Don was sitting with his sizeable family around the lazy-Susan style table in their suburban gentleman's farm, when the topic of Firing Mitch came up.

"Bill Weiss says Mitch is a Communist," Don started. He had been a Marine Corps Colonel.

"What?" popped up Jimmy, one of Don's four boys.

"And he's not the only one. Tommy Cohen says he's attacking the President..."

"Dad!" Jimmy was on his feet.

"They all say it. Mitch's bad for business. That he's dangerous. They say I should get rid of him."

"All the kids love Mitch," Jimmy lectured. "He's the one playing all the new music that they buy. You can't fire *Mitch!*"

So he didn't. Besides, the Bernstein interview was widely perceived as great work for a Local, and, in the spring of 1966, when WCAR signed the Carnegie Symphony to a series of syndicated in-concert broadcasts, they offered the job of weekly intermission host to good-old standup Mitch.

I submitted a list of ten questions for the opening show to Béla Czar's secretary. The brilliant conductor/music director was so high strung as we sat in his elegant green leather and wood-paneled Rockefeller Hall office, that while answering something challenging and confrontive like "How would you rate Severance Hall's acoustics?" he bent his gold Mark Cross pen so far in half it actually snapped.

In 1970, Béla Czar took sick suddenly while on tour with his orchestra in Asia, and died soon after landing back in the US. By then, interviews with jazz, rock, political and cultural figures had become a regular feature of my all-nighter underground show on 'CAR, *Hertz Happens.* My seven-year stint with the Carnegie Symphony was about to come screeching to a halt with conductor Eugene Ormandy, who complained about my beard and long hair—two weeks after I announced to Bennett that I was leaving Bargain Records. Then it was announced that Leonard Bernstein would conduct—his only time ever with our Symphony—in the official Czar Memorial Concert: the Mahler *Second* in the bucolic splendor of Daisy Center.

"Just a press conference? No interviews? Whataya want me to do with a press conference?" I asked Bennett.

"Hijack it, Mitch. Who's going to be there to challenge you?"

He was right. The local "classical" music media was not rich in derring-do. The press conference stumbled around in familiar territory as I sandbagged, letting my colleagues, the Music Critics and commentators, fetch the Maestro's predictions for the future role of the symphony orchestra. "A museum," he told them. Then I slickly moved the agenda:

"Pop music in the Sixties was greatly influenced by your own *West Side Story*, which did a lot of things socially as well as musically, and reached a spec*ta*cular audience, of course, on the Broadway stage and in movies." The usual get-em-on-your-side Gushorama. "Do you think that something like *Hair…* " I paused, searching for the polite way to put it, in awe.

"…could have a similar influence?" He made me sound good.

"Right."

"First there's a difference between *Hair* and 'something like it…'"

"Right."

"I don't think that *Hair* will have a lasting influence except for its form, or for*mat*, because it really doesn't have a form. I've seen *Hair* now for the third time and it's the first time I've liked it. I saw it in Vienna in the German language…"

"Did you like the music?"

"Not particularly, I like a couple of songs…the last song, and I like 'Frankie Mills' very much, very sweet song…wry and cute. None of it is of any particular importance, but something *like Hair,* as you put it, written by… *written…*really *written.* "

"The last time that you and I talked, we discussed a thing that you were working on, from Thornton Wilder's *The Skin of Their Teeth* that was…"

"…about five years ago…a sad subject, 'cause it all collapsed…in collaboration…"

"The question I ask is that with your unquestioned *powers* for communication in so many different areas and your ability to *write* music that would be better than *Hair*, presumably…" (groping) "…are you now interested in writing…"

"I don't think it would be better if I tried to write *rock* music, for example. I don't think I could write a better…or even as good…"

"You don't think so?"

"Probably not. I've never tried."

"What is the music of *West Side Story*?"

"It's not rock."

"What is it?"

"It's *pre-*…I don't know what it is…it's the music of *West Side Story*…" (chuckles) "I can't pigeonhole *that.*"

"Well, would you be interested in writing something that…that…"

"*Yes!*"

"…pretends toward…some kind of…the fashionable word is…"

"Yes…"

"…or the post-fashionable word is 'relevance,' that kind of…"

"Yes, that's what's been hanging me up, these five years since we talked, that's one of the reasons *Skin of Their Teeth* didn't reach completion. And I've had two similar projects since then on which I've spent anywhere from six months to a year on each one. One of them was an enterprise involving Jerome Robbins, based on a little Brecht play called *The Exception and the Rule*, which is nothing if not 'relevant' and, could have been, I still think, the most exciting theater piece that Broadway has ever had…and it just didn't work out, after a year of very hard labor. And we parted; gave it up. The third was a film project, an all-musical film, which I was planning with Franco Zeffirelli on the life of Saint Francis, and I spent six months on that one. And our ideas began to diverge more and more, and we saw after five months or so that it was not going to be possible to have any unanimity of feeling, so I had to give *that* up. And the result is that I have piles of music lying around of unfinished things and nowhere to use them because they're all so particularly specific, relevant to the given project. And in these cases the point I'm trying to make is that this 'relevance' problem is the one that usually hangs us up as collaborators, and I haven't quite figured out *why.* It may have something to do with our generation, with an unwillingness to *pander* to youth by pretending we are, because we aren't…we're the Pre-Hiroshima generation and the kids are post-…and a great unwillingness on my part to take advantage of current trends, sort of get on a bandwagon, do pseudo-rock nonsense. In other words, it's a matter of finding out exactly what I can do *now.* I would have known if I'd continued, if I'd continued after *West Side Story* and written the next show and the next and the next. I think by now…"

The dozen or so assembled scribes drew breath. Less than a gasp, it was nevertheless a collective intake audible on the tape, yet subtle enough to elude their conscious detection. The maestro looked down at the table. The moment hung in the late spring air. Then he sighed, a deep sigh as if from an excavation. I held my breath.

"…I would have found what I was looking for." A broad grin, a smile of release. "But for better or for worse, I did accept the NY Philharmonic at that point…"

"I do recall that…" Trying to help him find easier terrain.

"That was '57—that was thirteen years ago. Long time. And I was *ab*-solutely sure at that point that there were *dozens* of young kids around, composers, theater people who would leap in and take the next step after *West Side Story*, which pointed a direction, it seems to me, having broken ground that was fairly clear. But, instead the contrary has happened to the Broadway musical scene. It's retrogressed, fearfully; it's gone back to *Mame*s and *Hello Dolly*s, which represent the infancy of, and the infantilism of the American musical theater instead of having taken a step forward. There are a couple of exceptions to that. *Company* is one exception, by Steve Sondheim; *Fiddler on* *the Roof* made some attempts, but I don't think it's really first class material."

"But there are other kinds of 'relevance' without, as you say, pandering to a youth-market. You don't have to write rock 'n' roll music…"

"That isn't all I mean by relevance…"

"…or take advantage of the trends and trendiness of writing for the market, you could certainly do other things—it *seems* (of course it's easy to say)…"

"I'd have to pick up the pieces from 1957 now…" He looked at me, his face a composite of pure mammalian forlornity and radiant angelic hope.

The next morning I was sitting around in my nightshirt, drinking black coffee, and listening to "On Sir Francis Drake" by the Youngbloods when the phone rang. It was Carnegie Symphony Manager Bob Goldfarb:

"Lenny wants to see you."

"Lenny who?"

Was I, perhaps, stoned? It's possible, despite the early hour.

"Leonard Bernstein! He's staying down in Aurora, near Blossom Center. Give him a call."

I thought for a minute about recent rumors of Lenny's *penchant* for young men, then decided that with my scroffulent *muzhik* beard, long hair and munchie-generated crescent gut, I'd be an unlikely seduction target. So, rolling a couple of joints—Lenny'd been attacked in a Tom Wolfe piece on what the author called "radical chic"—I got in the mustard Porsche 911-6 I was borrowing and headed down the turnpike for Aurora.

"My contract with CBS is up for renewal in September," he began, "and this new person, this Cashman, this lawyer, is not necessarily a friend of our music."

Jeremy Cashman had just taken over the reins as President of Columbia Records from Lenny's old friend, Goddard Lieberson.

"He's just discovered rock'n'roll," I agreed, "So it's doubtful he has time for much else. I was in Puerto Rico when he waddled out on stage in a white Nehru suit to take the helm from Goddard. What a joke!"

"Well, we'll find out soon. We're going to ask for a Leonard Bernstein Department, funded by CBS. If they accept, they can distribute what they refer to as my 'product'…and I intend to do everything in video *and* audio…if they turn us down, we'll go over to the Germans—Polygram has made us a generous offer."

I was sitting there in institutional air-conditioned darkness at midday, trying to dope it out. Why is this icon sitting here telling me his business secrets? And: does he want my body? And: should I offer him a joint? Of course, he sensed my confusion.

"So, I'd like to discuss hiring you to run this new division, should they show the good sense to accept our proposal.

Yes! "And why are you asking *me?*"

I couldn't accept that this casual meeting with a local Carnegie hippie was seriously intended.

"You must know that I was impressed with what you said yesterday…and of course there was that fiasco with Buffone way back when."

He remembers! And he likes me!

"And when you asked about a new *West Side Story* I started thinking maybe you're the person to help me get to a project like that, find a suitable— relevant—script. Could you even write something yourself?"

Is he asking me?!?

"So I'm offering you a many-faceted job: produce my world-wide tours and recordings, look out for my interests at CBS and help me find a book from which to make a socially valuable theater piece for the present political circumstances. Conditional upon Jeremy's acceptance of our proposition."

"He'd be a fool to turn you down," I pledged.

"Turn *us* down," he ventured in friendship, "and he certainly qualifies."

We talked for about two hours. We never did smoke a joint. Nor did he ever make anything like a pass at me.

I spent the weekend in and out of his dressing room at Blossom, watching him rehearse the mighty *Resurrection Symphony* by his predecessor Jewish composer/conductor, the divine Gustav Mahler. Finally, Saturday night, soprano and alto soloists, Carnegie Symphony and Symphony Chorus filled the dripping Empire County air with a message to Béla Czar's distant but abiding spirit:

> *O glaube, mein Herz, o glaube,*
> *es geht dir nichts verloren!*
> *Dein ist, was du gesehnt,*
> *dein was du geliebt,*
> *was du gestritten!*

> *(O believe, my heart*
> *that no trace of you will be lost!*
> *What you longed for is yours forever;*
> *What you loved and would have given your life for!)*

He had asked for some of my writing and accepted my offer to write a *Dona Nobis Pacem* for his just-commissioned *Mass* for the opening of Kennedy Center. I dashed off some sample verses in what I thought was simple rhythmic popular style, based on the image of all generations of mankind inhabiting the Earth simultaneously, with the possibility that at any given moment, the Bomb could expunge Past, Present and Future in a single MIRV. A Peace Poem, talkin' 'bout:

> *…till Peace strides like a Panther…*

I had been impressed by his support for the Black Panther Party. Soon I had a letter from Schuyler Chapin, head of Lenny's New York-based production company, Amberson, confirming our potential relationship:

"Lenny has told us about you; that you're 'absolutely extraordinary' and I'm delighted to…etc., etc." And later, one from the Maestro himself, from Vienna:

I went to see Jeremy personally. I'm sorry to say he all but said 'Lenny who?' I fear our enterprise is at an end. I start talks with die Deutscher next Tuesday.

Thanks, B

By the time I got this fateful communiqué I had quit Bargain Records, been dumped by 'CAR, and gotten fairly well entrenched at one of the new breed of progressive rock stations that had surfaced in Carnegie, with my own air shift as well as an hour weekly interview show.

In the fullness of time Jeremy Cashman overcame being fired as President of Columbia Records for allegedly spending company funds on his son's ultra-Bar Mitzvah, to become a "Magic-Eared God" of pop music. "The Germans," as Lenny called them, went laughing all the way to the Deutschbank with the residuals from Bernstein "product." And I became a radio "personality" in what was becoming Album Oriented Rock, as I allowed The Counterculture to simply sweep me away in a new social direction altogether. My heart was off to L.A. and all that that entailed.

PART THREE

Hope and Fear are equally illusions.

—*Kadak Pawo*

Tree flew in to Los Angeles the week after Trout was fired. The genius production-kid from Carnegie finally arrived in the big time. While other rock stations offered jangly stoner-antagonistic commercials, Tree lovingly wove the music around the announcer's voice, creating totally original thirty-to-sixty-second stand-alone aural masterworks. I heard the spots as music, as mini-singles, and was drawn in by the levels and textures. Sometimes it was my voice, with maybe George Duke's electric piano behind me, or John McLaughlin's guitar, or an extract that Tree rescued from some otherwise useless LP. Counterpoint was not too pretentious a concept. Point against point. Tree himself couldn't explain it. He just felt it and did it.

He was untraveled, and unknown outside a tiny nerdly coterie in Carnegie. The Head was lying in wait for what he perceived as Tree's youthful college-less ignorance. Sniffing this, Tree's nostrils flared, and he decided to move down the hall from me, his only L.A. friend, into the Lido Hotel.

Adrienne and I had just been on our first real date, a showing of *State of Siege* at Charles Adikoff's little screening room on Sunset. The new Costa-Gavras movie was a true story of the CIA training South American cops to kill dissidents. I watched Adrienne with interest, looking for signs. I was pretty sure her politics were tenderfoot anti-war radical like my own.

She was a "Sixties person," as opposed to "straight." Wore jeans and her hair long. Smoked dope casually and socially. Shared general human attitudes, and so, I simply assumed, similar experiences. She'd been in the UCLA film class that Jim Morrison walked out of. One of us. She was one of us. Adrienne smiled softly when she saw me looking. Later I suggested we stop at my place.

"Okay," she said.

For the occasion I had gotten my old Caddy running, the funky but imposing black Sedan de Ville with "TONGUE" license plates, and we arrived at the Lido without disgrace.

When I opened the door to my "suite," Tree sat at the kitchen table chopping lines of cocaine on a Disneyland mirror, Minnie's likeness veiled in thin white granules. Slumped opposite was Don Hall, a part-time weekend jock at KURB, whose special love was film music, and who dealt drugs to the hip media community: weed, acid, coke, 'ludes, mushrooms, even peyote and opium, when the occasion required.

I turned to introduce Adrienne as the boys snapped to, and found her studying the large blowup of the "Naked Mauser," that the *Star* had presented me for my troubles. She produced a noncommittal face and came over to meet my friends.

We spent an hour polishing off the last gram or two that John had with him.

"Want I should go score some more?" he asked, barely conscious.

"Where is it?" Tree asked, before I could say a word.

"At my pad. Burbank. Just take a minute," he said. "On me."

"No thanks," I told him. "Tree, can I have a word with you?"

He levered his tall frame to a standing posture, whipped his long hair around in a circle, more of a strut than a vision-enhancement, and ambled off to join me at the big curved window that overlooked the singular squalor of back-alley Hollywood.

"Well," he began through desiccated lips, "it looks like Ms. Adrienne is every bit the goddess you painted her. Definitely statuesque…"

"Thanks," I acknowledged. "But I can hang with you cats any old time. While Adrienne's time may be limited…"

"So, like, could we bozos kindly get the fuck outta here? No problem."

Adrienne and I had our first night of love there on the floor of the Lido, and despite the usually deflationary affects of *la coca*, I found myself immediately whipping off my jeans, my purple silk Jockeys stretched tight across my extended longing. As the morning cracked and slowly spread over Wilcox and Yucca, a twin realization dawned on me: I would soon have to be up to drive Tree to KURB for his first day of work and I was probably in at least deep-like with this woman.

I turned off Highland onto Wilshire, smiling over at Tree. He smiled back, then flipped back into serious first-day game face. *It will be good for me to work with Tree again,* I thought as we rolled west. *He could use a friend right now, and come to think of it, so could I.* We approached the two odd little side-by-side office buildings housing KURB-FM.

"I still feel weird about running out on the gang."

"I can dig it."

"They were great, all the WURB folks. Threw me a far-out party. Renda even gave me a blowjob! Remember Screaming Queen Bitch?"

"Renda Mycznewicz, right? The lesbian."

"Right. Trout got her to blow me."

"At a party? In front of everybody?"

"Maa-a-an! No, in Trout's bed. First we did some 'shrooms."

"Really."

"Yeah, Tommy told me, 'Forget us, pal. Forget me, forget Carnegie. This is your shot. Like, how many of these do ya think you're gonna get in this life? Get on it!'"

"And here you are," the classic early Firesign Theater line we'd come to use as a rhythm lick between us.

Now I really felt it. My responsibility for his coming to L.A. in the first place, recommending him for the production manager job at KURB over a bunch of older guys, encouraging him to come, picking him up at the airport, helping him find a place to stay at the Lido, driving him over for this first morning on the gig.

We neared the brontosaurus that rose high over the stinky petroleum pits, glowering at traffic passing on the Miracle Mile, now falling to ruin, between the Art Deco May Company on Fairfax and the dinky station buildings. Then we spotted the men with their picket signs.

"*Fuck me* if they didn't finally go out!"

"Huhhnnnn?" Tree didn't know.

"I.B.E.W.! The fucking engineers! They've been working without a contract since January. Fuck!!!"

I felt a quick chill, a reminder of how liquid—like a sudden diarrhea—the transition from joy to mortal anguish can be. Tree didn't know exactly what a "scab" was, but he did know he was far from comforted by the sight of the eight or ten middle-aged men in windbreakers and plastic baseball caps trudging silently around in a flattened circle under the station's modest marquee.

KURB was a union shop, the jocks all represented by American Federation of Television and Radio Artists (AFTRA). It was my first trade union experience. My father had belonged to the AMA, a viciously conservative craft guild, and one he supported nonetheless with near-religious loyalty, honoring its exclusionary mandates despite his generally hyper-democratic world-view. Between his ethical example and Injury-to-One-is-an-Injury-to-All attitude I was perfectly pre-conditioned for the trade union movement. His Ethos had two features:

1) fundamentally anti-authoritarian personality;
2) First-Gen-American's commitment to egalitarian values.

He supported Negro doctors, and helped "colored" professionals buy homes in Baker Heights. He gave me a perspective far to the left of most classmates at my prep school. Though hardly a Red Diaper Baby, I was acquainted with Marx's famous, "It is right to rebel."

Actually, at the time of my joining AFTRA I had read almost no Marx. The Manifesto, and a few other readings in *Contemporary Civilization* at Columbia, was about it. My radicalism in radio had been built on a very slight prior engagement in the Civil Rights Movement as well as the usual readings—*Animal Farm; Hiroshima; 1984; Brave New World;* Kafka, Mailer, Brecht—and not much more. True, I had been raised in a household wherein the pocket-socialist *PM* joined *Life, Esquire* and *The New Yorker* as regular bathroom reading. I'd lived through the televised McCarthy hearings, condemned the banning of The Weavers and was a moderate follower of Pogo and Lenny Bruce. As a student of Philosophy, I had been trained in critical thinking, become an atheist, marched in local Civil Rights demos and been appalled by the growing US involvement in Southeast Asia. Later, I read Mark Lane's *Rush to Judgment,* subscribed to *Evergreen Review,* I.F. Stone's *Weekly,* and the *L.A. Free Press* with Ron Cobb's brilliant political cartoons. I had been devoted to R. Crumb, who was a frequent guest on *Hertz Happens!* back in Carnegie. But nothing more radical than that.

It was all of this that predilected me toward union militancy. As an AFTRA member, and through the open eyes of a would-be union activist, it was clear to me that I'd been set up by The Head in a covert and loathsomely clever way. Poor Tree, flown two thousand miles to break a strike.

"Just get out here, make spots, start your career. Ticket to the Big Time." He was six months from his twentieth birthday, in L.A. a day and a half. Being as tall as he was helped. People always thought he was maintaining. And maybe he was.

"That cold mother*fuck*er!" The rage of useless defeat. "That vicious union-busting shit-eating *Head!*"

I muffled our humbled oars, circled the block to avoid the guys, and I dropped Tree at the back door. He didn't wave as he slipped inside.

Suddenly, as I pulled out onto Spaulding, I was immensely sleepy, easier prey to guilt. *It's me,* I told myself. *My fool fault for setting his ass up.* Fighting to stave off a deep, nameless fear, I ruminated on a quotation:

To remove illusions is to set the stage for removing the source of the need to create illusions.

As I guided the old Caddy through the Superfly streets of downtown Hollywood, my brain was a brush-fire—flaring and fading, then flaring again. The issue of *Star* with the naked picture was just hitting the stands. There was a groundswell of support for this most recent sex-centered and thus audience-building provocation. My fellow jocks had been barely lukewarm, as usual, but KURB's Sales Manager plumped for turning the huge centerfold into a station poster.

Entering my Lido rooms, I heard the phone. The Filipino political exile that ran the desk had a message. "The Head wants to see you."

Norman Woodeheadd's office was the only authentic executive space that city-hippie KURB had to show for itself or, in fact, required. The small room was over-decorated and always darkened a la *'77 Sunset Strip*, and directly overlooked the La Brea Tar Pits. The Head would have blended well with the scaly critters buried outside his window. He was only five years older than I, but with his Michelin Tire-man physique, pasty skin, slicked down hair and penchant for powder blue or maroon suits (in an era of Levi-Straussian hegemony) he always looked like the delegate from the past.

"New York thinks we've gone too far with this sex deal. Somebody's gotta go."

I was blinking really fast. "Why me, Norman?"

He stared at me as if struggling to master his own mind.

"Come on, man."

Nothing. Just the cheekbones moving as his teeth gritted laboriously, holding back whatever he was thinking. Letting out the line.

"I didn't dream up the Naked Wall."

His gimlet eyes glared impassive. I ran with the hook.

"Or that damn parade. The Sushi, Coke and Panties thing."

"Mitchell."

"Norman, this is bullshit. Is it the naked picture?"

"Well…"

"Norman, you know damn well you guys okayed that picture yourselves."

"It's not that stupid picture."

"What then?" I was losing control.

"You know what, Hertz. Corporate wants all this foolish sex stuff stopped."

"But why me?"

"I can get you double severance if you go quietly."

"You told me to go ahead with the photo, damn it!"

"I'll let you keep an office here while you look for work. Otherwise…"

The Head proceeded, one-at-a-time, to fire the entire KURB staff, consigning their careers to the relative obscurity of National Public Radio, the TV Networks and feature films. Only The Head himself stayed on in commercial radio, transforming an indomitably outrageous freeform mind-altering broadcast jewel into a docile, enormously profitable, play-listed plastic-hippie corporate lapdog, until one of his secretaries accused him of beating her within an inch of her life. Then he became a Consultant.

As for me, the last thing I did was to work on part of the station's coverage of the Wounded Knee uprising. Then I headed off to find…more Fear, I guess.

Fuck 'em all! Fuck these infantile fears of the dark. Are there monsters lying in wait in the room? Why pray for someone else to turn on the light? Fuck these fears, this psychic darkness at noon. Blow it off! Turn on your own light. Be a lantern unto yourself! Anything beats living in fear. Wasn't it the divine Emiliano Zapata that said: "Better to die on your feet than live on your knees"?

However, while painting myself the Fear-Slayer, I would at the same time always question the role of my own desperation, masquerading as revolutionary appetite—fed-upness with my former life, a horrible sinking fear that I'd come down the wrong path and would give anything to change direction. But the ritual calling-out of fear, and the attempt to kick its ass, was exhilarating. Surely this stupid naked picture was my own personal symbol of Just Say No! to Fear.

The Mauser was there to accentuate the imperative, aimed point blank at that great stifler of thought, cruel jailer of souls, cold-blooded murderer of minds. *I WILL NOT FEAR*—*but* you *might consider it*. And as our grand-mammies used to tell us:

"*Sometimes you eat the bear. Sometimes the bear eats you…*"

This time, maybe, I was ursine enchilada, but deep down I *knew* that next time—maybe not *every* time, but *next* time—I would garrote that Grizzly.

Bowie's "Ch-Ch-Ch-Ch-Changes" was on the Caddy's AM radio. Tree was in shock from the taunts of the displaced union guys every time he crossed their picket lines. "Scab! Traitor! Hippie!" That and the dull realization that The Head had him doing the work of three guys. Three guys with families. Kids. Some of them Tree's age, probably. As we headed up past Curson, he looked sick.

"Can you go back to Carnegie?"

He stared off at the summer sun streaking the hills pink. Eyes bared, squinting slightly. In pain.

"Is your job still open at WURB?"

"Fuck it!" he finally grunted. "I'm here."

I nodded and headed the Caddy east on Sixth Street, past La Brea, across Highland, finally heading north on Cole, still bathed in slowly setting sun.

"What about you?" he asked at last.

One of the forces that brought us together was a shared interest in getting and staying high. Tree and I were only recreational users but we recreated a lot. We strove to bring that play-and-pleasure quality into the workplace and thus, through the work itself, to the audience. Drugs were a shortcut to positive energy. We looked at the straight world, with its degrading reality of draft boards and police, as survivable if and only if one was supplied with the proper admixture of inebriants.

"Let's get high."

The first thing I did after depositing my KURB severance check was move back into the Beachwood Canyon house, Senta had bought a house for her and the kids in low-middle-funky Venice. I fixed in place a fiendish denial-beaming smile for my erstwhile coworkers while I began the process of professional relocating. I cashed my life insurance policies, and started to make a home again. Tree moved in downstairs, where my three boys had had their own floor—complete with a kitchen and direct access to the pool. Adrienne and I shared the top two floors, and bought a rubber water bed. Smoked dope all the time. Drank a little. Coke when someone else had it. No orgy scene, or anything; just me and my new honey. A pre-nesting phase snuggle-fest. Pleasure.

Adrienne, with all those cute younger sisters, her lovely, long-suffering Southern Belle mother, and her father, with the presence of a giant. He wasn't really tall; maybe 5'11"or so, but big-boned, extra-stocky, and very, very strong. Handsome, with blue eyes and dark hair, he appeared every inch the man of action.

Stan Dresser had been in OSS in Europe for most of WWII, a demolition sergeant. Every night since the war, at least one or more of the perhaps thirty people he killed at close quarters would make a nightmare appearance. He'd turned down suitors from both the CIA and the Chicago Mob and began a series of romantic financial ventures that kept the family peregrinating across the Caribbean and then California. Diving schools, helicopter schools, diamonds, you name it. Stan had a whale of a time, but the family suffered. Adrienne attended so many schools by the time they landed for good in Burbank that her only friends were her family.

Through Tree, I retained a connection to the rock reality that was metastasizing onto Hollywood, with its publicists spraying free goods—LPs, T-shirts and comps, sometimes dope, all on somebody else's dime. In one valedictory 24-hour period I was taken to the L.A. Coliseum by the president of Green Finger Records, then to see Paul Simon, then to an after-hours party at a Sunset Strip bistro hosted by Mel Brooks where his new movie *Blazing Saddles* was being screened.

Our host had started the cocaine in the Mercedes 600 limo on the way to the game, producing a large salt-Baker, sprinkling the powder on a fold-down mirror, chopping continuously as we crept along the newly installed "diamond lane" on the Hollywood Freeway, handing each of us (there was a blonde "girl" publicist and the label's Art Director) a crisp new $100 bill, which we duly rolled and snorted the proffered thick white lines, each "chased" with Dom Perignon drunk from crystal snifters subtly branded with the Green Finger logo.

The publicist made a big show of lifting her denim skirt as she bent into the mirror, her marvelous thighs glinting white and firm in the darkened cabin, and we were all treated to long periods when her flower-print panties were on almost constant display. By the time we arrived in our upper boxes, we were internally adjusted to compensate for the tragic boredom of the Rams' offense, watching Lester Josephson gain 2.8 yards per carry as we passed the spoon there on the 45-yard line, in front of 70,000 sullen and sepulchral Rams fans.

That night I went to see Paul Simon at the Santa Monica Civic Auditorium. The promo man at Columbia was the guy who'd introduced me to Zappa, and had been a biz-pal ever since. So there I sat in the absolute front row of the Civic, coked-up pretty good. The tiny Simon perched on a stool no more than ten feet away, singing "Was a Sunny Day," "Mother and Child Reunion," and all the other great tunes I'd played for my radio audiences. Long, sad thoughts. *Have I blown it? Is it over?* Then comes my favorite, "borrowed" from a Bach chorale, "American Tune."

I don't know a dream that's not been shattered or driven to its knees…

The coke, the music. Lost in reverie shared with the beautiful hippie couple next to me, all in white, blonde hair co-mingling as they swayed to the soulful sounds, arms wrapped around each other—a unanimity of bliss. *Connected. We are all connected.* Suddenly, in mid-chorus, a disturbance. Elevated brain registered: *Turbulence; the hippies being moved, ushered out, connection severed.* Before I could react, another couple was ushered clumsily in: guy, maybe forty and bald, gray business suit and solid tie; woman, maybe thirty, with bleached hair and a yellow pants suit, taking their places to my left. Paul Simon sang:

Oh, but it's all right, it's aa-a-a-ll right, we've lived so well so long…

I glanced over at the guy. An earpiece with a little cord disappeared into his suit jacket. *CIA agent?* Then I reached for the coke bottle. At the interval, the hip-radio people coalesced at the front, stage-left. The coke dulled my humiliation for being newly dumped. Instead, I took a fierce, out-spoken radical posture.

"Who the fuck is this guy?" I demanded.

"Paul Somebody, the new PD at KDLR, the RKO Top-40 station," veteran Mal Freed put in mildly. "Why?"

"Sitting there with a plug in his ear…"

"Probably listening to his own station," said the ameliorating Griff Gonzo, KURB Perky Morning Guy.

"At a fucking Paul *Simon* concert?" I insisted.

"Maybe he's checking for dead air."

"Time's expensive at K-Dollar," put in Dr. Demento.

"Mitch is right. That's *fucked!*" said the voice of Tim Boye, the handsome young radical from KURB's closest rival, KBCA, part of the BCA (Broadcasting Corporation of America) network. KBCA had started the trend to changing the designation from "Underground" or "Progressive" Rock to "Album Oriented Rock" radio. AOR was an obvious attempt to transform our heretofore socially-minded concept of "Audience" into the market-oriented term "Demographic." A whorish corporate wink at the record companies before diving sackward together.

Tim was the designated house "firebrand," talking tough in a New Age-y kind of way, playing the few politicaloid album tracks the play-list would allow: "Street Fighting Man," "Woodstock," lots of The Who, Dylan and Grateful Dead. His worst sin of over-reaching was conducting what I called "un-terviews," putative interviews which somehow always manage to feature him:

TB: *"So, Joni Mitchell—what's the story behind 'Big Yellow Taxi'?"*

JM: *"Well, one day in New York…"*

TB: *"I was just in New York. Where do you stay? At the Chelsea? I love the Chelsea. What's the story behind 'Chelsea Morning'?"*

JM: *"Well, my friend Neil Young and I…"*

TB: *"I just played a Neil Young track before you got here; he was up here on my show last week…"*

On this occasion, still early in his ascendance to Official Throwback Plastic Hippie status, he was at least ostensibly taking my side, retrieving the shield of the fallen martyr.

"But he's got to keep tabs on his station." This statement of managerial solidarity was from KURB's Program Director, Matt Gatherer.

"He looks like a cop," I said.

"It's the New World Reality: Dig it!" said Tree, who had joined us with one of the KURB Music Librarians, a round curly-haired dolly with a shiny smile.

He wasn't invited to the *Blazing Saddles* party, but I figured if we showed up with the underage girlies we'd be okay, and my sense of things was confirmed by the cheery welcome of the Warner Brothers people when we show up at Hector's around midnight and joined the party. As the lights dimmed, the librarian found a way to lie down with her face in my lap.

When the three of us first set up house in Beachwood Canyon, we would go out together in my newly-acquired 1954 pink and crème Ford Victoria with Ford-o-matic. Tree would accompany, but he'd always dump us, in his never-ending search for female companionship. He was a hit at KURB with the jocks, and a smash with the advertisers, for whom he worked his razor-fingered magic, even if it was only a thirty-second spot for a Drag Race. "SUNDAY! SUNDAY!" And Tree was psychedelically good. Even in L.A. he was considered an artist. The jocks who sniffed at me had mascotted him after only a few weeks.

Tucked away in the big house under the Hollywood sign, we had our fun. Occasional guacamole and drug parties. Adrienne's pneumatic sister Lana asked if she could bring a boyfriend for a swim in our pool. I watched from the third-floor dining room as she stared up at me and slowly bared her twenty-five-year-old fleshly resplendence, tits first, then proceeded to give me and many of my grateful neighbors—it was a horseshoe canyon at 3:00 in the afternoon—an unforgettable fifteen minutes by fucking his luckiness blind before our envying eyes.

Senta had left behind the old Ivers & Pond grand in the huge high-ceilinged hall. I had started playing the piano again for the first time in years: Scarlatti *Sonatas*, Bach *Partitas* and the *Italian Concerto*, Handel *Suites*. I fired up the big Yamaha sound system and played Adrienne her first Mozart: the *23rd Piano Concerto*, with Friedrich Gulda conducting from the keyboard. She closed her eyes and took it in. I was beginning to improvise, in a primitive kind of way, on pop, blues, and even country. One time she started to hum along with something, broke into song and a lovely country-folkish voice emerged.

"You can sing!"

"I learned a few things in college."

"Like what things?"

"Oh, you know, the usual: Joni Mitchell, Joan Baez, some Dylan."

I started to pick out "The Song about the Midway" by Joni and it turned out Adrienne knew all the verses. Foraging through the piano bench produced *The Judy Collins Song Book*, and I paged through to easy harmonizing tunes: "Mr. Tambourine Man," "My Ramblin' Boy," "The Last Thing on my Mind," and "Deportee."

At first she had trouble with singing harmony, so I assigned her melody parts and I found a voice I'd never had as a Mozart/Schubert baritone, a soft but in-focus voice that could range above-the-staff with ease, picking out altogether acceptable folkish harmonies on song after song.

"Just listen, I'll sing melody and you see if you can hear a harmony part and just let 'er fly." With a little practice she did it brilliantly. We flowed together in unforced natural consonance. By focusing on blending with her, I somehow learned to accompany us both and sing at the same time, a combination which had seemed impossible to me till then, but which became the most natural of acts.

At the end of the month, I was commissioned to write a hippie-friendly booklet on Classical Music for Licorice Pizza, a youth-oriented So-Cal record retailer. I drafted a few chapters, including, "There are Negroes in the Museums" and "Opera Before *Tommy*," which met with such initial praise that I sold an old friend at RCA Red Seal on a series of classical LPs for rockers. He, in turn, went to his sister entity Random House and pitched my book to go with his projected series of LPs, with the result that I was shoehorned into a deal and began a rather funny and mostly informative tome: *Roll Your Own Beethoven: A Punk's Guide to the Classics.*

A week later, a battered yellow Rambler wagon pulled up to our hillside entrance and, direct from a trek to Mexico, came the Glovers: my beloved sister Lily, her husband Barney, their two girls and a babysitter.

I'd always been spooked by radical intellectual Barney. He was a charismatic lecturer, dazzling in synthesizing ad hoc vast quanta of Western civilization into an attack on US involvement in Vietnam. Barney was brilliant, under his control-obsessed blustering. In the few times we were obliged to accept social proximity, I tried to be as open to him as I could, without being drawn into a *mano-a-mano.* He had all the provocateur's tricks: talking over you, leering a long-toothed smile, and allowing a condescending giggle to overtake the answer to any statement you were foolish enough to be baited into making. He was also a world champion eye-roller.

When the Carnegie Symphony broadcasts fired me as Intermission Host, or rather, let me hear from others that I'd been replaced, Lily and Barney had come from Boston—in those days, full of poetry and revolution. We gathered with the Glovers at our parents' house. I'd begun to let my hair grow over my collar.

"Mitch...the Carnegie Symphony...I heard they dumped you." Barney started sincere, but ended with a characteristic nervous deprecating giggle.

"More or less…" I pondered the chasm.

"Do you think they're hoping for more or less revenue?"

"Probably just less embarrassment. Ormandy said I looked like a hippie."

"Oh, so he complained to the Symphony management?"

"I guess." I had only heard rumors. "No one ever called to explain."

"I'm impressed…" he burlesqued.

"I beg your pardon?" Now I'd gone and done it.

"…with the icy imperial elegance. Wouldn't have figured Carnegie for the chops to finesse that kind of kiss-off."

"I guess it depends on your analysis…" I was groping for a spacer.

"What is *your* analysis?" Barney was now chuckling openly.

"Is there more wine?" I shot a look at Lily, who held a bottle to a tiny mouth.

"I know what my analysis is," he lampooned. Why wasn't I surprised? "It's simply the ruling class closing ranks, and drawing the class-line across your butt."

"What are you calling a 'class'?" Not that I wanted to know. I'd always thought of myself as one of the leaders. Part of a ruling apparatus. I did not want to concede inwardly to Barney's lecture—that I was maybe one of the ruled.

"Marx defines a class as having a common interest, expressed in a system of social interstices."

"But lots of people are against the Vietnam War."

"Now that they see they can't win," he laughed in my face.

He was right. I owned nothing, beyond a mortgage. I'd gone to school with the ruling class, and they provided me a living—if I behaved myself.

Barney found the one-volume version of Trotsky's *The Russian Revolution* in a used bookstore, and insisted on buying it for me. That night, when I started reading it, a strange kinesthetic sense of wonder overcame me—memory and revelation that there was something else I needed to know.

Thus far my *Roll Your Own* book had been following predictable lines: hip-oid bio-sketch of the Top-50 "classical" composers, recommending major works (but not specific recordings). That night after dinner, Barney was tired and too fatigued for contention. I read him part of a chapter called "A Day in the Life; or, The Great Composers All Put On Their Trousers One Leg at A Time": Bach being required to teach the choir boys and mass-produce cantatas, Mozart pilloried by the Archbishop of Salzburg for writing "flesh-pot" music, Haydn wearing livery, Beethoven rooting for the French Revolution to wipe out his local aristocracy, and Prokofiev and Shostakovich swallowing Stalin's many knuckles.

Barney listened. I caught Lily fixing me with an unreadable gaze. We talked about how in 1917 Leon Trotsky had come back to help the great Lenin make the Russian Revolution. When Lenin died a few years later, the sullen secret policeman Josef Stalin had stolen the Bolshevik Party, and with it the reins of power from the far "superior" Trotsky, transforming the infant USSR into a jailhouse. Stalin had driven Trotsky into years of exile, finally managing to have him murdered in Mexico.

It appeared now that my sister and brother-in-law had become modern Trotskyists, which meant that they still upheld the Old Man's vision of overthrowing the Soviet Union from the Left, as opposed to from the Right with the CIA et al., by what Trotsky called "Permanent Revolution." Before his assassination Trotsky had founded a "Fourth International," a new, tiny but global revolutionary organization dedicated to this (what seemed to me to be) Sisyphean task.

Barney and Lil were deeply involved in this. First, they had been young faculty anti-war activists at Boston University before moving to Niagara State and becoming really political. Serious. The Anti-war movement was splitting between the majority who sincerely wanted change, and the crazies, as they called them, the anarco-minority of Rage Monsters. My sis was part of a serious revolutionary cadre that eschewed terrorism, adventurism such as the infantilism of Abbie Hoffman's "cultural-revolutionary" YIPPIES, as well as the macho-strutting "Weathermen." Lil and Barney had started out in Students for a Democratic Society (SDS), then came out into the worker-aping but Stalinist Progressive Labor Party and thence joined a small group that split Left out of Trotsky's own but degenerating American grouping, the Socialist Workers Party (SWP).

Before they hit the road for Big Sur, they gave me the name of a guy to call about joining a study group. I had always wanted to be able to say I had read *Capital*. I was at Columbia at the height of the Cold War, so the Communist Manifesto was all I knew of Marx and Marxism. In the early Sixties, when I had turned my back on academe and was clerking at Bargain Records, young Marxist professors had been popping up on campuses all over the country. Slowly, since the time of the Cuban revolution, and at the heart of the antiwar movement, there were more and more astonishingly well-informed graduate students.

There seemed to be a whole school of New Left academics spontaneously emerging from Noam Chomsky's brow. Everywhere you looked there was a Black History or Women's Studies Department. So crowded was the field that rival Black nationalist groupings were shooting each other across town at UCLA. At a time when rebellion, embedded in "rock-attitude," was becoming universal among young people united around opposition to the Vietnam War, the study of Trotsky was for me just the next step.

Things went okay between me and my Random House editor until I began to mistake a work of popular journalism for a pulpit. It was my compulsion in this period to say whatever was on my mind without apparent regard for consequences. My editor loved the first half of the manuscript, but then the class-struggle perspective began finding its way in. One day, she sent it all back, with a note:

"Who do you think you are? This is not the book I committed to. Please return the advance…"

When the Trots asked me to join a picket line at the Gallo Brothers fields outside Merced, I decided to just say "yes" again. I squeezed myself into the back seat of a '58 Falcon between two kids in their mid-twenties. This spontaneous turn towards the working class also meant leaving Adrienne alone with Bruno, who was visiting for the entire weekend—their first time alone together.

When we got to the line it was already scary. Hot muggy morning in the Central Valley, "America's Breadbasket." Helicopters overhead, the Gallos in a robin's egg-blue Coupe de Ville with a white vinyl top. Local cops looming everywhere. And, throughout all this twittering Breughel of a scene, beyond our line, the pickers—some UFW rank and file, some Gallo-herded scabs— kept picking. Their stoop-labor mocked my big-city radical posturing. The Trotskyist position was to give "defense" to the UFW, but not support to their call for consumer boycotts of grapes. "You can't organize housewives," is what we were supposed to be telling the Left. But we showed solidarity with the

Farm Workers physically, putting our bodies on the line. Trying to shut us up, keep us off the picket line, were two or three different groups of jeering Maoists, some honest left-folk trodding the line, who thought we should Just Act Nice. Scared the shit out of me.

Meanwhile, I was being retrofit with a history of Left regroupment since the time of Marx/Engels et al. in the First International; a history that few Americans outside university Political Science or History departments knew, and with a decidedly Trotskyist skew. We Trots were seen variously as "Ultra-left," "sectarian," "splitters and wreckers," "Agents of the Mikado"—some closer to the truth than others. We saw it as our job to pursue Lenin's strategy of "revolutionary regroupment," which meant that we showed up at every Left event we could and did an "intervention," that is, we took the unpopular line of holding out for Trotsky's "Permanent Revolution" in the face of every imaginable variant of what we considered Reformism (pronounced *Ref*-orm-ism; never Re-*form*-ism). Echoing the words of the French Revolutionary plebeian chorus in Peter Weis's *Marat/Sade*:

"We want our Revolution…NOW!!"

Thus we opposed the entire Left *from* the Left. An entire range of fake revolutionaries pushing some brand of bureaucratic accommodation with the bourgeoisie: Stalinists and Maoists (fundamentally identical) pushing two-stage revolution; Nationalists of all colors, ethnicities and genders, pushing some kind of inclusionary token. The Trade unions (UFW, Air Traffic Controllers, etc.) we saw as well-intended but misguided efforts to win the masses to a passive away-from-the-worksite-and-therefore-disoriented strategy of boycotts and harmless protest, ultimately leading to token "black faces in high places," a toothless Farm Labor Board or some such paper solution.

We spent two nights in Central Valley motels together, and I found I had a lot in common with these "comrades." They were mostly younger than I—Sixties kids whose draft resistance had grown into permanent professional contempt for a system, they had decided, that caused the wars and everything else they hated. Maybe so.

When I got back to L.A., Adrienne really teed off, screaming at me, hurling shoes. How could I leave her alone with Bruno? I started to retreat as I always did, until I saw her crying. Bruno was banished to the perimeter for the while. Though I was still out of work, it somehow felt okay, like maybe it was acceptable to think of myself as a proletarian revolutionary first. Anything else would be my Day Gig.

After months of mournfully watching the swimming pool turn darker and more bilious green, I sold the house for small profit, half of which went to Senta.

In the serial cohabitations of '74—Tree, Adrienne, me and later Bruno playing musical residences—we would have fourteen combined addresses in the next five years. First we happened, by dumb luck, upon a tiny white frame gem with a succulent-filled yard on Eastern Canal, in Venice, with a bonus for Tree—a solarium, a glass-walled circular sun-house at the front, facing the canal, which was filled with thousands of waddling, ack-ack-acking ducks. I discovered I had twin hernias, a condition that might hamper a would-be revolutionary's scrambleability, so I opted for a bilateral herniotomy and spent the days in the sun recovering and contemplating Lenin.

Tree and I were still tight, the odd kind of connection that develops between men half a generation—fifteen years—apart. I was a little too young to be Tree's father, and a little too old to be his brother. On our endless freeway cruises he almost always drove, tirelessly bullshitting about music, politics, and sex. I tried to synthesize it all, forever compiling and refining Mitch's Rules of Motion, in which I would explain how everything worked "despite what they taught us in Civics class."

Sometimes I would fulminate at painful length, lecturing him on some point I was still trying to figure out myself. The fact that he had never gone to college allowed me some room to improvise a precarious metaphysics for his rolling captive benefit. We'd ride the twelve Didionic lanes of L.A. freeways to the desert, to the ocean, to the mountains, in a stoned mobile symposium on some aspect of freedom as seen by the New Mitch. Tree worked mostly in the area of what he considered religion, having been raised by a churchgoing divorced mom. He began to see this more broadly as The Realm of the Spirit, and felt a personal duty to insert a deity into discussions of Marx, Trotsky or Wilhelm Reich. These he'd never encountered before and they, with Darwin, were my favorites in those endless rappin' parabolas.

Dealing with God like that gave me pause, but it was Tree's only defense in what he may have felt were personal attacks. Having to square his white-bread Divinity with Orgone and the Rate of Exploitation at 85 miles an hour did me good, though. It moved me away from Militant Atheism and more toward Yogic Materialism.

We liked playing Searcher and Little Searcher.

Bruno was in deep shit, reportedly running roughshod over his brothers. Senta had taken to her bed, lying there in a daze while the three little pumas plundered the place. I hated what I had done to us all by leaving them, and agreed to take him to live with us. Our bijoux canal-side residence was too tiny for Bruno's wide berth, so we planned to move again. I would be missing the initial phase of this domestic adventure while attending my first national political conference, in the Midwest. The night just before I left, Tree, Adrienne and I were lying on floor, watching *WKRP in Cincinnati*. The wounds from my surgery had been pretty painful, and I was wafting around in opiates, as well as the usual pot, when I suddenly heard a clear loud voice:

"Go ahead, touch it. Touch your incision!"

They looked at me. It was two weeks post-op.

"Put your hand down there," the voice urged.

Why were they staring at me? Where was the voice coming from?

"It feels better," it said.

It does feel better, I thought. *He's right. I like that voice.* My fingertips crept back to the lower abdomen, probing for pain, but also recapturing the terrain in the name of pleasure. *Feel down there. Feel good. Opening the border, sensation seeping back. Melting.* And still the voice, disembodied but searching for a home, keeps up its ringside reportage.

"Yes! Yes! There! Lower, lower…there! Where the pain was!"

They stopped looking at me and Tree turned the TV up.

Later, we snorted some pink speed that Tree found in his dresser drawer and went back to my tiny quarters: just room for the redwood waterbed that Adrienne and I shared and the new Fender Rhodes "88" I'd bought out of the *Recycler*, a swap-meet of a weekly paper where bargains, if not guarantees, could be found.

Tree lay down in front of the old Vox stage amp I'd picked up to play the Rhodes through. I noodled the keys, arpeggiating aimlessly, and we commenced one of our Cosmic Post Mortems on the mystery of the disembodied voice.

"Splitting out a separate person, part of yourself," Tree opined.

"It was *far out,* I mean, hearing this voice from *way* outside my head, so that the whole part that would have heard it, inside, in the sinuses or wherever, wasn't there, you know?"

"No resonance."

"None. Apart. Not me at all, at *all.* "

"Like the time you dropped the Honda on Franklin?"

The year before, just before breaking up with Senta, I'd crashed my 750 cc bike at 5:00 a.m. on the way to do an air-shift at KURB. Riding down out of the canyon on Beachwood half asleep, I failed to notice that they'd watered the surface of Franklin until I hit the corner. One Big Wiggle and the bike went over and began to plane eastward on its right side, showering sparks. I somehow managed to hop up on the left side and, holding the one available bar, went on down the line.

As I surfed past two ladies waiting for a bus in the dim morning gloom, I could hear a scream—one that cracked the dawning day wide open with a rooster-shaming screech of shock and dismay. Sitting there tickling the 88's on Eastern Canal a year later, I could still hear the voice of that phantom rider calling out its emergency update:

"He's all right," to the concerned public transit patrons.

"He's all right." It was, of course, my own disembodied voice.

"In a crisis your third eye pops out and speaks," Tree said.

"Wanna buy a metaphor?"

"Oh, fuck you."

"Just kidding. You know, maybe it's just denial, just a retreat, dividing out a persona, an independent observer, recoiling in horror from my own stupidity. Pointing back at myself, saying 'he did it.'"

~

When Bruno and I came back to town from the conference, we went to our new straight-o ranch house in suburban redneck Venice. We found Tree and Adrienne toasted way past someplace else. While we'd been gone, they had moved all our stuff to the new place. It had been a catastrophe; they were bummed and wouldn't get off it. Bruno and I recoiled. He'd been bouncing around cross-country for ten days, between rescue and revolution. One of the things we expected people to do back then was "go with the flow," and kids were no exception.

After a few days I knew what I had: a classic triangle with the extra-cost option of a Greek chorus. We let the games begin. *Moto perpetuo* with Penal Colony implications. Endless three-cornered emotional billiards, and none of us had a cue.

We wrangled on regardless, anger everywhere. I tried to say yes to all, whoever was asking. Always defending Bruno, whenever I sensed a threat-to-my-baby in her tone of voice. We'd have plates-of-the-earth sex, and in the afterglow, she'd just happen to tell me something he'd done. We were all intense people, and everything resulted in instant escalation. By the end of the first stress-blasted month Tree, bummed by the endless relay of blame, showed us his dust, finding a modernish bachelor beach pad about a block from the ocean.

One morning, when Adrienne had some toilet time-share grievance with

Bruno, she started screaming at me in our cheap ranch-type kitchen. Adrienne slammed out the door, rattling the sizable glass pane. I began to exhale with a grimace, but she returned. Back in: SLAM! Out: SLAM!! SLAM!!! Five times! Ten! Bruno was yelling in his room, then came running out crying. He ran into my back and fell down. I dropped to my knees as her voice, like a wounded monster, roared out at me.

"YOU ASSHOLE!" And then at Bruno: "You hate me! You want to see me gone! Don't you! Out of your life for good!" slamming the door. This time the big pane cracked and a large shard flew past us and crashed.

"Don't you?!" and slammed it again. Glass sprayed everywhere.

Again. Only the hibiscus-patterned curtains blocked the direct spray of glass as it covered the room. I covered Bruno and waited. Finally it was quiet. The next weekend she came back to get her things.

That Halloween—Walpurgisnacht, by god—Tree came over just after dark to take my two younger boys trick-or-treating. The Pacific breeze, ten blocks from the beach, was stiff. Whatever few leaves the season had left whirled past the window in sudden updrafts. He parked his '73 Pinto Runabout and started up my driveway. Tree said later that what he heard was unearthly. Ghastly. He stood rooted, bound to honor his own childhood Halloween phantasms that overcame him in this ghostly suburban mini-elegy.

It was just me, wailing on the Fender Rhodes, screaming through the Vox pointed out the door into the still gathering Night of All Hallows. Chilling, howling, violent—yet arcing off into longer and longer phrases which folded out into a kind of Serenity, intensely presenting itself as a worthy partner to the night.

Tree covered his ears, pushed his way past this undulating electronic wall and gamely tried to shoot the shit with me for a couple of minutes, but I wasn't really there. I was out, hovering above the roofs of Venice, lifting my sorrowful angry keen, absent of strategy.

I had first met Bonnie Hansen-Duello at the Summerhill alternative school, which all three of my boys attended. Her daughter, Céline, was in Bruno's group, and I felt pulled to her right from the jump. A petite henna-redhead with tiny birdlike features and the moves of an Olympic gymnast, she was a fast talker with a fist of a voice, the kind you expected to be accompanied by cigar smoke. The younger daughter of a hot-shit builder, she was openly outraged that her vulgarian father had actually gone and made buckets of money.

"So, big deal! So he built the Sawtelle Towers. Like, so fuckin' what?"

Bonnie was Studs Terkel in tutu, a dance instructor married to an as-yet-not-in-power Sandinista, Augusto. He was a thin, dark poet/intellectual from a prominent Nicaraguan family who wanted the *gringos* out of their way, so that they might exploit their own countrymen much more efficiently. She was, in any case, separated from Augusto, who was currently stationed at a base camp in Honduras, or was it Santa Barbara?

When Bonnie came into my stranded life with her about-to-be-vacant Ocean Park beach house, my ears had gone up like an infield fly. Turned out her father the builder had bought her a cute little Topanga Canyon retreat, and her Pacific-side rental on Wadsworth was available. I came to inherit her rental of half a beach house for $200 a month. *Two hundred.* I had heard of her dance activities and knew she was seeking an accompanist. Right after Adrienne slammed out, I played a simple piano audition for her and within half an hour we were cuddled up on my rectangular waterbed. We were soon stuffing her nether lips with abandon. Her first post-coital words, even before my breathing regularized were:

"What am I doing with a Nice Jewish Boy?"

"Lady," I ventured, "do you have me wrong!"

She tended to encourage the Orphic side of me. Interesting, the relationship between anger and fun, as if sexual connection itself was an act of defiance. I had fucked her: *so there*! She had spread it around a bit: *so there, too*!

I saw Tree a lot in the months after he moved out. Adrienne, perforce, had found herself a place in West Hollywood where I would, despite everything, still find myself invited. Tree's place had wall-to-wall carpeting, floor pillows, one huge white leather couch, and the corner horn speaker cabinets his mother had shipped out from Carnegie. And, of course, his round waterbed—*locus classicus hippius.*

He'd meet me for an early breakfast before going in to his new gig at KCST, the new plastic AOR station on the Sunset Strip. Good money, heavy spot load. Neither of us mentioned Adrienne.

The Wadsworth house was a beat-up two-story frame, divided into rentals, up and down. The upstairs neighbors were Martin Michaux, a dedicated French painter of *les cowboys,* among other objects of American *arts ordinaire,* and his extremely foxy Los Feliz Jewess of a wife, Linda, whose ass sent me into paroxysms of acute infectious glossolalia. Bruno and I went up to let them approve us as co-tenants.

Neighbors on one side were a film actress famous for her advanced social views and her reformist politician second husband. On the other side—packed in tight as only beach real estate can be—lived a repulsive, bulbous ex-Santa Monica cop, "Dint" Sweeney, and his abused/abusive family of hollerers. The actress and her hubby cast the Sweeneys as The Workers.

Trotskyists, of course, did not consider cops part of the workers movement, considered them enemies in fact, and intervened ferociously with other groups' attempts to organize police unions, but I let that go. The actress might not have recognized a proletarian if he bit her in the ass (and lots of them would have loved to, from a salad of motives). We were left with the incessant din. At first I tried to make nice with them:

"Mr. Sweeney, I'm your new neighbor, Mitchell Hertz."

"Wadja say?" opening his front door to greet my repeated ringing. "Turn that down!"

The bellowing TV from inside continued so he pushed his immense animal bulk through the doorway and onto the stoop to address me.

"Watsa problem?" His voice was bullhorn strength and flat.

"No problem, Mr. Sweeney, just wanted to introduce myself," I said, extending my hand. "Your new neighbor."

"Yeah."

He wasn't looking at me. His eyes focused somewhere way over my head. He made no effort to accept my handshake. Just then the door banged open and a woman of almost equal girth leaned out, and spoke two words.

"Dinty; food."

She withdrew with a bang.

I pocketed my hand and went back to my porch.

Bonnie told me she'd had to sand the floors to rid the hardwood of grease from the Harley the previous tenants had maintained on a stand in the living room. Few of the windowpanes were uncracked, many covered with children's stick-on patches. Only the thinnest plywood sheet served as my and Bruno's common bedroom wall. But I wasn't kicking.

While her husband was out Sandinizing, Bonnie became a major presence in our lives—my employer, lover, co-parent, fellow armchair revolutionary, and music-loving companion most weekdays and into the nights. We would pick up Céline and Bruno from school, and drive to one of the dance classes that she instructed. I would accompany, and our grudging offspring played more-or-less together.

After class we'd cruise west on the Santa Monica Freeway into the setting Pacific sun, then north on the PCH, to climb the canyon up to her new Topanga cabin, tucked away in a small clearing. She cooked Central American delicacies, and then all four of us would crash on floor comforters for the night. In the morning, a neighbor who taught at Céline and Bruno's School added them to her carpool.

One time in late winter of '75, Bonnie drove our kids and me in her battered old BMW up to Big Bear, where she had rented a cabin for the weekend. The intrepid, fun-loving Bonnie thrashed the 2002 up the winding mountain roads, us in the front smoking joints, our kids, the lovely but provocative seven-year-old Bruno and Bonnie's lovely but nervous daughter Céline, interacting unevenly in the back seat.

Leaving late on a whim, we managed to find the cabin in the frozen darkness, and settled as best we could with the makeshift gear we had grabbed as we left L.A. Sex with Bonnie was almost always a problem. For one thing she was tiny all over, which could have provided an allure of its own, a sense of challenge, a virginal channel compression and all that. But the second factor was her insistence on using a device called an IUD, and denying that it was ripping the end of Mr. Johnson to little shreds. I exaggerate the damage, but like most people I approached sexual activities for fun, and the balance of pleasure and pain is critical. To feel a sharp twinge on the head of your penis every time it was fully inserted was not conducive to regular repetition. At first I tried female repression and avoidance strategies from Doris Day movies. But how many times can you say "Not tonight" without reasonable back-up?

As a last resort I tried the truth.

"It pinches me," I finally told her.

"It can't be me."

"I don't see anyone else in there."

"Come on, Mitch. *I* can't feel it."

"Of course, *you* can't feel it; it's not your dick!"

"But it fits flush."

"Okay. I don't know. What's your theory?"

"Are you tired of me?"

"*Bon*-nie!"

"Are you? Are you thinking of Adrienne?"

"We promised not to mention that."

"Then what?"

"I told you. There's a sharp piece of plastic back there playing a Paganini *Caprice* on my cock every time I go deep. I'm sorry. That's what it feels like."

"Well, you don't want me to get pregnant again, do you?"

"*Bon*-nie!"

Unfortunately she had a dainty little mouth full of teeth, so while I could offer her oral pleasuring, I could not accept the equally torturous returned favor from her.

I kissed her good night and held her lovingly in the mountain stillness.

After a shivery wine-and-comforters first night, we arose, drank flagons of the over-roasted Peete's coffee Bonnie loved so much, then headed, for the kids' sake, to the toboggan run on the other side of the mountain, down at about 3500 feet. We parked and dropped some acid.

By now it was noon in the mountains. Hot, and the snow heavy and dripping wet, widening spring green peeping through the gray-white. By the time we'd sloshed across the parking lot, Céline was approaching hyper-whine, Bruno kicking away wrathfully at the mud, and the LSD-25 Bonnie'd handed me with my Half-and-Half was beginning to CHUKKA-CHUKKA in the sudden broiler of a sun.

I opened my army jacket, wiped sweat from the griddle of my brow, squinted up the path leading out of the lot, and was amazed to see a caravan approaching. I beheld a scene from the Ancient World, a princely convoy of Persian merchants, richly dressed in cured hides and silk, camels and stallions from Araby. I could hear their hooves.

There was part of my brain that realized that it was a group of Iranian students. We'd seen them when we pulled in, parking their 404 Peugeot. Down the mountain path they came, dark and handsome, dressed like rich Europeans. Sons of satraps of the Shah with beautiful skin, dark hair and a sprinkling of beards. I watched them float toward us as in a dream. I felt myself swaying gently as they approached. Bruno drew instinctively nigh. Bonnie and Céline were off tinkling laughter just at the limit of audibility. The riders pulled up. We gaped at the richly accoutered apparition. Then I watched as a large white man, with an air of quiet rural authority, rode over to address the hallucinating father with son.

"Mind takin' this hoss over to the gate?" he asked, offering me the reins of a tall chestnut mare. "We'll meet you over there." And then trotted off at the head of the Persian legion.

I was struggling with familiar bugs-in-the-head stuff, which, under normal circumstances, would have strongly vitiated against sudden or unusual activities. But the way the morning was going, I just naturally hoisted little Bruno onto the front of the saddle, put my boot in the stirrup and grunted up behind the boy.

The ride across the quarter mile of parking lot was endless but uneventful. My brain, of course, was performing the first act of *Aida,* but the rocking motion of the big horse was comforting, and when we reached our assumed destination, I snuggled up to spidery Bruno, and we sank together into reverie. I sat there on the parked and placid palomino, cozy and warm in the sun. Baking and cuddling my boy, quiet in a haven surrounded by the frenzy of vacationers extracting the final fun from the last snow of winter.

The horse shifted its weight gently, and Bruno broke our private silence.

"Dad!" he whispered shyly in his reed-like voice. "We're falling off the horse."

"Of course we're not falling off the horse."

"Da-ad…"

Bruno was just getting to trust me in my new custodial role and still wanted to please me enough to keep him, so he consciously tried to avoid pissing me off. But he could indulge me only when his own pressurized universe left space for accommodation.

"Bruno, we're just on a little incline here, a bit of a hill…"

"Dad…"

By that time it was clear that we were indeed falling, rotating slowly, almost languidly a degree at a time, as the cinch—obviously left untightened by the owner who'd intended us not to *ride*, but to *walk* the horse to the gate—kept slipping, rotating until we'd reached a point where I could neither deny the certain immanence of our fall, nor prevent it.

In the end I just decided to succumb to the flow. I created a basket of my left side, elbow and shoulder, and absorbed the rather stunning blow that the tarmac delivered when it came up to meet us. I escaped with a small number of fairly deep bruises, which, lasting for several months, served to remind me of the folly of inattention, loving or otherwise.

About the best thing that emerged from Bonnie and me was the confidence I developed in my ability to improvise at the piano. Modern dance, especially Martha Graham technique, which Bonnie taught, had a simple foundation: First it contracted, then it released. You established the basic meter—double or triple, usually—which I figured I would assign to the left hand in perpetuity. I could let the right hand slave to the pulse in the left hand, the contraction/release modulation of the dance itself.

Contract *AND* release *AND* contract *AND* release. Contract/release.

Like a worm slithering its peristaltic way

I would begin with a simple two-or-three-note repeated pattern in the bass with the left hand. Then, when it was firmly planted in the dancers' movements, when they began to groove co-jointly, only *then* would my right hand—keyed to the patterns of moving limbs—begin its sub-mental adventures. I would gaze meaningfully at Bonnie, and then at the loveliest bodies that I had staked out for deeeeep inspiration—and my right hand would begin to speak. This incredible, elevated kinesthetic state was my leading consolation and best central energy.

Meanwhile, Adrienne and I continued to see each other. In fact, looking back, I can't really believe that I handed her so much guff in those days, or why she chose to put up with it: attending Bonnie's class semi-regularly, even going to the ridiculous length of having *planning meetings* with me and Bonnie, scheduling weekend leisure hours, dividing me up between them.

"I'll bring him back here at two; that gives you twelve hours from…"

I was becoming more political, taking a more active role, bringing Bonnie, Tree, or Adrienne to various forums—and even some gritty demonstrations organized by the Trotskyists. There are no hornier women on earth than the dedicated activist/socialist women who hit on you for a sex-act, day or night. So little rookie-pol me was floating into a pussy-pool a mile wide. They weren't all glamorous, by any stretch of the imagination, but that was the good news. That randy energy, an unselfconscious intelligence, and an ability to speak forthrightly all combined to make most of them plenty attractive.

And it was restorative, I thought at the time, to experience feeling wanted without having to get up on my hind legs, as I'd been trained to do around women, putting on my standard poodle high-heel, ex-Jewish tap dance just to get laid. It also gave me the room to look around and compare Adrienne with other women, to check out the difference between love and formal programmatic agreement. But in time it got old for me, alibiing my often-recalcitrant Johnson, holding it out taut and trying to squish it in soft. *Feh!*

That summer there was a national conference on a state college campus in Michigan. Thousands of pages of bound discussion documents were handed out to comrades. Reading them was entering another world, more remote than the veritable phase shift from Los Angeles to Ypsilanti. A world of factions, fights, splits, tendencies, tiny propaganda groups where a single word could spark a debate lasting all afternoon. Comrades signed up to speak on "rounds," round after round after round.

So we were sitting around between plenums in a little student lounge in one of the dorms, and an actual student was sitting at a serviceable spinet trying to pick out the piano Intro to "Imagine" by John Lennon, still a current song at the time. Over and over, he got the first few notes then missed. I was in a leatherette couch cluster with a group of fallen-away Catholics listening to their stories about the nuns beating them with pointers, and worse.

"Like this one Sister Mary Matilde. I'm sure she had the hots for me," Sparky Benedetto from the Bay Area was testifying. We were all drinking straight tequila. Small shots—we had a late afternoon session on the National Liberation question. "Always making me hoist my skirt before she strapped my ass. Never even thought of it till I met Judy. She'd had the same thing happen in Providence."

"No shit? You girls had that crap?" asked Joe McInnerny from the New York Local. "Guys never had problems with the Brothers."

Gales of laughter.

The student was still trying to play the "Imagine" intro. I went over to him and asked could I try. He slid over. I sat down and after a false start, it just came out. The young guy was glued to my hands, deciphering the fingering. I kept going. The comrades started to wander over and join us.

"Imagine no possessions...I wonder if you can.
No need for greed or hunger, a brotherhood of man"

The young Japanese Detroit organizer had been watching. She came to my room at 3:00 a.m. with a fifth of Old Overholt, paper cups and what you might call a bottomless hunger. She fucked me till I was ready to cry.

˜

What was left of my career was stringing for a generic weekly rock radio show, called *In-Studio*, conducting off-mic interviews and running to LAX with the tape to be over-nighted to the producers in New York. They paid okay, and with my accompanist money from Bonnie and the other choreographers I played for—slim by any but Calcuttan standards—I could pay for Bruno and my expenses and eke out minimal child support. I was still a pretty good interviewer, but the show aired nationally without my voice, or even an "interviewed by" credit. The one time I actually heard the show, it was neither richly nor imaginatively produced.

I was also retained by record companies *de vez en cuando* for various projects, but never a *job* job. I remember an office in the then-new Warner Bros building in Burbank, alone at the end of a silent empty hall, working on the *Barry Lyndon* soundtrack, and writing articles on Stockhausen for rock journals, Warner Brothers house organs, etc. Repeated efforts to re-up a publisher for *Roll Your Own Beethoven* kept aborting and a new low was achieved when Adrienne left to discover Europe.

˜

One night sitting with Bonnie in a remote hot springs, transfixed by the desert sky, and peaking on her LSD, I developed these deep abdominal yearnings, these empty-belly cravings for my boys: *"I…need…to…touch…them…need… pull them into me…into the hole in my center…need to…hold them inside me… want to…hold…them…hold…"*

I would just reach out to them in the sky. Floating in the clear starry…

touch them, pull them into the chasm in my hollow gut. I could never tell Adrienne. She wanted children of her own. I thought to share it with Bonnie. Tried and tried, but my throat parched and closed, my tongue retracted, folded back on itself, words frozen and stored. Though she seemed content to offer sweet solace for the moment. Refuge but not release.

When Bruno and I moved in together on Wadsworth, without Adrienne, I treated him like a baby, a sweetheart, a long-lost friend and confidante. The night we arrived at the funky beach house, we skipped down the street, and across the public parking lot that was all that separated us from the ocean. I danced with Bruno in the surf, sun setting pink on the rounded white buildings trimming Santa Monica Bay. I felt a moral imperative to store this ecstatic vision away against the day when I might not recall the blessed impulse that could take hold of a man and move him to live for such feelings.

Everything was easy. I sat in the bamboo-curtained, glass-enclosed front porch office and wrote with the door wide open, walls lined with the complete works of Lenin. Bruno left his bike on the stoop at night without benefit of lock. We seldom used keys. I struggled to understand his problems by applying imperfectly digested Marxian social thought.

As soon as we were settled, I took Bruno out of Summerhill, the private school, which I considered too unstructured for a boy who had such problems staying focused. They sent him home before noon two or three times a week. I would pick him up from the Palm Street public school and take him on radio interviews—introduced as my road manager—and he would wander off to ride the elevators at the Holiday Inn on Highland, or to explore the hip corporate halls of CBS or Warner Records, while I committed Maria Muldaur or Neon Park to tape. He fell asleep in the just-built L'Ermitage as Leo Sayer recalled art school in perhaps excessive detail.

One bright Venice morning over liver, onion and eggs at Nupar's on

Windward Circle, I tried to explain this to Tree. "This is the life that he's going to be leading. This is the way society *is* today. I cannot protect him from cruel reality. I didn't *create* bourgeois society; I only have to *live* here."

We were sitting at the counter, watching the old German cook shove browning potatoes around the grill. Nupar's always gave me the sense of a new world—plus or minus—infinite varieties. A short walk from my new house was the waiting coziness of the all-accepting hash house. Slumped among the regulars, drinking coffee, conferring in quiet clumps as the busty young waitresses handed down the heavy china plates: hippie-artist types, bearded, parti-colored get-ups, the full bloom of Sixties efflorescence; gentle old Venice-Beats, tired and bent over their *L.A. Free Press;* Vietnam vets, with anger-tightened faces, lava pools or agates for eyes; the outlaws, dope-dealers, bikers, pirate record sellers, herbal medicine hypesters, psychedelic hairdressers, record company promo men and other con-persons. An entire generation tied together with a rope of hemp, a certain so-what look, and more hair than the average accountant.

I loved the illusion that we had created our own culture—counter-cultural, alternative, anti-society—take your pick. But I could only kid myself so far. The war was ending, the youth culture being slurped up into the next corporate marketing configuration. By pulling out of Vietnam, the Establishment had only strengthened itself by burying differences. I felt at home in this bohemian milieu, but with my lace-up boots and cord Levis, I fancied myself way past that—a worker.

Tree pulled his long hair back and over his shoulders, where it would do less damage to his Italian sausage omelet.

"We *all* have to live here. But you wish you could spend more time with Bruno, don't you? Whatever you think of this society."

"Yeah." Tree was not afraid of challenging my ass when he thought I was kidding myself. "If I don't keep a high consciousness I could be eaten alive by guilt."

"What's that? What does 'high consciousness' mean?"

"*You* know." I knew he was baiting me. "Focusing on the way things really are, not getting into morality weirdness over abstractions."

"Right and wrong are abstractions?"

The door opened and a group of bodybuilders trouped in from nearby Muscle Beach. Smiling vacantly, they seemed to be saying: *We don't have to worry, we're the lions.* I couldn't help gaping at their inflated bodies.

"Look," I said finally, "I spent ten years with a woman I didn't love, okay? I mean, I loved her, but, like, I just let her be my little mommy-nurse. I slept-walked into parenthood…I've got to under*stand* this shit scientifically or go on making these same idiot mistakes the rest of my life!"

Tree shook his hair, the way people with ultra-long hair always seem to do, men as well as women, and compressed his lips, as if holding back what he really wanted to say, something unpopular.

"What do you think Bruno makes of all of this, those endless political jamborees you sit through, the demos…?"

"I dunno, man. Why?"

"I don't know either, babe. I'm just wondering what must he think."

"What did you think when your dad walked out?"

Tree gave me that little head jiggle. Opened his mouth to speak, thought better of it, turned to stare at me for a second, and put his fork down. "In a way I was glad. I got to have my mother to myself…"

"What about your sister?"

"She was pretty much my kid, too, but…"

"But?"

"But I felt pretty helpless. Exposed, I guess. I hate the word 'vulnerable.'" Tree's voice sometimes stuck in his throat. The vestigial trace of a youthful lisp lent it a sincerity that made him even dearer.

"Weren't you always pretty big?"

"Yeah, but dorky, too, ya know. Pudgy. Bruno's awful small for his age."

"Don't worry. He'll be fine." I wanted us all to be fine. "Sometimes I wish I had all the things I gave up; everything I had before he was born."

"How did you feel when you had it?"

"I sleep easier now, I guess. Except now I have to think about *him*. It's like…all those things you hid from or ran away from when you were a kid…all the things you thought you'd never have to deal with ever again. And it turns out we're condemned to go through all of it—not try to elude it, but actually come to some kind of *resolution* of it—as a parent. Your nervous system is so totally fused to your kid's, ya know? It's so much more intense as a 'grown-up' to go through it *with* him. Yuck."

"You'll get the hang of it. You can't learn it all at once."

"I know, I know. I think he'll be okay in the long run. He'll make a very valuable adult—if he survives this bum-of-the-month tour with me. But it's so hard for him now; he's got trouble in school, trouble with his mother and brothers. He just can't seem to main*tain*. And it's so hard not to blame myself."

"Self-pity ain't the ticket, Pops. Guilt either. Plus, are you telling me you should'a stayed with Senta? That double-message dogshit you were peddling with her? That's what fucked up the kid in the first place. All that fakey cooing you cats were doing when I first met you; gimme a break! I gotta tell ya, it always drove me *ca—razy!*"

"Yeah, yeah. I had to get outta there. It was killing me. I was washing black beauties down with Haig & Haig. But I was no great shakes as Daddy then, and I've got nothing to build on now. And Adrienne's no goddamn help!"

"It's worse with her," Tree ventured. "She acts like his older sister."

"And then I get to be in the middle, my favorite! I fuckin' hate it."

"What does Bruno think of all your different women?"

"He shines it on, mostly, I guess. He has no illusions. He's bored. Sometimes my upstairs neighbor with the great ass comes down before breakfast and hops in next to me while he watches *Sesame Street* on the end of the bed."

Tree looked sad, too conflicted to say the obvious.

I glanced up at him and said, "I don't know, it never *seems* weird."

I took Bruno with me to dance class, and for a time the two of us would leave with various young women dancers, Bruno to sleep on one side of the 1/2 inch ply, me and the succession of ballerinas on the other. They dug it—the dancers, the teachers and the studio people—this modal, hypnotic, lyrical George Winston-meets-John Cage-meets-wrong-note modern dance music. And sometimes, when it clicked, when I relaxed, I dug it, too. Once in every class someone I was playing for would privately catch my eye. Sometimes they would kiss me up after rehearsals.

Bonnie got me a part-time paying job with the L.A. Department of Parks and Recreation as accompanist to municipally offered exercise and dance classes as well as other civic festivities.

Mostly I'd play at different Westside city facilities, on humble uprights, for an hour or two, three or four afternoons a week. I also played in more atmospheric private studios—but the city gig was more reliable. I needed the coin. Often at the private teachers' gigs they would pass the hat after a two-hour continuous session that might net me three dollars, I swear. So I was happy for whatever the City could provide, despite the dismal morale of the premises.

One bright winter morning an incident befell me that I would come to see as marking the end of the Hippie Era as I understood it. I was scheduled to accompany a class for Norma, a luscious forty-something who'd been trained by the Divine Martha Graham herself. She was subbing for Bonnie as a favor—her usual environs were far grander than the Venice Pavilion, a large round brick community structure in almost unusable condition. I loved to play for the refined and fleshy Norma, my eyes licking her curves as she moved. *"Contract! AND…Release!…AND…Contract…AND…Release! AND…."*

So I arrived a little early with a big paper cup of Venice coffee, and took my place at the spinet at the rear of the stage. Smiling to a few other early arrivals, I instinctively edged the piano away from the men's room behind me—stinky this morning, I noted. Once, twice I pushed the small blonde instrument, and yet the stench followed, curling my nasal hair.

Norma flowed in, wrapped in Dance Aura, waving me a cheery hello as the class gathered around her. Again I pushed the piano farther yet from the apparent source of my olfactory distress. Then I began to tinkle and trill, warming my tendons against the ocean morning air. I began a combination of scales and broken chords with my right hand, the decrepit soundboard flat and dull, needing to be plonked really hard. Then my left hand strode downward from Middle C: *Boom-pa, Boom-pa, THUD! Squish, THUD* again. Without thinking, fixed on Norma's soft face, I tried again: *Boom-pa, Boom-pa,…SCHLOOOP!!*"

In a flash I understood why the stink kept following me. Though my mind rejected the conclusion, my sensorium told it like it was.

A quick glance confirmed the underlid presence of copious human excreta gracing the hammers and soundboard. With the cognitive evidence, my moral sense awoke: *The lumpen filth!* I raged. *Attack on culture! War on music! Crime against mankind! Too cruel to be dismissed.* Then came a thunderous shudder up from mid-gorge, profound physical revulsion, and finally, an apparition:

Primitive man, loins unencumbered, approaches the mechanical *diabolus in musica.* Throws open the window to its soul. Squats athwart its portal. Rises once! Twice!! Three times!!! Pounds the ribs over his sacred heart. And, at the height of his ritual dance of denunciation, lowers himself one more time into the chasm separating Man and Nature, releasing his excremental contempt for the despoilers of the One True Life. An act of elimination by one already eliminated socially, I presumed. A rejection of our society-as-it-is-and-has-been-too-long!

He grunts a final curse:

I defile your ways.

I obscenity in the milk of your mother;

I desecrate the totem of your ancestors!

Accursed, smothering death-in-life, hypocritical,

exploiting, cowardly imperial monster of a civilization…

I SHIT IN YOUR PIANO!!!

In late '74 Tree's career had a growth spurt. His new station loved him, overworked him, underpaid him, and sent him off to train the new production guy at their Detroit outlet. When he took his vacation at the end of that rather pleasant tour of duty, he decided to drop into Carnegie.

Welcomed as Big Noise from the West, he paid a state visit to our old stomping grounds, the returning prodigal major-market AOR success story, and was shocked by the changes. WURB was now all-white and all play-listed. He described it to me as "Greaser Rock" excluding all black music except Hendrix. They were in bed with the major labels, the promoters, Major League Sports teams, and mostly *Rolling Stone*, where they mysteriously were named "Rock Station of the Year" five years in a row. Seems they owned the market. Working Carnegians had little choice but to obsess on football, canned beer and the cravenly commercial entity that had encrusted the magical WURB that Trout had built.

Tree said he almost wretched at the sound. Instead, he called a telephone number I had pressed upon him before he left. The phone was answered by Anne-Marie Bernac, our lovely erstwhile babysitter, who, now eighteen, still lived with her family across the street from the old Hertz place in Carnegie Heights. I hadn't seen her since her inevitable ripening, but had a feeling that he would appreciate the introduction. Tree ended up driving her all the way back to L.A.—and falling in love with her in three days of deserts and separate motel rooms.

The plan was for her to stay with me and Bruno for a while, to mollify her parents, but when they got back, they found that Adrienne was somehow re-ensconced with Bruno and me in the Ocean Park house.

I had tried to act casual, but Adrienne's month running around Europe without me had been worse than I could have imagined. Tree had no kick, since Anne-Marie just naturally moved in with him. She was very subdued, and reluctant to initiate a conversation, but such a deep warmth, if not ever quite actual fire. So sweet! Such a tender young soulful morselette! Olive skinned, full-lipped and beyond voluptuous. Tree couldn't stop thanking me for hectoring him to call her.

I was out of money for the first time in my adult life, and acting the novice scuffler. I now faced the stern evidence that I had formed a functioning human genetic grouping, uprooted them from their extremely comfortable home, moved them across a continent, and abandoned them while liquidating the operation's assets, all in the breathtakingly brief space of fewer than two years. Ten years accumulation of labor power, money, insurance policies, furniture and clothes, as well as one of the most extensive private record collections in America—30,000 LPs of every imaginable type: jazz, blues, folk, spoken, rock, but mostly classical. I had seven or eight recorded versions of each Mozart opera. Twenty or more versions of the late Schubert Sonatas. Plus, imports from everywhere: weird Stalinoid Eastern European labels like *Qualiton, Suprafon, Melodiya* as well the usually Western European labels like *Voce dal Padrone, das Alte Werk, Electrola, HMV,* etc. And rare, out-of-print early LP transfers of 78 rpm originals, like Carnegie Symphony conductor Béla Czar playing the piano, and still sealed cartons full of new releases from all the major and most of the minor labels. Gone.

Gone, too, were the remembered symbols of power—titles, secretaries, credit cards, a de Tomaso *Mangusta* and an S-1 Bentley. Gone. Senta had gotten a little cash and a few furnishings out of the divorce: some beautiful Persian rugs, the parlor grand, Tiffany lamps, real German deco stuff. All gone.

Then our upstairs neighbors, the Michauxs, had a crisis. We had become almost friendly, as neighbors sometimes will. Martin liked to use Bruno to pose almost naked and covered with watercolors for his more abstract paintings that might include lobsters placed strategically at various points of my son's epidermis. I would be there to chaperone, you might say, but more to ogle the scrumptious young Linda, his wife, Bonnie's closest friend, who smoked Gauloises, always had a *vin blanc* at hand, and loved to talk about art and politics. Her dad had been a Stalinist sympathizer who actually took her elder siblings to the USSR to live for much of the Thirties.

Linda loved Andy Warhol and his school. Saw the Factory as a Social Movement. At the depth of my resentment for anyone who had chosen to work within the system, I delivered this judgment over a glass of Moselle: "Warhol will be remembered mostly as representing the low point of a decadent society in its death agonies."

She began to cry. She was a lovely girl, twenty-five and smart and devoted to ecstasy, but with a lot of pain in her life. I was a little afraid of her situational ferocity, in defense of a freedom of thought she worried I, like her father, would sacrifice for political goals. She'd been in Paris in 1968 and seen the French Communists sell out the General Strike, and she was tough. Our few previous talks had been contentious, but I always learned a lot. Her tears were something of a shock and a revelation, but I was still thinking mostly with my dick back then, so I reflexively began to backtrack:

"Well, in the sense that Warhol's a surrealist and wants your conscious mind to go away so he can deal with your subconscious, I can see his contribution," I conceded, "like forcing you to stare at the Empire State Building for eight hours until the pain that's trapped in your psyche by the compulsive socialization that's already destroyed his life can come out, screaming 'PAIN, PAIN, PAIN,' or something."

"Or something," she said, daubing her eyes and refilling my glass.

Her husband the painter, who liked his alcohol even more than she, was in the habit of strolling the boardwalks in the evening, taking in sunsets and the sounds of the native Venice drums. One night, on a lonely stretch of bicycle path, he passed a group of surfers smoking, toking and boozing around a fire barrel. One of them called out. Laconically he turned and gestured in a way that only Parisians can, with a contempt that can deny the very personhood of the recipient.

Continuing to put distance between himself and the group of rowdies, he was struck between the shoulders by a well-aimed wet sneaker. He went back to return the shoe and was beaten mercilessly. Two days later he packed his bags for France.

For a brief time thereafter, my mornings were qualitatively transformed by Mme. Michaud slipping downstairs and into my bed. Then Bonnie found out, issued a stern ultimatum and Linda withdrew. Then Bonnie's Sandinista husband reappeared in L.A. to denounce her as a "whore" and "disrespectful" (sic). She promptly fled with Céline to a life of dance in San Francisco. And I hooked up with Amnesty International and the Partisan Defense Committee to work with class struggle political prisoners, torture victims of various juntas and American assets worldwide. I seemed to be withdrawing from Tree's world, the universe of commercial entertainment. On the one hand, becoming a Marxist in my head, and on the other hand orienting towards a real person's job.

I've never seen an unhappier motherfucker than me as a cabdriver. My day started at daybreak in the cold of the Red Top Cab Company yard on Electric Avenue in Venice, trying to pour congealed oil into frozen sumps. Check in, fuel, bribe the Dispatcher and clock out. Drive back home to pickup Bruno. Drop him at early day-care. Then a ten-hour shift of propane-fueled, disorganized vehicular grab-ass, including stopping at LAX to pickup the endless river of Trotskyist press, pamphlets and other documents for my political co-thinkers, while dashing for fares. Then waiting at cabstands, pickling in anxiety. Hoping the two or three dollars I grease the dispatcher every morning would do me some good. The day would not end until after racing back to pick up Bruno from the Ocean Park Day Care Center before it closed at 6:00 p.m., dropping him off at home, sprinting as fast as I could with my big old propane tank in the trunk back to the Red Top yard to clock out, before going home to randomly derived dinners.

I'd come into the house with a headache and an attitude until I'd gotten dinner for Bruno and in the process, thrown back a half bottle of Cuervo Gold, or whatever I could find. Then I'd impersonate a human long enough to get Adrienne to go to bed with me. I did this six days a week.

I was moving closer to the Trotskyist movement, a noble, if abstract, revolutionary tradition—the ultimate egalitarians, at least on paper. But it was one thing to have Trotsky's *Transitional Program* on the nightstand and yet another to actually live the life. My old friends avoided me like the guy in *Li'l Abner* with the rainstorm permanently over his head.

"Go do your proletarian-and-pissed routine for someone else," Tree said.

Yet, Tree's next girlfriend, his beloved April, bore that very heritage. He met her at the birthday party Adrienne threw for my fortieth.

The guests were typically heterogeneous—from some of the Beach Boys, who came in tuxes directly from the Grammies—to a bickering brace of multicolored Bolsheviks—to Adrienne's sexy sisters—to the divine Carla, the Veronese gypsy from one of Bonnie's dance troupes, riveting us with a topless, flaming, sword dance to the *Black Orpheus* soundtrack. Panning the room, the birthday boy proclaimed himself well pleased. Adrienne was giving me pleasure despite my puckered pusillanimity, rallying my friends to succor me in trying times. Blessed be the party-givers.

Anne-Marie went off to college, back in Ohio, and by the time she left April and Tree were seeing each other. She had actually been a member of the Trotskyist's youth group, which is where I'd met her. Moving in with Tree, who'd just built his warehouse studio over on West Washington in Venice, was the beginning of her gradual but total break from politics. He knew she had not been at all shy sexually during her career as the young revolutionist and suspected that even she and I had been lovers, though he did not need to know.

Politically, though, I was definitely what they referred to as "periphery," never taken seriously by the lifer cadre. But *I* took it seriously, perhaps because I needed it to explain my life. I had nothing to lose. I'd given away or sold everything I'd ever had except that old blue leather jacket, and my books.

After the briefest of honeymoons on Wadsworth, things with Adrienne and Bruno began to deteriorate. Talking with Adrienne was seldom helpful.

"He's impossible," she'd tell me in a death-conquered voice, and try to change the subject.

"If you could just try to approach him with love…" I hear myself plainting.

"I'm not his mother. He's *got* a mother."

"Just try to be his friend."

"His friend? He *hates* me. Don't you see the way he treats me?"

"He just needs love. Just like you and me, baby."

"He needs help, Mitch. Professional help."

The three of us together were always tick-tick-ticking away, awaiting the inevitable blast. He'd get nervous and do something provocative; she'd explode. I'd ride to his defense. Very little of this behavior was in play when Bruno and I were alone together, which was a lot.

"What's her problem, Dad? She's always mad."

"She doesn't mean it, son. She can't have kids of her own, and…"

"Why not? Why *can't* she have kids? You hump her all the time."

"I don't know, Bruno. Maybe we'll find out. We're trying to find out. But she doesn't mean to be mad at you."

"You don't know, Dad. You don't know what she's like when you're not here. You don't hear what she says."

Senta went on welfare, and I made my child support payable to the D.A.'s office. It was summer, and I sat on the sun porch, typing the draft of my first writing assignment for *Vanguard Worker*. The L.A. local had been asked to provide a historic piece and, since I was "in Hollywood," I was given a shot at it. I'd haunted used bookshops and amassed a tiny library of source material on the post-war blacklist "Witch Hunt" period.

The Hollywood 10 were the "Unfriendlies," ten film directors and mostly talented screenwriters like Dalton Trumbo and Ring Lardner, Jr. who refused to name names before the House Un-American Activities Committee. They tried to invoke their Constitutional right of Freedom of Thought to avoid self-incrimination as well as protect their friends and colleagues who, before and during World War II, had contributed time and money to pacifist, integrationist and anti-fascist "popular front" organizations. Some of these groups turned out to be fronts for the Communist party of the USA. My article explored the relationship between the ostensibly revolutionary CPUSA and the often-pampered, far-from-proletarian Hollywood liberals whose famous names could promote and help finance the activities of these groups. It was an organizational question: how did the Party co-ordinate (or separate) these distinct groups: cadres, on the one hand, and "dupes" on the other?

It wasn't going well. I'd never written a Marxist analysis before, didn't know what they expected stylistically, and could never resist a cheap gag line ("no shot too cheap; no stoop too steep").

Then one of the neighbor Sweeney kids, the apparently Latino son of the gigantic Orc, Dinty, started working on his lowered '63 Chevy next door, with his blaster set just under maximum volume: *CHAKA-CHAKA-CHAK-KONG!!*

I tried to put a filter on it, like the fabled Japanese behind rice-paper walls, but my nervous system was backed up with undeliverable messages. After a polite trip to the neighbor's curb, in which the slobboid teenager just looked at me, rolled his eyes and sneered, I went back in the house and turned up the stereo: Stravinsky as revenge. *The Rite of Spring* consumed the entire weekend before Labor Day.

Then the rest of their family got into the act. Part of me pitied them. Lumpy, coarse Irish-Mexican-American; taught obedience from the cradle with the single strategy of cuffing their ears. The resulting auditory impairment accustomed them to shouting as normal communication. Their house was packed in tight against ours, maybe an arms-length away.

My sister Lily was in town from New York with needle-melting back pain. I took her on a round of Southland spine specialists. She slept on the once-furry black couch in the front room. After three weeks she still had no diagnosis, but she felt better. Perhaps helped by the distance from her disintegrating marriage, two little girls, and no job, trapped in the big house on the campus of Brooklyn College, where Barney taught. I hated to see her in pain. A dishwater blonde like me, but smarter, prettier, and gutsier. She complained about my neighbors, too. Their radios and assorted grunts and howls kept her awake.

Still, she was up early that last day, singing in the old tub-shower, ready to meet Dick Deutschmann, my old pal from Baker Heights who was in town for a week-long conference. I suspected Lily and Dr. Dick had been lovers way back. My mother assured me, "She's too fastidious for that sort of thing."

Lily and Adrienne went to pick up Deutschmann while I finished typing the first draft on the secondhand Smith Corona 250 I'd found in the *Recycler*. The neighbor kid—or a different equally hippo-like one—was washing his car at the curb, blasting beneath his porch window. *CHAKA-CHAKA.* I tried to focus past it, mentally putting the red ball of irritation inside the blue triangle. *Only a few pages to go. Just go out and talk with him…*

"Could you turn that down a little, please? I'm trying to work."

No response.

"Hi! Can you hear me?"

Sullen look. His hose accidentally gives me a short burst.

"Hey!" I yelled, took one look at the cold contempt in his face, and turned to go back into the house.

It seemed to get quieter, but then the back of my head was blasted forward by a barrage of huge heavy metal power chords, obviously turned up louder than I ever thought possible. I took a deep breath…and then…I. Just. Snapped. A metallic river rose up into my mouth, then slammed out through my teeth in a torrent of curses ricocheting off the steamy street:

"You fucking Idiot! Shut that shit *UP!*"

The giant slope-shouldered youth turned slowly, stared truculently at the raging middle-aged man. His sloppy sister gazed cow-head-over-a-fence at the scene from her front stoop, my agonized outburst barely rising to her impaired threshold of audibility. She managed a bored and callow sneer.

"YOU FUCKING MORONS! I'M FUCKING THROUGH WITH YOU PEOPLE!! *PEOPLE*? SHIT-FOR-BRAINS MONKEYS! YOU'RE ONE STEP UP FROM BARNYARD ANIMALS!!!" I stamped back into the house. As I crossed the doorstep they turned the gain up on the blaster.

I turned on my big stereo, dragged the *AR* studio monitors to the windows, lifted them to the sills pointing broadside at the neighboring Sweeney home and put on the last movement of the Beethoven *Ninth*.

Oh, Freunde, Nicht diese Töne
Sondern, lasst uns angenehmere anstimmen und freundenvollere…
("O, friends, not these sounds! Let's sing something gladder, more full of joy!")

The baritone, the chorus, the tenor. The orchestra. Louder and louder I cranked the big silver amp. There was a life-positive energy, a bright flashing potency, loosed in the room, roaring out into the quaint little street. I stood pinned to the back wall, shaking—scared by the intensity of my own anger, hyper-ventilating, afraid to move.

"Alle Menschen werden Bruüder
Wo dein sanfter Flügel eilt."
("All men are brothers in the haven of your wings.")

Lily, Adrienne and Dr. Dick came home to find me quivering, heart rate and respiration way elevated, face alternating between flushed and chalky white. Later I calmed down enough to go to an Amnesty International meeting, hoping to clear my head.

When I pulled up to the house after the meeting, I saw my sister, my lover and my best friend all waiting for me, looking nervous. Bruno was there on the sidewalk, downcast. Turns out the three of them had let the ten-year old convince them "his dad did it all the time" and dropped him at Tommy's #5 burger stand up at Ocean and Pico. I felt the river begin to gnaw on the levee when they told me the lumpo neighbors had struck back, and reported Bruno as an unattended juvenile. The Santa Monica cops had come, picked Bruno up, and searched the house. They'd returned just as the police were leaving.

I totally lost it, sweeping up the terrified Bruno and dragging him to his mother's house, where I deposited him on the front porch—sweating and screaming at Senta to take him and keep him. Back at Wadsworth, I collapsed, a dis-integer, incapable of self-maintenance, out of solution.

I woke up in the heat-baked apartment of the L.A. Organizer of my political group, who tolerated my class-alien presence. It was deepest August, scorching hot in the tiny Hollywood Boulevard walk-up. Here, sleeping on the floor, I resigned myself to a life of activism. All else having failed, I determined to commit to the life of a Professional Revolutionary. Nothing terrorist, thank you, just the traditional factory-gate labor activities favored by American organizers since the Wobblies.

It felt good, re-integrative, even. Within weeks I found a cramped old place in a not-too-funky eight-unit building on Parkman, just south of Sunset in Echo Park. For a few weeks I lived that boring L.A.-backwater life, finally deciding to volunteer for a transfer to the Bay Area, where I might be useful in the coming General Strike.

I was sitting in my unmoved-into place, nursing a San Miguel dark, and listening to Eric Dolphy, Roland Kirk, and finally Sonny Rollins's *Freedom Suite*. Cartons of books, records, old files in heaps. My one remaining Persian rug, from married life in Carnegie, rolled up and limp as my life, leaning against the kitchen wall. Waiting for a call, I was supposedly on my way to the Bay Area, where they were getting me hired in to Long Shore. When the opening came, I'd be gone.

I sat there taking stock as the sun set over East Hollywood. *Physical shape—decent at thirty-seven. Newly repaired double hernias. Good upper-body strength. But my hands! My piano-playing fingers, soft palms and weak wrists.* I was terrible with blisters, always wore a batting glove. *Maybe they won't make me lift the heaviest stuff right away.* I had flashes of myself disoriented in the hold of a boat, crates cascading from a broken container above my head. *And what about attitude and demeanor?* Suddenly I felt like an even geekier and more preposterous George Plimpton. A Paper Prole.

Just then the phone rang, a call from Sascha "Fabulous" Strauss, my old pal from my KURB days, now plying her anything-but-rough trade in the world of network late-night television. On what might have been my last day in Los Angeles, or polite society in general, she was telling me she was now an associate producer on an NBC music show called *The Midnight Special* (after the famous Leadbelly song). They appeared to have, *mirabile dictu,* a job opening:

"It's *per*fect for you, Mitchell. And Marv'll love you. He's *fab*ulous!"

"Who?"

"Marv Tweed, our Producer-Dir*ec*tor—one of a kind. You'll get it in a *heart-beat*."

"You know I've never worked in fucking *tele*-vision."

When did she get duped into TV? Remembering her father's connections: Jack Benny, George Burns, and years of contact making as Paramount's Head of Publicity. Nepotism Alarm. Sneer.

"Here's what to *wear*: Cord jeans…"

"Come on, Sascha."

"…Sports jacket…Got a tweed one?…and penny loafers."

"Penny loafers!? *Yikes!* What's the job like?"

"Simple. You're really the writer, but to not pay Guild scale they give you 'Creative Consultant' credit in the crawl. The guy you're replacing was Co-producer. Did you know Marco?"

"Creative television, eh? Is that like airline cuisine?"

"Mitch…"

"Or family business?"

"Don't be a *dork.* You write the show, work with the hosts, the big acts, help in booking, you work on the "Tributes" with me…"

"Tributes?"

"Our hottest segment: you'll love it! Mini-documentaries, like short bio-pics, you know. Don't you ever watch the show? You help interviewing and check my scripts, maybe come to editing. Can you be down here tomorrow at 2:00? I want you to meet Marv…Got a pencil…9000 Sunset…twelfth floor… 'Brent Lukerman Productions.' Got it? See ya!" (Click).

The phone rang again. My organizer.

"Looks like we're in for a wait, Mitch. Harry Bridges is trying to make a deal with Alioto behind the workers' backs. Just sit tight."

"How long could it be, Joe?" I wanted to know.

"A week. Maybe more. Looks a bit iffier than before. Hang in there." He hung up to go organize someone else.

Two days later, Marv Tweed was smiling expansively from behind his antique desk. He offered a laconic question or two, looked away, frowned, another question, then beamed.

"I like you!"

"I like you, too," I sought to assure him.

"But I can *hire* you." He laughed and all his face shook, the sense organs enlarged, as if in florid adaptation to a permanent state of pleasure-harvesting.

"Feel free," I encouraged.

"Eh?"

Marv Tweed, from the one-word evidence, was Canadian and the owner of a hearing aid.

"I said 'I'd like that a lot'."

"I may have to have another operation. I keep getting water in the inner ear."

I wondered how he shot, much less edited, the first major network music show.

"Mostly by vibrations," Marv answered my silent query. "I feel the beat through the floor." Lavish smile. "Does that sound odd? I started on drums as a kid."

"When'd you get into TV?" I was glimpsing a new world.

"Right out of school. I always knew I wanted show business. I never even considered university."

Looking across at fleshly Marv in the stately sensuality of his generous office, floor-to-ceiling windows on two sides, gazing out at the Sunset Strip rolling east, I felt giddy, tongue-tied, and out of place, despite my resurrected herringbone and Bass Weejuns. I smiled desperately, remembering to take a deep breath. Then one more and I began to relax a little.

"I must tell you I don't know whether I can even do the work."

"Sascha says you're perfect."

"What does the job entail?"

"Eh?"

"What's the gig?" I asked, louder.

"You're my assistant."

"What does that mean?"

"It means you're hired. We tape in three days."

"No kidding?"

"It'll have to be approved by Brent. You know about Brent?"

"Brent..."

"Brent Lukerman, the owner...Executive Producer."

"Oh, okay...Right! Yeah."

I didn't know, but I was sure I'd find out.

"I'll call you tomorrow to confirm, but you're hired…Great!"

He rose slowly, appearing relieved. I liked this soft, overweight man ten years my senior.

"Great," I said.

The next day when Marv did call, it was to tell me that Brent Lukerman had *ex post facto* cut my salary from the proffered $500 to $350 per week, still big money to my thirsty ears. I accepted it just like that. Marv picked me up that evening outside my unmoved-into Parkman rooms in a cherry 280SL, and treated me to a Dodgers game and a $100 sushi snack for two at a new place on La Cienega. I brought along the field glasses I'd bought the last season that Senta and I'd followed the Browns together. At the sushi bar I gave them to Marv in the name of friendship.

Up at *The Midnight Special* offices, Brent Lukerman, dressed *always* in Levi's, gingham cowboy shirts and Tretorn tennies, was the *líder máximo*, guiding our endeavors from the vastness of his enormous offices. *Billboard* magazine had the whole floor below us, and we were *married* to the charts, as well as the famous "TV-Q" ratings system, which registered an act's presumed audience acceptance. Marv was in charge of getting the show on tape, but Brent pretty much dictated everything else: host, guests, running order, when a male voice could answer the office phone (never). Marv's approach was to deal with the crewing, shooting and editing, and let everything else—all that money and power—flow through him, or at least around him. He led by example. On tape days you were glad you had Marv's veteran hand on the wheel. But I was left to figure out what he wanted me to do from what he avoided. Directors have a healthy contempt for Producers, I noticed, and they seemed to have trouble respecting themselves in that role.

Everyone on the production staff except me had been raised in the business, through family connections, and had years and years of experience being talent coordinator, associate producer, production assistant, or whatever. I didn't even know what their job titles meant. Walking in cold I felt once again like a hick.

At thirty-seven, no longer possessed of the driving ambition that fueled the careers of my co-workers, I had to run to keep up, trying to avoid detection, while picking up whatever chops I could in the process.

Self-consciousness tended to limit my real strengths; deep firsthand knowledge of music and a programmer's love-of-audience/love-of-self confusion, like Trotsky's fatal inability to distinguish himself from History.

Sascha had made me welcome with signs and banners my first day, "Mitch!! What a Guy!" Placards and all. The P.A.'s and cute receptionist dug me and flirted around my little office, but the Talent Co-ordinatrix, "Kitty" Veneziana, copped a snippy little pose.

"Sascha says you never worked in TV. What *have* you done—other than *ray*-dio?"

"Nothing, really." What could I say?

"Well, I'll let you know what I need from you."

I shot Sascha a look. But she was gazing dreamily at the homes perched atop the Hollywood Hills.

And then there was Faye Mermelstein, rhino Brooklyn Jewess with no fuse at all. Faye took the opposite tack. She "loved" me right away, telling me point blank, "I have a lot to learn from you." I knew at once I was in for it.

We taped two days every two weeks, fifteen hours a day at KNBC in Burbank. Two straight days of an intensity that took my yokel breath away. There were hundreds of Union people governed by arcane bylaws and grievance procedures; the schedules that needed to be observed like Orthodox Jewish dietary proscriptions; the network; the Late Night brass; the Mensa-oid Standards & Practices censors in blazers; the guest musicians, bands, hand-wringing managers, record label reps, publicists, hopeful groupies and—behind it all—Brent Lukerman's championship ego.

Not a place to fuck up. The huge sound stages with their thousands of lights, cables, mics, the gigantic pedestal cameras, the four sets of risers so we could tape Dr. Hook while Black Oak Arkansas or the Captain and Tennille or K.C. and the Sunshine Band or The Commodores were setting up.

I hied myself unto Fred Segal, one of the first Melrose boutiques, and, telling the young kid who waited on me I'd been in Levi's and T-shirts too long, would he please dress me hip, walked out loaded down with pairs of Chemin de Fer flared jeans, Santa Cruz Imports shirts of gaily checked Indian gauze, and an early Ralph Lauren corduroy jacket to wear on tape days as a sign of rank. In the production hierarchy Book of Order, role identifiability was a sacred principle. Thou shalt *look like a producer!*

I loved Wolfman Jack, the venerable late night growler from Mexico and L.A.'s fabled pirate AM radio past who had been hired on as the show's M.C. He was a major figure in international radio syndication. I remembered him from the KURB days, and an eye-opening soiree he'd thrown for David Bowie when the *Ziggy Stardust* tour played the Santa Monica Civic. A big, gruff-but-tender kinda guy with just enough brain cells, Wolf had a total rock 'n' roll heart, but he gave us all fits by not learning—after four years with the show—to dispatch the simple Intros and Promos off the cue-cards in fewer than multiple takes. This was not cost-efficient. We taped him last, after breaking most of the crew, keeping only one or two of the five camera setups we used for the music acts.

In my weekly I tried to write him up into a kind of bent Jules Verne-ish character, some kind of rock wizard. But Wolf was an old dog, and less than eager to learn new licks. The Wolfman persona had served him twenty years already, and he trusted it—anything new would have to fight its way into the act. Still, he always praised my writing, often rising to the occasion before the camera and poppin' my Svengalese buttons with pride. There was the time that we were taping some promos for one of those cheap "Best of" compilation shows that we began to rely on more and more. I had been ringing the variations on "be there or be square" lines close to exhaustion and was hoping he'd do something moderately cool with "be there, or *c'est la guerre*," like take a grand pause. Something with timing. Be funny.

"I can't quite get the tongue around it," he bitched affably to the darkened sound stage. "Who wrote this stuff?"

He knew who fucking *wrote* it, and was invoking the question that has given writers Blinking Sphincter Syndrome since the dawn of time.

I came over to the stage to reassure him from below the camera, and we restarted tape. My rabbit ears were flattened back side'a my head.

"5…4…3…(beat) (beat) 'BE THERE OR…(uh) SEST…SEST LUH… LUH…(laughter)…GRRRRRRRRRRrrrrrrrrrr!!!!"

The Midnight Special "Tributes" were another matter. It was a time before music television, before "videos." Lacking the possibility of TV exposure elsewhere, the Biggies flocked to us: Aretha, Loretta Lynn, Johnny Cash, Johnny Mathis, Jethro Tull, Elton John—even, one day, Jerry Lee Lewis.

I kicked back, and let Sascha do the off-camera questioning while The Killer sat at the piano mugging and noodling these outrageous right-hand licks. She was wrapping the interview without touching on the still semi-*verboten* area of his famous incestuous honeymoon trip to London. Sascha shot me a pregnant look: all yours, big shot.

"Jerry Lee,'" I began. "Uh…I'm sure you've been asked this before, but this is like a biography of you, ya know, and we, well, I have to ask you to tell us again about marrying your thirteen-year-old cousin and flying her to Europe with ya for a honeymoon…"

"*That's right!!*" Lewis thundered. "*That's* right! *Everybody* says 'She's thirteen.' Go ahead and talk about it. Everybody said she was thirteen! Thirteen! *Every*body! But not one damn soul, not the papers, not the BBC…*no*body had the balls to mention the plain truth that she turned fourteen the very next day! God *Damn!!*"

"That's a take. Aaaannnnd a wrap." Marv's *suavecito* voice reached us over the intercom from the booth. "Thank you, Jerry Lee."

About this time, illuminated by a bolt of karmic lightning, my old partner Tommy Trout appeared in Hollywood. There had been no keeping him down, of course. After his mugging at the hands of The Head in Carnegie he'd been rollin', rollin', rollin'—bringing David Bowie to Carnegie to kick off his first stadium tour; then on to conquer New York as that most satisfying anomaly: the too-cool black player in white-boy rock 'n roll. Trout arrived in L.A. as VP of Promotion for a hugely successful English rock label distributed by Warner's. We partied some and put together insider trading-type talent swaps: he'd give me "A" list talent for the show if I'd tape the "C" list newcomers he was priming. This scored me some serious points with Lukerman.

Our staff practically lived at the Roxy, the town's new classy rock club, where most of our acts played sooner or later. We got to tape them before or after—at their convenience, basically. We'd walk over two or three nights a week—it was just across the Strip—and get free dinner, unlimited bar tab, and usually drugs from record company shills. Then Lou Reed or somebody would come on and we'd maybe get ideas on how to shoot him. Or maybe not.

I was totally digging the *chi* that performers put out. Dealing with their handlers and other apparatus connected the "lowly me" with the "powerful them," if only as conduit. I was admitted to the circle of the potent, but only if I could reach out and link hands with my neighbor the publicist, the VP of *Late Night*, the *TV Guide* contact—you get the picture.

Producing for a huge national audience, tapping the rock viewer years before MTV was, on one level, stunning. We fancied ourselves as sharing the duller side of the leading edge with *Mary Hartman, Saturday Night Live* and not much else.

I'd been hired in the first place on the presumption of my ability to bring in the hip acts. When I joined the staff in the summer of '75, they were just mending from a rather rude Dylan jilting. Marv had gone down to Florida and shot Bob with Joan Baez, Roger McGuinn and the unique artistry of Bob Neuwirth—who claimed to have given Janis Joplin her first real orgasm. But someone in Dylan's entourage thought it was "too commercial," and pulled the plug after the taping. Likely it was Neuwirth. His performance on the pirate tape Marv dubbed for me shows him with, shall we say, least to lose by nixing its airing. I soon got Booker T. & the M.G.s, James Brown, Bonnie Raitt and Judy Collins, so I'd had my little triumphs, but I knew Brent was looking for bigger and better.

To this end, I'd hooked up with Island Records, Bob Marley's label, who wanted us to shoot a huge political concert Bob and the Wailers were giving in Kingston to promote an oppositionist candidate for Prime Minister. Island would pay for everything: travel, film crew, staffing. Marv and I would fly there, shoot the live event, fly back to L.A., edit and turn the film around for the next week's *Midnight Special*.

I was so proud of myself that when I went to Brent I couldn't completely mask my satisfaction. His secretary gave me an appointment for three days later, so I went back to my bland office and cooled it. I worked on a script for a Willie Nelson/George Carlin show.

At the appointed hour, I opened the heavy doors, entered the darkened hangar, scanned for and finally found his command center on what looked like the horizon, trekked across an enormous expanse of rugs and hardwood. When I came within hailing distance, I was met with what I took to be Brent Lukerman's head.

The big chair turned slowly to face me.

"Got something I think you'll like," I said. Brent, still on the phone, looked up dully and motioned me to sit. After a five-minute wait I put the Island film proposal before him.

"Exclusive for a year, Brent, costs us nothing. Island covers it all."

"Who is this again?" He looked away at something on his desk.

"Bob Marley and the Wailers, live in concert in Kingston, probably all kind of big name guests. Island has the rights. Marley's a god to millions of people. All over the world. Like Ali."

"*I* know who Bob Marley is." Brent was always bland.

"So?"

"He's nothing."

⁓

We didn't go to Jamaica. So I called my old friend Jay Largent, now a budding producer, and I pitched him a different idea:

"We'd do it tasty," I told him.

"No *Midnight Special* logo."

"Okay…"

"No Wolfman."

The more thoughtful of the late-Sixties folk-rockers had heretofore eschewed the obvious smell of commerce which exuded from most elements of the show. It was ninety minutes weekly of very well-shot, studio audience live-to-tape Hit Parade, tasked primarily with not losing NBC's numbers coming out of Carson on Friday nights.

"Maybe just a soundstage look, like *Hard Day's Night*."

"Yeah, okay…"

"Tell Robbie I want the *guys* to pick the guests, but my idea is to do their roots: Ronnie Hawkins sits in or does a solo set…Muddy, whoever they want, Jay."

"We could talk to *Bob* again…"

Bob Dylan, was, of course, still the Kahuna, the target of *all* those who would exploit (including us, to be sure), yet able thus far to run clear of commercial music business's baser emoluments. Untouchable. If I could get him to reconsider, or better, if he'd come on and do a set with The Band… Bloodstone took me to meet The Band's spiritual leader and amanuensis, Robbie Robertson, at his oceanfront residence in Malibu Colony.

"Like, Levon could introduce Muddy, Garth could bring on Neil Young, you could all accompany Joni, or Bob…I think the guys might go for it. "

Robbie listened, and thought. "We've got some big decisions coming up, anyway," he finally said.

Bloodstone told me on the ride back to town that after all these years of touring The Band was fixin' to pack it in, and that maybe, between the two of us, we could build a TV show suitable to the occasion. But the next week when I phoned him my calls went unreturned.

Adrienne and I were living apart again. I had a place in East Hollywood on Mariposa, a half-block north of Fountain. Downstairs was the kitchen and a room for the rented upright, couch and books. Upstairs was a tiny place for my mattress on the floor and windows on three sides. I could see the top of Beachwood Canyon. My neighbors were mostly Latino families. Scientology had bought the old Cedars of Lebanon Hospital down the street (where George Gershwin had checked himself in one afternoon in 1939, and died of a brain tumor the next morning), and was painting it a baleful industrial blue.

Adrienne and I saw other people, but I managed to keep in touch, between busy taping days and Roxy-hanging, and sometimes partying pretty furiously with the invincible Trout.

One day he kissed me on the forehead and said, "You love her. Do you know that? You're in love with her."

"Why do you say that, Trout?"

"Maaa-aaan. Dig yourself. What are you?"

"What am I what, Tom?"

"What are you? A-fucking-sleep? You are totally in love with the woman!"

I'd been thinking about her as an enemy, almost, a person who wouldn't give me what I wanted. Although she did let me surround her body quite often. Wasn't it enough? Was I certifiably sex-crazed? Was I insatiable? Was it the drugs? I felt way sweet on her, but there was something else, too.

"I don't know, Trout."

In the two weeks after our meeting with Robbie Robertson, while Brent Lukerman's mouth watered, and my credibility hung in the balance, I had but one call returned by Jay. And when he did call, it was to announce that his old pal Marty Scorsese had agreed to direct a feature concert movie of our idea in San Francisco on his Thanksgiving break. Robbie would produce what was being billed as *The Last Waltz*.

I took the news well, I think. In even my short time in TV, I had learned to think hierarchically, developing a sense of my relative cloutlessness.

I managed to wangle a job for Adrienne's younger sister, Lana, as receptionist with the selfsame young Mr. Largent. The two of us planned to travel to San Francisco as *The Last Waltz* came together. I would have killed to sleep with Lana. She had pulled off her T-shirt in my presence once too many times, smiling her toothy grin as her mammary fascinations beckoned heavily below.

When she told me she had some pharmaceutical methydrene she was bringing along, I hastened to forget to invite Adrienne. It was a working trip, I told her, but booked one room in the New Otani for Lana and me.

It was an epic party. Cocaine was the Power Drug of the new epoch. People bragged of blow in the Carter White House. Backstage the Winterland Arena in San Francisco was awash in multiplane elevations of spirit. Eric Clapton, Paul Butterfield, Bill Graham, George Harrison, Annie Liebowitz, Emmet Grogan and The San Francisco Poets (effectively purged from the final cut of the film), Mo Ostin, Albert Grossman and every major cinematographer in America. Out in the Arena, the San Francisco Symphony played Strauss waltzes for dancing. Then, somehow, the assembled stars of rock managed to join the paying attendees in a sit-down Turkey Day feast for thousands.

~

The weekend was to have an even longer lasting impact on my life because of two accidental meetings.

One was bumping into Sandy Durnit, because he stumbled into my path outside Winterland, between Van Morrison and Neil Diamond.

"Mitch, man, it's great to see you!" nodding his characteristic bass-player manqué nod. "Come on up to the room," waving to include Sascha, who was up there as an aspiring booker, and Lana. "Got some blow."

It was some of the sorriest *coca* that ever disgraced a mirror, just stimulant enough to start his brilliant babble.

"We got this radio show here in The City," he said, wiping some errant spittle. "Right here on Market Street. *The Planet Daily* like the newspaper. Can you do our L.A. interviews?"

"Yeah, well Sandy, ya know I'm working on *The Midnight Special* right now. Takes most of my time."

"Just a 60-second feature. Syndicated. Alternative radio. Five times a week."

From the heights of my Network TV gig I snooted, "This blow is disgraceful," I said, making a face. "Gimme your card. Maybe I'll call ya."

That night I finally got my chance with lovely Ms. Lana. We had both been ingesting regularly of her pharmaceuticals and had not been to bed since we arrived. I was just finishing a Drug Moment wherein the inebriate looks the substance in the eye and sees him/herself looking back. A bond of similar elements is consummated. What is it about this intoxicant I like? What is there of *me* in this powerful methamphetamine? What indeed? The result was my scribbling on a yellow pad this proposal for a late night TV show called *Are We Keeping You Up?* That took about forty-five minutes—we'd snorted the whole bottle by then—while Lana got ready for bed.

In my mind's eye, I saw Lana's weighty mammae, just as they were when she showed them to me up at our pool, hefting them and staring at me all the while. I was squeezing them delicately in my palms-turning-to-fists as her nipples popped through between the fingers. She screamed a drug-and-passion-filled cry of pent-up lust as I pawed her roughly, her mouth gaping, thighs soaked with her love for me long-withheld for mere convention. "Give me some rockin' cock at last!" she crooned as our lips and tongues and holy sexes enfolded.

But in reality what she did was utter a tired, cranky *Mi-itch!* at the touch of my first finger on her wool-encased leg, and it was off to my own bed for me.

The second meeting was a stumble-into situation with Darcy Waters, a tall thin Santa Cruz ex-rock piano player aspiring L.A. clothing magnate. A cool, refined and handsome house-hippie kinda guy friend of Lana and, it turned out, currently dating none other than my Adrienne!

"She's a peach," he told me smiling slowly.

"Yeah."

Damn! That does it. But, what is it? Something was going on down deep, but cocaine, pharmaceutical methydrene and sleep deprivation were preventing a reliable report. Was it jealousy? Rejection by Lana? Somehow through all the layers of mood alteration, I knew all I needed to know. Saw her "peachy" face, her heart floating in sweet memory. *This shit has to end!*

I was off for L.A. in the early morning, leaving most *Waltzers* to sleep their rock Sunday off, dream their rock dreams away. I was winging my way back to my Adrienne, who received me *senza rancor.*

Back at 9000 Sunset, things were twittering with *The Midnight Special* pre-production scheduling—the speedup before Christmas Break. Brent had handed us a New Year's Special he'd somehow conned the network out of, co-hosted by Doc Severinsen and Gladys Knight, to write, book, shoot and edit concurrent with normal weekly production. I was still political enough to riddle the obvious rude-boy riddle: since we were working almost double-time to jam everything into the can before the break, could we expect to be *paid* for this "vacation," as it was being formulated in our humming little Strip-view hive.

My co-workers looked at me with a perfect blend of pity and scorn, and briskly moved the agenda. You can be certain that it was an unpaid hiatus that greeted us with a holiday bray, presented to us demurely by Brent's accountant after he had jetted off to Vail. Tooodle*ooooooo*ooooo! When the toasted staff dragged itself back to the office, we found gift-wrapped boxes on our desks. Brent had honored us with cardigan *Midnight Special* letter sweaters with a show logo on the arm in orange. I heaved mine out the office door, over the receptionist's desk and onto a pile of *Hollywood Reporters* in a rack by the front door.

Adrienne, by now a full-time Montessori teacher, had fled her apartment— a West Hollywood single where she'd been dangerously voyeurized—for the security of a crude, claustrophobic little wreck of a railroad flat back down in Ocean Park. It was sunless, approaching the truly dismal. Her roommates were April, Tree's lover and occasionally still mine, and another Montessorian from Colorado named Janet Planet.

When they moved in together that fall, Adrienne asked me if I'd refrain from coupling with April on-site. By then I was merely another name in April's Leporellan catalogue. I told Adrienne I'd go her one better, and chill with April *completely,* a rare instance of Seventies selflessness. I'm not sure April ever noticed.

Not until the rainy season were the depths of the house's squalor truly revealed. Built on a desert, L.A. features not hot and cold, but dry and wet seasons. So, after Thanksgiving the storms began to blow out of the Canadian Northwest, and the three young ladies began a months-long siege of the landlord to repair the roof, and ultimately got themselves thrown out. Christmas of '76, I found Adrienne in this bitter swamp, roommates dispersed to Long Island and Petaluma. I'd thought to wash away the hiatus blues with a bag of magic mushrooms someone had given me. Despite her head cold and messy sinusitis, we chewed them up with a little Cuervo, and tripped and talked all night. It was late the next day—winter's light giving up to early evening—when we surrendered the warmth of the comforters for the dank tarn of Eln, and rose for some nourishment. I got up without my pants and padded to the john still with last night's head. Halfway down the hall I stopped.

"I didn't know you wanted me to marry you."

"How could you not *know?*"

"I just never thought about it that way," coming back into the faint light of the kitchen.

"Then why have you been saying no for five years, if it never entered your mind?"

She was putting on the kettle for herb tea in her light green chenille housecoat. I left her there, slouching off back down the hall to the toilet. Outside the early December rain drove against the dirty panes. I questioned my eyes between the streaks on the medicine chest mirror. My feet were freezing. As my urine arced down into the bowl, I felt a heightened sense of the grace of life. I shook off my prepuce with determination, and opened the door to the hall.

"All right."

She looked up from putting the tea tray down on the rickety 40's metal tube table in the dinette.

"All right what?"

I looked down the hall at her and felt lightheaded, then pulled towards her by a gentle but irresistible force, until even in the dullness I could see her eyes.

"All right, let's get married."

"What are you saying?"

"I'm saying, 'let's do it'!"

Next day we rushed off to find a place to live, and came up with a weird old two-story beach house at 27th and Ocean Front Walk. Actually, our part of the house—the back—fronted on Speedway, that mangy but populous little alleyway behind the beachfront properties, with only a glimpse of ocean from the second floor bedroom. It was more than we wanted to pay, but I was working steady so we took it and didn't look back.

Adrienne was sick, and I stayed with her until the new place was ready, bringing tea and orange juice—along with a purple cashmere engagement sweater that finally raised her spirits. I noted a true polarity, more than a simple "chemistry" in our relationship: whenever I was hot, she was cold, and vice versa, when I was down she always knew how to pump me up—and the converse. So now, as she convalesced under my ministrations of course, I began to get sick. I'd been regaling her with plans for the wedding.

"How's your Mom going to like having Wolfman do the wedding?"

"You mean officiate? Is that legal?"

"No, but I'm not getting Church and State involved here! But we'd already have done a legal blitz-o-ceremony downtown."

"I guess…"

Adrienne's pretty face was still, but behind her honeyed eyes she was seeing her mother, a sweet displaced Southern belle, a woman passing through life as if expecting to stumble upon lost Tara around the next corner, react to this open perversion of What Is To Be Done.

"Okay…he could play, like, Rock Minister. I'll rehearse him."

That night my fever deepened as the skies opened, the rain dripping into pots and pans that ringed the old bed as we slept. Around midnight we were awakened by sirens and red lights circling the wet walls as firemen thumped down the alley to the big modern apartment house that blocked our westward view. I decided I was dreaming and went back into a deep fungal sleep. She fed me boiled eggs in the morning and that afternoon when the phone rang I was beginning to feel better. It was Marv Tweed calling to tell me I'd been fired. A week later he, in turn, was whacked. Downsizing.

I could have pressed Wolfman to keep his promise, but that ate it in big pieces, so I went back to the Ouija board for someone to officiate.

"I got the name of some stately black judge."

"Uh-huh…"

"Judge Baker, someone's uncle. Guy with pear-shaped tones. He'll do a simple civil proceeding, before we do some serious partying."

She was dubious, thinking she'd have trouble clearing the ante bellum censors.

We went ahead and hired the Miramar Hotel in Santa Monica for the first Sunday in March. Then, two weeks before the date, "Judge Baker's office called. He's decided to go to Portugal, or somewhere."

Adrienne and her family had been good sports up to this time, but were now pushing a Sherman Oaks rabbi they'd heard about.

Out of comfortable alternatives, I asked around for a name, and was sent to a young clergyman at a proto-politically correct church in Ocean Park. Despite my worst fears, he turned out to be thrillingly tudeless.

"Tell me what you're thinking," he began.

"I was thinking I want to exclude any reference to divinity," I said appreciatively.

"Okay."

"Do you have anything like that?"

"You're the writer," he said mildly. "Why don't you write what you want and I'll read it?" I loved him.

Tree took us into the KCST studio where we spent the night producing the intro and reception music segments. My sister Lily came in from Fun City representing my mother and father, who were too "sick" (I accepted their definition) to travel. All three sons had been bought flannel suits. Aged Aunt Selma was beaming. Sweet cousin Noah Guilford was down from San Anselmo with a pair of hand-blown goblets and a bottle of Peruvian flake. We received lots of blow. All the Dresser sisters and their concupiscent girl-chums were in Sailin' Shoes mode. We partied all week before the blessed event. Marching powder flowed like menses. It was 1977. I played the cheap rented spinet in our barely affordable Oceanfront residence, and we all sang.

Sunday, March 6, dawned perfectly calm. By afternoon, the sun was licking the poolside palms at the Miramar, and the Pacific glinted golden in the middle distance, full of promise. The music before the ceremony included "The Emperor Waltz," Keith Jarrett's "Hymns for Organ," and my friend Michael Hoenig's "Departure from the Northern Wasteland." The previous night's party was rekindled as a starter-culture for the grander revelry in store for relatives, colleagues, comrades, coworkers, collaborators, co-writers and buddies from diverse realms spread through the bi-level area. From the old Hollywood bar, with its photos of Ronald Colman and Barbara Stanwyck and dark velvet booths, guests strolled down onto the reception level, flowers everywhere in the mid-afternoon brilliance.

The crowd—from black autoworkers to television directors with many layers of lounge lizards and random malingerers in between—swelled with the music, approaching the verge of spontaneous group levitation as show time approached. The room energy was tipsy, surging, bubbling, swirling. Don't forget snorting. The young minister made his appearance at three o'clock.

The ultra-elevated well-wishers were presented with the need to execute an abrupt hairpin 180 in order to deal with a clergyperson. He stepped forward as the hubbub slowly began to simmer down. Tree pushed the "Play" button and the opening bars of the slow movement of the *sixth Brandenburg* came somberly out into the afternoon air. That was enough for Adrienne who, without letting the "march" establish, grabbed my hand tightly and dashed off toward the makeshift altar, where we arrived in seconds, the rest of the wedding party, equally elevated, huffing and puffing behind us.

I had written a classic New Age do-it-yourself ceremony— poetry and not *too* embarrassing sentiments. Mostly it was short.

SCRIPT:
1) ROBERTO ALMEIDA: AD LIB INTRO AND READING
Shakuhachi solo: a mediaeval Japanese tone poem in multiple tableaux. Describes the meeting and mating of deer.
2) INTO: REV. RICHARD FONDA: WEDDING POEM

RICHARD:

Welcome to our party! Take a look around!
You see yourselves and we see us…
Everywhere we look.
Tell us why, tell us why,
The mountain dreams beneath the sky.

Rejoice! You, the very particles of our life.
You, the sparkling prism of our love.

Welcome to our party! Take a look around!

We look at you and see ourselves…
Our table vanity ringed in lights
And you looking back.
Gathered in lumps and bumps, in bodies,
Friends of all models and shapes…
We love you, our friends, and you love us…
A good thing to know in front.

Rejoice, you molecules of our otherwise atomized lives.
Your gravity is our specific weight.
You need only ask,

Welcome to our party! Take a look around!
We seek and find our love's certainty
In the people whose faces bleed past us like children's drawings
On a moving airport sidewalk.
Tell us why, tell us why,
The mountain dreams beneath the sky.
Rejoice with us, our friends.
You are what we got when we went out
Looking for a whole lot less.

Unfurl that brow:
"Everybody got a laughin' place," and
You can't stop the setting sun
With the small of your back.
Things do change
People can grow
Love has a way of improving the odds.

Tell us why, tell us why,
The mountain dreams beneath the sky.

Come, oh, our common gladness,
Kissing all our needing lips
With smiles warm and fine,
And all our lives with your resonant ease.

3) MUSIC SELECTION:
BRANDENBURG CONCERTO NO. 6: SLOW MOVEMENT

4) ENTER BRIDE, GROOM, PARTY

INTO: REV. RICHARD FONDA READS SHORT STATEMENT
(MUSIC FADE UNDER.)

RICHARD:
Adrienne and Mitch, your presence here today symbolizes your commitment to
defend, preserve and develop the deep love and trust the two of you share.
We are glad for you, knowing you have worked hard for it.
Four years of founding the relationship you now openly and joyously cherish.
Four years of retraining each other to feel more and fear less.
Trying to use the Past as a guide to the Future,
while the Present blew in through chinks in the wall.
You come here today to celebrate your love with your friends

and to assure them of your shared commitment to growth and self-respect.
And, needless to say, to boogie-woogie.
Mitch, a deeply traditional man, has the traditional ring.

6) BRUNO OFFERS RING CUSHION TO MITCH
(RING BUSINESS.)

7) RICHARD:
Good Luck! You're married!!!

8) THEY KISS

9) MUSIC
1) FANFARE: (THE KISS.)
2) CANNED APPLAUSE: (THEY SEPARATE.)
3) "THE ENTERTAINER" (COUPLE LEADS PROCESSION TO
DANCE FLOOR. CUE: SISTERS).
4) J. GEILS: "DO YA WANNA DANCE?" (OPENING LINE ONLY.)
SMASH CUT INTO:
5) BOB MARLEY AND THE WAILERS: "LIVELY UP YOURSELF"

As I said: mostly it was short.

Adrienne was so coked-out that she left all our wedding presents behind in a room at the Miramar. By the time she finally remembered them two or three days later they could not be accounted for. There had been no formal honeymoon. Then, no newlywed game. Finally, no income.

I remembered my meeting with the brilliant, sputtery Sandy Durnit at The Last Waltz. *The Planet Daily* took on new meaning in the light of my new marital status and Ocean Front Walk rental payments, so I called the big galoot, got hired quickly enough, and made arrangements to take over as the show's L.A. correspondent.

Then I got my first taste of the adrenalinated energies of one Stan Christopher.

Tough-voice Stan took the phone from Durnit as soon as I'd signed on, and lost no time at all in sharing his frustration with working with the overweight, pop-eyed alternative media ideologue who was our nominal boss:

"I need to zip his fucking fly for the boy genius. How old is he, thirty?"

"I've never really worked with him before," I phumphered. "He seems to have a good brain."

He was verbalizing what I'd always, despite a respect for his intellect, felt about Durnit, *in fondo*. Also, I was older, and marginally more respected than Stan. My reputation served to keep Durnit's fabled flakiness in check somewhat. Stan, in his late-middle apprenticeship couldn't as yet manage.

"Brain as such," Stan allowed.

"He has good ideas…"

"You've never worked with him, man. Half the time I just throw his fat butt outta here, tell him 'go make calls from home. I'll cut the tape.'"

Stan had heard my first batch of tapes by then. I guess he thought I was a pretty good interviewer. He wanted to find a way for the two of us to co-function efficiently, leaving a largely executive role for the Recovering Creative Person.

Phoning to Stan in San Francisco, I stood at my desk in the place Adrienne and I'd been forced to take on Olympic, a traffic-blasted in-town artery. Far from the no-longer-affordable beach, I looked down at the Carthay Circle Church and the coming and going of hip-dressing Alcoholics Anonymous attendees, saying:

"I liked the distinction Rechy drew between cruising and hustling. It's not that different for us breeders."

"Like it or not." Bonding.

Stan—long, straight pure blonde hair to his shoulders, an ex-Army hippie, had read John Rechy's *Sexual Outlaw* with unusual compassion for someone associated, however peripherally, to the manly aura of rock.

Unlike most of the newsmen I'd met at KURB and its rivals, who were basically surfers with functioning verbal skills, Stan was a walking, talking compendium of anti-establishment fact, folklore, fantasy and far-fucking-out fiction. He simply was Mr. Radical Media, making it his business to know every inch of the Nixon tapes, the Pentagon Papers, all of Jim Garrison's research into Dealy Plaza, all that stuff. Plus, he was the kind of music lover I'd always wanted to know—the guy who loved music whose charm escaped me—Al Di Meola, Jean-Luc Ponty—and thus could turn me on to surprising shit. Finally, he was a committed advocate of recreational drug use—for psycho-spiritual pursuits, exclusively.

So it was exhilarating hanging with two younger outlaw males for whom pleasure was life: Tree, and now the amazing white light of Stan Christopher, with his piercing blue eyes, blonde mustache under a straight but distinguished nose and a voice from Newscaster Central Casting. But what the voice said! The content was there—outrage for days! If unduly shaped by the primitive inversion of Eighth-Grade-Civics-Class worldview, into an oh-yeah? pugnacity that challenged, intuitively and viscerally, American government policies and functioning norms. On occasion I grew tired of his seemingly endlessly serial Eurekas, as occasionally happened when he got so turned on by his own rap that he couldn't shut it down and couldn't hear anything else.

So I was back doing interviews, careful, this time, to keep my voice way off mike. Like a film director, I surmised, calling instructions from out of range.

I did two hundred and forty three interviews in that thirteen month period, mostly for Stan and his various syndicated radio news shows. I like to think of this work as having been at least in part investigative broadcasting. It *wasn't*, of course, in the strictest sense, at *all*, but we did deal with controversial issues and exposés some of the time. We sought out and interviewed writers, reporters and other *real* investigative types who *were* doing the daring, original work. We merely passed it along to whatever share of the youth market was listening to our syndicated ninety-second-chewing-gum-spot imbedded daily radio features. Nevertheless, Stan, Durnit and I routinely acted as if we were on a Mission from Somewhere.

I started keeping records of my *tête-à-têtes* with the very first one—a character actor named Michael Ansara, acting as semi-official spokesman for a film called *Mohammed, Messenger of God*. I drove my silver Renault R-5 with the 100-watt Pioneer system Tree'd help me get, listening to Chick Corea's *My Spanish Heart*, to this faceless modern condo in Calabasas on a bright March afternoon, and listened to him deliver a soft *apologia* for the Islamic "Revolution." Basta. I gave the cassette to Stan and Durnit the next day, but it was never used.

Then came Robert Downey, Sr. the white director of *Putney Swope* (one of the hippest pieces of film ever seen, especially in '68). He was being sponsored by the Los Angeles International Film Exposition ("Filmex"), one of the only decent L.A. cultural institutions of the Seventies. Filmex was premièring Downey's absolutely maniacal new feature *Moment to Moment* which I recall only faintly but pleasurably, but which ends with this amazing pullback from a window scene of the guy with the huge nose from *Swope* and a middle-aged woman actor, called, in the film "Mme. Frogroise," I believe, snorting cocaine from a *major* sugar bowl with matching soup spoons, crossing arms àla Heidelberg beer mugs, and gleefully packing their sinuses as credits roll. The interview—the first using my new Nakamichi 550 portable—was duly edited into *The Planet Daily* Show #481, and I was duly awarded $50.

Soon to follow was a talk with Samantha Eggar, who was starring in the new Canadian film *Why Shoot the Teacher?*, co-starring Bud Cort, then coalescing a cult around *Harold and Maude* and *Brewster McCloud*. Miss Eggar's triumph had come with an Oscar nomination for her role in William Wyler's 1965 *The Collector*, costarring Terence Stamp, followed by *Walk, Don't Run,* and my personal favorite movie featuring animals yanked about from spot to spot by piano-wires, *Dr. Doolittle*. We dealt superficially with the problems in the post-Studio System Hollywood, and we also took on the Woman Question.

A big part of the interview process, of course, is relations with publicists, some of whom were more charming than others. My favorite was Regina

Kroll, round and luscious, with long honey blonde locks and a huge smile. Revisiting the talent swaps I'd done with Trout for TV, I had also worked some trades with Regina: she'd slip me "names" normally too big for my radio show, and I'd interview marginal people who just might turn into a show for us. She'd call to invite me to her clients' screenings and we'd sit in the back of the room burrowing in each other's clothing. Innocent flirt-petting, but infinitely preferable to cruelly watching *A Bridge Too Far,* for example. Anyway, Efram Zimbalist, Jr. was one I doubted they could use in New York, given their Youth Culture orientation, but I figured: *What the hey! He'd been a bigger star than Edd "Kookie" Byrnes on 77* Sunset Strip *in the Fifties.*

His gray eminence went dutifully through his paces, flogging an undistinguished Xerox televenture, while Regina and I stifled respectful yawns. About twenty minutes in—sensing he was content with his hypescraft—I asked the obvious:

"In view of the revelations of the improprieties that have come to light regarding the FBI under your friend, J. Edgar Hoover, have you reconsidered the value and nature of your long personal relationship with The Director?"

"Well," he postulated, "a lot of what you hear is poppycock, of course, and *listen!*—you have to remember there was a 'Communist Conspiracy' back then; you had groups like 'the Letterman' and the 'SDA'" (sic, sic, sic). It was too sad a spectacle to laugh, although Regina managed a snort of ambivalence.

We were forever running around New York and San Francisco, talking to the heavies, trying to get them to say something Out There, useful to our audience, whoever *they* were—whoever would sit through the Trident commercial.

I saw our frenzied, probably self-deluded activities as trying to do something my father would have been proud of. Something like what *he* did. Serving people someway, healing some part of them. And I *know* Stan thought of it that way. I loved working with him. His respect for my ideas and, implicitly, the way my mind worked was a welcome change from the rote anus-sharing in the Network/Studio "relationship" hierarchy.

Then our little syndicated feature was bought by the dope magazine *Stoner*, which worried me credibility-wise, but for a while their checks cleared, and living was easy. I'd fly PSA redeye to the Bay Area every once in awhile and stay with Stan on his rented houseboat in Sausalito. Nights we'd stay up drugging and mad-rapping and then take the ferry to The City in the morning, passing Alcatraz drinking dark strong coffee, the gulls cawing as they swooped low over the wooden deck, floating in the windstream.

From our ferry San Francisco looked so romantic, the city swimming in the cold young sunlight. We took the bus up Market to the office-studio he shared with Durnit. One night *Stoner's* publisher, one Tim Forskein, came out from New York and performed the ultimate four-hour New Left more-radical-than-thou circumnavigatory speed-rap on the new *Planet* editorial policy. Since he didn't seem to understand *any* of the concepts he was freewheeling through I figured that either he had burned too many brain cells and was terminally inchoate, or, he was some kind of cop or other narcotics recycling agent. A frustrating night, the four of us Monster Verbalizers penned up there in the cramped hippie-squalid office suite, listening to him elude, side-step, outrun, and finally avoid every one of our concerns re: the future of the enterprise under his recently acquired aegis.

I realized early in the marathon gum-bumper that the truth was going to be tough to extract from this fake, and pretty much tuned out, letting my mind stroll down the corridors of alternative futures. I'd drop back into the discussion just to be sure I wasn't missing something of timeless value, but it was all pretty much the same Al Haig redux blah-blah/woof-woof.

Back in L.A. after caucusing by phone, the three of us decided to take direction from *Stoner* Sales Manager, a short Lower East Side Italian who, though essentially a conduit from the then-lucrative paraphernalia market was apparently Forskein's *de facto* spokesperson, and he would always tell us "go for it."

Six months later Tim Foreskein was found with a bullet in his brain. Counterculture Pleasure Warrior or dope-cop? A corpse either way. By that time the show had been bought and sold a couple of times and was now owned by a creepy little syndicator called D.I.R. in New York and titled "Direct News," a name which, at least, succinctly captured Stan's in-your-faceness. He had gone to New York as Producer and done hour specials on the Jonestown catastrophe and Abby Hoffman in hiding.

We would work together for about two years, first in San Francisco; then for a New York syndicator, Stan as Producer, me as West Coast Person. We had a happy run, telling ourselves we were somehow a continuation of the countercultural vector, which combined with the mainstream demographics to produce high-consciousness audiences/populations, before the chewing gum sponsor ankled. Stan garnered a borderline straight News Director job in a decent local FM outlet, from whence he wondrously vaulted into the belly of the network as an anchor on CBS's alternative news/feature service.

And I was, once again, nowhere.

At first, things with Adrienne were cozy and nice. She was more relaxed as the Honest Woman. She'd been running all her life, ready to get some rest. Happy teaching at Montessori, coming home to me with the star of satisfaction on her forehead, smiling, kissing, hugging at night at home when the Boulevard was quiet. I had managed to talk the generous piano dealer Abel David into giving me credit on a new Yamaha upright grand to replace the endless dogshit rentals. We sang together that first in-town winter.

Sex was always perfect. More than occasionally enhanced by drugs. So it was blissful until the first wave of job wobble.

10:00 a.m., second pot of coffee time in our studio-apartment on traffic-angry Olympic. I was reading Charles Champlin in the *L.A. Times* when the phone rang. I picked up and heard the news: our little show was dog-meat. The sponsor decided we were "wrong for his target audience" and our New York syndicator bailed, dunking us warninglessly into the shit-can of History. My stomach flap-flap-flapped.

But came a palliative thought: Tree was trying to get me to be host/ producer for *Rock World*, a popular but vapid radio show he's been producing, an hour-long weekly, syndicated internationally. They did all the production down at Tree's studio in Venice, a newly converted warehouse. I'd be working at night, in deference to his few daytime clients. We'd be there all night every week. All night. Every week. But I needed the work.

The current host of *Rock World* was a bland but ambitious broadcasting school clone, who opened every break with a windy, empty rap: "I'm here in Hollywood with…Billy Joel," or whoever, and sank steeply downward from there. If I took over, it had to make an abrupt one-eighty. The owners didn't seem to give a shit what the show sounded like as long as none of their 200 AOR FM subscriber stations canceled as a result—highly unlikely because the stations took money from the sponsor in exchange for airing the show with their spot embedded.

Our first show was Warren Zevon. It was April, 1978. "Werewolves of London" was his big hit. His sideman and co-writer, cult guitar-god Waddy Wachtel, was on fire. Linda Ronstadt had recorded several of Zevon's tunes— "Hasten Down the Wind," "Poor, Poor Pitiful Me," "Mohammed's Radio," and most notably "Carmelita"—enough to confirm his membership in the young, white L.A. neo-country/folk-rock matrix that included Jackson Browne, Lowell George, The Eagles, Carla Bonoff, J.D. Souther and Andrew Gold—but Zevon was distinguished from these mostly rad-libbers by a kind of unconscious but passionate right-wing anarchism. A spoiled Hunter S. Thompson, if you will.

Tree and I came up with a tape of "Werewolves" live at the Roxy to open our first *RW*, which, along with a new audio logo, gave the show a spaceman sound.

"And his hair was perfect."

Zevon's label's Publicity VP, another ex-Carnegian, sent a note:

"Mitch, man. Best show ever, man. Do it *to* it!"

We were off and running, at least our noses. Cocaine was back from

Hollywood's Babylonian past, now *the prime Powerperk*. Behold the flow of influence in a room—backstage, at a club, agent's office, wherever Power lurked. The ebb and flow of the white powder to and from the bathroom. People excusing themselves, one at a time or in pairs. A One-on-One meant finding a 'girl' who liked coke, confiding privately that you had a quantity, finding a suitable location, and then letting her fuck you for the drug. Simple as that.

Power. A hierarchy defined by sugar bowls, dealers and tiny silver spoons. In the Seventies, cocaine was a continuation of the marijuana-thing: the rock 'n' roll lifestyle, an attack on straight values, an aspect of alternative consciousness: this was not your father's inebriant of choice. Mirror, mirror. Whatever you told yourself, you didn't let yourself be left out of the coke-line.

Monday morning, I reported to RATWorld headquarters for my weekly meeting with my Executive Producer, Louie Lipton. Lipton, a lop-eared working-class Jew from Southie and a pretty nice guy, began the exact same incantation week after week:

"Ya doo'n a faaabyuliss jawb, Mitchell. I loved th' last show…"

I thought he was sincere, but then so were the five $100 bills he snapped off from a modest roll, and placed side by side on his cute roll-top desk.

"Thanks, Louie. You're a man who knows what fabulous is," I told him before he got nervous and picked up the phone again. Then I scooped up the bills.

I gave the money to Tree, who bought the drug retail—in little colored origami wrapped grams—and we had a G for each of the five sessions it took us to write, record and edit the one hour show. We started in the late afternoon. I drove my $2,000 Alfa GT to this first floor loft from which, with typical ferocity—born of the stubbornness to do it with his own hands—he wrought an authentic hippie production den.

Here he slept, with his darling April on a raised dais crowned by the giant waterbed, round and toasty warm. He was twenty-five, living his dream of hip L.A. media. Tree made far more money than most kids his age—especially hippie kids—plus he gets freebies to everywhere. Tickets, comps to the Roxy, the Whisky, the Forum, the new covered Universal Amphitheater. His studio was replete with rock: T-shirts, posters, wacky New Age *objets d'art*, "men's" magazines in orderly piles.

April's books are there, too: Lenin, Trotsky, Rosa Luxembourg, James Cannon, Grasmci, et al. They filled the tiny raised "bedroom" platform to the edge. Above the bed an old early Toshiba color TV hung by chains from a girder. A Honda 550CB middleweight motorcycle leaned at the entryway poised to finesse the crowded summer beach streets. Outside, a Pinto Sportabout in British racing green, with vinyl top, sunroof, wide ovals and Ohio plates. Stylin. Pleasure Temple of the Young Hedon.

But pleasure was not what drugs were for at *RATWorld*. It's hard to say exactly how the actual cocaine-based granules we inhaled nightly functioned in the psycho-social vortex we occupied. A way of entering that unique, hollow head of death that cocaine dependably engenders in humans? The same head as the average listener, maybe—someone, some kid, some lone and lonely dickhead somewhere in America, loaded on Ludes, or reds, or just kickin' back, takin' bong hits of Thai stick or Oaxacan, starting the second 6-pack—someone fleeing Corporate Type-A-head on the way to Anywhere Else, watching TV with the audio off and listening to radio.

Out. We all want out. Out of the Las Vegas culture that thinks that Vietnam is fine as long as you keep it off television, of the suburban security guaranteed, air-conditioned nightmare of denied feelings and objectification, of the world of Better-Thans and Stronger-Thans and Richer-Thans and No-You-Can't. Death on Lay-Away.

No! Out! No Frank Sinatra. No Nixon. No Mom and Dad. Tune out; fade out, zone out, check out. Light out for somewhere else, where the smell of brain cells soaking in Booth's or Tanqueray don't rot our olfactory bulbs. Out of sight, out of our minds, out to getcha, outer limits. Whip it out. Out at the plate. We outta here.

The audio gear Tree managed to assemble for us to work with was primitive. two-track Ampexes, mostly, early stereo from the mid-'Sixties and a pretty basic Tascam board. He recently put in some sound-processing stuff, too, dbx, some Dolby and additional EQ, echo and reverb units as well as a couple of decent new Technics cassette players with logic. We made do, but it was all hands-on, manual and laborious, with much duplication of effort, endless waiting and boredom.

Tree cut the interview into basic track segments. We planned the running order of tunes, I wrote intros, outros and little linkage pieces, while he sat cutting lines of blow with his favorite tool—employed with uncanny proficiency on tape and flake alike—the single-edge razor blade. Symbol of the age. Iconic.

The walls were lined floor to ceiling with metal record-racks—two copies of most of the current rock LPs, plus jazz, classical and modern music, as well as the usual production library staples; sound effects, oldies, comedy, ethnic music and recent and classic soundtracks.

He had an especially fine ear for the texture and dramatic qualities of instrumental music, the inherent emotionality, the language of feelings that was accessible if and only if one paid attention.

Tree did; and his work always reflected that radical, awake and emboldened freshness that was the essence of the Hippie Way. *Who cares how "we always did it"; let's fuckin' do it right for once! Right now! Right here, damn it! Let's act like we care about our audience as living, breathing, even thinking individuals (however wasted) not just numbers for the demographers and media buyers' mill. Let's use our feelings!*

Tree was a joy. A guy driven enough to want to make his work perfect, but always motivated to take chances and the extra effort to turn his mistakes into inspired risk-driven innovations.

A typical *RW* opened with a choir singing *Gaudeamus, igitur* fading under Groucho Marx remembering his college days, from *Duck Soup*, into our psychedelic audio logo, panned wildly in concentric three-sixties into my Opening Intro.

All this production took time and energy, and that's where the Peruvian marching powder naturally came in. We limited ourselves to a G a night, but usually about 3:00 or 4:00 we ran out, and ended up breaking out some of the generic speed he kept in his dresser, which, in our condition, was routinely chopped and snorted up as more of the same.

Only a little more blood in the nostril distinguished the amphetamines from the previous stimulant.

We called it quits around 6:00 a.m., when lovely doe-like April rose for work. The nights began to blend into one long struggle against the stubborn and resisting program which only by Friday or so will finally start to take shape. Six nights, all night. Sometimes, in the low-tech inefficiency of his set-up, I waited for him to finish an edit for hours, amusing myself with *Hustler* or *Penthouse* or *Gallery*, trying to give myself a hard-on, despite the drug-induced torpor.

I never thought I was an addictive type, if there is such a thing, though one of the turning points in my life was kicking tobacco. My father, the lung-man, could polish off a pack and a half of Luckies or Pall Malls a day. While I was working on radio *and* running the record stores, I'd smoke at least a pack at the office and then I'd go on late-night radio and smoke another pack: Old Gold Straights—real men *hated* filters—or maybe one of my father's even more toxic brands. I'd close the mic switch, light up a Camel, look down into the ashtray and see one already fuming away—or maybe even two.

By 1967 Senta had already lost three fetuses, I guess we should call them, and when she started the blessed swelling with what turned out to be Bruno, she revealed that my smoking in the house, especially before breakfast, gave her the dread nausea.

I tried to quit, but my staff came to me and said, "Look here, Young Master. Please start smoking again immediately, okay? You're a hopelessly impossible asshole without your nicotine."

So, a drooling, dribbling mess, I had gone right on back to one of the universal forms of addiction—along with sugar and caffeine—dried tobacco leaves. But I could hear Senta's extreme discomfort.

I was on the squash courts of the Racquet Club in the old Windsor Arms Hotel. 235-pound Don Goodman, my boss and fifteen years older, was kicking my little butt mercilessly wall to wall. Adrenaline was singing its revenge aria in my diminished cardiovascular *palcoscenico*. My chest heaved with pulmonary fatigue. 11-5; he was killing me. Passing shot. Point! 12-5. I pulled up at the back wall, dripping wet and beginning to give in to a deep wracking cough. My non-racquet hand flew out to intercept the phlegm that shot projectile-like from my opened throat, and caught: two giant green frogs of mucous. I decided once and for all to quit smoking.

But as soon as this was accomplished I felt a small trap-doorlet open in my mind and heard this sly weasel-voice begin to intone:

Aw, c'mon, Mitchie. Ya just bought a fresh pack 'a' Pall Malls. Why waste a quarter? G'wan 'n' smoke 'em. THEN y' c'n quit. Y'c'n always quit, kid!

I knew I had to squash the weasel. I *knew*. If I wanted even a modicum of self-respect, I'd have to skin the motherfucker right here and now. *Slam the door in his sleazy face! Yes! Turn away now.* Don came over to see if I was okay and I returned the favor by staging a sturdy little rally to bring the game even, 12-12, before losing 15-13. But a moral victory was assured. I dumped my half-full pack of Pall Malls in the locker-room trashcan on the way out to Don's Mustang. He drove me home and I marched down the twisty drive thrilling to the prospect of the announcement I would make to a grateful Senta.

When I opened the drawer under the kitchen telephone and found an almost full carton, that crimson wrapper with the fake coat of arms and Latin motto: In Hoc Signo Vinces. *Jesus! With this emblem will you conquer? Up your ass! Constantine's code was it? Some kind of blessing of the departing Crusaders. So we're somehow supposed to colonize our lungs for the ancient Tidewater tobacco barons tranced out on chivalry and Our Lord. Gimme a break!* As I thus inveighed, I began to hear the high lonesome whine of the weasel again:

C'mon, Mitch, man. Don't be such a stiff. Think of Bogie, man! Think of

Brando in The Young Lions. *Yeah! Rolling that sweet-looking thing around his lips till you want to race to the john and either fire one up or clip yer carrot, or both, whichever comes first. Or Belmondo, or—God it's sexy!*

Get the fuck outta here!

You used to smoke reefer...

Beat it!

What are yuh—some kinda faggot...?

It was a milestone in my human growth, which, perhaps interrelatedly, had been pretty skimpo up till now. Therefore, I say I'm not an addict-*type*, unless you count my predilection for pleasure in all its known forms. But is the relentless pursuit of pleasure *necessarily* a non-Family-friendly kinda deal? I pledged to myself in the shower of a quaint motel in San Francisco that all future activities will contain some mixture of:

1) Value; and, yes,

2) Pleasure.

I read Albert Lowen's excellent *Pleasure*, an openly and proudly Reichian book in which the author's master and shrinker, Wilhelm Reich himself, would have been pleased. I read it then, having throughout the mid-Seventies immersed myself in Reich's opus: *Character Analysis, The Psychopathology of Fascism,* and especially *Sex-Pol,* in which Freud's brightest student describes his work in setting up free sex/health clinics for Berlin youth in the 1920s. State out of the bedroom! Sex as a birthright. Life as the result. Love and Work. See how nature makes the things we need to do to sustain ourselves and our species—eat and reproduce—pleasureful? Tends to encourage human persistence in these survival-requisite activities, no? Consider the alternative.

Tree chopped the coke on the mirror on his workbench. He held his hair back from his skull to lower his nose to the mirror, snorted two thick lines, slid me the mirror and went back to cutting tape. I took the mirror, swirled the finely chopped granules into two monster bombers and SNORFF! Then the other nostril: SNORFF!

It's 4:00 a.m. If Tree had modern equipment we'd be done by now. I'd be home in bed with Adrienne. Fuck! When was the last time we were together? We need better gear. Multi-track board; better equalization. Compression. Compress the sound. Compress the time. Less hours. Less work. Less cocaine. More rolling in my sweet baby's arms.

I noticed *Penthouse Letters* open on the bench next to me. A slender blonde impersonating a high school cheerleader bent over, her deliciously juvenile butt offering to kiss the camera's face. I got hard. I looked over at Tree lost in his edit. The next photo showed the counterfeit teenager demurely dividing her fuzzy cheeks for our delectation, smiling over her shoulder, knowing what I was thinking.

I was thinking of April. She was twenty when I met her in Niagara. Provocative long blonde plaits. Slender young body. We only did it a couple of times. She loved the sex act, and—with an infinite pool of "comrades"—had a lot of practice. Yet she was faithful to Tree. *How'd he like to watch me fuck her?* Cocaine loosing the snaky predator, the moral outlaw, the psychic daredevil. Nasty limit-smasher on the prowl for greener pastures of dominion.

That's why I did the drug. It fueled the drive to pierce society's social skin—*give it a good prick! Taboos-R-Us. My cock a divining rod for repressed fear. Sic 'em! Root out the hypocrisy with bold action, sexual defiance! Fuck your mothers, boys! Your sisters! Watch your wife cumming forever, fucking your bowling team! The Astronauts! City Council! Cumming in rainbows of Lemme Outta Here! Take and give without fear! Take this little faux teeny-boffer in* Penthouse. *Whoever, wherever. Whenever, whatever! Be ready to cruise; lose your shoes! Pay some dues to the crews of losers. Give it all away! Hoist butts in the air to Freedom forever!*

No. *Just the show. Finish the damn show.* Every week we were a little later dropping the master off at the pressing plant, until only hours separated delivering one show from starting the next. I longed for sleep, oozing fatigue toxins. I slide into zzz-land at the odd family gathering, seeing my kids only when they can come to the studio on an early evening. The sensation of rotting, walking, talking decay. Living to work, or merely for the drug?

Adrienne just wanted desperately to conceive. We'd been passing like kites on an early spring wind, flapping by happenstantially, bobbing round each other's lives, tangling the other's line. Schedules, deadlines and my drug use combined to keep hostility covert and well-deflected into other areas, notably Bruno.

Bruno was back with his mother. Senta had re-married—a guy named Fred Potter who really hated me and referred to me only as "That Loser." Fred was one of the early computer geniuses, and a decent enough man, but he sometimes attempted to discipline all three boys—especially Bruno—with the shame and guilt routine he learned in rural New England. He was reported to have treated Bruno to such life-giving affirmations as:

"You know what *you* are? You're a *liar!* You're a liar *and a cheat!*"

I forever promised to take Bruno to live with us, but I could barely afford our little one-bedroom studio in Carthay Center. Adrienne, with her fertility stalemate, was in no rush, either.

At about the height of the mid-August heat wave a boiling schism erupted at RATWorld. Our bosses, two Jewish guys from Medford, were screaming in the office. Paychecks start bouncing. No money. And No Money meant no money for drugs. *In extremis* I let our Executive Producer Louie Lipton talk me into siding with him against his partner Freddie Schmutzer. I never paid much attention to the business side of RATWorld operations; it seemed so hopelessly inept and flabby. The partners' acumen was limited to begging or feeble attempts at bullying. But one day Stan ("The Bold") Christopher came vaulting up the Olympic studio steps on some kind of assignment for a new CBS Radio "youth" network New York.

"Sounds like it's time to light the blue flame, pal," he tells me when I sketch him the dilemma. "One'a these guys is stinkin' up the place," he solemnizes, "and you gotta get up off your haunches and burn him out."

"They're so small-time their paranoia actually smells; 'are we gonna make it in Hollywood?'"

"Poor suckers." He shakes his fine blonde pageboy.

"Poor suckers is right. Both of them. There's no Good One."

"Wasn't it Louie you said was okay?"

"Precisely. And not a dust particle more."

Stan comes over with me to RATWorld Headquarters for what would have been in normal times my usual weekly visit. But with the "shortness of pants," as my Uncle Arnold used to call being broke, we were Pure Scarcity Vectors. We drive over in the new navy blue 530i RATWorld has just leased me, trading spoons on the way up La Brea, north to the rotting storefronts of Hollywood Boulevard and east to what must have sounded like the big time to the Bean Townies: Hollywood and Vine. Same building as Motown.

I swang the princely Beemer into the World Federal Savings lot and parked. Stan was pretty cooked, so I must have been too. Our teeth were sparkly.

We went to see Louie, in his dim, fear-haunted office. For the first time I noticed his Red Sox ashtray.

"Mitch. This is fucked."

Right in front of Stan he started whining, begging me to throw Freddie out.

"Please, Mitch. He's killing me. The bastidd is killing me. Freddy's killing the damn show." He looked ready to cry.

I looked to Stan. Eyes brimming, laughing in short silent snorts through pinched sinuses.

"Do it, Mitch!"

"What, *me?* Dump *his* partner? Tell me why he'll go for that?"

"He will, Mitch," says Louie. "He just will. He just *will*." Louie seemed closer to tears. He looked down at his cheap desk.

Stan beamed across the top of Louie's lamp. "Yeah!"

Things were approaching breakdown. *Too little sleep, money for drugs but not for payroll. Now no money for drugs! Wait a minute.* I walked across the hall—pausing for a line with Stan—into Freddie's larger, more moguloid lair—walls full of gold record plaques and framed RATWorld ads from Billboard, etc. Schmutzer was behind his imposing leather shortness-obviating ego-platform of a writing desk.

He was a less than imposing man. Balding at 30, with the unfortunate combination of stooped shoulders and potbelly, he choose to cover the whole with whatever the guy on the second floor of Fred Segal's told him to buy. Freddie looked down at me with mild pique.

"Time to go, Freddie," I tell him with that hollow, mock-heroic coke-voice I recognized as my host-persona from the show.

"Whatta you want? Get-the-fuck outta heah, okay? I don't need anotha problem."

"No, pal. It's you that's the problem. Now pack up your stuff. We don't want to *see* you down here, got it? Go make your calls from home."

Echoes of Trout and The Head. In the car later Stan told me, "You were beaming that clear blue light you beam sometimes when you really bear down, y' know?"

Whatever that meant. But Freddie did it. He left fairly quietly, too, and for a week or so things were better. We got a few back-pay checks. The show got to the pressing-plant on time. But then it was back to slow-pay, long hours and I literally collapsed, handing off my job to the unspeakable Sandy Durnit. He lasted less than a month with Lipton, who rattled easily. Then the show quietly folded for good.

⁓

I went into therapeutic seclusion, though Tree characteristically struggled on till the end. I cast my net and pulled together a little production company to do "long-form" radio work, mostly artist portraits and specials. Together with Tree and Deirdre O'Connor, we called it *Aural Tradition*.

Deidre was a trip: the brilliant, punky widow of one the great pioneer "outlaw" jocks: Tim O'Connor, who'd been on the "Further" bus with Kesey and the boys, and twenty years older than Deirdre. To me she was hipness itself. Still in her early twenties when Tim died from Life Excess, she was struggling to raise her son Micah and, I knew, casting a knowing eye on my guiltily elastic relation with Bruno.

"Why don't you just *take* him?" Deirdre wanted to know.

"Our place is too small."

"Getta bigger place, pal. He's suffering with Senta, fucking up his brothers. She's ready to freak. So what's the deal?"

"Can't afford it. I'm… *you* know how it is."

"I couldn't afford it either, man. Just get a place for the three of you and *find* a way to afford it."

Using *The Last Waltz* documentary we'd done for Warner Brothers, and a few of the better *RATWorlds* as calling cards, we elbowed our friends in Promotion, mostly Warner's and Columbia, to find us budgets to make 60-minute specials on their college market artists.

I was still angling to take what I considered "my" rock interview format into infant cable television. Working with *Midnight Special* pals, Marv Tweed, whose credibility as director was unchallenged, and Sascha, to deliver talent; I took meetings with HBO and Showtime—the only real games in town in those early ground-floor days of the narrowcasting medium.

We had a breakfast meeting at the Polo Lounge with the decision-maker at Showtime, sombody Major's daughter. I was carefully prepared with a list of deliverable artists. With me was the head of Warner Brother's video department, in what I hoped was a power move. The two ladies and I sat there making snappy bi-coastal hierarchy-repartee over our eggs Florentine as Chevy

Chase floated by, then Bette Midler. Finally, the lady from Showtime studied the Warner's artist roster briefly and chirped:

"Good. Let's do all the comics! Comedy's hot."

Steve Martin, Lily Tomlin, Martin Mull, Pryor, the original *Saturday Night Live* cast, Cosby. Of *course* we don't have the video rights, bitch!—other than a few promo clips! We say we'll get back to her.

Concentric peregrinations.

Tree and I did a long, rambling, but detailed and exquisitely textured hour-long show with minimalist composer Steve Reich, on the occasion of the debut release of his masterpiece *Music for Eighteen Musicians.* God knows who aired it, but my old pal at Warner's, Lance Guilford, liked it enough to hire Tree and me in to do Pat Metheny for the space-jazz label ECM, which WB has just picked up for distribution. *New Chautauqua* was his latest and the show introduced it and him.

This was going to be our *capolavoro* to date, we figured, and Tree was contemplating making capital improvements to the tune of a multi-track board, new noise reduction and editing equipment which would kick our new production company off in style. Plus, Elektra-Asylum ordered a major Judy Collins audio-bio to accompany her LP, *Hard Times for Losers,* so we were definitely *happening.* The sales manager of the hot audio design house laid a big discount on Tree, who proceeded to buy racks and racks of little boxes with buttons and lights, and the future was lit groovily.

At about the same time, Tree and April's affair was experiencing yo-yo turbulence. Tree was such a horn-dog that control around women was, for all intents and purposes, out of the question. It was virtually impossible for him not to pursue any woman who was moderately attentive, and then he felt instant remorse. Yes, he loved April intensely, but as The Sweet put it so succinctly:

"Everybody ne-ed
Satisfaction guaran-te-ed.
But everybody want
Part a' the AC-TION!"

To prove his love for her, he fell for the time-pickled tradition that many sheepishly coughed up a couple-o-months of salary to participate in—giving your girl diamonds. Being young, and an Ohio bumpkin, he naturally went for a dodgy deal some friend of Adrienne's brother was hustling. He bought her a pair of near-pecan sized glass-cutters that seemed obscenely perfect. Diamonds!

As a result of this otherwise blameless romantic extravagance, he then could not afford the multi-track board we needed. *We can live without it,* I rationalize. *At least it makes Tree happy.*

We started the arduous task of laying in music under Pat Metheny's voice to illustrate influences and other points of his rap, and as the hours groaned painfully on, it was obvious to both of us—though tensely unspoken—that a four-track capability would have made life a lot easier.

A few days passed and Tree asked if he could use our apartment to meet someone. On the appointed night Adrienne and I went into the bedroom when the person rang the bell and came up. *Mork and Mindy* was new on ABC, and we wanted to check out the rumored-to-be-insanely-gifted Robin Williams. Tree came in and joined us just as the show was over.

"What was *that* all about?" I wanted to know.

He smiled a cool-daddy know-it-all smile.

"So?"

"So, I sold the diamonds."

"You sold 'em?" I held back my question about new equipment.

"Four-track city, My Brother." Tree's eyes sparkled jewel-like.

"Right on!" I smiled the smile of relief.

"She's coming down on Saturday to bring me cash."

"You get your price?"

"Yep."

"My hero!" *Now we would COOK!*

It's Friday, hot for late March, and I leave the studio for the drive out to Marv's, up the Coast Highway. Tree promises to have a trial mix of Side Two when I get back.

"Cool. I hope it's the last time you'll ever have to play mad-scientist with this shit."

"You got that right. Next week, the mother lode arrives. I ordered twenty-thou of the coolest gear ever conceived by homo-technoid. But I'll have fun with my trusty razor blade while you're gone."

I wait in the Alfa in front of a locked gate to Marv's beach house for about an hour. He never shows. I give up and head back to Tree's in moderate disgust. I pump along, retracing my steps down the PCH—the little coupe grooved into fifth—when a traffic backup at Topanga brings me up short. I creep along southward an inch at a time, pulling the shift lever out of first into neutral every few seconds. The engine temperature edges into the red. Alfas; one loves them for other qualities.

It is still early, so I turn off at Sunset, which looks clear. The engine can cool off on the straight shot back into the city. *I'll call Tree when I get back to my place and see if he is still fa-tootzing with the mix.* I watch the temp gauge as the coupe climbs Sunset up past the Self-Realization Fellowship, past Will Rogers Park and into downtown Pacific Palisades. By Chautauqua it has dropped down into the black, and I'm free to enjoy the curving trail back to town.

I've loved the gracious green gardener-intense *paseo* ever since we came to L.A. Now, just a few years later, a barely accredited Angeleno, I am coming back in eastward, past UCLA, past the Hollywood feudality of the Bel-Air gates, west and east, through the banked esses west of Whittier, then into Beverly Hills, where Sunset ran straight and broad, a splendid stately river edged by trees and a central island of grass, past the old, pink Hotel and the mansions and finally *ffwhoosh!* Out onto the carnality of the Strip, the Business office towers, Hamburger Hamlet, Hornsburg Jaguar, the Cock and Bull, Gil Turner's Liquor, the Roxy and Tree's ex-station KCST on the north side of the street. I turn down San Vicente—an avenue I love for its universally applicable hypotenuse, all the way down to Olympic.

It takes almost an hour from Trancas. *Better park around the corner. No parking on Olympic after 3:00.* I park, trudge inside to relieve my bursting bladder, then phone Tree, watching the six lanes of slowly building traffic pouring in and out of southern Beverly Hills-adjacent.

I bet he's mixing something outrageous, cooped up alone with all our recreational chemicals. Maybe he's wearing cans. The ringing goes on and on while I conjure up images of goofy-smiling Tree nibbling on a Thai stick. Then I hear a click, then violent scrambly knocking noises, CRASH! CRASH! CRASH! And then the most baleful sound I had ever heard. Tree's voice—terribly, awfully altered.

"Mi-itch…" and a kind of bubbling noise, then the banging again and other urgent colliding jumbled sounds.

"Tree!?" Shock beginning to take me.

"Mi-itch…"

"Tree? What *is* it…"

"I…They shot…Shot me…come…" A crash, then silence.

Stunned. *What is it? What's happened?* Mind races ahead. *Fever. Fastest route to his studio. Plot! Find car keys. Then: call Senta; get an ambulance rolling and call cops. Head for Santa Monica Freeway. No crashing, no getting stopped. No fucking cops.*

What's happened? Is this fast as I can go? Faster. Did he plug himself by accident? He's still alive. Will I deal with it okay? Will I be okay? What happened? Tree had a .45. Did that dumb fuck shoot himself? Still alive…his voice so shattered on the phone…still, he recognized me. Answered the phone in the first place, so…how bad could it be? Cops'll be there first, so I won't have my mettle measured. He was alive/answered the phone/sounded okay…what? Sounded okay? Ghastly! Ghastly and from Beyond, from that world, not this. Cold throated and dry. No, the dumb fuck! This'll set delivery date back at Warner's. The stupid fuck! A real kid move. Cops cops cops. Is there dope in the place? Fuck! A friend is visiting from up North with bags of Humboldt! Big bags. Trash bags of herb. Oh fuck!

Anger comes as welcome relief. *Now I'll have to deal with bales of marijuana, and fucking pigs rooting around, busting us while whatever minor flesh wound Tree may have self-inflicted becomes a raging torrent of gore.*

I catch third gear and put the Alfa into an easy semi-slide at about sixty through the Bundy South off-ramp and down Centinela, then west onto Venice Boulevard into the afternoon sun, flailing the little coupe from lane to lane again, mashing the throttle to the firewall, the engine howling at the 6000 rpm redline.

I make the turn at West Washington and see the back of the red and creme paramedic van. Looking down the drive to his recessed studio, I see the front door flung wide. In the gigantic surge of adrenaline that grips me I abandon the Alfa and sprint down the drive.

The paramedics are squatting off to the right near the file cabinets, working to fit a stretcher with metal support rods for IV's. Then I turn and see the blood. Tree is lying, alone, unattended in a motionless ball on the floor.

Blood is everywhere. His hair hangs wet over his face. I bend over and smooth it off his forehead. He is still breathing. Gasping. When he feels my hand on him he says my name.

"Mitch," he chokes. "The diamonds…find the diamonds."

"Don't talk."

I bend down over him, holding his head. Feelings rush: longing for my own sons, a brief flicker of wanting my own father, then gratitude that it isn't me on the floor, and immediately the love of still being whole, then a transcendent love for all humanity, followed by a deep revulsion to the thought that *it was humans who have done this.* Tree lies there in a lake of his own blood.

He looks up slowly with a tiny smile. I stroke his face but the paramedics move me aside, telling me they've failed to reach UCLA, but they'll keep calling them by radio from the van, otherwise they'll take him to Marina-Mercy Hospital, which is a lot closer. They hurry him onto the stretcher, install the IV's and are out the door with him in seconds.

"Stay here and wait for the police," they say.

⁓

As soon as they drive off with Tree I start to reconnoiter the place I left just a few short hours before, now irreversibly transformed into a scene of stark, ugly terror. Lots of things are broken or strewn across the otherwise orderly studio. And the blood. Not just the pitiful puddle of my partner's life energy from which his body has just been lifted, but a number of big drops—splashes really—that lead toward the back, our working area around the tape machines in the studio proper. I walk back, following what looks like a trail leading to the back door. The phone rings. Our friend from Humboldt County, calling from the Arco station on the corner. He'd been driving up as the paramedics roared off, and wants to know about his trash bags. Come get 'em fast, I tell him. I hang up and call Senta and Adrienne.

I notice the back door open, blood on the jam. Blood in the alley as

I follow the splotches, beginning to thin to drops in the dried mud of the hundred yard drive that runs behind the short row of commercial spaces. The trail leads south, back out to the street, across West Washington, fewer red droplets now, but steady and easy to follow, down the sidewalk, around the corner to the side street, one of those nameless suburban beach ways between the Canals and Venice Boulevard. And there ends.

There is also an empty space at the curb, where a car might have stood. Across the way a neighbor cuts his grass behind a wire fence.

"See anybody running out here maybe a half hour ago, maybe bleeding?"

"This couple came runnin' over here," he tells me without hesitation. "Guy was like holding his pants."

"His pants? Where?"

"Right around his crotch," he says.

"Was he bleeding?'

"I was upstairs," he points over his shoulder. "Saw 'em from up there. A woman was with him. Running. They was running.""

"Was either one bleeding?"

"Guy's crotch looked wet. That's what I thought. Coulda been blood."

I scrawl down his name and sprint back to the studio. The herb-friend is there, a half-hysterical look in his pointy olive features. He's pulled a big white Econoline van up to the back door and is throwing in bags of weed.

"At least we don't have to flush any of it," he offers.

I look at him. The cops will be here any minute. He slams the sliding door shut, hops in and drives off. I never see him again.

The LAPD arrives as soon as he's pulled away. Two uniformed officers. One has a steno pad out. I am orienting them when April calls. I tell her what's happened as calmly and inconclusively as possible. She gulps; she will be right home. I take the two cops to the bloody trail and walk them over to the next street. The neighbor is still mowing his patch of lawn. He tells them what he told me and we walk back to the crime scene. Other cops have arrived by now and are taking pictures. I tell them what I know, not much. April comes in, takes one look at her ravaged home and goes limp. I hold her slender body and try to comfort her.

"Gotta call Tree's folks," she whispers.

I manage to keep April from getting entangled in questioning. We both have basically bad cop-attitudes. I convince her to find out which hospital he's in and to go stay with him till I can get free.

We crowd around Tree's bed in Intensive Care that first night, imploring him to fight for his life. He is in this outrageous pain, far beyond the dulling power of the opiates they keep him full of. He has taken five bullets: one in the thigh, one in the arm, two in the gut and one in the chest. Three .38s and two .45 slugs left him a complex of damaged fiber, threatened organs and potentially lethal infection.

He will be lucky to make it through the night. We are drawn into his suffering, caught between wanting to hide from its terror, and the challenge to drive it away. He tells us every way he can of his desire to die. He implores us.

"The pain," he mouthes. "Let me go. I need to go. Let me die."

But we will not let him slip away peaceful into surcease. Before the startled eyes of the ICU night crew, April climbs up onto his big motorized bed, overhung with tubes and monitoring devices, and begins the chants of exhortations, the rousing supplications—"Live! Live!" The demands upon his spirit to persevere. When morning comes he is still extremely critical but he is still there, and the incredulous staff, doctors, nurses, even the cops, have to admit his condition has stabilized.

A day later Tree's family arrived from Ohio. As awful for me as watching his struggling the night before, seeing the panic in his mother, father and younger sister's faces even before they get a look at him was worse. I felt the deep, fearful hurt each time as I went through the anxious briefing process for them. Only the father, the engineer, made an attempt to cover his grief. We were all in shock.

For the next two weeks Tree improved, spiraling ever-upward toward recovery. We stayed at the hospital full-time for five days, sleeping in the halls outside his ICU. Adrienne and April came before and after teaching their classes, but his family and I pretty much lived there until we were told that the immediate deep crisis was over.

He was still in horrendous pain, and sitting with him, holding his hand, the brief exchanges with him, mostly by fiery eye contact, were especially tough on his parents. I had to force myself to go in there. Mostly it was April and the family.

Near the end of the first week, Lieutenant Hathaway, the detective from the Venice Division who was nominally heading the investigation, called me into his office.

"Well, Mr. Hertz, a little good news. We got the shooter…or, one of the shooters, prob'ly. Like some water?"

"No thanks, Lieutenant. Good work! How djoo guys do that?" I tried to work the bonding side of the street.

"Thanks." A short good-looking guy with tight blonde hair and a remarkably tweedy suit, alcohol-tinted nose and almost intimate kinda attitude. He took my arm and walked me into a small, sweat-and-tobacco lined conference room with a dangerously low ceiling, and locked the door.

"Yeah, he checked himself into the VA Hospital in Westwood the same day he shot your partner. Claimed he was, ya know, walking along Pico and someone just drove by and shot him."

"Just mindin' his own business, right, and someone drives by and plinks him in the nuts?"

I was relieved, but found myself wondering: Why had he locked the door?

"Right. Looks like Tree got him where it hurts."

"Who is he? Who's the guy?"

"Hollywood street trash. Burglar, dope dealer, small time white filth."

"Anything about a girl?"

"Yeah. The VA says there was a girl with him when he checked in….."

"Great!"

"…but she faded. Before we could get there, she beat it. We'll get her."

"Well, that's over, right?" I started to get up.

"Not exactly, Mr. Hertz." He motioned for me to stay seated.

"Well?"

The detective fixed icy blue eyes on my own blood-shot pair.

"We got two eyewitnesses positive ID-ing *you*."

"*Me?*"

I looked over at the locked metal door. The airless room took on an even less savory aspect. The smell of despair. Of fear. Of failure of nerves. My stomach rocked side-to-side, my knees double-jointed and uncertain.

"Wha…?"

"I know, I know. You couldn't have done it. Where were you that day about 2:30?"

"Are you fucking shitting me, Lieutenant?"

Something about the situation made me think butch expletives would help, strengthen my resolve, maybe. I was trying to concentrate on demonstrating the absurdity of what he was saying. *Stop. Wait. What, me kill Tree? Be serious, shit-biscuit!* But my nervous system wasn't granting me access to due reflection.

"*We* know you didn't do it. But we got these two neighbors—a guy and his son, say they heard gunshots, went over to check and saw you come out the front door."

"*Saw* me? I was in my car driving back from the beach."

"I know."

He was writing on a pad. *Fuck!*

"Anyone in the car with you?"

"I told you this already, Lieutenant. Come *on*. I was alone."

"Right."

"Do you really think Tree would let me in his ICU room if *I'd* been the one that shot him?"

I held on to myself enough to keep the room from gyroscoping, but the walls were calling to me, calling my name. Beckoning and threatening in the same gestural moment. Turning to *confiture,* to exquisite sugary ooze. Closing in on me, pulling me closer to its sticky sweet danger. *Too close!* My arm hairs rose in a sucro-tropism, pulling me into its deep vortex. *You will come to us! You will come within these walls.*

"Well, *I* believe you, but we don't have positive ID on Lester Fike, this guy in the VA, ya know? And we do on you."

"And…?"

"And your buddy has an attitude about he don't wanna talk to cops, won't let no cops in the room…"

"Yeah…?"

"And we need him to ID young Mr. Fike here."

He waggles a small pile of photos. Upside down, I see a thin wispy-blonde face with meager lips and flimsy white mustache.

"Well, I'll see what I can do. Ya know…"

"Mr. Hertz, this is a homicide."

"What do you mean? The doctors say he has a great chance…"

"*Hah*-micide, Mr. Hertz."

I weighed my options. "Okay, Lieutenant. I'll talk to him for ya."

I was scared shitless. I admitted to myself that I had been sand-bagging, letting others take my place at Tree's bedside far too readily. I kept my visits brief, and encouraged April and his family to precede me. I'd physically *be there* all the time, even sleep there. But I kept my personal one-on-ones to a minimum.

I was directing, I told myself, not co-starring. The job was to do our best to save him, despite the predictions of the cops. A hope arose, a hope that by saving Tree we were saving ourselves, our own truest hope. And also saving that idea we had held on to, that we were in new times—that this was a hopeful age.

Tree was in a tiny ICU gestalt of monitors and tents, tubes and masks. A nurse was adjusting the flow of some liquid. He was dozing. She looked at me looking.

"Mitch," he said, but with only the top part of his voice, thin and unsupported—but not a whisper.

I turned from the nurse and put my hand on his arm. The skin was cool. "Love you, Tree. Love you so much, man."

"Mitch," he said again.

I just looked at him, and saw Florentine beauty in shades of white, and drank him in, pain and all.

"They just want you to look at the mug shots. That's all."

"Your picture be in there too?" His voice was giving out.

"Don't know. They'll be here a coupla minutes is all. No stress."

He nodded okay.

"You can make it," I said, trying to keep our eyes locked. "If you want to."

"Sometimes I do want to." And he went to sleep

So the Lieutenant came in a little later, Tree fingered his assailant and cleared me, but the moment in the locked room continued to resonate.

The next days were very compressed, trying and exhausting. I helped coordinate family functioning, dealt with the cops, notified Tree's friends in the Midwest and L.A., called an old Carnegie radio colleague, now a *macher* at *Radio & Records*, to raise money for the hundreds of thousands that the weeks in ICU would cost.

One day the alleged shooter's alleged girlfriend showed up in the ER lobby looking smacked-out, asking for Tree and holding something in her purse. I went out to hold her till the cops got there, but once again, she vanished into the ether.

There were long speechless nights with his anxious loved ones. For the first few over-nights together we followed Tree's every movement. Then drifted into the sad dullness of the wounded. One night when things seemed stable, we all went over to Tree's studio. April was moving out—couldn't bear to stay there and found a room, "till Tree gets out and we find a new place," in Santa Monica.

We gathered to consider the potentially ruinous financial calamity the diamond thieves had wrought—and to bless the few pieces of property April is wanting to move out with her to her new place. The night was cold and as friends and family sat, ghostly echoes played off the denuded walls of the suffering studio. Most of the electronics were already carted off to be sold for expenses. We talked about what we considered possible futures: best case, mostly, how April would find a rental for the two of them and dedicate herself to nursing him back to whatever health he might still achieve.

The Venice air was damp with the beach spring's longing for summer. The emptiness before the arising of the next form, the next moment, the next phenomenon. The womb of all life. Empty. And sad.

Our voices echoed softly and in the darkened studio our shadows loomed portentous on floor and wall alike. Then a vapor arose to surround us and our talking ceased, an eerily transcendent sensation. As if his absence, in that cold moment, had pulled the energy out of the room. To get our attention. Bring us to order. We sat there in its thrall. Feeling whatever we missed most about him. The wind off the Pacific slapped the darkened skylight.

Finally Tree's mother reached out and pricked the tightly-drawn sausage casing wrapping us tight, with a single sentence:

"What do you think happened?"

I didn't want to be the one who answered, but the silence that met the question was so total that I finally say, "I don't know, but they likely just shot him in the process of stealing the diamonds. He probably went for their gun."

"But there were *two* guns."

"Yeah." I realized that my feet were being drawn to the exact spot where I had always been sure the shooting took place, in front of the old green file cabinet he'd bought used at a place downtown and where there'd been a small but very deep puddle of blood when I'd found Tree lying fetal just a few feet away. "I think maybe he'd turned to get the diamonds out of their hiding place in one of these files," I extemporized. "And turned back to face at least one gun."

They were listening. The room seemed darker.

"He must have been *pissed* when he saw she'd brought a guy with her."

I could see him letting them in with a self-disgusted snark on his face. I glanced at April, who frowns, and looked away.

This is the life we chose. The Great Out There. Greed for Experience. Me, too. I live that way too.

"Now, here he was getting definitively thwarted, ripped off. Beaten, he was feeling desperately beaten."

Around the room, I saw grim faces and pain.

"And getting pissed. Pissed at himself for acting stubborn and losing. Humbled and shamed. And pissed at doing something stupid." I looked again. We were floating in the cold, hanging in wet air, eyes wide.

"Probably grabbed for the gun and took a slug for his efforts, but who knows? Coulda been both of them, guns drawn, maybe high on drugs—hard to say. But he shot the guy in the balls! I'm happy about that; I'm not ashamed to say."

"Have you ever thought that if your car hadn't overheated, you'd have been there the same time the thieves arrived?" Tree's father asked. "You might have gotten shot, too!"

"Or prevented the whole thing," his mother said carefully.

Standing there it all came together for me: the struggle, the exchange of shots, the second gun coming into play, the noise, the smell of powder and fire, the blood. *God! Had I let this happen to my friend? My young charge? My…* My mind flew to my own children. How safe were they, living in Venice, with the culture that spawned the Mansons and many lesser human pus-buckets passing as Hippies? And with a mother they could always overpower and outnumber? *Am I responsible for Tree? Haven't I tried to warn him?* I thought about the blood. About one of my kids swimming in it. Saw once again Tree's tiny smile as he recognized my hand on his brow. I looked quickly at his family. *Do they blame me?*

If we had spent our weekly drug budget on the studio instead of sending it up our noses, April could have kept her diamonds. But that was not the point. Tree and I had come here to live a (supply adjective) Life. We were not so much producing a show for itself, but as a way of supporting, even fostering, this Life.

Drugs were central. A way of reaching the goal before the steeplechase starts. *Be happy now. THEN do the work.* It was all about character. Inebriated character. Shortcut to Fully Human. Blame. *Tree did drugs before he met me back in Carnegie.* Guilt squirts out.

How much is my fault?

My mind flipped back through the files rapidly. Paused at Carnegie—soon after leaving the world of retail, when I met Tommy Trout and we began that fateful stoned relationship cemented by opium, hash, and lots of weed. And by talking—about music, race and politics.

"It's all about Youth Culture. That's how they see it," Trout had said.

"Yeah?"

"Yeah, so that's how we see it too, 'cause that's what they're paying for."

"So?"

"So, they don't know what they're doing, of course."

"Yeah."

"Yeah, but *I do!*"

In the absence of drugs as a *lingua franca,* almost as a mode of conveyance, I wouldn't be here at all, would never have met Trout, wouldn't have met Tree. It was not an excuse—just one aspect of the truth. The truth, which also included the life I left, which was precisely what dope helped me forget in the first place.

And what about my career? Would I have had any success crossing over from Classical Music radio to Underground Rock without dope as the transitional object? The ritual of public roach-passing was a terrific leveler, a show of good faith, of bonhomie, even communal consciousness. Sharing the Earth.

But I *was* guilty. Guilty of not taking my life seriously, of only being *against* things. Of letting myself steep in anger, and its co-efficient, self-pity. Unlettered nihilism. And I was Tree's closest adult male friend.

I resolved to share the convalescence chores with April.

We had another week of Tree wheeled in and out of OR's as his various organs—mostly liver—exceed their limits. Surgical measures were required to help him deal with the stubborn bullet-scattered toxins that refused to leave his system in peace long enough for him to heal. But things were so improved by the end of the second week I let Deirdre throw a fundraising barbecue at her place in Brentwood. Radio people, musicians and half the cast of *The Blues Brothers* movie were invited for the Sunday evening bash. Post-Vietnam solidarity of a sort.

Saturday dawned sunny and clear, a spring treasure of a morning with high winds and cotton ball clouds. Tree's sweet mother begged us to take the day off.

I slept late, had brunch at a new diner on La Cienega, and took Adrienne to the County Museum. A perfect Southern California day—art and the natural beauty of the park surrounding the museum and adjoining tar pits. We sat in the park, smelling the faint aroma of the sprouting jacarandas surrounding my lucky ass in the Wilshire District sun.

I considered my life and what I'd done with it. *Am I proud of what I've become? Am I justified in having hope? Will my boys remember their Daddy as some blow-hard loser? A guy that basically copped out? Joined the 'Sixties as a way of lying down on the job?*

What was I hoping in the first place? To somehow liberate myself?

Who ya kiddin? You gave up on your life a hundred times. When you quit your job. When you started smoking dope. When you gave up classical music for rock. And why? Because it was easy. Simple. Because you had no real business training and couldn't ride out the crisis at the record stores and keep your role in the community, your marriage, or raise your children right! Just a lazy over-age, flake-hippie.

I looked up and saw Adrienne sitting quiet among the bougainvillea, just now beginning to flower. And the jacarandas. *The jacarandas!* She smiled over at me and the park lit up. I let her smile warm me.

It almost made me think I've done the right thing in leaving my past behind in Carnegie. Despite all the struggle, all the loss, all the drifting downward in society, career and all that, I might have done the right thing. That I'd freed the part of me that was the best, that had been frozen, or at least submerged for all those years in abortions and the marriage that was supposed to save me from them. The side that loved freedom, sweetness, beauty and my truest self. The side that didn't need all the things that my father robbed me of by squeezing me out of my family, so he could have my mother to himself.

I had a vision of my father as a giant baby, an enormous infant, elbowing the infinitesimally tiny me away from my mother's breast, my birthright, my legacy, my life-to-come. In that moment I felt for him the compassion I felt for Tree's poor family—desperate, and needing to find some kind of peace. My father at peace, with my mother to suckle him. *It's okay. Couldn't be any other way. Let it go. Love him. Love the baby in him and in yourself. Let it float away and float with it. Keep floating. You joined this Sixties-thing to do just that. It was your last call for something you thought you needed, something missing. A feeling that comes out when you broadcast, when you connect with your audience, every time you open the mic switch the energy that comes through your earphones, in from the ether, from the hearts of all the listeners (whether they know it or not), from the Universe. Forming a circle, a loop, an ocean of courageous energy, a home for your heart.*

At least a fair chance.

At least a hope.

I thought of my own hope, my leap of Faith into the spirit of the new generation, the "baby-boomers" they called them, born after World War II, not before it like me. I somehow joined those kids, those dreamers, followed their glowing spark. I had been sure that wherever it all went it was better than where it came from, where I'd been going, what they saved me from.

But where am I now? Where were we all, as Students For a Democratic Society gives way to Gene McCarthy, then George McGovern and Bobby Kennedy and finally the mild and conciliatory Jimmy Carter? *Please Please Please. Where is the hope? How can I live when everything I left behind is coming back, the same thing with a different name?* Malcolm X and the Panthers gave way, under a hail of bullets, to Martin Luther King, murdered the week Bruno was born, to the slippery Jesse Jackson and far worse.

My hope was sputtering. My choice to join this life, to cast my lot with these "kids," these "hippies," these "radicals," was in danger of being seen as a stupid-but-tragic, life-ruining mistake. A cosmic blunder. Another case of Mitch running to a daylight obscured by clouds. Running wild and directionless. Following his heart, or fleeing his fears and ignorance?

Adrienne watched me, the love in her face mixed with uncertainty and dismay. Then she smiled. And I smiled, but couldn't help thinking that as far as "The Kids" went, my lovely bride would probably never have a kid of her own. Just my three, with all the jealousy and resentment that might entail. *I've fucked every Dixie cup on the West Coast trying to bring fertility to her poor insides, frozen or scarred. She wants a kid so desperately. Can I give her what she craves? God knows I blow hot and cold. She will go have it without me anyway, if I wouldn't fuck on till the end.*

Tree is my son, like the three other boys I abandoned in Venice. But this one, this beautiful young man, bursting to give himself to the world through his handicraft, must survive, as a beacon, to all the sons and daughters of America, awakened by the shared hope of all, the liberating call of the Sixties, even as it everywhere succumbs to the power that hates talent, the fear that devours love, the war that vanquishes peace, the profit that fuels it all, for ever and ever.

Oh, bullshit! I stopped myself, as Adrienne knelt in a flowerbed, bringing a deep red rose to rest on her delicate cheek. *Bullshit! It's not about profit! It's about me and who I am. Do I know? Or do I need this generation of young babies to tell me? Do I need these lame-ass identity politics? A retrofit role in some movement? Am I a hippie? A Beatnik? Militant? Broadcaster? Father? Lover? What? Say it, Mitchell! Say it! What? A seeker? Dreamer? Runner? Cosmic liar? Pick one.*

"How ya' doin', baby?" Adrienne was a few feet away as I awoke to her proximity. Her arms closed around my neck, dark eyes seeking to hold mine.

"You look down," she said.

I tried to smile. "Think we should head back?"

"We could stay a few more minutes." She looked hopeful, smiling up at me, her dark straight hair framing her perfect face, the smile lighting it from beneath. The gardens surrounded us in quiet and majestic green.

We come home to our Olympic apartment at twilight. I put on water for tea and the phone rings. It's Tree's mother.

"He's gone."

I stand there. I know I say something. Something comforting and assured. But what I feel is different, an immense downward pull, like falling straight down. My stomach tightens in distress, the nausea of dying dreams. A bitter slick covers my tongue and throat. The warming glow of the day sharply fades, betraying the illusion: the end of self-deception.

Holding the receiver against my chest, I feel my heart knock vainly against surrounding sinew. Feeling what we knew all along, what I knew when I walked away from the comfortable life: that we were dead men anyway, or, if we were lucky, it would turn out that it was society that was dead, and we the live ones. Now what?

An image floats up to me. We had just started the Metheny mix, working intently as a raging spring storm revealed leaking warehouse ceilings. Despite the cold and clamminess, the guitarist's fresh young music and unencumbered remarks had inspired us. Messengers of Spirit! Bringers of the Good Vibe we!

Almost finished, but weary from our toils, we decided to break for the day, and Tree walked me out to my car. As we emerged from the moldy wet concrete of the studio, the rain had stopped in Venice. I crossed West Washington to the Alfa, got in, blipped the engine and opened the window to wave good-bye.

He was standing there, tall and straight, a little more filled out at twenty-six than he'd been as the teenager I'd met back in Carnegie, but still arboreal, after all those years. Water dripped off the roofs. Just before I caught first gear, I looked up. A deluxe rainbow saluted us from the western sky. I pointed to it and he looked too, and nodded, and smiled.

"He just…left us. He was there and then, the next minute, he was gone."

His mother's voice is so very gentle. So light. Over Olympic, the clouds convey a sunless concern to the waning day. A wind springs up. Suddenly the leaves are fluttering everywhere.

About the Author

Martin Perlich has worked at the fringe of media
and the arts for most of the last forty years.
A minor folk-hero in Cleveland radio in the 60's,
he came to Los Angeles in 1972 to discover that
Hollywood only played one way: straight (to the bank).

He produced underground radio, public and network TV,
and feature films, while conducting some of the most admired
broadcast interviews of the 70's, 80's and 90's.
All the while he pounded away on the *Adequacy Quartet,* four
novels chronicling his efforts to follow his heart
while those around him were losing theirs.

The Wild Times is the first of these.

Martin still lives in and broadcasts from Los Angeles.

!

@

#

$

%

^

&

*

( )

+

=

< >

;

" "

...

?

.